I0768519

A JOURNEY PAVED IN SHADOWS

J.E. ELLIOTT

Copyright © 2024 by J.E. Elliott

All rights reserved.

No part of this publication may be reproduced, distributed, or transmitted in any form or by any means, including photocopying, recording, or other electronic or mechanical methods, without the prior written permission of the publisher, except as permitted by U.S. copyright law. For permission requests, contact lue.thoughtsofagoblin@gmail.com.

The story, all names, characters, and incidents portrayed in this production are fictitious. No identification with actual persons (living or deceased), places, buildings, and products is intended or should be inferred.

Book Cover by J.E. Elliott

Illustrations by J.E. Elliott

By J.E. Elliott

<u>The Divine Shadows Saga</u>
A Journey Paved in Shadows
The Light of Evenfall

Written in my blood, washed with my sweat, polished with my tears.

Western Armiria

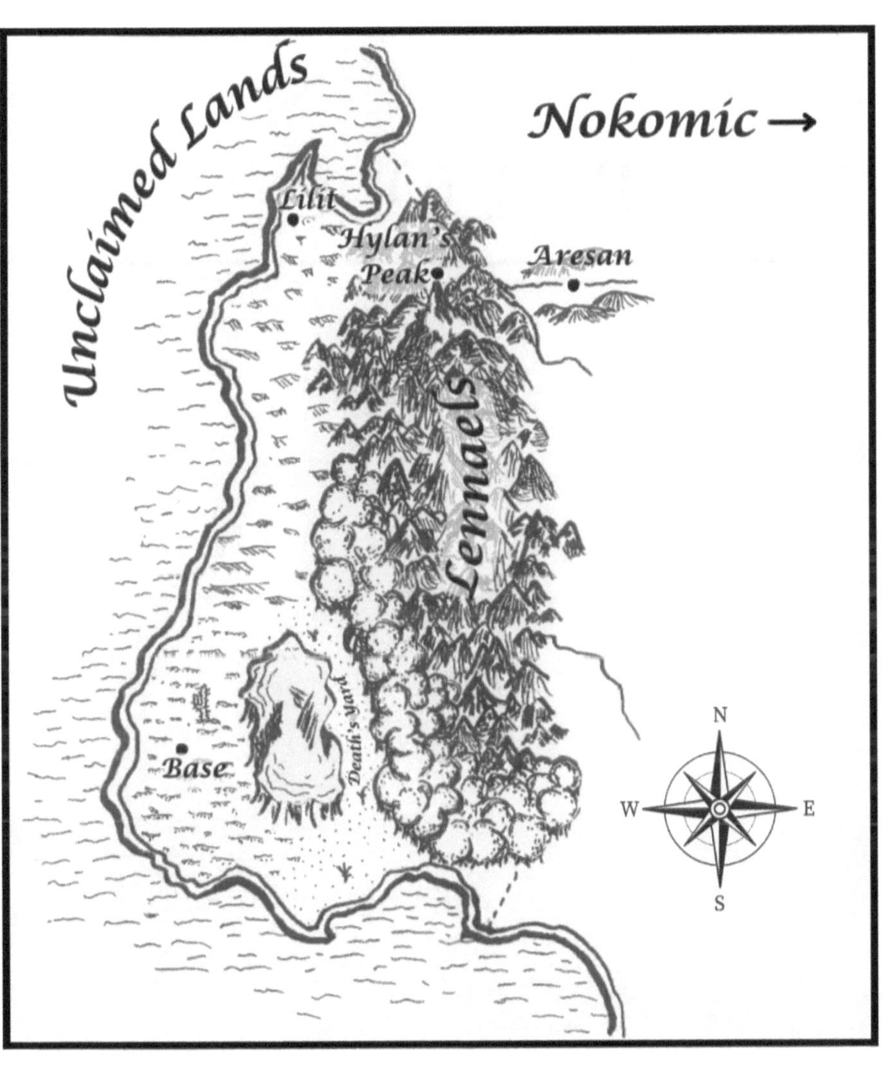

Unclaimed Lands
Nokomic →
Lilit
Hylan's Peak
Aresan
Lennaels
Death's Yard
Base
N
W
E
S

Part One

Blizzards

Chapter One

A piercing wind tore through Rin Nowell's jacket. She buried her face behind a stiffening scarf as her quick breaths turned to puffs of fog. The snow danced around her body until she blended in with the world blanched white. It inched up her legs with each minute, but she still trudged along the mountainside. She tugged her jacket around her shivering body until her legs inevitably buckled.

"Gods on high!" she cursed as the contents of her bag scattered all over the blanketed frost. "Couldn't you have picked someone else's day to ruin?" Her possessions disappeared beneath the snow with alarming speed. She reached for everything at once, but when she shoved the food and canteen back inside her bag, a sudden wind sucked a tattered piece of parchment out of her satchel. The paper flew past her ear and into the storm. Without a thought for common sense, Rin dropped everything and jumped on her feet. She leapt after the paper as if her very life depended on it.

The chase was trying. Rin grabbed at the wind, just missing the page by a hair's breadth, hoping not to lose it in the towering conifers. Icy panic clenched her heart.

She took a deep breath and prayed against gravity. *Jump, Rin, jump!* Landing hard on the ground, a freezing sweat broke out over her body. She forced her legs to lunge forward. Arm extended with fingers outstretched, Rin grasped at the paper one last time. Her panic softened with relief as she felt the smooth parchment between her fingertips. She tumbled down into the snow with a *thunk*, her ginger hair sprawled over the ice beneath her. Breathless she laid, thanking every Divine in the book.

A smile stretched across Rin's face. For a moment, things seemed alright, like she'd make it through this in the end. Yet as she examined the paper, her heart sank. Tears swelled. The vicious winds tore the map in two. Rin stared at the wall of snow. There was nothing there but defeat.

The whistling winds hollowed her mind. "It's okay, everything is okay," Rin forced herself to say as she reached for her bag behind her. "I'll just get off of this mountain, then find some help and ask for another map and—" Her fingers searched, only finding the numbing bite of snow.

Her bag.

Her bag was gone. She must have tossed it aside in the panic of chasing the map. Not only did that bag hold all of her food, water, and clothes, but it also contained all the information her father had given her before she embarked on this godsforsaken journey. A journey that now seemed like it would be the death of her.

Rin fell quiet, nothing to fill the silence but the howling wind. She stood and fought off tears.

People warned her gravely about this quest—about the dangers of traveling Nokomic alone and about losing her way and ending up in the middle of nowhere. Rin ignored all the worrisome villagers who tried to keep her in Aresan. They didn't understand—they weren't the ones searching for their mother.

Rin cut the thought short. Crying wouldn't solve her problems, nor would dying only to cause more grief for her father. She had to press on; she was bound to head down that cursed mountain at some point. "What goes up must come down, right?" she mused. There, she would get the help she needed. All she had to do was make it off of the mountain.

Chapter Two

R in couldn't help but remember how she ended up on this mountain. The arduous land she trekked was just as cold as the argument that sparked the journey.

She had been sitting at home months ago, watching the late summer storm brewing beyond her bedroom window.

The entire valley of Aresan seemed to sway with the wind. Even the Lennaels far west rattled with each crack of thunder. The petrichor was strong enough to make its way between the wooden boards of her house, tempting her to sneak out through her window and let the rain soak through her soul. She wouldn't even bother with her cloak. The thought passed when the dreaded echo of footsteps approached her door. Rin sighed and placed the scrap of paper into the book on her lap. She took a deep breath and closed her eyes to savor the few moments she had left with her thoughts.

Three knocks sounded on the door, followed by the creaking of the rusty hinges. Rin kept staring at her closed book, eyes glued to the red leather binding.

"Are we okay to talk now?" her father asked. He remained in the doorway. He hadn't even changed out of his field clothes yet.

Rin lowered her forehead to her knees, biting her tongue at the risk of tears swelling again. She prayed she could sink into the bare floor she sat on and disappear.

"Rin," her father said carefully as he took a step into the room. His eyes were heavy and dark. When was the last time they had known light? "I know how you must be feeling right now—"

"Do you?" Rin ground out before she caught herself.

Adrian Nowell dropped his gaze to the floor. "Yes, and that's why I'm here right now." He walked to Rin's side and sat down beside her against her bed frame. He tried to catch her gaze but gave up and decided on the window ahead instead.

Rin sucked in a burning breath; her throat tighter than a knot. She drew her head from her knees and focused on her reflection in the window. A mirror image. Rin was always baffled by how much she looked like her father, from his ginger hair to his green eyes. However, while his were rich as a forest, hers were radiant as an emerald. "I can't stay here. I know that this is our home and there's a life here for both of us, but—"

"Erin, there's more to it than comfort and security," her father interrupted. "I'm not trying to hold you hostage here. You don't understand."

"No," Rin said, sharper than intended, "I don't understand. Because you never tell me why when I ask!" She threw her arms to the ground and heaved herself off the floor, a surging anger seizing her chest. "I could understand if it was because Nokomic is dripping with crime! I could even understand if it's because you need me to help tend the fields and animals the rest of the season! But Da, those are such easy excuses to give and you've never given them! I'm twenty years old now. All I want to do is find my mother and ask her why she left us twelve years ago!" She marched to the window, digging her nails into the splintering wood, and turning to face her father. Oh, how her head rang in that anger. "One night she was here, and then I wake up and she's gone forever and I'm never told why. I've waited for so long. I've given you as much time as I could so I wouldn't rip up those memories for you, but you have to meet me halfway." She shook her head, rubbing her palms into her damp eyes and brushing the fray of her short hair out of the way. "I have to know why she left, Da."

Her father stared in silence, his brow creased downward, his lips tugged in a frown. Rin didn't think his joy ever fully returned in the last decade. "It sure takes the Flames of Ashnagz to get you going," he murmured, a grin twitching at his lips, "I don't know the last time I saw you this angry, Rin."

Rin blinked; her guard tossed to the side. She slid down against the wall facing her father. The fire in her chest died. "I—I didn't mean to yell at you—"

Her father shook his head. "It sure takes a lot… just like her." Adrian Nowell looked up at Rin and smiled warmly. "Look, I know that I've been a little… unfair with all of this. But you have to believe me when I say I don't know why she left, either." Something in his expression shook at the memory. Rin's chest panged with guilt immediately. He stood up before she could say anything. "Follow me," he said, then walked out of her room.

She trailed her father past the crackling fire in the hearth and into his study, lined with shelf after shelf of books, scrolls, atlases, and trinkets Rin couldn't even name. Surely there were far more books than any other villager in Aresan possessed; far more than any farmer ought to have. Da refused to sell any of his things from his time as a scholar in Croft, even if it seemed as out of place in their little cottage as a raging storm in the middle of summer. While her father walked behind his desk, she slid into the chair facing it. The seat was as large as it was comfortable, and as much as it dwarfed her frame, it was her favorite spot in the entire house.

Her father walked to a chest placed against the back wall and fumbled through the contents for a moment before he finally pulled out an envelope once sealed in yellow wax with a flower of lavender in it.

"What is that?" Rin stared at the envelope, the purple pedals stirring a faded memory.

"Twelve years ago, when your mother left," he said, carefully holding the broken seal, "she left this map." He slid a time-worn piece of parchment into his hand.

Rin jumped to her feet. Her father offered her the map. She took it gently. A thousand questions flooded her brain, but she only managed to grab one. "Why did she leave this?"

Her father scratched the back of his head, shrugging his broad shoulders. "I'm not sure." He sat in his chair, the wood groaning under his weight. "Your mother told me it was too dangerous to be around her and she needed to leave in order to protect us. She was leaving for a village named Lilit outside of Nokomic's reach, where the Resurrection couldn't find her. This is one of the few maps that marks the village. I think she meant if there was ever an emergency, that she would be here. That's only what I could assume. She left in such a hurry, she didn't have time to explain." A decade filled with sorrow stole the light in his eyes. Rin swallowed hard.

She couldn't take her eyes off the ink that marked Lilit on the map. "Do you think..." she glanced up as a smile spread over her face, "do you think she could still be there?" Her eyes were cautious, yet optimistic in the candlelight.

"It's been a long time, Rin," her father said. He watched her eyes dim to a look of defeat. He took a deep breath. "I wanted to go after her... but I couldn't leave you. Lilit is only a three-day journey around the Lennaels. I would have to stay here and take care of the farm, but... I believe it would do you well to travel there and see."

Rin's heart nearly pounded out of her chest. Her head whirled with excitement, and she had to sit down for a moment to calm herself. "Are you saying... I might finally see Ma again?" She tightened the grip she had on the edge of her shirt, holding her breath, waiting for his answer.

"Yes, I am," he said with a grin.

Rin sprang up from the chair like an excited goat. She cried with delight and ran back to her room, throwing various clothes onto the bed.

"What should I bring? How many clothes? Do we have any water pouches, or should I go buy a new one?" Her questions became incoherent ramblings. Barely being able to stand still, Rin struggled to grab the buckles to her satchel. Her excitement guided her throughout the house. She went through all of her drawers, shelves, and closet. Just as she was about to run out of her room to raid the rest of the house, Rin's father walked to the doorway of her room, trying his best to look excited for his only child. Rin took a step back, and her eyes softened. She wrapped grateful arms around her father and rested her head on his chest.

"Thank you," she whispered, tears collecting in the corner of her eyes. "I'm coming back, though. I would never leave you, not when you still have the rest of Nokomic to show me, not to mention the continent, and all of Armiria."

Her father smiled and put his arms around her. "I know," he said as he kissed her head. "But Rin... I was going to ask if you could—"

"Finish out this season with you?" Rin let go and smiled widely. His eyes were as red as hers. "Of course."

Her father smiled and nodded, pulling her back into his bear hug before he let her run back to his study to examine her mother's map.

Rin was excited beyond containment. For once in her life, she would not have to wake up to the only valley she's ever known. The roads east were too dangerous to travel, but the west? Her kingdom's problems didn't reach west into the Unclaimed Lands. The thought was exhilarating.

Chapter Three

The evening sun crept behind the horizon's frown, marking its inevitable defeat of breaking through the clouds.

The more she walked, the more Rin hated herself for her dull-witted attempt to divert from her original path around the base of the mountains. The landslide blocking the valley below was fresh and treacherous. Finding her way through the mounds of unstable rocks and mud would have taken twice as long as simply climbing the lowest summit of the Lennaels, that was, if a snow storm hadn't crept upon Rin. Even for someone accustomed to the Lennaels, crossing through the snow would have been a hellish task, so for Rin, perhaps impossible. The mountain itself made Rin's stomach twist, as if it was trying to blow her right off its side—something she tried not to take personally.

The sun was nowhere to be seen for hours, licking a numbing chill up her bones. Rin kept her hands tucked in her arms where her pits offered enough heat to stave off frostbite. She longed for the sweet fields of green and warm breezes. Just the mere thought of the sun's scorch tricked her senses into forgetting the harsh weather for a split second.

She walked blindly, graced by the divine Yath Ha that she didn't wander off a cliff. She passed through the occasional sprawl of withered trees and navigated dips in the terrain. Rin even decided the mountain would be quite beautiful if it were not for the heightening chance of death and the fact that she had looped around the same path twice.

"Okay, Rin. You've been going in circles for who knows how long." She sat down on a jutting rock, hoping her legs would not refuse to stand later. "At least I know which way not to go anymore, right? I mean, mistakes are only steps to make toward progress... or something like that," she said aloud, trying to remember what Da used to tell her as a child. It barely ruffled a smile. She pulled herself up using the low-hanging branch of the tree beside her.

"Just keep your legs moving," she said out loud. The cost of giving up crushed her spirit, and a decade-old dream of reunion. She would get down from the mountain and find her mom. Rin exited the scattered woods.

She took a small rock and scratched a big "x" into the middle of the bark, the same as countless others she had marked along her path. *That should do it.* The grove cleared into a vast field of snow.

Rin scanned the clearing for any threats. Her heart skipped a beat. Halfway across the clearing, she saw a silhouette hidden behind the veil of icy flakes. She looked around for any sign of a house. Nothing. Profanities flooded her mind as she refocused her attention on the person heading her way.

Can they even see me? she thought, squinting for more details.

Whether they were walking to her, or in her direction, Rin wanted to prepare for whatever could happen. But there was nowhere to hide, no one around to help her, nothing to do other than wait.

Wait.

Wait.

Wait.

The snow was an anchor on her feet. She didn't want to make any noise, but her stiffening joints made her want to scream out as the wind violated her body. She didn't care if she was frostbitten or going to lose a limb from the cold. All she wanted was to feel the grass caress her body in the fields of her village. If she couldn't do that at least one more time, then she might as well die right there. At least that's what the dehydrated, food-deprived thought whispered in her head. Rin marched through the snow. It crunched like eggshells under her boots. Just as she came close enough to see the brown leather of the figure's jacket, she stopped. She tucked her head behind her arms, guarding her face from the abrupt gusts of ice.

She inhaled as deep as she could before her lungs stung against the frozen touch, then closed her eyes. "H-hello?" she called against every objection in her head. She swallowed the trace of moisture left on her tongue. "I think I'm lost... Do you know the path that leads down this mountain?"

Chapter Four

In spite of the bitter storm, a trail of footprints laid behind Zarus Lowwenth. The Lennaels were far from a hospitable host on a good day, but to call this night *hostile* was putting it kindly.

Zarus glared at the gathering snow ahead. His raven hair twisted wildly in the wind, frost enveloped his coat, and the wind watered his eyes. He ignored it. The Lennaels' threats were empty to him... its dangers meek. He was more interested in the sudden aroma that pulled him from his home.

Zarus closed his eyes, inhaling the raging winds. "It couldn't be..." His face twisted in disgust. He hadn't met the scent of humans in ages. The doubt in his mind rattled with urgency, guiding his step toward the wind.

His stomach churned.

They can't be too far. I'll catch them before they even know I'm here. Biting down on the oily panic in his gut, Zarus lunged forward in a breathtaking stride. The blinding snow became a curtain concealing him and his hunt. Suddenly the unbridled dread knotting his chest swelled into his mind. Pandemonium flared in his head. Every step toward the stench caused the siren in his mind to amplify. He couldn't suppress it.

His body weakened.

Zarus's legs buckled, crashing hard into the snow. His hands shook violently. He felt as if his head had been cleaved open.

"Please don't..." he muttered to himself through clenched teeth. *It's just an animal——it has to be an animal.* Zarus couldn't convince himself. He pressed his hands against his head, falling deep into the panic that blinded his judgment. Memories of distant screams flooded his thoughts.

He bared his teeth against the clamor. He bit down on every nerve raging, every pound of his head until it finally became a whisper in the wind.

Zarus remained fallen on the ground with lead for lungs before he gathered the strength to drag himself out of the dense mound of snow. It was another few minutes before he stood.

As if the mayhem had never been there, Zarus gathered his resolve and continued tracking the scent until it led him to the edge of a field.

Chapter Five

"Can you hear me?" Rin called through the storm.

Her teeth gritted, she wanted to scream——out of frustration, anger, pain, or the agonizing wait for whoever was out there to answer.

"I need help. I have no idea where I am, and this storm isn't helping the matter!" She called out as loudly as she could, thinking the snow might muffle her voice. Little did she know the person ahead couldn't have been twenty feet away.

Her voice cracked. "If you could just tell me where we are, I'm sure that I can figure it out from there. I don't want to be a bother but—" Rin stopped in her tracks. She saw two eyes that resembled splashes of freshly poured wine. She faltered against the beating stare. She was almost grateful the falling snow masked the rest of his features. Something screamed in the back of her head to run.

The snow was already above her knees. She couldn't afford to stand in the open terrain much longer, yet she knew better than to turn her back on this man. She slowly began to step back from the silent silhouette.

"Who are you?" he asked.

"What?" Rin replied upon instinct.

"*Who are you?*" the man demanded. A low voice composed of shadows. The ferocity in it shook the mountain without ever raising. He pronounced each word thoroughly and clearly, and Rin couldn't decipher if it was an accent or not. But it was impatient.

"Rin," she mustered more sheepishly than intended. "My name is Rin Nowell." She only now noticed how rapidly her teeth were chattering. Audible enough to scare off the wildlife, if any wildlife was foolish enough to be caught in this weather.

"What are you doing on this mountain, Rin Nowell?" He didn't idle in conversation. Perhaps he was as cold as she.

Freezing. It nearly slipped her tongue, but she sensed that sarcasm would not earn his favor. "I was traveling, and got lost."

More silence. He was weighing her answer.

Another gust of wind crept through the curtain of snow, pricking away at her raw cheeks. Rin threw her arms up to protect her face. The pain of her glacial skin raged against her patience. Why was he taking so long? It wasn't a hard decision: yes or no. Would he allow her to go with him, or would he leave her to be buried? Or maybe... Was he lost too? Her gut twisted at the idea. Rin cast it aside from her mind. If she was going to die, whether by the blizzard or the hand of this bloody-eyed stranger, she would try to keep a level head in her last moments.

"Please," Rin pleaded, "I can barely feel my hands..." The sympathy card couldn't hurt at this point. Not when it was true.

The man said nothing. A throbbing pain welled in her head as her stare dropped to the snow, but the sensation dulled to memory. Rin looked up and nearly jumped to find that the man had moved closer. He studied her——his stare, so forbidding that Rin had to bite down on the urge to look away from it. Yet she had trouble simply not staring, albeit a little wide-eyed. Now that he was close enough to look at, she found a horror in front of her.

He looked akin to a wraith blending into the night, searching and studying her with that haunting gaze. Raven hair that spilled past his shoulders. Ghostly skin which sang nightmare. An expression that held the impending promise of harm.

Rin knew she was out of options. A sickness grabbed hold of her senses. Something inside her writhed against this like-wraith, yet she still couldn't convince herself to look away. It's not everyday you see a nightmare while awake. The shock trickled out of her gaze. His confusion subsided, and the nightmare-of-a-man stiffened. She opened her mouth to speak, but his voice silenced her.

He lowered his head, eyes closing tightly, like the words tore apart his insides. "Follow me," he sighed rather begrudgingly. Without giving Rin the chance to squeak a reply, the man turned around and stalked off to the field's edge.

The blizzard raged. Rin struggled to keep up with her escort——who didn't appear too concerned. She followed his tracks. It was only this man and herself on the mountain, which sent a rather unnerving shutter down her spine.

She tried to focus on anything but the chill reaching into her bones. *Who are you? Why did you help me? Where are we going? How do your tracks look like you're gracefully walking across the snow rather than trudging through?* Whoever this person was, he needed to focus on safely returning to shelter.

Rin tried to catch up to the stranger, but tripped over a snowdrift and fell flat on the ground. She tried to grab his arm for support, but he walked on and made no effort to help catch her.

The man nodded his head toward the bottom of the cliff, not caring about Rin's glare as she picked herself off the ground. "Down there," he said, "that's where we're headed."

The cliff, which Rin had only noticed after she finished patting the ice off of her hands, dropped to a small valley two hundred feet below. A dilapidated house stood within. She almost didn't catch her frown; it was going to be a long night.

Chapter Six

Zarus navigated the way down the cliff-side's winding path. He didn't concern himself with the girl's constant slipping. Yet, he couldn't help studying her. It was apparent she was no threat, but there was something about this human that stole his interest. She didn't notice.

As they closed in on the trail leading into the valley, distance no longer skewed perception: the old castle grew with every step. Rin gawked at the edifice, but Zarus had seen it a hundred times.

The ground hissed with every unsteady step the girl took, threatening to shatter the ice-coated walkway under her. Zarus rolled his eyes and strode seamlessly across the slick surface.

He pushed open the grand doors. They made their way into the foyer, the two of them tense and unsure of what to do. Zarus scowled once they were standing next to each other. This female's presence was odd, but he couldn't figure out why, proving irksome. Zarus closed his eyes and pinched the bridge of his nose. Frankly, he wasn't sure why he even brought her here.

Why?

The question echoed through Zarus's head. He hadn't intended to help her. He didn't want to approach her. Once he saw her silhouette in the blizzard, everything told him to let her die in the storm. Yet here she was, standing beside him with an air about her that called to him, and two emerald eyes pinned on him. He broke their gaze and walked into the sitting room adjacent to the foyer.

***

Rin stood in awe. She judged the house so easily at the top of the cliff, but quickly realized her mistake with every step until the castle's spires towered over her. She imagined what it looked like before time had taken its toll. Bricks and wood, that's what she was used to seeing at home, but the manor was stone. Crumbling stone at that. It was sad; no landscape, not even a tree. Only frost decorated the dreary castle.

It became apparent the walls inside hadn't held well over the years, but they kept out the unrelenting wind. She noted a grand staircase at the far end of the foyer, too dark to see past. Two rooms opened on either side of the entrance hall. To her left, Rin thought she saw a few glass shelves stretching from floor to ceiling, an array of disheveled books scattered about; undoubtedly the public studies she often heard of in magnificent homes. The room to her right was too dark to see anything other than a chair or two; perhaps a sitting room.

It was clear neither of them knew what to say. The man's expression soured as he turned to start a fire in the sitting room, and Rin realized she had been staring at him too long. Blood rushed to her cheeks. Desperate to ease the discomfort, Rin ruffled her mind for ideas.

"How, uh…" she struggled, the chill still holding firm on her throat, "how long have you lived here?"

The man looked over his shoulder. Rin couldn't tell if he was annoyed or disinterested. She sighed and followed her host into the parlor. The couch was filthy enough to suffocate, so she sat on the floor. Rin lifted her legs to her chest and miserably waited for the warmth to return to her body. She lowered her head to her knees, exhaustion a final weight on her shoulders.

Every time Rin's eyes gave into the temptation for sleep, the drafty house woke her again. She didn't have the energy to check the state of the fire. How long had it been since she sat down? Her mind no longer cared about vulnerability. Just as she was about to fall asleep, a physical weight fell on her shoulders

She tilted her head up and saw the man's boots tread back to the cold fireplace. The man's worn leather coat draped over her like a gown, still laced in ice from the storm.

Rin grabbed the edges of the coat and pulled the warmth around her face. The scent of the man filled her senses, striking in her mind something all too familiar. She inhaled more, drumming up the oddest memory of old books.

A flicker of light distracted her, and she looked up to find a fire blazing in the hearth. The heat soaked into her body.

"Warm up." The man stared into a corner opposite of her direction.

Rin watched him for a moment. There was something about this man… something that she pitied. The thought lingered as she moved to sit before the fire, putting enough distance between herself and her host to keep her anxiety at bay.

The fire thawed Rin's joints, letting her body relax after a day full of stress. Her face softened with contentment as she felt the heat's touch against her outstretched hands. The intensity of the flames roared bright enough to light the room. It danced upon both of their faces, desperate to fight off the shadows, yet this man kept his gaze away from the fire. *Does the light bother him?* As if he sensed her thoughts, he turned to the fire and watched the logs burn.

"I don't know," he finally said.

"Hm?" Rin hummed, not taking one lick of the flames for granted.

"I don't know how long I've lived here." Phantom chains held his stare on the hearth. His tone, however, not dreary, sounded as forced as malfunctioned machinery. Yet beyond the fire's gleam, this man's features actually weren't that daunting. He had almond eyes and high cheekbones. Intense as his demeanor may have been, the lines of his face appeared smooth next to the fire. Rin didn't feel like she was speaking with the wraith she met in that field, but rather someone in his late twenties.

"How do you not remember?" But before she could marvel at her lack of manners, the man stood abruptly. He muttered something under his breath, something Rin wasn't given the chance to question.

"You'll have to make do with the lackluster light. I don't have many supplies here, but use whatever you find in the room to your liking." His voice was strained, as if he was in pain. He crossed the corridor to the stairs at the end of the foyer. His movements were unsettling, like watching the injured attempting to hide a limp. He glanced at her over his shoulder and spoke so low Rin struggled to hear his words. "I'll return shortly."

She assumed that was the end of the conversation, but he stopped before he stepped onto the staircase. He didn't bother to look back.

"I'll try to answer whatever questions you have when I return." With that, he ascended the creaky stairs. Rin was left alone.

She thought about following him, but lost the idea as her eyes crept shut. Before she knew it, the crackling fire lulled her into a deep sleep.

***

Rin opened her eyes, waking from her sound sleep. Her head swayed as her eyes adjusted to her surroundings. Still the same jacket over her shoulders, still the same bitter temperature that she fell asleep in. However, she was not in the same room. In fact, Rin found herself standing at the top of a rather decrepit staircase. There was an odd sense of familiarity to it, but when she tried to look over the railing of the loft to the bottom, all she found was darkness.

A curious tug of her mind shifted her gaze. A dusty hall stood before her, decorated with frost and lit with stale moonlight seeping through a window across from her. She struggled to find the lines of where everything started and ended. The entire room hazed together. Darkness seeped down from the ceiling. Dread poisoned her mind. She feared becoming one with the lifeless scene that surrounded her. There were only two directions she could go: down the hallways leading east or west. Darkness welcomed her either way. She had to make a choice. A strange breeze pushed through the east hall. It snatched her attention, chilled her mind. The draft sent Rin's skin crawling.

She could have sworn she heard a voice.

"Help me..."

Ice pierced her mind. She took two steps toward the east hall. Four doors split on each side, all leading to nothingness. Rin watched the hall meticulously, searching for anything that could have been the origin of the voice. She stared and stared until her eyes burned, but not even the shadows shifted.

That couldn't have been him, right? *Rin thought to herself. Whatever voice she heard—if she had heard a voice at all—it belonged to a child. Its innocence and clarity didn't belong to the brooding man that saved her. Then another question welled: who called out to her? And why, in all of Yath Ha's greatness, were they pleading for help...? Rin wasn't sure she wanted to know the answer. That whisper—the helplessness of it cut into her mind like a hot knife. The sorrow that it wrung out corroded her heart. Without another thought, she walked into the hall.*

The air sat heavier here, swimming with an unnatural resonance. The hairs on her arms stood on edge. She prayed that her mind was just playing tricks, but a numbing fear struck a far worse discovery. She heard something so weak and fragile that she expected it to be another pitiful plea. Instead, the faint whisper grew into an orchestra of voices crying out in blistering agony. Rin's eyes feverishly darted around the chamber; nothing... nobody. The chorus persisted like steel cutting into her skull. The blaring voices grew louder and louder with her every step. How many were there? How many screams was she hearing? It was unbearable! And then, rising above all others: 'Run.'

Rin's body trembled as the cries amplified with warnings and hysteria.

'Get out!'

'Don't leave me!'

'We'll have to risk the storm!'

'It's getting closer!'

Rin yearned to run back to the staircase's lick of light. Tears flooded her eyes as she forced herself to press forward; she needed to help the child. The acidic burn of vomit crept up her throat as the yowls bounced off the walls. The pain, the pleas, the terror of whatever had happened to these people... Rin felt every bit of their hopelessness. Her heart pounded through her chest, her breaths short and quick. She closed her eyes. All she wanted was to collapse and scream.

Just when she thought she would surrender to the terror, when the bellows were so loud that they reverberated in Rin's chest, it stopped. Everything stopped. The screams, the pressure, even the feeling of desperation had fled her senses. Slowly, Rin opened her eyes. She stared at the doorless room before her: the end of the hall.

A staircase lingered in the corner to her left, but all Rin could do was stare into the empty room. There had been a door, but it was hanging on by a rusted hinge, cracked and splintered in the center of the frame. A chilling draft pushed against her body, freezing the sweat lining her forehead. Shadow veiled it, and she had trouble finding the lines of detail. Her nose wrinkled as she inhaled the musky aroma. Just enough moonlight leaked through a window, illuminating a crumbling hearth on the far wall.

Rin took one step onto the threshold, but the hiss of ice retracted her step. She felt that ghastly sense of dread poisoning her blood. It numbed her core with winter's breath. Suddenly, like a match striking, a flame flickered in the hearth. A flame that emitted no light, offered no warmth. Rin's heart froze.

"Run, Miss... Please, run away. Save yourself and just run..." Young, pained, fearful. The same voice as before.

Rin pivoted around and sprinted out the door. She flew down the hall, right past the screams of the damned. She raced for the stairs. Her head was spinning, her breaths stabbed her lungs, and she longed for home. No longer was the want of adventure resonating in her heart like a hopeless bell. All she wanted was to be off that gods-forsaken mountain. No more voices, no more mysteries, no more warnings.

Tears rolled back to Rin's ears as she burst into the open landing of the staircase. She sprinted right for the battered stairs and jumped for the bottom. It was a heartbeat too late before she realized it; the further down she fell, the wall of darkness grew. She couldn't do anything to stop herself from flying into that wall—a force so tangible that Rin's body jolted at the impact.

Her vision fled. She felt herself twisting and turning and writhing as she fell further and further into the nothingness below. It was impossible to ignore the screams now; impossible to stifle the overbearing panic grabbing her chest. Rin attempted to join the choir—to cry out for help, but the shadow smothered her. Nothing left her lips. Not even a whimper. She struggled to calm her breaths, struggled to do anything other than let panic engulf her mind. Her senses fell muted and crazed as she fell further and further and further.

Chapter Seven

Rin prodded the kindling into the hearth after she started shivering again. The storm still roared beyond the crumbling walls, yet she felt as if she had been ripped away from the castle and thrown into a frenzy of horror. She sat on the floor silently before the light, occasionally letting herself glimpse the man who sat on the couch. His crimson eyes pierced her each time.

Rin was never one for nightmares. When she awoke in a cold sweat to the man nudging her shoulder, asking what in Ashnagz she was moaning and groaning about in her sleep, her face nearly matched his eyes.

A dream. It had been nothing but a bad dream. Yet again, her host saved her. He was the one to wake her up from that gods-awful dream, after all. She didn't know how, but Rin was determined to pay this man back... eventually. Until she figured out how to do that, her mind didn't seem to stray far from the remnant sounds of an imaginary child's warning to run—

"I almost forgot." The man broke his silent stare after nearly half an hour. He reached over for a blanket rolled up into a tightly wound cylinder, and tossed it to her. It landed on the ground in front of her feet. She muttered her thanks as she met his stare, but guilt twinged a frown.

Rin winced, unable to give anything in return for his kindness. "Will you allow me to come back and repay you once I make it off this mountain?"

"I don't think that would be wise, Rin." He spoke with directness and intensity. Rin couldn't help but feel the need to cower.

"Because I already got lost up here once?" She chuckled, but wondered if she should be joking at all. There was something about his rigid stare and aggravated tone that kept her from trying to tickle a laugh out of him.

"Something like that," he murmured. She tried to decide if it was dread ridden on his face or simple discomfort. He looked away before she could tell. "What were you hoping to do before you got lost? There's not much to see on the mountains." The road from her thoughts to reality was rocky and rugged; she had to take a moment to process the question.

"I was traveling to a village on the other side of the Lennaels to find my mother." What might Cissrey Nowell have been doing at that second while her daughter froze? Rin's stare fell to the floor as she continued. "I took a wrong turn and found my way up here. This storm came out of nowhere, and I was going in circles." She couldn't believe how much had happened in one day. She flicked her gaze back to the man sitting in his chair, face devoid of any empathy. A huff filled her lungs, rolling her eyes to the fire again. What ever happened to answering any of her questions?

Rin unraveled the blanket as annoyance soaked in. She couldn't tell if it was once soft, or if it simply was never a pleasant fabric to begin with. Giving up on this man and falling back asleep crossed her mind, but she didn't want to while her host was still in the room. She still knew nothing about him. Rin tried to hide her irritation, but what did it matter? He wasn't paying attention, anyway.

"I, uh... I think I just wanted to see the world a bit, too," she added, staring into the fire again. She shrugged. "It's always been just out of reach, you know?" Rin thoughtfully bit the inside of her cheek; even back at home, she never said that out loud. Funny how strangers bring out unspoken truths.

"There are some maps here that you could take with you. I have no use for them." Rin glanced at him with a raised brow.

What do you care? She thought, but said, "What if you need them?"

"The chances of that are very unlikely, Rin." He was staring at her again, the same unsettling way he had when she first saw his eyes through the snow. Rin had a hard time meeting the gesture, but what really stuck out was her name. *Rin*. He kept repeating it, like she was a distant memory he was trying to recall.

The ghostly man spoke flatly. "There's a lot past the mountains—truths and myths. A map of the Unclaimed Lands could mean the difference between life or death." He broke the tension by placing his gaze on the fire. It was hard for Rin not to wonder what forged such an austere expression. "But you should know, it's dangerous to travel these paths alone. You never know what you might run into."

"I take it you know from experience." The possibilities teased Rin's mind with both horror and excitement. Zarus paused and she feared he had fallen back into a spell of silence; but to her surprise, he kept going.

"You could say that." It was clear he was referring to her, which was a curious thought in itself. Before she could ask, he stood up from his chair and found a place on the floor near her side. "Where are you from, Rin?" The change of his tone struck her blind side, as if a weight had been removed.

Why so casual all of the sudden? "Around a day and a half east of the mountain base." Rin spoke carefully. She might have told him something personal, but still wasn't keen on giving anything more than needed. Hearing herself addressed by name again poked at an impatience that had been building up for a while as well. "I'm curious. Do you have a name, or should I keep mentally referring to you as *this man*?"

"It's *male*, not man."

Rin furrowed her brow at the correction. "And your name?"

"...Ia sien Zarus Lowwenth."

I am called Zarus Lowwenth.

The words flowed off his tongue like a gentle breeze, as if built for the language of Caenlin. Merchants and travelers passing through Aresan used to speak it to reel customers in. She never delved into the dead language like her father, but picked up on small phrases. Maybe he was a scholar? Undoubtedly there was still distrust in his eyes, but Rin supposed revealing his name was a good sign. "Why are you looking for your mother?" Zarus asked.

"To ask her why she left, or to make a fresh memory with her," she said thoughtfully, sleep tugging on her mind. A yawn escaped.

Zarus considered her words, the wind beyond the walls howling at the mountains. "Why seek someone who wronged you?" His voice was a hush. He closed his eyes and lowered his head, thinking.

Rin stared for a moment at the sudden change of tone. "I wouldn't say *wronged*. I don't even know why she left... I'm trying to save the judgment until after I speak with her." She studied the pain in his expression. This *male* was troubled—deeply. He acted like he wasn't in the same world as her half the time. He bounced back and forth between balanced and broken. The brief conversation was pleasant, but Rin could not settle the unparalleled fear she felt the moment she stepped foot in this castle—this hollow, frozen castle—not even when she thought she was going to die earlier that day. She dropped her stare.

"I should probably get to sleep..." Rin sighed. The conversation was over.

***

Zarus glanced at Rin as she dozed off. He tried to keep calm, but his breath was lead. His pulse grew wild, like the uncontrollable winds outside. His head throbbed in the same rhythm as that siren. He tried to ignore it, tried to occupy himself by figuring out who this girl was. All in vain.

"*Not now...*" He seethed, shaking as if the storm had made its way into the crumbling estate.

He couldn't take his eyes off of the fire. He stared at the burning wood as the flames and smoke engulfed it.

A frigid wind crept into the parlor.

***

Zarus whispered something. Rin tried to investigate the fearful tone that emitted from the fearsome male, but another chill rattled her bones at the sight.

The like-wraith had come back to play. Motionless, he sat, shadows wrapping around his back like a veil. Unblinking, he stared into the heat of the fire so long that Rin's eyes burned for him. A mild tremble caught his hands. The longer she watched him, the more she saw the horror clawing at his insides. Pity panged through her heart. He was a statue carved of stone, crumbling from the inside out, pain etched through its grooves.

Just as Rin dug up the will to attempt helping this male, her host lurched over in a frenzied cry. The entire mountain must have shaken with him.

"*Stop!*" He staggered to his feet. His eyes were clamped, his head rocking. Zarus slammed against the back wall with enough force to crack the outer boards. "*Just leave me be!*" He opened his eyes long enough to look at Rin, misery cracking the whites, then sprinted out of the room and up the staircase without an utterance. His footsteps crashed against the steps. Rin sat alone with the fire, face pale as snow. A sickly knot tightened in her gut.

Rin was certain of one thing: Zarus was not screaming at her. While she sat there, unsure of what else to do but watch where he ran out of the room, the faintest whisper of a child continued to roam the spans of her mind.

Chapter Eight

Zarus stumbled up the stairs, blinded by the crushing weight in his head. He whipped around the edge of the loft's railing and headed to the east hall. An uncontrollable shiver shook his bones as he ran past the four doors. He cut a sharp left and made for the top of the staircase tucked in the corner.

It was a race against time, and time was not playing fair. He rammed into the last door on the third floor and slammed his hand against the frame. He gulped down the air like it was his first breath. The floor shook beneath his feet—a sickening sensation swirling in his head. He darted into the room, slammed the door, and slid down against the back of it, his breath clouding before his lips in utter mockery. A thin layer of frost started growing over his fingers.

"*Why now*?" he seethed.

No one answered. No one ever answered. He forced his eyes to open and look across the quarters. The mirror. He needed to get to the mirror. He pushed forward like his life depended on it, roaring against the cleaving pain.

***

Rin followed the sound up the staircase to the open hall overlooking the foyer. She ran down the east hallway, past the four doors until she reached the room on the very end. However a chill crept along her spine, halting her step. She stared at the room. And then the four doors she had passed along the way. This was the hallway from her nightmare. The door behind her had half fallen off. The hearth was identical to the one she dreamt of... but there was no voice emitting from it. No flame dancing in it. With difficulty, she tore her disbelief away from the scene and climbed to the next floor.

Zarus's commotion had silenced. Rin carefully walked across the eerie corridor until she found a door encased in ice. The frost bit into her hand when she grabbed the handle. The ice had sealed it shut; she couldn't even twist the knob.

Rin bit her cheek. Zarus was broken; even with how little she knew of him, that part was obvious. She could see his shadow under the door and gave the knob one last twist until the ice cracked open. She slammed her weight into it, banging it open against the inner wall, the hinges rasping sour notes.

An old desk rested along the wall, the top barely visible with the stacks of books and half-melted candles. Shards of ice transfixed the ceiling, growing downward like crystals in a cavern. A mirror on the far wall caught her gaze. The ornate craftsmanship took Rin's breath away. The engraving alone was as fine as the minute stitches of embroidery—carved from a material so dark that it absorbed the light. Barely a smudge of dust laid on the flawless glass. Rin stared at herself. It stirred a feeling of unease. Maybe it was her lack of sleep or the darkness surrounding, but for an instant, she saw the mirror cast a glow. It was ever so slight, but possessed a thrum of power, nonetheless.

Rin glanced down below the mirror and gasped. Zarus lay motionless on the floor, arm stretched out toward his reflection. It appeared like he was dragging himself toward the mirror. A tangible pressure weighed on her chest. Her head throbbed and her breath hitched in her throat.

Rin fixed her eyes on his unmoving body, waiting... willing him to show some sign of life. The situation called for panic, but somehow she forced the tremble from her hands. If this male really was injured, or worse, she would have to abandon her anxiety. She shut the door behind and walked toward him.

Zarus stirred when the door creaked shut. Prying himself up, he placed both hands on the mirror and leaned his head against it. Rin thought her eyes must be playing tricks on her, for she swore the reflection rippled.

Zarus growled, but shame dabbled with his tone. "What do you want?"

Rin felt dazed. "I don't really know," she admitted, taking a step closer to him. "It seemed like a bad idea to leave you alone."

Zarus slowly turned to her, a shadow falling over his face, leaving an ominous flash in his eye. Rin instinctively shifted back.

"Do I frighten you?" he tendered.

Rin stared at him for a moment. There was no use in lying. "If there was something to fear, it would have harmed me from the start. You concern me."

"Enough to make you leave?"

"Enough to make me find help."

Zarus stepped into the light shining through a smudged window. "Do you stay here with me, or risk the storm and go meddle with those lowly insects for help?" His eyes narrowed with abhorrence.

Was there no other option? Rin felt a sudden dizziness overcome her. Everything he said fluttered around her head until she pinned down something to focus on. "Insects?" she repeated, shaking her head. "You act like you're not even—" Fear shook her voice. This stranger, resembling a shadow of a wraith, eyes red as blood, alone and broken in the cold. Male, not man.

"Not even human?" Zarus offered dryly.

Rin couldn't speak, she couldn't even move. All she could do was stare, the whites of her eyes rounded. A chill ran through her core.

Zarus bled the tranquility of the night dry until his smirk grew into a laughter of mockery. He took a step closer until he towered over her. His face was void of any morbid amusement, save for the cruelest curve of his lips. "Don't make me laugh, Rin. Haven't you figured it out yet?"

Rin stared back into his nightmarish eyes. *Not human. What else is there to be?*

"Why do I call them insects?" he snarled. "Because their order is flawless, their community is perfect, but if something different comes around the nest, they won't hesitate to label it as a threat. They'll do anything to get rid of it. It could be as harmless as an odor. Sometimes it's even willing to help, but they still wipe it away. Even if it's one of their own. And what's more, Rin..." Zarus paused; a sigh of disgust escaped. "Humans are worse. They have attachments to those around them, to their friends and family, but have no trouble cutting those bonds the moment they don't like something about you. The moment you're perceived as a threat. Any relationship you once held: severed."

His expression, the pain within, pulled on her heart. Yet it alarmed her. There was still one thing Rin didn't understand. "Why are you telling me this?"

He stared as if unaware he said anything to begin with. "I'm not sure. You're one of them, after all." His voice trailed into thought, eyes glancing down with inquiry rather than remorse. "I haven't spoken to anyone in quite some time... What year is this anyway?" he asked, changing the subject at such a pace that Rin barely kept up with him.

"It's the year... 541?" Rin asked herself more than him.

Her host's face fell unamused. "You don't sound sure about that."

"Well, maybe if you had the day I've been having, you'd understand that I'm not exactly working with all my brain power right now," Rin's words bit harshly. Zarus said nothing, didn't even bat an eye.

"Is everything okay?" Rin was afraid of his response.

"AP?"

"What?" Rin uttered. She felt her cheeks burn red as his frown morphed to blatant annoyance.

"541 AP?" He emphasized, each word sharp as a needle. "Is it five hundred and forty-one years After Peace?"

Five hundred and forty-one years since the last peace treaty of the continent was signed, and the calendar started anew. She nodded slowly, exhaustion weighing heavily.

"541..." Zarus muttered to himself, his hand sweeping his hair out of his eyes. Rin wondered if he was trying to convince himself it was true.

"Only a few months till the new year, actually," Rin added. "Are you alright?"

He ignored her. "I know it's been a long time, but 541? That's too long... has that much time really passed?"

His eyes trailed to the elegant mirror behind him. Rin found herself unable to articulate the curious feeling of sorrow that the beautiful piece evoked. Perhaps it was the grandness of the mirror shoved in an abandoned castle, or maybe the glow that glued her eyes to the lonesome glass. She stared at the mirror as silence befell them. Two separate reflections stared back, a world apart.

Just when Rin opened her mouth, three thunderous knocks echoed throughout the halls of the estate. Zarus's attention ripped away from the mirror. His face drained of color, his eyes widened. A moment passed where neither of them moved, but he eventually led her to the top of the stairs overlooking the vast atrium. Zarus's wan expression assured her he wasn't expecting company.

What on Armiria could be outside right now?

She turned to Zarus, but whether it was rage or terror shaping his face, Rin knew not to say anything. He refused to take his eyes off the front door, even when he spoke.

"Find a room and hide."

Chapter Nine

Rin saw the fear on Zarus's face and ran to the closest door she could find. A small closet in the corner of the open landing. The weight pressing down on her head returned. She placed her ear against the cold door and listened to the blaring silence.

***

Zarus glanced towards the closet. *Don't come out,* he channeled.

He sighed and walked down the staircase through the foyer. The presence looming outside the castle walls was suffocating. His hand went for the handle of the door, but he stopped before touching it. This meeting was inevitable. He knew that. His heart thundered, the trembling of his hand returned. He furrowed a brow, trying to find a reason he shouldn't turn away. The temptation to ignore the knock nearly won over, but he hesitated. Rin.

His mind urged him to just leave her, to let her fend for herself and deal with the consequences of finding her way onto this mountain. He wasn't responsible for her well-being. Yet he couldn't leave her to face a monster alone.

Zarus scoffed. He yanked the door open with such force, the iron's screeching protest panged throughout the empty halls. "Why are you here?" he barked at the black-eyed demon towering beyond the door.

Eretimis Havilurce smiled, completely unfazed by the insolence. "It is nice to see you too, Zarus." Zarus couldn't say the same. He merely snarled at the repose. The demon looked him up and down, the snow falling off his long ebony hair with the movement. He looked exactly the same as the last time Zarus saw him; from his square jaw to the bulk of his frame. "I would expect nothing less than you running off to such glacial conditions." Malice whorled within his almond eyes. This male donned no armor, sported no weapons. He wore a black tunic, a belt made of gold fabric around his waist. His demeanor denoted poise, regality held in his appearance, but that didn't mean he was harmless. It was all a mask that could slide off faster than a heartbeat.

"*Why*." Zarus was unwilling to play along. Not this time. He stood on edge as the newest visitor of the night smiled at him with soulless eyes.

"Why do I always come back?" Eretimis's smile twisted. The male's low voice was as sinister as it was tranquil; the calm after a battle.

Desperation. Zarus nearly said it, but he knew it could spark unwanted conflict. "There's nothing I can do for you, Eretimis." The moments that passed were slow, digging into Zarus's restraint without mercy. The malevolence staring back at him knew it, too.

"But you see, Zarus, there is," the male said with a sharper edge to his voice. "Your mind will help me guide a new age. No matter how far you run, I will always make it back to your door. However, I clearly stayed away too long this time. You lost your manners."

Zarus outright scoffed. *The cold is far more than you deserve.* Although the words never made it past his tongue. As if royalty itself were standing before him, Zarus stepped aside and let the demon walk into the castle. A knot tied Zarus's chest, tightening his breath. The unwanted guest paused in the middle of the foyer and turned to him.

Zarus tried to suppress his dread, tried to keep his demeanor and thoughts void of stress, but the pound drumming in the back of his head was ferocious. A gusting wind pulled his attention back to reality. He forced the door closed against the worsening storm, sucking in a deep breath, only to find Eretimis studying the hearth.

"I have never known you to sit in the light for comfort, Zarus," he commented offhandedly. Ill intent lurked behind each word.

Zarus hadn't thought about the fire. He pretended to be unscathed so as not to lose composure. He forced himself to walk closer to the demon.

His stomach rolled. Their eyes met. Eretimis's unreadable—hollow. The longer Zarus stared into that familiar face, the more he remembered the last time he stood before this monster. When everything fell apart.

His guard unraveled. *Not now. Keep it together for a few more minutes.* His head split in two, his composure escaping through the cracks. "I will never stand beside you again, you traitorous leech," Zarus growled. "You are not welcome here. Leave."

"But Zarus," Eretimis said, holding his hands up in feigned offense, "if I did that, then how would I find the girl you are hiding?"

Zarus felt his heart drop and he couldn't explain why. He pretended to be unamused, but he spoke too tightly. "There's no one else here." He felt icy sweat forming along his spine.

The demon's dark eyes flickered at the invitation; he accepted it blissfully and looked down the desolate hall. "The room stenches of her; in fact, the whole castle reeks." He stepped down the threshold. Sadistic delight molded his expression. "So where is she tucked away,

Zarus? And why are you trying to hide her?" Eretimis looked back at his host.

Zarus snarled. "There is no one else here, Eretimis. Trust me when I say things won't end the same way as last time if you stay here any longer." There was no room for discussion.

"Save the melodramatics, *uhlandyi*." Zarus's temper riled at the name. "I will leave if you want me gone that badly, but do not think this is the last time we meet." At that, the male stalked across the corridor and opened the door. Zarus stepped out of his way without objection. He gritted his teeth against the wind that crept through the open door. It was only against the bone white backdrop of the blizzard that Zarus noticed that there was something different about this demon from the last time. What used to be skin warm as the desert was now drained of saturation, as if the pigment had slowly leaked out. Eretimis glanced a dark eye over his broad shoulder before he walked out. "I think it would be wise to get rid of that human before I return." Eretimis let out one last vituperative smile, then shut the door behind him.

Zarus immediately let out a sigh as the demon's presence disappeared. He trudged to the sofa before the fireplace and fell into it. The weight on his mind gradually dissipated, his headache fading.

"You can come out now." His fingers pinched the bridge of his nose.

Snow began to cascade from the ceiling.

Chapter Ten

'But Zarus, if I did that, then how would I find that girl?'

Rin's body turned to stone. How did he know she was there? This stranger sent a chill down her spine. His voice moved through the air like oil running across skin. The thought of this person finding her was enough to invoke raw fear.

The conversation continued back and forth, but she heard none of it. Her head spun out of focus. She set her eyes on the darkness around. Rin calmed enough to hear his farewell. And then silence as she slumped to the floor. A few moments later, she heard Zarus's voice.

Get up, Rin.

It took a while for her to muster the strength to leave her only sense of security in that closet. Her host was lying back on the couch, eyes closed, and the bridge of his nose pinched. And snow? Snow was falling inside the house.

Zarus slowly sat upright. Neither of them spoke. She studied the lines of his face; more taut and troubled than when she found him beneath the mirror. "Old friend?" she finally asked.

Zarus snapped faster than a bear trap. "That bastard is no friend of mine."

Rin hesitated. "How does he know that I'm a girl just from my scent?" It seemed like a decent start. Zarus had already implied he wasn't human, so maybe this newcomer wasn't either.

"A human nose is too weak to catch the stench." His tone was short and stressed as he stood up and walked to the windows. Rin didn't have the energy to take it personally.

"Is he some sort of animal?" she asked, trying to imagine what he looked like, but the only thing that appeared in her head was darkness. It was more than merely a dark nothing. Nothing would have been more settling. Cold, swarming darkness with no form and no life... Zarus's voice pulled her back to reality.

"You could call him that, but you would risk offending every animal alive. There are many beings that can sense beyond your abilities."

"Okay then, why was this non-human here?" Rin felt a tinge of annoyance at his vagueness. "Is he here to hurt me?" She dared to let the question slip her tongue.

Zarus sighed. "He won't find you." Rin was startled by the sudden sincerity. The flames in the hearth painted shadows along the contour of his face. "He's a demon, like me. I've known him for nearly all my life." Spoken with as much enthusiasm as a prayer to Vulyn, host of the dead.

Oh, no big deal. Just a *demon* out and about on the mountain, making menacing threats against her. Rin's insides twisted. "Why should I be gone before he comes back?" *And why is he coming back if you don't want him to?*

The like-wraith said nothing, his eyes narrowing as he thought. She could feel her heart drumming on, leaning in closer for an answer. "Do you really want to know who he is?" Zarus finally asked. Yes, she did, but the warning in his voice caused her to falter. A world of demons didn't sound like something she should dabble in. Did she have a choice at this point? He knew she was here, threatened her should he find her. Rin hadn't realized her head started nodding until she saw disappointment on Zarus's face.

Clearly, he didn't want to talk about this demon, but by the Divine Lhaerem's judgment, Rin could sense the importance of it. For her own good, she did not back down, even while seeing the distress it wrung out of Zarus.

He sucked in a deep breath before speaking. "The Dark Tyrant Eretimis is a demon who came to this world a long time ago." Each word sounded like a stab in his side. "He and I have a long history." Rin watched Zarus cross his arms and lean against the wall as he spoke. His eyes focused on nothing in particular. "Ever since I met him, he's wanted me as his underling. So much so that he has hunted me down and searched for me across the world. He tried to convince me to join his plans, and eventually..." he paused for a moment, "eventually I agreed. He was my mentor, but it didn't last long. I left on bad terms, and haven't seen him since."

"Until tonight?" Rin asked tentatively.

"Until tonight," he nodded.

Rin watched his sadness grow. She moved closer to the fireplace and sat down, running into the snowflakes still frozen in the air. Rin opened her mouth. "What does Eretimis want you to be a part of?"

Zarus glanced at nothing in particular. "Change. Some kind of change. He leads his followers to assault Armiria, claiming it's an effort to get revenge on humanity for what they did during the Crimson War. It's a lie. He was always hiding something, but I escaped before I ever figured it out. He holds a stronghold in the north, out of human perception."

Crimson War? Rin furrowed her brow. When were humans ever at war with demons? "Why did you need to escape?"

Zarus let out a sharp sigh, uncomfortable with an uncomfortable topic. "He tried to kill me. I think that warrants enough cause to flee." Her eyes widened.

Rin dropped her stare and bent her knees to her chest. Another question sprouted, one she didn't want to ask. "What happens if he finds me?"

"He would kill you."

The world fell still. Rin's fragile resolve dwindled into sheer nausea. She finally gave into the desire and touched the floating snow, desperate for a distraction.

"Kill me?" Rin repeated, panic flooding her voice. Zarus nodded. "Why? What did I ever do to him?" She shook her head back and forth in hopes it would wake her up from this hellish nightmare. "What am I supposed to do? I can't just wait here for him to murder me! But the storm isn't letting up..." Rin's desperation was apparent, but she didn't care. Not when some murderous demon was going to kill her! "Oh gods, oh gods, oh gods..." she whispered as she buried her tears into her knees. She hugged around her legs so tightly the muscles were going numb. At last, Rin looked up only to find Zarus staring down at her.

"Is it too much to ask that you keep it together?"

Tear-streaked, Rin opened her mouth, but couldn't find the words.

"Did I not just say he wouldn't find you?" Zarus asked rather directly.

Rin wiped a tear from her cheek. She didn't get it. "Why are you helping me?"

Zarus waited to answer, unsure of himself. "He's caused enough strife for enough people."

Rin's lips straightened. "I'm sorry for what he did to you," she said. Having Eretimis show up at his doorstep couldn't have been easy.

Zarus growled bitterness. "I don't need your pity, Rin." He hushed his aggravation and started pacing across the parlor. "We need to figure out a way for you to make it through this storm."

Really? Maybe she hit a sore spot, but she was only trying to be considerate. She just couldn't win. "My supplies were lost to the storm. Even then, I don't know how to get down this mountain." Rin frowned as she racked her brain for any ideas worth mentioning. She had a feeling that brainstorming with Zarus was an endeavor in itself.

Rin took a deep breath, resting her head on her knees. A mere hour of sleep wasn't doing much to help the situation. She fidgeted with Zarus's jacket in her hands, feeling the worn leather against her palms. She forgot she was wearing it.

"I've got it!" Rin yelled, disturbing the pensive room. She couldn't suppress her laugh as Zarus's red eyes rounded. "What if I made my way down the mountain smelling like something else? What if I smelled like an animal?" Zarus narrowed his eyes, unsure of what she meant at first, but he then looked at the coat over her shoulders and understood.

"Masking your own scent," he whispered. "You're not as foolish as I thought. It might work." Rin offered the demon a rather obscene gesture. Her smile didn't fade; not when she found a way for herself to live.

Zarus muttered to himself as he ran through the possibility. "I have no way for you to smell like an animal. Maybe wearing my clothes?" he suggested, pacing across the room, but he frowned. "It wouldn't be enough. All that's left... would be blood."

What? Rin's smile fell. "What about blood?" she quickly asked.

"If you wear my clothes and blood, it might be enough to hide you." The breath left her lungs, her stomach churned. Blood, of all things, was not something she took well to. Just the thought of it made her queasy.

"Um, Zarus?" she tried to catch his attention.

"He might not fall for it, though," Zarus continued on, too transfixed in thought to hear her.

"Zarus..."

"But under the right circumstances of the storm..." He turned to her, a sly smirk curving his lips.

Rin attempted to smile back, tried to enjoy the all-too-rare smiles that made Zarus actually look approachable. She couldn't even force a grin. "Y-your blood?" she stuttered.

"Do you know where we can get someone else's? Of course my blood," he snorted. "Why?"

Why? Rin opened her mouth, but had difficulty finding any words for a moment.

"Because you'll get hurt!" she blurted. "Y-you can't just wipe your blood on me! How are you going to get it?" Rin shook her head. Cutting him up couldn't be the only solution.

Zarus shrugged. "A little blood loss won't kill me," he said. He acted as though it were a casual subject to him—using his blood as a tool. Rin listened in horror, and she wasn't even the one who would be cut. "The only thing that worries me is that no one is ever in this area, so even if he were to smell you as a demon, it wouldn't be believable..."

Not only that, but Rin let out a sigh as she thought of another drawback. "It wouldn't make sense if there were two people emitting your scent either," she frowned, swatting some of the snow in the air. "Having you be in two places at once would instantly give it away." So much for a brilliant idea. Maybe it was for the best; she felt guilty. In fact, she felt bad about everything that had happened. Instead of just packing up and leaving, Zarus felt the need to help her escape

Eretimis's malice. Rin fell back into the chair beside the fire. "Why are you going to so much trouble to help me? I mean, wouldn't it be easier to give me a map and point to the nearest town?" Exhaustion muffled her words. "I may have gotten lost, but I know how to read a map." When she opened her eyes, she scrunched her nose back at the demon. "What?"

Zarus looked at her as if she spoke through a foreign tongue. "How far did you travel before you got lost?"

She stared at him blankly. How on Armiria was she supposed to know? *She* was the one to get lost. "I remember the sun being out on the paths near the mountain's base, then this storm struck, and after that I really couldn't tell. It hit so quickly, and all the sudden I ran into you." She shrugged. "How come?"

He shook his head. "This is Hilyan's Peak, Rin. The highest point of the Lennaels. The closest town is halfway down, at least two days on human foot. How did you think you could cross it in one day?" It was a good question, but Zarus was just as confused as her.

"We're at the top?" she dared ask. Rin felt the color drain from her cheeks, yet her head burned like the flames in the hearth. "No, that can't be... I wasn't even trying to pass over the mountain!" She rubbed her temples as a splitting headache swelled. This entire evening felt like she was trying to climb a ladder, but someone just kept adding extensions so she would never get to the top. Only she had gotten to the top, but the top was *not* by any means her destination.

"How long will it take to get to the bottom?" Rin dreaded the answer.

"Well," Zarus began, regaining his stoic composure, "a few days if you really rush." He rubbed his fingers against his closed eyes. "Leave it to a human to make such a mistake."

"I'll be buried in snow before he even finds me..." Rin whispered.

Zarus's eyes stirred in calculation. "If you left right now, maybe you could make it. I can't sense Eretimis outside, but something tells me he has an eye on this area." He looked at Rin in a movement so jolting, she nearly jumped. "It's decided then."

Rin rose a brow. "What's decided?"

"I'll guide you down this mountain. You'll still have to have my blood on you, though. The less trackable you are, the better."

It was an effort to keep her mouth from hanging open. Guide her down? Zarus was far from a social person. Yet he was willing to escort her down this dangerous and uncertain path? She met his stare with wide eyes, only to find the last thing she expected. Curiosity. It sent a shiver up her spine. With this male's hatred for humans, his interest in her only appeared morbid. He was a danger in his own right.

"Just don't hurt yourself too badly," she quietly pleaded. She would either live or die tonight. Zarus offered some strange sense of safety that she couldn't afford to deny.

"It's only pain," he said, his voice carrying like the wind's whisper. "It fades."

The front doors cracked and moaned with the surging winds. It stole Rin's attention, an oily fear spreading through her gut. She couldn't look away from that old rickety door. "What if he's out there right now, just waiting for the perfect moment?" She shrank further in the chair. Eretimis was a demon, and something told Rin that their strength in legends had not been exaggerated. She would be helpless.

Zarus rolled his eyes. "I already said he will not find you," he muttered as he stood up and made his way into the shadows of the house.

Rin couldn't help a grin from forming as she jumped up and followed behind.

Besides, how many people can Eretimis really get to help him kill one person?

Chapter Eleven

R in stood at the massive door in wonder, holding the lantern close to Zarus as he unbolted the latch. He slid open the heavy door, her heart pounding at what might be on the other side. The rusted rollers sang and an orchestra of metal sounded through the halls.

As they walked through the door, Rin raised the lantern higher, revealing shattered glass on the floor and cracked furniture strewn about. Zarus was unfazed. He walked through the mess to the cabinet against the far wall. Rin waved away the dust that clouded the air and saw an assortment of timeless treasures. Fur capes, satin robes, leather coats. There was even a pair of mud-caked boots. None of which were Zarus's, apparently. *So whose were they?* He handed her a leather coat lined with fur. She removed the one he had lent her, grateful for the warmth of the fur.

Rin wanted to ask about the garments, but before she could open her mouth, Zarus turned and took her through another corridor. They made their way down a narrow staircase and ventured past a decrepit greenhouse and a dingy kitchen. Zarus finally stopped when he got to a desolate room made of stone. There was a rug discarded in the corner. Had it been spread out, she would have never seen the trapdoor in the center of the floor. Zarus opened the vault and led her down a ladder into a room so cold that she nearly froze to the bones. As she scanned the room, she was stunned by enough weaponry to arm a militia.

She wondered once again; just who in Armiria did this castle once belong to?

While she gawked at the swords, lances, bows, and remaining armaments stored, Zarus walked to a section of knives on a table. He found a silver dagger decorated with ornate carvings.

Rin had never seen such a blade; made not for work, but death. She was too mesmerized to realize he was lowering it to his palm. Zarus sliced the steel into his flesh. Blood rushed to the surface and streamed down to the stone floor. A tocsin sounded in her head.

Zarus remained silent, looking at her ashen expression.

Woozy, Rin cleared her throat enough to speak, but words failed her. Slowly, her head nodded up and down. The male just sliced open his hand, for Yath Ha's sake. She shut her eyes, left in a sickly haze as Zarus wiped the blood across her cheeks, forehead, and hands. When she finally stifled her queasiness, she glanced at his hand. Blood still rushed out. After a brief argument that even demons could get infections, Rin tore off some fabric from the bottom of her undershirt and wrapped his hand. He didn't protest. And as a show of his gratitude, Zarus offered her a scimitar in return. The peculiar curve of the blade bent the lantern light. She held the crimson handle with a firm grip, following the black veins lined in the material down to the red gem set in the pommel.

***

"It would be easiest to cross over the mountain," Zarus said to himself as he gazed into the crackling fire. The sun was now reaching over the horizon, and although Rin hadn't slept a wink, she was just happy for the night to be over. He asked, "You're going to the other side anyway, right?"

Rin nodded, forcing a smile to her drowsy expression. "I don't care how we go. I just want to leave this snow behind and live to tell it." Not letting her exhaustion grow too far, she stood up from her chair and stretched her legs by the dying hearth.

"Then let's leave. I don't want to stay here any longer than we have to." Zarus gathered up the few maps he had snuffed out of the castle and placed them into a satchel. The nearest town was a day's walk if she could keep up with his pace.

She tried not to think about the ravenous growl of her stomach when Zarus mentioned they would have to find food along the way.

Rin bit back the shiver of a sudden draft. She looked up and found Zarus standing before the hearth. Snow smothered the flames until the fireplace was dark and cold once more. As the snow gradually stopped, Zarus was met with her toothy grin.

"So you *were* causing the snow inside before!"

"First time you've seen magic?" he asked with the slightest grin. Rin couldn't help herself. She nodded so violently; her head rattled. However, confusion spread across Zarus's austere features. "Is it not common anymore?"

"I've only heard it in stories." Her smile deepened, which lasted only until she felt the dried blood flaking on her cheeks. "There's a dangerous reputation around users from what I've been told. The Resurrection likes to snuff them out."

"The Resurrection?"

Rin furrowed her brows. "The organization that's been terrorizing Nokomic for the last seventy years. They held rule over the government until the last decade or so." Zarus simply shook his head. Rin stared suspiciously for a moment, but shrugged. "I heard a rumor that a user lived in my village many years ago, but we never crossed paths."

"Pity," Zarus whispered.

A spirit of inquiry plastered over her face. So if magic *was* real…

"Hey, Zarus," Rin said softly, "what is that mirror for?" The question may have seemed out of nowhere, but it had been bearing on her mind all night.

Zarus blinked a few times, clearly not expecting the question. "I'm not exactly sure," he finally admitted.

Rin raised her brow. "Then why did you run to it before?"

"It absorbs the excess of my magic that I can't control, but I don't know its original purpose," he said, breaking their stare. He paced around the parlor, the wooden floor moaning with each step until he halted near one window. "It allowed me to escape Eretimis once."

"How?" Rin asked a little too quickly.

"It teleported me away," Zarus said to her reflection in the glass pane. "I don't know how it worked, nor where it took me. It was probably used for travel. The thing must be ages older than me."

Rin met his reflection's gaze. "Where did you find it?"

"In an abandoned Aeliun fortress; that's all I wish to say of it."

Aelius the ancient empire that split into Nokomic and Damrok? How old is he?

She had read the empire fell to ruin because of a sudden attack on its capitol over a thousand years ago and caused the stir of tension in the continent today.

He turned around, changing the subject. "How's the blood?"

Rin lifted a hand to her cheek, feeling the crusted blood flake off of her skin. "It's dry." It still didn't sit well that someone else's blood covered her, but she found not thinking about it helped... sort of.

Zarus strode to the front doors of the estate. "It will have to do. The sun rises lower every night now, so we shouldn't drag our feet about leaving."

Rin tried to prepare herself for what would come next. She wrapped her coat around her torso and straightened the collar around her neck. After tugging on her pack's strap and patting the hilt of her scimitar beneath her coat, Rin nodded at Zarus. "Now or never."

The doors opened, and the sun's pale light flooded in. The storm hadn't let up at all. Rin longed for nothing more than to shut the doors and relight the fire. She took a deep breath, ignored the drumming of her head and heart, and forced her legs to push through the snow.

"Stay close to me." Rin could barely hear Zarus's call over the winds. He walked out the door, somehow staying leveled on top of the snow's delicate surface. She swallowed a deep breath and followed.

Divine above, help us.

Chapter Twelve

The next day and a half was treacherous.

Whether it was making sure Rin hadn't been buried alive or they hadn't picked up unwanted followers, Zarus was constantly looking over his shoulder. The snowfall pressed down. By late afternoon, the storm lightened enough to find their first stop. One of Nokomic's many outposts in the Unclaimed Lennaels: a small village tucked into the side of the mountain halfway to the bottom. Snow piled against the wooden cabins throughout the village, undisturbed and fresh. No one was in sight. After the better of an hour of going from door to door, Zarus found a sign frosted to the entrance of a shop.

Season worse than usual.
Back when snow melts.

Zarus busted down the wall of a cottage so Rin could stock up on whatever dried food had been left behind. They rested briefly and left before sundown. His goal was to reach the next outpost before nightfall. But the sun slid behind the horizon too quickly, and the blizzard raged on.

A sheet of white surrounded them, the snow reaching Zarus's shins. He looked for his companion, but the thick veil was deceptive. "Rin!" he called.

"What?" she shouted, redirecting her step to his voice.

"You're moving too slow! Pick up your pace!" Damn his tongue for shouting so mindlessly.

"What did you say? The wind is too loud!"

"I said you need to—"

"What?"

Zarus staggered against the surge of vexation. The girl was tired. Her slowing pace announced it loud and clear. Too long. They had been in the open for too long.

"For the love of those damn gods you worship..." He trailed back to Rin, startling the girl as he appeared out of nowhere. Without giving her a chance to open her mouth, Zarus grabbed her wrist, trudging onward.

Rin squirmed in protest. "I can walk by myself! If you would just slow down—"

"If I slow down, Eretimis will find us and you'll be dead!" Zarus barked.

As if the deities themselves wished for his failure, the world was smothered in a cloud of snow that Zarus couldn't escape. Rin wasn't much to pull, but the snow was still piling. He spewed profanities at the world, but forced forward. Twilight was the final straw. They needed shelter.

"I can't see anything. This wind is tearing apart my eyes," Rin stammered.

Zarus sighed and narrowed his eyes against the brutal winds; he didn't even know which direction they were heading. He had an idea, but it would cost them.

They'll find us if I do this...

The other option was being found right here, right now, in this hellacious situation. They would be as good as defeated the moment

Eretimis's followers showed. Zarus cursed. Whatever the outcome, they needed the risk.

Zarus closed his eyes against his better judgment. His face stained with focus. His mind surged with a feathery force that rang through his soul; a siren urging him to act. A dome formed high and wide around them, the snow and wind locked outside of the protective shell. Rin's head lifted curiously at the sudden tranquility.

"What's happening?" she asked.

Tension coursed through his body, lining his muscles and steeling his bones. He couldn't even open his eyes. His magic wouldn't be able to hold for much longer.

"Do you see a cave?" Zarus managed through bared teeth. Rin heard the strain in his voice and didn't question further. It felt like an eternity while she searched. Drafts broke through the dome. His grip was slipping.

"Quickly, Rin!" he yelled.

"Straight ahead, one hundred feet," she squeaked. "Zarus, what is this—"

His eyes tore open, and the dome was gone. The blizzard assaulted them without remorse. Zarus grabbed her arm and sprinted forward. He searched for the opening in the mountains, until finally, the gaping cave appeared like a gateway to Ashnagz in the distance.

Fatigue was all Zarus knew when he burst into the hollow. He nearly dropped Rin, but she freed herself of his grip just in time. He crashed into the cavern wall, and slid to the ground. Through heavy breaths, he looked at Rin. She appeared fine, but confused.

"We'll head back out in a few hours," he said, finally calming his lungs, "rest for now." Zarus glanced outside at a snow so deep it reached three quarters of the way up Rin's leg. *She thought she could travel through this?* He *tsked* at the thought. Yet he still couldn't figure out why her presence called to him. She was a book he couldn't put down, a misfortune that couldn't be ignored.

It was hard to focus. His head throbbed, his body felt numb. It had been a while since he used magic of that magnitude, but if he would have known it would cost that much energy... Rin stepped away and returned with the broken floorboards she had taken from the castle, knowing there would be no firewood to find under the snow. After a moment, the faint glare of a fire caught his heavy eyes. Before he fell completely asleep, Zarus heard a murmur in the wind and jolted upright.

Jumpy. He was just jumpy, he reasoned with himself. He looked over and saw Rin watching him.

"You should try to sleep," he muttered, stifling a yawn.

Rin shook her head. "I don't think I could if I tried." He knew the feeling all too well. "Can I ask something? Out there, you stopped the snow from raging around us for not even two minutes. Why did it drain so much of your energy?" She studied his face with tender eyes, the firelight sending a glimmer throughout the emerald fields.

Zarus barely mustered a mumble. "Creating my own snow and controlling that which nature throws at me is completely different. One is made from my magic, handcrafted by me, the other forms without my ability. It's easier for us demons to manipulate what we create."

Rin considered him for a moment as she poked the fire. "You nearly passed out once you hit the ground."

A sigh escaped his lungs. "Demons don't draw magic from nature. I haven't controlled the elements like that in years. I'm surprised it even worked."

"Thank Yath Ha it did."

Exhausted or not, Zarus couldn't help the scoff from his throat. "I wouldn't waste your breath."

Her head cocked to the side at a curious angle. "You don't believe they exist?"

He couldn't even manage a sigh. "I know the gods sit high in their paradise and watch our world with a studious eye. That's the problem."

"What do you mean?"

Endless questions. His head throbbed with each passing moment. "They're aware of the Flames bathing our worlds, and yet sloth consumes them like a poison." Rin's eyes widened at the insult. He went on. "Always one to judge the mess, always one to punish, but never one to stop it in the first place. All powerful, all mighty, all lies."

Silence swelled like an infected wound. Zarus's eyes finally slid shut, the world hushed.

Rin interrupted his revelry. "Why would they stop us? They gave us the means to live peacefully, prosperously, and we ruined it. War, violence. It runs rampant in Nokomic every day—let alone Armiria. Between the Yath Ha and their Attendants the kaetha, how can they stop us when we insist on destroying ourselves?"

She continued. "We act on our own accord. Imagine a world where the will of someone else is forced upon you. Nothing would be genuine. We're made to be free. It's our choice what we do with it."

"Correct me if I'm wrong," and he rarely was, "but wasn't it the *Attendant* Anöwe that taught us our wicked nature? The Two Creator's very own divine counselor." It might have been a lifetime ago that he cared to study theology, but Zarus never forgot. "The gods who write the universe know everything that was, is, and will ever be. They knew he would corrupt us. Wouldn't you call that allowance?"

Another pause. Another moment of consideration. Not once did Rin Nowell lash out at his blasphemous ideas. "Yath Ha created us to be free. Why wouldn't they create the kaetha in the same way? I won't claim to understand how the gods work, nor the details of the beginning of time, but I do know that the kaeth Anöwe didn't force us to act on that knowledge. It was also Yath Ha that gave us the means to defeat him."

Something heavy sat in Rin's stare. Zarus watched the girl for a moment, but let the conversation go. So young, so naïve. She had no idea what she spoke of.

She eventually settled close to the fire. "Your magic was beautiful."

Zarus's eyes slid shut. The fire faded into warm hues and his thoughts grew thin.

***

The shadows raged to smite—pushing and breaking the light into submission. Zarus didn't care if they burned out anymore; he didn't need them to see. He walked through the twisting halls, his hand pressed against the pain in his side.

He'll pay. I'll cut him to his knees and force him to pay for this.

A trail of crimson followed behind, letting every demon within the fortress know Zarus's location. They weren't foolish, though. They had seen what happened when they crossed him. He rounded the final corner that led straight into the throne room.

He'll pay.

Zarus approached the doors, clenching his bloody torso, and felt all the rage, all the pain, all the wrath he had done so well to keep hidden all those years—too many years. This was it. This was how it was going to end: revenge.

The yearn for blood raged in his soul. His hands felt of ice, his head fire. Zarus reached for the doors. There would be blood, even if he didn't make it out. He heaved the doors open.

There was nothing inside the throne room. No throne, no demons, no tyrant. Only the sickening heat of wildfire.

Zarus looked around, finding himself not in the throne room of the fortress, but in the Nokomai city of Xandra. He stood before the Temple of the Divine. Ash buried the ornate steps, corpses, and debris. Fire engulfed the city square. Smoke, skin-melting heat, screams and cries. He heard the clashing of steel; a battle. He tried to move, tried to get out of the path of the oncoming flames, but his feet wouldn't budge. Zarus broke into a cold sweat. There was nothing he could do. All the while, beastly silhouettes formed in the smoke. They roared, they hissed, they surrounded. The shadows stepped in line with the fire, inching closer and closer. It was only a matter of seconds.

The flames nearly licked his feet, but before he burned, everything faded into nothing but blinding darkness. It wasn't hot, nor cold; it was nothing. He could manage nothing. He'd lived with it for centuries. However, something stirred. Whether it was a breeze or the slightest glint of vision, there was an undeniable energy.

Zarus...

There it was again.

Wake up...

A shiver up his spine? Zarus couldn't tell...

Rin needs you.

He winced at the realization. A voice; it was a voice speaking.

Zarus, danger is near. Wake up and protect Rin.

A tiny whisper in the back of his head; faint, yet so apparent. And then suddenly the floor dropped beneath him. He fell endlessly into a dark abyss.

***

Zarus's eyes slowly opened. That dream again… but something else. What was the last part? His head ached, and he had to put forth a sum of effort just to keep from dozing back off again. Rin was lying on the ground, curled under a blanket. The fire she huddled around was now a pile of embers.

Urgency bucked him like a horse. Zarus jumped up off the ground and ran to the cave's entrance. He searched the outstretching fields of snow, adrenaline rushing through his veins. The snow hadn't stopped, but there was no sign of demons. Once he was certain no one had advanced while they slept, Zarus made his way to Rin.

Anyone could have attacked us and we'd be none the wiser.

Zarus put a hand on Rin's shoulder and stirred her. "Wake up, Rin. We have to leave."

She groaned, her eyes still closed. Zarus understood she had gotten very little sleep lately, but if they stayed in one place for any longer, they would risk their safety. Someone could've already found them for all he knew. Zarus shook her again. She yawned, rubbed the sleep from her face, and carefully stood.

"How's your hand?" she asked, letting out another small yawn.

Zarus looked at his palm. He unwrapped the cloth stained with browned blood, then flexed the muscles in his hand. "All better," he said, showing Rin the skin unmarked by a cut or scar.

Rin marveled as she rolled her blanket. A frown drew over her expression.

Zarus traced Rin's gaze. The snow was still coming down, and showed no sign of stopping. If he didn't know any better, Zarus would have thought the Divine were intentionally slowing them down. Something other than the storm weighed on his mind.

"It's strange," he muttered, his eyes focused on nothing in particular. "There's a disturbance in the wind, but I can't sense anyone through this storm..." Zarus fell silent. A shrill wind blew into the cave, disturbing what was left of the fire and sending the embers flying. A shiver chilled his spine. "We'll get snowed in if we stay here any longer." He looked to see if Rin was ready, only to find fear. Zarus sighed. She was still new to all of this, only human.

"Are you sure we should leave now?" Rin asked as she met his side.

Apprehension tied his tongue, but Zarus nodded. "We're a sitting target here. If we stay, we die—"

One step. One step was all he made when a sudden chill snaked along his spine, climbing inch by inch until the world fell out of his senses.

He collapsed.

Chapter Thirteen

The wind howled, the same blizzard running corybantic around Rin. Except now Zarus was lying on the cave floor—unresponsive without a trace of focus in his unblinking eyes.

Rin cursed, dropped to her knees, and attempted to wake him. No matter how many times she shook him or screamed his name, Zarus would not answer.

"Dammit, Zarus! Just wake up!" she shouted.

What even happened? One moment he was talking and walking, the next he froze solid. His expression was blank, no glint in his eyes nor flick of his brows. Nothing. Rin growled another curse before she grabbed Zarus's shoulders and dragged him back to the dying fire. She searched through her bag for something to wake him. A scent, a sound, a feeling—*something*. The storm raged outside, and the harrowing idea of being buried in this cave snuck into her frantic thoughts.

There's no way in Ashnagz I can carry him through this snow.

Biting the inside of her cheek, Rin gave up and elevated Zarus's legs with her pack.

***

Zarus jolted awake, only he couldn't see a thing. He tried to sit upright, but his body was numb—paralyzed. Not even his neck would turn.

Where am I? My body, my voice... What's going on?

Magic was nothing new to Zarus; he had spent countless years mastering his ability to break free from the spells of demons. This spell was potent. Excruciatingly, he wedged his eyes open. Only they were already open. There was an aching fluctuation of light and dark. His sight didn't return, but he could feel the world around him.

Where's Rin?

The more he attempted to move, the tenser his joints grew. Panic crept into his chest. He attempted to recall what had happened before he fell, but something interrupted his search.

Out of the darkest corner of his mind, a bitter laugh sounded as though it rang through water.

Who's... there. It was an effort to direct his thoughts. His mind felt like lead.

"You've chosen interesting company, Zarus." A sinister voice hissed from the dark. "I can't help but wonder what purpose you have for traveling with this human." Bitterness poisoned this being's tongue. "I'm sorry, but you'll wait here until I come back for you." His voice hummed a throaty chuckle before fading away.

Leave her alone! Zarus growled through the walls of his mind. As much as his mind struggled, pulled, even twisted; he could not free himself from paralysis.

***

Rin tried prodding Zarus's arm with the burning embers of the fire. Nothing stirred him awake. She paced the cave, hoping an idea would come to mind. What if he didn't wake up? What if she was left to navigate this gods-forsaken mountain alone? Rin was so lost in the panic swelling in her heart, she hadn't noticed the silhouette approaching outside until it stumbled through the piling snow into the cave.

"H-help me," the man stammered. "Help me, please..." He lurched with each step, nearly crashing down as he stammered towards Rin. Frost stretched from the bottom of his jaw to the top of his forehead. His dark brown hair hung stiff at the end of his braid. She stared at the man, no older than she, so close to death.

"Lhaerem's grace!" she squealed. "How can I help?" Clearly, this man needed immediate care. With the next town being so far away, there was little she could offer. And Zarus. He was in dire need as well... Rin ran to the man, wrapped her arm around his waist, and carried him to the fire.

It can't be Eretimis, can it? I mean, this man is half frozen.

She stared at his frozen hair and frostbitten skin. A sickening picture to see what almost became of her.

***

Whatever was holding Zarus in place was stronger than he could break. It felt like he was tied down, but he couldn't see anything binding him.

Get to Rin. Get to Rin!

Only a demon would know him by name. Zarus knew Eretimis wouldn't come back on his own. That wasn't how the Dark Tyrant worked. He would send another demon to track him down and kill Rin.

In the midst of struggling against paralysis, an idea struck Zarus. Calmness suddenly replaced strain; he inhaled deep and full.

The air around him chilled, creating a layer of frost over his entire body.

***

"W-warmth," the man stuttered, weakly lifting a shivering finger to the dying fire.

Rin pulled the remaining kindling from her pack and worked to relight the fire. Perspiration formed along her brow. "What can I call you?" she asked, trying to instill a sense of calm in the situation.

"Tatsuo," he said, unable to stave the shiver from his voice.

"It's nice to meet you, Tatsuo." But she paused for a second, re-thinking her words. "Although it would have been better under different circumstances." Rin shook her head at herself. "My name is Rin."

She focused on the fire, making sure not to stumble with the stress; she could only assume Tatsuo focused on not dying. The discoloration of his skin was severe.

Somehow, her trembling hands managed to spark a flame.

***

Rin's voice echoed. It was faint and far away, but it was there.

Zarus's magic encased his entire body. His eyes were no longer pained by the blinding light changes. His head didn't ache, his mind felt sharper. He waited for the frost to spread a little more, when finally he found what he sought. Wispy threads of magic became visible under the frost's touch. They wrapped around his entire body.

Zarus pulled himself up with every ounce of might he possessed. His muscles felt stiff as stone, but he had crumbled stone before.

Finally, he heard the snapping of frozen threads. He freed his legs and arms first, then his torso and chest. His senses whirled back into focus as the final thread broke.

His eyes were open toward the cave ceiling, the icy floor nipping his body. He heard Rin's silvery voice flutter through the air and his heart welled with relief. She sat at his side. She was alive.

***

"Might I ask what you were doing on this mountain?" Tatsuo asked as he tugged her blanket further over his shoulders. "It's dangerous to be here alone."

The fire was barely holding. Rin ran about the cave in search of kindling, but the cave was dim. "I made my way here by accident," she carefully said, scooping up a brittle twig. "I almost died, but then he found me and took me back to his castle." She gestured a nod at Zarus. "Eventually, we were forced to flee. We've been traveling down the mountain ever since, and then Zarus randomly passed out a few minutes ago."

Tatsuo tilted his head up at the mention of Zarus's name, just enough that Rin noticed the action. He didn't ask more, but something told Rin to move away from this man.

Tatsuo sat right by the flames, his gaze plastered on her. "Heavens, what happened to your face, Rin?"

It was only then that Rin remembered the blood covering her face.

***

Move, dammit, move! Zarus's fingers bent ever so slightly, but the paralysis was stubborn. He might have regained consciousness, but his body was slow to wake up. *Get out of there, Rin!*

***

Rin touched her cheek, dried crimson flaking off her face. "Oh, uh... well, we thought it was best to cover myself in Zarus's blood to mask my scent." She still shuddered at the idea. "After all, demons can smell humans just like animals can." Exhaustion stole the words out of her mouth. A minor panic seized her. Though to her surprise, Tatsuo inquired nothing of the casual mention of demons. He didn't even seem fazed. His narrow eyes fixated on her own through the flying embers. "And then I ran into you."

'There's a disturbance in the wind.'

Zarus's words echoed through her mind like a kiss of death.

"Is something troubling you?" Tatsuo asked through the glare of flames. He gave her a honeyed smirk, flashing his jaw backed by fangs. A familiar pressure weighed down on Rin's shoulders.

***

Zarus felt the magic distort the air. He tried to yell, but nothing came out. His forearms finally moved, but what good would that do when this demon attacked Rin and he couldn't reach her?

Zarus took a deep breath. He forced a whisper. *"Run."*

***

Tension flooded Rin's body. Only the hand of the gods could have allowed her to hear Zarus's warning.

Her throat was dry and stiff, her tongue no better. "N-nothing is troubling me," she stuttered rather unconvincingly as she recklessly backed further into the cave, away from Tatsuo.

Tatsuo stood slowly. "If nothing's the matter, why are you running?" he asked, a morbid curl to his smile. He sprang forward, grabbing her arms and pulling her close enough to feel his blazing breath on her cheeks. She cried against the crushing strength of his hands.

"Really? What *are* you running from?" That malevolent smirk sprawled across his face. Rin gasped as Tatsuo's brown eyes faded to a piercing chartreuse. His pupils narrowed into slits and his skin thawed to a warm fawn. The brunet braid bled fiery red. Talons grew where human nails once were and dug deep into Rin's skin.

The male transformed nearly every one of his features right before her tearful eyes. A demon. She tried to yank herself free, but his deadly grip crushed her arms.. The scimitar hung uselessly at her side. Rin stared into Tatsuo's eyes as she realized that this was it; there was nothing she could do to stop her demise. Her heart pounded furiously, a siren screeched in her mind.

Tears flooded her eyes. Rin closed them, not wanting to see her death.

***

His body's paralysis was a minor feat to conquer when he saw Rin's first tear fall. Zarus pried himself to his numb feet, weakly stumbling toward the girl he promised to protect.

"I'm going to rip you to shreds," he snarled.

Chapter Fourteen

Rin kicked wildly at Tatsuo as Zarus stumbled, but the assailant caught her leg and snapped it into an unnatural angle. The crack was sickening. He released her, and Rin cried out as she slammed to the ground. Zarus's soul shattered at her pleading expression. He hadn't reached her in time.

"He won't save you, human," Tatsuo seethed, lurking back into the shadows of the cave.

Only one thought was in Zarus's head: get to Rin. He rushed forward, but barely caught the glint of the staff before it smacked into his chest. He fell backward, head hitting the ground first. Tatsuo stepped out of the darkness and smiled, a spear in hand.

Who is this demon? Zarus tried to think of who Eretimis might have sent, but he couldn't recall Tatsuo.

"You know," Zarus growled, pushing off the dank floor of the cave and forcing himself to stand, "you're really beginning to piss me off." At that, his magic prowess brewed within the well of his mind. Depthless fog welled from the palms of his hands, and he instantly directed the magic's course toward Tatsuo.

Tatsuo dodged out of the waves until he landed face to face with Zarus. "Did all those years of hiding make you slow?" he taunted.

Yet Zarus stood his ground, refusing Tatsuo to near Rin.

"Fine, if you won't move, then I will!" The demon lunged, his spear aiming for Zarus's heart. It was a sloppy attack and he overshot his target. Zarus grabbed his arm and threw him away from the girl. Before Tatsuo tumbled to the ground, he regained his balance, taking one long stride for Rin.

***

Despite the misery in her leg, Rin could move. The pain should have been unbearable; yet the more she forced herself to crawl to her good leg, the more something inside of her felt different. Or new? A tingling inside her head that spread to her leg. It soothed her.

Adrenaline? But that wouldn't leave me calmed. I mean, it's broken! But—

Rin hadn't noticed either demon moving her way. Suddenly Tatsuo was an arm's length away from her. However, instead of maiming her, the demon collapsed. He shrieked, wrapping his arms around his abdomen where a fountain of blood welled. Zarus—a like-wraith—stood above Tatsuo; dark mist dissipated around them. Crimson trickled down his fingers. Rin couldn't comprehend how Zarus skewered his hand through Tatsuo's stomach.

Terror flooded Tatsuo's reptilian eyes. "H-how did you do that?" shouted the demon, blood pouring through his arms. "How did you move so—"

"Don't waste your last breath on foolish questions, kid," Zarus said in a low tone, unsheathing the dagger at his belt. Then Tatsuo's hands shifted along the spear before Zarus noticed. The assailant blurred from Rin's vision, only to reappear a hair's breadth from Zarus.

She gasped when she saw the spear now sticking out of Zarus's chest.

Back to his feet, Tatsuo stumbled against the cavern wall, blood dripping from his mouth. His words were a whimper. "*You'll pay for what you did.*"

An up-surge of heat engulfed the cave. Zarus's eyes widened. He yanked the spear from his chest, plucked Rin off the ground, and sprinted into the storm. She didn't hear what he yelled before a wall of blue inferno lit the maw of the cave.

Chapter Fifteen

The blaze singed the sky. Rin struggled to free herself of Zarus's unconscious body, which had shielded her from the explosion.

"Oh, get up, Zarus!" Tatsuo yelled hysterically, a firm arm wrapped around his impaled stomach. "I thought you could hold your own!"

Rin pried herself free as Tatsuo stumbled to them. His glare narrowed when he saw her leg, eyeing it suspiciously.

She glanced down, her brow furrowing too. Her leg was no longer bent at an odd angle; in fact, it wasn't broken at all. Rin shook her head and pulled her attention back to Tatsuo.

"Why do you want to kill us?" Rin asked. "What could either of us have done to make you this desperate? You need help." She gestured to the demon's bloodied tunic. "Just walk away."

Tatsuo scoffed. "You don't know a damn thing about that demon, do you?"

"I would be buried ten feet below this storm if not for him." She didn't need to know any more.

"Foolish girl," Tatsuo hissed as he limped forward. "You've done a good job digging your own grave. But Zarus won't be the one to bury you in it."

"What makes you say that?" Rin's temper spoke before she could catch it. His blood still poured, his face contorted with each step. He wouldn't make it long.

Tatsuo growled, low and cold. "I'm going to wake that monster up, then force him to watch as I slit your throat." Rin saw a flash of red, and suddenly Tatsuo hovered over Zarus behind her. Rage dug into her mind like this demon's talon had her arms.

I will not die today!

Everything went dark for a split second. She blinked hard, her eyes instantly focusing on blood. Blood trickled down to the snow from her scimitar's blade. Her hands trembled against the weapon's weight. A gash tore across Tatsuo's back, drawing pools of red deeper than the demon's hair. A shriek echoed off the mountains. He whipped around to the girl holding the blade behind him.

"Sneaky," Tatsuo muttered through blood stained teeth.

Rin trembled backward. She swallowed hard. *You're in deep shit now, Nowell.*

Her knees were on the verge of buckling. Every ounce of strength drained from her body. Rin barely lifted her blade again as she evaded Tatsuo's strikes. Fatigue reached deep into her bones. The only reason she was still alive was because of the severity of Tatsuo's injuries. He was slowing down. How long would that last until her exhaustion won over?

"Don't you know how to do anything but run away?" Tatsuo yelled as his fist crashed into a snowdrift. Rin leapt out of the way just in time. Drenched in sweat and robbed of breath, she leapt behind a mound of snow, praying he did not hear her gasps.

There's no use, she thought amid her racing pulse. She needed to get to Zarus. The only chance she stood was with him by her side. Injured or not, Tatsuo was just too fast. She couldn't slip past him. Rin slowly peeked above the trench. Her eyes followed a trail of blood a way's off where Tatsuo searched for her. His back faced her, but he'd react in a heartbeat if she tried to charge. How much blood would he lose before he fell? What on Armiria was driving this demon to such lengths? She ducked down and studied the gathering of trees a few yards ahead.

Rin's eyes suddenly lit up. She shoved her hands beneath the snow and searched the ground for something—anything—large enough to make noise. A single, measly stone, but it would work. She chucked the rock into the grove. It hit the evergreens with a rustle loud enough to scare a bird. Rin didn't wait to see if Tatsuo took the bait.

She jumped out from the snow mound and ran for her life in the opposite direction to Zarus. She reached for the unconscious demon, a tingle spreading through her arm and into her hand so hot it burned. It wasn't fire, but the strange feeling riled her blood; heat not painful, but soothing. Her hand grazed Zarus's back, but she wasn't fast enough. A hand wrapped around her shoulder. Tatsuo threw her backward, her head spinning wildly against the impact.

"You're stronger than most of the humans I've met," Tatsuo commented, a wall between her and Zarus. Rin clenched her teeth and tightened her hand around the scimitar. "Although you have a point. Someone is sure to find us if this goes on any longer..." Before she could stand up, the demon was level with her eyes. Tatsuo opened his mouth to speak, but Rin didn't let him. She balled her fist and slammed it into his jaw. His head knocked back, his body following suit. She leapt to her feet and held her blade toward Tatsuo as steadily as she could. Yet suddenly her vision blurred and her body swayed. *Where did this come from?* It was as if her body wanted her to give up and die.

"You have a brutal punch," Tatsuo remarked as he rubbed his jaw, a fresh line of red dripping from the new split in his lip. "You know, you've caused me more trouble than I expected..." Something of empathy lined his words. "I'm sorry he dragged you into this, but—" Before she could consider the guilt in tone, Tatsuo's chartreuse eyes writhed.

Zarus suddenly stood behind the demon, his unmoving hand crushing Tatsuo's shoulder to the bone. "You should have run away when you had the chance."

Tatsuo's sincerity bled dry. His pain and disgust welded into raw hatred.

***

It felt like he was diving into the most ravenous Flames of Ashnagz while wading through ice bearing waters. Zarus's body drowned in the sensation as soon as his eyes opened. Not an inch of his body was in pain. Torn muscle, bleeding arteries; Tatsuo's spear had pierced through his chest, but he felt nothing. He didn't think twice; he used that newfound comfort to kick the back of the demon's knees, sending him to the ground.

"Maybe you're not as daunting as the legends make you," Tatsuo barked through heaving breaths. He failed to break free.

"Rin," Zarus kept his gaze on the male below, "leave this field and find somewhere to hide." He had already noticed the dread etched into her stare.

"Why?" Her grave eyes plastered on him.

"Because I doubt you want to see what comes next."

Rin shook her head. "Why can't you just let him go? He won't be able to follow us..."

Naïve child. "He'll go crawling back to Eretimis and tell him our location. Even if he somehow makes it back without dying, Eretimis will slay him like a dog. Trust me, he'll find the death I give him a mercy." Zarus rattled Tatsuo's shoulder to keep the demon's fading mind awake. He had lost too much blood.

Tatsuo's bite was harsher than he expected. "I would *never* do anything for that bastard," he hissed in one last weak attempt to free himself. The words tolled surprise. Zarus released his captive, letting Tatsuo crash into the snow. "If you need it spelled out, then I'd sooner die than do a favor for the Dark Tyrant." Tatsuo slowly enunciated each word. Zarus's eyes narrowed as the urge grew to snap the demon's neck.

He felt Rin move to his side. "If you're not working for him, then why do you want to kill us?"

Why does it matter?

"Because this monster cares about you." Tatsuo glared at Zarus as he sat up. He wiped his thumb across his chin, catching the blood. "I'll make him watch you die, then kill him, too." Tatsuo suddenly pressed his hands together, extending both arms. The air distorted like the heat of a fire. A ruby spear formed in his hands, armed with a jagged white blade and a wine red sash tied around its neck.

Zarus yanked the weapon from Tatsuo's hands and pushed him back down before he got to his feet. The weapon was remarkable; only the hands of Hraesan smiths could have forged such a spear. Zarus had no recollection of the demonic blade. After he finished examining its metal staff, he dropped it in the snow before Tatsuo.

"Why do you want me dead?" Zarus asked flatly.

"You really don't remember, do you?" The demon's eyes narrowed into cold steel.

Should I?

When Tatsuo sensed Zarus's confusion, he dropped his stare to the snow. "I guess I shouldn't be surprised. I was just a child back then."

He paused, then looked up to Zarus with a loathing stare. "You killed my father and mother right before my eyes." Rin stiffened beside him.

"What were their names?" Zarus asked, crossing his arms.

"My father was Hiromitsu Kurosawa, my mother Nariko. They fled from Eretimis's reign of tyranny on Eroz and hid here on Armiria. They threatened his power so he sent *you* to slaughter them!" Tatsuo barked his blood onto the snow.

Kurosawa. Their faces instantly flashed through Zarus's head. The dragon and *narikaah*. He had never officially met them, only heard tales of the mighty name, but Zarus hadn't killed the couple. He hadn't been given the order to. A chill ran through the air. Zarus glanced up, finding Rin's growing distrust.

"I didn't kill them."

That flame in Tatsuo's eyes sparked again, simmering and burning into his heart. "How can you say that? You murdered them in front of each other—in front of me! The Shadow of Evenfall ripped them away from me, and he doesn't even remember!" Zarus saw Rin sway as the air thickened with dormant magic. Her hand wrapped around the hilt of her scimitar.

Zarus didn't falter. "I don't remember it because *I* did not kill them." His eyes narrowed as a spark of pain flared back into his chest, but his voice remained level.

"I *saw* you there three hundred years ago!" Tatsuo snarled.

Zarus's eyes nearly rolled at the words. "I wasn't on Armiria three hundred years ago. I was stuck somewhere on Eroz." He spoke through his teeth, desperately keeping his attention off of the pain seeping back into his chest.

Tatsuo froze; the spear slowly made its way back into his hands. Not as a threat, but a comfort. "How can that be... He looked exactly like you!" His voice was void of hatred, denial taking its place.

"I don't know," Zarus muttered.

Silence claimed the mountain. Rin's voice finally chirped up beside him. "Is he done trying to kill us?" With a quick glance, he could tell everything had caught up with her. Her sweat washed away all of his blood from her face. It hadn't done a thing to protect her.

"I don't think he could if he wanted." Zarus took one last look at Tatsuo Kurosawa's ashen expression, then walked away.

"What are you doing?"

"What does it look like I'm doing?" Zarus retorted. "I'm getting you down this mountain."

"Aren't you going to help him?" Rin asked, grabbing his arm and pulling back. "He'll die if he stays like this!"

She doesn't understand. Zarus shook his head. "If he wanted to live, he should have stayed away from me."

"How can you say that? He was only attacking because he thought you killed his parents." Rin dropped to her knees, examining the injuries inflicted on Tatsuo as the demon sat motionless. A small part of Zarus sympathized with the male. Three hundred years was a lot of time to waste, only to fall back to square one; he would have killed to learn more about his parents as well. However, it wasn't his concern. Yet Rin still called out, "Aren't you the slightest bit curious why he thought you were the one to murder his parents?"

He halted; a sigh already escaped his lungs before his hands wiped the frustration from his face. Zarus promptly, though lacking any enthusiasm, turned around and rested Tatsuo back into the snow. He didn't look at Rin while he recited a healing spell, especially not when she had that sly grin on her face. He had to work on healing his own wounds, too. But something crossed his mind amidst his tethered focus.

He asked, "Rin, how is your leg not broken?"

Tatsuo was injured, gravely, but he was still the son of a half-demon and a dragon. So how did Rin stay alive the entire fight and somehow overcome a broken bone?

"I thought you healed me," she shrugged. "You yelled something about it before the explosion."

Zarus's hands fell still. He looked at Rin in a moment of perplexity. It was true he had started reciting a healing spell as he carried them from the explosion, but he blacked out before he could finish it. Furthermore, the spell was for himself so he could finish the battle against Tatsuo...

They both stared at each other for a long moment before Zarus started healing the male who had just tried to kill him.

The sun glowed above the horizon. The night was finally over, a new day had begun.

Chapter Sixteen

Rin stood at the edge of the cliff, taking in the sun's warm embrace. Yet her mind did not quiet. The tremble did not leave her hands. And the memory of blood and fire did not ease from her mind.

"So?" she heard Zarus ask from behind. "Can you see anything?"

Rin scanned the horizon but didn't find any villages. "Nothing but the sun."

Zarus's frustrations were apparent, but it was nice they weren't directed at her. From the moment Rin had finished wrapping Zarus's chest, he had been carrying Tatsuo over his shoulder. She could only imagine what type of exhaustion he was working against, up and down hills, over a frozen lake, and through the unforgiving snow on the ground. Every time she offered to take the load off of Zarus's shoulders, he refused and said they couldn't afford to slow down. She pretended it was just because of her leg.

Hours later, when the sun had risen higher and Zarus stopped to rest, Rin ran ahead and spotted a village not too far away. It had been about two days since she sat in an actual house, and even longer since she slept in a proper bed. Everyone was in need of a good night's rest. She turned on her heels and rushed back to deliver the news.

"There's a village just ahead!" Just ahead was a warm bed and a warm bath waiting for her. She winced as she waited for Zarus to chastise her volume, but he said nothing. "Zarus?" She took a seat next to him. His face was buried in his hands. "Did you hear me? We can find food and shelter there."

She had a feeling they were getting closer to the mountain's base since the snowfall had eased, and now, seeing the village proved it. Rin wanted to sing with joy.

A full minute passed. Rin figured the demon had dozed off while he waited for her to return, and she did not intend to disturb him. Instead, she moved to where Tatsuo laid and switched out his bandages. It was odd to find that she was walking on her leg with ease, and yet Tatsuo's wounds were still healing. She had pondered it all morning as well. Once finished, Rin had to resist the urge to fall asleep. Though before her head dipped, she jolted.

The most subtle of whispers resonated in her ears. Rin glanced at Zarus. His hands still buried his face. She inched closer to hear what he was saying.

"It doesn't matter if it's convenient, it'll only cause more problems... The snow isn't as bad this far down. We could just find another cave and avoid it..."

Rin sat beside Zarus and stared at the snow under her boots. "You don't want to go into town, do you?" Zarus lifted his head with little reaction.

"No."

Rin stole a quick glance and found nothing but dread in his eyes. "How come? Is it the people there?"

"It's not the people *there*, it's the people *everywhere*," he corrected sharply. "It's the people in this town, the town at the bottom of the mountain, and even the town on the other side of Armiria! It's everyone, Rin, everyone!" Zarus's voice shook Rin's chest.

"What happened to you to make you so sad?" Rin's tongue slipped her manners. It wasn't her business what happened to this demon, and it certainly wasn't the time to discuss such matters. But the question was out there, lingering in the air between them.

Zarus answered with hefty silence until he finally sighed. "You learn that everyone is the same once you live long enough."

Rin watched Zarus's muscles tense, and clearly saw how uncomfortable this topic was, but that didn't answer her question. "Did the people in this town ever do anything to you?" She looked to the sky, where more clouds were beginning to form.

"Does it matter? They're humans. I can't tell a single good story about any encounter I've ever had with a human—"

"Not even me?" Rin interrupted. "Then why did you offer to help me? It doesn't make a hint of sense."

No matter how many times she claimed to not be curious, or tried to convince herself it didn't matter, Rin still had an unsettled feeling in her gut as to why Zarus was so willing to help her. He saved her life so many times, yet hated humans with a passion. Now that she was mixed up with Eretimis, and the half-demon who had a grudge against Zarus, she felt like she needed to know more about the demon she befriended. Just as Zarus was about to reply, Tatsuo shifted subconsciously.

"He's going to wake soon," Zarus said instead. "We need to get to an inn before he does. It'll be easier to hide the pointed ears and fangs while he's out." Zarus rose to his feet.

"Last time I checked, there were no inns inside caves." Rin yawned as she hopped off the log. Vexed and tired, the demon glared at her, to which she returned a grin. "Are you sure about this?" she asked.

"No. But if it'll shut you up, then the dreaded interactions will be worth it," he huffed, lifting Tatsuo over his shoulder.

"You're overdramatic, do you know that?" Rin flung her satchel over her shoulder, then led the way. When she turned back to make sure she had grabbed everything, she saw Zarus wince. "Are you okay?"

"I'm fine," he muttered, rather unconvincingly. Rin glanced at the fresh blood on his shirt until he rolled his eyes. "Why don't you try healing three people after not using the spell in two centuries."

Rin held the bite on her tongue and started heading toward the village. She could hardly contain her bliss at the thought of a fireplace, but it then occurred to her that they had no money.

She turned to ask Zarus if he'd be willing to work for lodging, but halted by the fear seizing his composure as they neared the outer houses of the village. He didn't like humans, and maybe even demons, but she never imagined that they would make him so uncomfortable. She might have considered letting him off the hook and finding yet another cave to stay in once evenfall settled, but Rin felt that hiding with humans would be safer. They could pose as regular people for the night and then be on their way in the morning. "So, what are you going to do after we get to the bottom of the mountain?" Rin asked, attempting to distract him. "Are you going to head back to your castle?"

He took a minute to think. "No, that place is as safe as Mortality's Edge now."

Rin's nose scrunched. "What does that dangerous place have to do with this?"

"Eretimis knows where the castle is. If I go back, he'll show up again eventually."

Rin arched her brow. "So you're going to find somewhere else to hide from him?"

Zarus shrugged. "If I disappear, it's only a matter of time before he finds me. I don't want to face him."

"Is he too strong to face?"

"It wouldn't change anything if I did." He adjusted Tatsuo's body over his shoulder, keeping the struggle from his voice. "Nothing would be different if I fought him or if I ran away."

Rin glanced back and found a lonesome ghost rather than the fearsome wraith she had been traveling with. She looked ahead once more, speaking clearly. "Zarus, if Eretimis didn't think to find you on a frozen mountain knowing your magic, I think you're giving him far too much credit."

Thankfully, she picked the right words, because the slightest smile curved Zarus's lips as they approached the outlying property of the town.

Chapter Seventeen

The evening air was crisp by the time Rin and Zarus dragged Tatsuo's body into town, found an inn, and got themselves situated. It took even longer for the half-demon to wake, so Rin rested while they waited. Thankfully, Tatsuo hadn't tried to kill anyone when he woke up. He reacted very calmly to Zarus's voice being the first thing he heard as well, although he was shocked to be alive. Even more shocked when Rin told him that Zarus was the one to heal his wounds. Yet the stubborn demon still had the nerve to ask her to leave so he could question Tatsuo in private. She was still muttering to herself about it as she combed through the busy streets.

Rin marveled at the night life of Illice, one of Nokomic's outposts in the Lennaels. It wasn't a gaping city, but people flowed through the town. There were street performers, vendors, shops, paved roads. Even in the icy weather, people still walked about the streets. Rin refrained from indulging in conversation and didn't walk into any of the shops. She was still being hunted, and although this was a town of humans, Rin didn't feel like pressing her luck after last night. So she made her walk short. When she finally made it through the sweaty sea of people coursing about the inn's tavern and up to their room, she didn't knock. She was exhausted, and the inn was so warm. She wasn't going back out even if Zarus wanted to keep more secrets from her.

She silently swung the door open. "Oh, hello," Rin said awkwardly.

The half-demon sitting with his legs stretched on the bed smiled at her.

She quietly shut the door and sat on the edge of the second bed, spinning her thumbs around themselves, biting her cheek at the silence strung about. "Do you know where Zarus went?"

"He muttered something about searching the town for threats, but that carriage wreck of a male could have gone anywhere," Tatsuo replied as he crossed his arms behind his head.

Rin nodded. Casual conversations with someone who had blatantly tried to murder you weren't an everyday occurrence. "So, I've been wondering..." she said tentatively, "how did you find us?"

Tatsuo flicked his serpentine eyes to her. "The other day, Eretimis found Zarus on the top of the Lennaels after three hundred years. Not only that, but he was harboring a human with him, who I can only assume to be you. It didn't sit too well with the old bastard. See, he wants Zarus to stay his hateful self." He swung himself onto the edge of the bed, fishing for something deep in the pocket of his tunic. "The Dark Tyrant doesn't want Zarus growing soft, else he won't be useful. Shortly after their meeting, Eretimis sent out this." Tatsuo stopped fumbling and passed a folded slip of paper to her. Rin nearly choked on the spit in her mouth at what she read.

Zarus Lowwenth has hidden from Hraesah's grasp for 300 years.
Now he has finally been dragged out of hiding. He was found with a
human on Hylan's peak of the Lennael Mountains.
Orders have been given that, should anyone find the treacherous demon
and his companion, the human will be killed and Lowwenth will be
delivered alive to our Liege Eretimis by whatever means necessary.

The rest read about rewards and currencies. A bounty. A bounty laid on her. Her head spun at the news. She ran to the window and barely opened it in time before she hurled. Hopefully no one was strolling in the alley below. Rin slowly trudged back into the room with a tremble in her voice. "How many people know about this?" she forced herself to say, still wiping her mouth.

A frown formed on Tatsuo's slender jaw. "As many that would listen. I'd guess a lot if word of it got around to me."

Rin shook her head. Zarus mentioned demons would be after them, that Eretimis wouldn't come back personally. But this? How many demons were hunting her?

Tatsuo must've seen her face drain of all color. Alarm welled in her gut as he leaned closer, but the tone of his voice soothed her fear. "Hey, you have Lowwenth with you. That means you're off to a good start, right? And don't count me out just yet. That tyrant, he's responsible for the death of my parents."

It was like watching life outside of her body. Rin eventually looked at him. "Why did he kill them?"

Tatsuo sighed, letting his arm drop from her shoulder. He plopped onto the bed across from her. "My parents moved to Armiria when I was born in order to escape Eretimis's reign in Hraesah. My mother was a dragon, but was married into the demon kind through my drag-on-demon father. They thought his rule would only bring disaster, so they left their world behind to keep me safe. They always liked humans and were labeled as *sympathizers* by Eretimis. A rebellion formed on Armiria that they sparked, so Eretimis had them assassinated and end-ed the rioting." Tatsuo's voice trailed, a desolate hush that muttered the last words. "I thought it was Zarus at the time—everyone knew he carried out Eretimis's dark deeds—and spent my life searching for him. I was wrong. There was sincerity in what he explained that leads me to believe him, even though he would probably deny it. He offered to help me figure out who killed them, but told me to wait until he finds me after you're safe. That's not going to work. He may not be the demon I thought he was, but he's not leaving me behind." It took a moment, but the desolation fled his tone, and a smile returned to Tatsuo's face. "And since I'm sticking around, there's no way in Ashnagz's Flames that I'm letting you get killed."

There was something about a friendly smile that soothed Rin's mind. "Why? Because you're curious about me?" Just like Zarus.

Tatsuo wrinkled his nose. "What? No, because you're my friend."

Rin raised a brow. "I am?" She didn't mean to sound so rude, but seeing as Tatsuo tried to end her life last night...

"I mean, yeah," Tatsuo shrugged, rubbing the back of his head. "You convinced Zarus to save my life out of sheer kindness. I don't get to make new friends all too often, so I'll jump on board whenever I can." He offered a sheepish smile, and Rin was more than grateful to accept it.

"Okay, I trust you." She smiled back.

Her smile disappeared when she saw smoke trailing under the door. Less than a heartbeat later, an explosion tossed her across the room.

***

Rin felt the weight atop her before she heard the panic or felt the heat. She slowly opened her eyes to the blazing debris of the inn. She was stuck beneath the wreckage.

Her chest tightened. She couldn't finagle away the beam pinning her leg down. Her head rang. The smoke was gathering in her lungs; the fires were spreading. Rin truly thought one of the kaetha reigned down from Lyhrëon when Tatsuo's silhouette appeared. He threw the burning debris out of the way, stepping through the fire like it was nothing more than puddles of rainwater. The half-demon was relieved to find her alive. He lifted the beam with unfair ease, then guided her out of the hellish smoke until they were safely away from the ruins of the inn. Only a wicked bruise hindered her leg.

The whole town bathed in havoc. People ran to vanquish the spreading flames and rescue the injured. Tatsuo and Rin made their way through the frantic streets until they finally found Zarus submerged in battle with a demon skeletal enough to lie in a grave.

Ice coated the stone pavement of the town square. Right when Rin and Tatsuo walked into the battle, Zarus forged a rod of ice from his very hands and threw the sickle between his opponent's eyes.

The grotesque being was neither male nor female. They moved unnaturally, as if a darker force possessed their skeletal figure. The demon hit the ground a moment later. Rin ran to where Zarus stood above his opponent, but the felled demon stirred below.

"Uh, Zarus..." Rin whispered as the long, gangly body on the ground twitched.

"I see it," he grumbled as he wiped the sweat beading down his brow.

The demon's oily brown skin resembled dried leather. Grisly long teeth, hollowed eyes, a blank and thanatoid face. Their emaciated body was ghastly and twisted. The skin around the gaping hole in their forehead slowly grafted itself together. Steam sizzled from the wound, the blood cauterizing.

Rin, Zarus, and Tatsuo slowly backed away, and she knew by Zarus's expression that he didn't know what was going on either. Tatsuo summoned his spear from thin air, and Rin's hand rested on the hilt of her scimitar.

"You little pest," the skeletal demon hissed from the ground, "do you know how many more souls I'll have to collect to make up for that?" Slowly, they rose to their feet. Their bones looked like they might tear through the thin, leathery skin. Their ribs jutted about at all angles, and Rin's stomach twisted when she heard the cracking of bone and tearing of skin along the demon's back. Legs resembling those of a spider tore out of their spine. The sight made of nightmares didn't faze the nightmare that was Zarus.

"Stealing souls is a bit of a cheap trick." He scoffed.

Stealing souls? Rin thought.

The demon barked a bitter laugh. "It'll be the least of your worries when your friends are dead and you're back in Eretimis's clutches, Lowwenth." The demon lunged. Not for Rin or Zarus or even Tatsuo, but for the civilian that ran into the town square.

The adolescent boy looked at the ice and blood covering the ground with disdain. "You're bloody magic users!" he cursed. "You set these fires, didn't you?" But the disgust was short-lived. The tip of the demon's spidery limbs jutted out from their back and stabbed into the boy's chest. Rin watched the life drain from the villager's face; color and emotion all bled dry until there was nothing left. The boy's soulless husk hit the road long after he was dead. Rin stared in horror as the spindly demon turned back to face her.

Blood and violence seized the square. Zarus and Tatsuo fought off the demon; Zarus with his ice and dagger, Tatsuo his fire and spear. The two landed their attacks, and it became clear the soul stealer was not prepared to fend off two opponents at once. For every slash and jab that pierced through the demon's thin, emaciated body, the soul stealer used the extra limbs on their back and found a new victim to rob. Just as the boy had fallen, each villager who wandered too close fell as an empty husk over and over. The demon's extra limbs extracted the souls, and the souls were then used to heal whatever wounds Zarus and Tatsuo inflicted.

"If you won't use that blade, then *get out of here*!" Zarus barked at Rin as she tried to inch closer to their opponent. A trickle of crimson ran down from his cheek.

"Excuse me," Rin replied, "but if it weren't for me and this blade, you would be dead! Oh, wait, you wouldn't remember because you were *unconscious* while I fought Tatsuo! Besides, *where am I supposed to go?*"

The blade of Tatsuo's spear sliced into the soul stealer's arm, calling forth a head-splitting shriek. "Would you two stop bickering and help me kill this bastard!" he growled, teeth bared and face dripping with the black blood spraying from the soul stealer's body.

Rin gritted her teeth as the strangest thing happened.

Delve into the power that sleeps within you, child...

Rin's heart leapt from her chest. A voice in her head, but not from her. She didn't recognize the voice, but who—

Tatsuo yowled as the demon's ghastly nails slashed into him. He parried the soul-stealing limb with his spear just in time. Ice seized Rin's spine. She needed to stop the stealing of souls or this fight would go on forever. Tatsuo's attack was the perfect distraction. While Zarus and Tatsuo advanced toward the demon's front, Rin swung around to their rear. The soul stealer didn't notice her until she unsheathed her scimitar and sliced clean through all three of the soul-stealing limbs on their back. Inky blood sprayed into the air. Their rage flashed toward her, but Rin was already swooping down, evading the demon's razor-like nails.

Zarus advanced. Three quick jabs of his dagger—upper thigh, abdomen, throat. By the time the demon lashed out at him, Zarus had already slipped behind Tatsuo. The half-demon directed his spear toward the night sky. The tower of orange flames stretched toward the heavens, illuminating the town square and burning the flesh off of the demon down to the bones.

Rin's stomach churned against the shrieks from within the inferno. She watched the heat devour the demon's body. She couldn't help to think she might have shared the same fate only one night ago.

The veil of night reclaimed the town square. "Recover from that, jackass," Tatsuo spat as the blast died down. He approached the seared soul stealer and lifted his spear to their throat. However, Zarus caught Tatsuo's arm before he delivered the killing blow.

Zarus dropped to one knee, grabbing the demon's raw neck. "You're going to deliver a message to Eretimis before I let you die." He tightened his grip, keeping the demon's attention sharp. "Send all the demons that you can muster from this world, send them in waves and shadows and armies. I'll rip them all to shreds. The only way I'm coming back is when you get off your throne and drag my corpse there yourself." Zarus let the half dead demon crash to the ground. Rage burned in his eyes.

The same fear inspired the soul stealer's strength. They dragged themself away from Zarus, more exposed bone through melted skin than Rin cared to witness, then stumbled off into the night. It wasn't until the soul stealer was out of sight that Rin placed her hand on Zarus's forearm. Softly, just enough of a reminder to come back to reality. Minds were a terrible place to get lost, and she could only imagine the labyrinth that shaped his.

Rin glanced behind her. The town was still putting out the fires. Barely anyone had noticed the fight, save those who died because of it. Neither of her companions looked too great either, covered in blood and soot and ash. She didn't want to know how she stood in comparison. Another long night, and once again, it appeared they had traveled to the pits of Ashnagz and back. Zarus eventually stood up. Tatsuo met Rin's side, an arm wrapped around his bleeding abdomen.

Rin spoke quietly. "No more towns. We'll just endanger whoever we meet." She forced herself not to focus on all the lives lost at her expense.

No one protested. Rin cast one last glance to the two beings surrounding her, then began the trek of putting the town of Illice behind them.

***

Lanterns lined the hall, a monstrous chandelier topped the high arches of the ceiling. Ebony walls blocked the world outside, and all eyes present in the throne room fell focused on the burned soul stealer that barged into the Dark Tyrant's court. Not a single soul spoke as the emissary delivered their message, too curious to interrupt.

Eretimis smiled from his foul throne. "So the traitor believes he will only return to the fortress dead."

"There is one more thing, my lord," the soul stealer croaked from the base of the dais, "a third member travels with them. A *narikaah* by the looks of it." A murmur spread throughout the room, but it hushed.

A vicious scoff rang about the hall. "He thinks we're weak?" The white-haired demon standing beside the throne laughed. "How many demons has he defeated? One or two? A child could do that!" However, the demon's boast cut short. Tension fell over the crowd, a tension made so effortlessly by Eretimis's silence.

The tyrant rose from his dais, each step echoing along the walls as he walked to the half-conscious demon below. He stopped before the wounded being and grabbed their neck. Eretimis held the demon off the ground, leveled with his dark eyes.

Low and forbidding, he asked, "Did I give you permission to stay?" He tightened his grip on their charred neck, blood and fluids pressing out of their burnt skin and dripping to the floor. The soul stealer's glazing eyes struggled to keep focus. They remained silent, waiting for the allowance to speak, not daring to breathe without permission.

Eretimis continued. "Did I say you could die here? You failed to bring me what I asked for and dishonored me in the process... the only reason you are here right now is because your victor allowed it. What gives you the audacity to lie here and besmirch my floors with your wastes?"

"M-my Lord, please... have mercy—"

Eretimis's voice cut sharper than a blade against flesh. "Mercy was fed to you by the hand you were supposed to bring back in chains. So you force me to ask again, why do you think you can stay here?" He narrowed his eyes, malevolence bleeding out from their depths. The demon braced themself, but death never came. The displeasure passed from Eretimis's expression, replaced by a smile so calmly deceitful. His hold on the soul stealer released, letting them crash to the cold ground. Eretimis returned to the grand throne.

Moments passed without a whisper, all eyes plastered on the Dark Tyrant. When he spoke, the room quaked beneath his voice. "For whatever reason you choose to remain here, it appears you need encouragement to leave." Eretimis narrowed his empty eyes. Shadows pulled from the corners of the walls, bleeding the color from the room. Darker than a moonless night, the shadows encircled the soul stealer, barking and growling, taking the form of snapping teeth. A new sense of fear plagued the soul stealer. Wounded or not, they took off sprinting for the arctic world beyond the fortress walls, but to no avail. Eretimis nodded his head, and the snarling shadows chased. Powerful jaws tore through skin and snapped through bone. Black blood sprayed the floor and walls. No one flinched. Eretimis listened to the torturous screams until only a smudge of blood remained on the floor. The beasts dissolved, the shadows returning to the walls, color returning to the throne room. He turned to the demon who spoke out earlier.

"You think this is child's play, Errogan? Then have Zarus Lowwenth kneeling before me in a day."

The white-haired demon smiled. He nodded graciously, then put an arm across his chest and bowed. "I'll return by the sunrise after tomorrow, my Lord."

Chapter Eighteen

The three unlikely companions continued on their journey down the mountain, hoping to find a cave to rest and warm themselves in. Rin tailed the single file, watching as the moon emphasized the drastic differences in the silhouettes ahead of her. To her, their differences were far beyond physical appearance. It was impossible for her to contain her curiosity. "Why don't demons need sleep?" she asked.

Tatsuo explained demons need sleep, they can just withstand more stress on the body than humans, especially stress on the mind, since that's where their magic wells. However, they still needed sleep—much more than they had received recently.

Before long, they happened on a cave. Tatsuo volunteered to search for firewood. He returned with his arms full. He stacked it loosely and ignited the fire with his magic. Thick smoke filled the air. Rin bathed in the warmth. They both agreed to keep watch while Zarus reluctantly closed his eyes.

"...So after I finally got my sleeve out of the machine, my dad never let me work in the fields alone again," Rin laughed, finishing her story.

"I think the only times I had to be supervised were when I practiced with my fire. I nearly burned down a forest once. My parents found me panicking and trying to put out the flames by cupping water from a nearby stream in my hands, then pouring it onto the fire one scoop at a time. I would have assumed a dragon and a *narikaah* would be proud to find their son playing with such magic. I was sorely mistaken." Tatsuo ran his fingers through the flickering inferno, playing with the tips of the flames. He laid on his side across from Rin.

Rin laughed at the image of a young and distressed Tatsuo, desperately trying to extinguish the forest he had set ablaze. The word he had just taught her danced through her head—*narikaah*, a dragon-demon. What his father had been; what he is.

"So can I ask you something?" Rin returned her attention to Tatsuo.

"Anything," he replied.

"Why are you choosing to stay with us? I mean," she paused. Tatsuo was a joy to have around, but the thought lodged in her throat as they had just met. "It's dangerous for you to be here. Wouldn't it just be easier to live your life without fear of being killed?" Rin closed her eyes as she lolled next to the fire. "Why not just fly away?"

"Well, first, I can't fly. I sadly inherited my father's inability to transform into a dragon and will always be stuck on the ground in this body. But..." Tatsuo thought it over for a moment, his eyes leading away from Rin and into the fire. "I honestly have nowhere else to go," he shrugged, but smiled. "There's the option to start a life somewhere, but I've never really been to any of the demon colonies in Armiria, and any family I have left is unreachable. I had a partner when I lived in the east centuries ago but he... well, the humans of Dìghao are known for their longevity, but they don't live this long. You and Zarus, you're all I have right now." The smile in his eyes faded. "I want to help you find your family," he said distantly, "so you can at least be with yours. Plus, I tried to kill you, so it's the least I can do."

Rin fell pensive. She couldn't imagine going through what Tatsuo lived, and was still living through. Even Zarus. Somehow, they both kept going. It was baffling to see their strength. As silence fell over them, she wondered about something he said.

"What did you mean by *demon colonies on Armiria*?"

Tatsuo looked confused. "I mean I never sought out the demons in this world."

Rin stared at him in disbelief. Did she hear what she thought she heard? "Zarus told me Eretimis came here from another world, and then that he was trapped in a different world three hundred years ago. There's a different world that exists where demons come from?" Excitement fueled her words.

"Mm-hm, aside from Armiria," he mumbled. "Don't humans know that?"

"Not that I've heard!" Rin almost shouted the words, unable to mask her elation. She threw her hands over her mouth as Zarus shifted in his sleep. "What are they like? How many are there? Who lives on them? How do you get there?" The questions flowed from her tongue, not allowing Tatsuo to answer before she asked the next.

"I don't know what it's like," Tatsuo chuckled, answering when Rin stopped for a breath. "I haven't been to the other, and Eretimis keeps the only way to travel between them to himself. My parents were among the last ones to travel here, and I believe that's only because they found a hidden passage different from Eretimis's way. There're only two worlds, though. You've got Armiria, for humans and shifters; and then Eroz, for demons, fae, and dragons. The realms aren't strictly for one species, but it's what the main population consists of. The shifters don't have a major region where they live in Armiria, but Eroz is broken up into two prime territories: the fae inhabit Milganos in the north, and the demons have control of the southern lands called Hrae-sah. The dragons tend to keep to themselves wherever they roam."

Rin stared, dumbfounded. She could only picture Hraesah as a dark, somber place. All of its light shaded by grim clouds; everything weathered and fallen. *What would a land of fae creatures look like?* Humans told stories of fae, of their tricks and beauty and love of nature. She'd figured them just as real as demons until now. She'd never even stepped foot into Nokomic's capital, Xandra, but the possibility of viewing a world completely different from Armiria, to see Eroz... it was unbelievable.

Her eyes grew heavy. She desperately tried to keep talking, but she was drunk with fatigue and even she didn't understand the slew of words she was trying to say. Tatsuo laughed, and within seconds, Rin slipped into a deep sleep.

***

"Is she asleep?"

"I think so," Tatsuo replied, his tone relaxed.

Zarus took a deep breath. Sending that message to Eretimis dug up more memories that he intended. Nightmares of the past woke him a while ago, almost the whole time Rin and Tatsuo were talking. He didn't want to interrupt them. He sat up and looked outside, only a sliver of moon to light the mountain.

"Did you get any sleep?" Tatsuo asked, prodding the fire.

Zarus rubbed his palms into his closed eyes. "Barely."

"I saw you awake for a while."

"So why didn't you stop talking?"

"Because," Tatsuo said, adjusting so he faced Zarus, "she needed to talk, and I wasn't going to stop her."

Zarus nodded. He was well aware he wasn't much for conversation. He sat up against the wall of the cave. "I honestly thought I had gotten away from all of this." A sigh rolled from his lungs, as desolate and somber as the night before him.

Tatsuo shook his head. "What are you talking about?"

"I thought I had finally gotten away from Eretimis." Zarus rubbed the grogginess out of his vision. "It had been nearly three hundred years since I last saw him, and I thought it was over... it was foolish of me."

"Not foolish, just optimistic," Tatsuo assured. He stood and put his hand on Zarus's shoulder. "Look, I know you like to keep to yourself, but you know you don't need to, right? You're not alone in this anymore." Zarus glanced at Tatsuo's hearty smile. He should have felt better, should have had some of the weight lifted off his shoulders... but this wasn't a game. More players wouldn't make a difference, and he was sick of enlisting them. They were up against Eretimis. *Eretimis.* The only way people have ever beaten him was by running out of his reach. Even Tatsuo's parents tried. Zarus didn't have anywhere else to run. How long before he gave up?

"Try to get some more sleep," Tatsuo smiled, and Zarus realized he had been silent too long.

"I'll be fine. You should rest as much as you can," Zarus mumbled as he stared at the dark world beyond. Why would he want to sleep when sleep only plagued him with memories? "You haven't completely healed."

Tatsuo argued, but ultimately called Zarus a *'stubborn mule'* and accepted defeat. He took a place by the fire, while Zarus remained by the mouth of the cave, listening to the wind's whispers.

Too many players... He knew what he had to do, but knowing and doing were two vastly different things.

Chapter Nineteen

Rin woke up the next morning feeling refreshed for the first time in days. The rising sun shone down into the cave. Zarus was the one to greet her. Tatsuo's heavy snores weren't surprising, but something about that day felt different. She had especially high hopes, and felt that the fresh light of morning was a good sign. Too many of her mornings had started in a storm lately.

She scraped up a quick breakfast from their remaining supplies, then woke up Tatsuo, who nearly ran her down when he smelled food. She couldn't help but notice that Zarus seemed less than enthused. He looked more disconsolate than usual. He wasn't the most talkative to begin with, but this?

They stayed put for an hour before finally packing up. However, traveling uninterrupted lasted only until a group of demons stood in their way. Rin charged headfirst into battle, swinging her scimitar wildly at the four demons in a fit that left them gaping at the meek human. Yath Ha answered her prayers, for Zarus picked up on her attempt at a distraction and conducted a blizzard of ice followed by Tatsuo's inferno. With the help of a lowly human, the demons fell. The group of bounty hunters were strewn about the snow well before the sun reached its peak. How many dead bodies had that been? Rin barely batted an eye at the battlefield. The idea of getting used to the sight of corpses didn't sit well.

"They deserve the fate they chose by helping the tyrant," Zarus uttered so easily when she asked why the demons had to be killed.

Tatsuo's answer was slightly more comforting. "Some people won't stop if they're let go." Rin wondered what merit that had, seeing as she and Zarus let him go. She supposed Tatsuo had been a special case, and a case that didn't fall under Eretimis's rule. The rest of the afternoon was rather uneventful. They traveled downward towards a clear pass between rocky cliffs, but Rin sensed tension in the air. A weight. Not of magic, but mood. She studied her companions, wondering if either of them had noticed it. That's when Zarus halted his step.

"Is something out there?" Rin called out as she shielded her eyes from a glacial gust of wind.

She heard a distant sigh, though not of the usual aggravation. "No, it's just..." the words jumbled in Zarus's throat.

Rin said softly, "If this is about the demon delivering the message, I'm sure he did. I mean, he seemed pretty scared—"

"It's not that," Zarus interrupted, glancing toward her. Rin saw his wan face, and dread immediately settled in her chest.

Unaware of the tension, Tatsuo spoke. "Do you think we could take him if he shows up?"

The worry disappeared from his face. Zarus stared at Tatsuo straightly.

"Is that what's bothering you? The thought of Eretimis showing up?" Tatsuo asked. Rin considered this. Zarus had directly challenged the demon, but for a tyrant who had so many pawns, would he do it himself?

Zarus's expression was static. The words deflected right off of him. He finally spoke. "We?"

"Yes, *we*," Tatsuo spit the word back as if it were sour. "Do you expect me to sit back and watch if he comes?"

Zarus didn't answer. Rin tried desperately to read his thoughts, but he was just as good at hiding them as she was showing them. He held their stare, but ultimately surrendered it to Tatsuo by turning away and walking forward. "This is my fight. No one else needs to get involved."

"What?" Tatsuo blurted in disbelief. He grabbed Zarus's shoulder, pulling him to a stop.

"You heard me," Zarus replied. He pulled his shoulder out of Tatsuo's grasp.

Offense stained Tatsuo's tone. "Are you kidding?" He ran in front of Zarus's path before he could walk away. "Didn't we just have this discussion last night?"

Zarus merely glanced down at Tatsuo's hands, unfazed by the gesture. "It doesn't concern you, Tatsuo." He tried to walk past, but Tatsuo's step blocked him.

"Are you really arrogant enough to believe that you can stop Eretimis on your own?" Tatsuo's bite was harsh. Rin ran between the two and tried to calm Tatsuo down, his shouts overpowered her voice. The *narikaah* pointed a finger at Zarus and took a step closer. "I know the things he's capable of. I've seen them firsthand! And I know that you've never beaten him before and always seem to fall back to your knees for him! *So why do you suddenly believe that any of this will change?*"

Rin froze beneath the thunder of Tatsuo's voice. His outburst didn't widen her eyes. It was Zarus. His stoicism drained away, replaced by a stern ire that drew out his scowl by lengths. Fists took the place of hands, held so tightly his knuckles turned white and his posture went rigid. Rin knew what darkness he contained. She felt it. Felt the hairs rise on the back of her neck as Zarus squared his shoulders, tensing his muscles as he tried to suppress it. Rin was certain he would snap. What Tatsuo said struck deep. Zarus still didn't meet Tatsuo's stare. He stared silently at the snow on the ground.

Tatsuo's anger broke down. "Why are you so against my help?" A forlorn hum rang through his words, but he did not falter.

Rin glanced back and forth between the two demons. There would be nothing she could do if they attacked each other. Maybe she could convince Tatsuo to flee, but reason with Zarus? Those blaring red eyes spoke nothing of reason.

Zarus held his tongue. Rin saw his self control fading, but he caught himself.

"Zarus?" she said, softly.

Zarus finally met Tatsuo's eyes, cut-throat and blatant. "You're not strong enough."

Rin's mouth nearly dropped. An icy wind rushed past her exposed skin.

Tatsuo scoffed. "And she is?" he growled, gesturing to Rin. "You're going to have a human fight against the most dangerous demon in the realms because I'm not *strong* enough to stand by your side, after all the strife you put her through?" There was a sick sense of humor in the question.

Zarus didn't laugh. "You're not fighting in this, Tatsuo—no one else is." Zarus pushed him out of his way. "This has nothing to do with you; nothing to do with *her*. She's only in this because she was with me. I don't need another person getting in my way. I don't need another life to save."

Rin didn't know what to do. Zarus was leaving and Tatsuo stood staring at the snow. The silence raged, and she couldn't find the words to replace it.

"I'll only get in your way, huh? Fine." Tatsuo straightened his back, watching Zarus walk away. "I guarantee that won't ever happen again." He turned around and walked in the opposite direction.

Rin's chest clutched. She did nothing to stop them. She glanced at Zarus. He stopped in his tracks, but didn't look back. A light snowfall cascaded from the heavens. When she looked back at Tatsuo, he was gone.

"Rin," Zarus said quietly, trying to sound confident or maybe unfazed. She saw right through it. "I'm getting you to your mother, and if that's somewhere Eretimis will find you, then I'll tear the world apart until you're safe from his reach."

Rin flinched. It was a promise too intense for two strangers. A promise she knew he meant. But nowhere in that promise did Zarus ever say that he would defeat Eretimis.

Chapter Twenty

T he base of the mountain grew nearer with each step. While the air warmed with the scent of soil and pine, Rin couldn't muster a smile. She missed her talks with Tatsuo. She also knew that engaging Zarus in conversation was close to impossible. Then again... *Can't hurt to try*, she resolved.

"Hey, Zarus?" He didn't answer, but slowed down until she met his side. "Is there a limit to how much ice you can create?"

Zarus took a moment to think it through. "I honestly don't know," he admitted. "I haven't found my limit, but that doesn't mean one doesn't exist. For a while, I tried not to rely on it."

Rin considered this; she had noticed he favored daggers in battle. "Does it save your energy?"

Zarus sighed. He didn't wish to chat, but she needed it. "No, it's just..." he paused for a moment, unsure if he wanted to continue. "I learned when I was young and less experienced that I shouldn't rely on my magic. Trying to control it takes a toll..."

Rin's nose scrunched at the comment. "That's stupid. You're blessed with this amazing gift. Why on Armiria wouldn't you want to use it?" She felt a twinge of envy. "Surely you experiment with your powers when you're not fighting. No one really gets to your skill without training."

"I used to," he said, "a long time ago."

"Long ago, like before you lived on the mountain?"

"Long ago like before I worked with Eretimis."

"Why did you stop? I mean, your magic is amazing. Why not learn more about it?"

"My magic scared me," Zarus admitted. "I didn't know what it was or how to use it for years. All demons have a power that comes naturally to them. That was ice for me. It was easier to learn, as well as spells. But the shadows... only purebloods can wield them. Eretimis said it was too much for me then. I couldn't control it." He paused. Rin was met with emptiness when she glanced at him. "I haven't had a need for them until you showed up."

Rin pressed her lips together. *Am I the only reason he's done anything in the past three hundred years?*

"Rin?" Zarus noticed she was deep in thought.

"Hm?" She looked up from the snow. Had he said something?

"I asked if you're getting the hang of that blade." He gestured to the scimitar's hilt protruding from her coat.

"I think so. It's still a little awkward when I first swing it, but it gets easier the more I use it. Tatsuo even gave me a few tips last night—" Her voice faded, replaced by a pang of sadness. The anger in the *narikaah's* voice still echoed in her head. Rin peered through the mist with thoughts of Tatsuo.

Zarus sighed. "I had to make him leave, Rin."

"I'm sure you had your reasons," Rin said a bit more aggressively than she intended. She didn't see how having Tatsuo's help was a bad thing.

"I know he's a decent fighter and was better at holding a conversation than me, but he's too young to die in a battle that's mine to begin with." He searched for the right words. "At least now there's no chance of him getting hurt."

Rin felt a fragment of the pain he felt. That didn't sway her. "Who are you to make that decision for him? Tatsuo knew what he was getting into. He dealt with Eretimis's actions firsthand, but still stayed. He chose to help us." Zarus didn't respond. He didn't even look at her.

Ahead, Rin saw where the ice of the mountain stopped and the gathering of trees and wildlife started. She sighed, rubbing her palms into her eyes. "Do you really believe Eretimis is undefeatable?"

"I do." He didn't hesitate.

"Why? He has to have some sort of weakness, right? No one is invincible."

"If no one's figured out how to kill him in the last two thousand years he's ruled Hraesah, then I don't think there is a way." He paused for a moment like he wanted to say more, but didn't finish his thought.

Rin shook her head. No one lived without weakness, and even if someone did, then that was all the more reason to need extra help. Her life depended on it. Yet she would likely never see Tatsuo Kurosawa again. Anger simmered beneath the surface, but she forced it away as the greenery caught her eye.

The underbrush was thick and untamed. The forest must have stretched for miles over the hills at the foot of the mountain. She couldn't believe it. After four days of snow mounds and disorienting blizzards, the end of this gods-forsaken mountain was in sight. Rin bit the inside of her cheek and waited for Zarus to lead the way.

"We aren't crossing the entire forest, just slipping through the edge," he said bleakly. He walked to the forest's shade without another word—back to his usual self.

Rin started to follow, but something caught her eye where the snow meddled with the underbrush. A shimmer glared under the sun. Zarus didn't appear to notice, but she veered her step to it. At first sight it looked like a simple piece of garbage, but once she stood over it, Rin saw a sword.

"Hey, Zarus," she called, "come check this out." She could practically hear his eyes roll at the tangent, but he made his way over without much complaint.

"We don't have the luxury of time to be staring at the snow, Rin."

"I know, but what do you think this is doing all the way out here?" She picked up the sword. It weighed far less than she anticipated. Her hand ran down the flat of the double-edged blade, feeling the grooves and incises rise and fall beneath her fingers. She lifted it into the sun. The silver steel nearly blinded her as she inspected it. The crossguard twisted around the hilt beautifully, smoothly transitioning to the black leather grip. A celeste gem rested in the pommel. A feat of true metal work, for inscribed along the ricasso was the etching of some foreign tongue—a tongue of which she had no recognition. It was a blade out of fantasy, not reality. Too pretty to be affiliated with battle, in Rin's opinion. The weathered edges proved otherwise. She glanced up to see if Zarus was as intrigued as she was. The opposite met her.

Zarus's face twisted in horror. He drained further of color as he locked eyes on the sword. He nearly lost balance, but caught himself, stumbling ungracefully in the effort.

"It can't be..." he uttered.

A sickly panic seized Rin's gut. "What's wrong?"

Zarus kept his focus on the silver sword. "It can't be... no," he repeated. He reached for the weapon, taking it from Rin's hands as if holding an artifact. His hands trembled as he ran his pale fingers along the blade. There was recognition in his eyes. And the way he held it left no doubt in Rin's mind that this was a sword of war.

"*Why* is this here?" His hands choked the hilt, as if he could suffocate its unwanted memories. His trembling body and shaking breath betrayed him. Zarus dropped to his knees. "This *can't* be here!"

Rin tried to reach out for Zarus, but fear paralyzed her. A shadowy mist flooded from his hands, spreading across the snow and stealing the warmth from her body. This was worse than all the other times he had snapped or fought off their enemies without mercy. There seemed to be no outlet for the pain and anxiety Zarus felt at that moment. What had overcome him? The thing that made him fall silent before an utterance of it. The thing that hollowed his eyes and emptied his soul.

Rin rushed to her friend's side, realizing he was gasping for air. Without breaking his stare from the sword, Zarus reached into his coat and drew out the dagger he had been carrying throughout their journey. Both hands trembled, making each respective blade shimmer in the light. He stared at them the same way she had stared at him when they first met. Rin saw the carvings in both blades. Her heart pounded. They read the same foreign language, shined the same silver steel. The two blades were probably forged from the same steel.

Rin tried to snap Zarus out of it, tried to take the sword from his hand or pull his focus away, but there was no calming him. He sank deeper into oblivion.

Rin looked around frantically. They were out in the open—prey for the taking. "Zarus, you have to get up. We can't stay here any longer!" She tugged on his arm, but he didn't budge. Not until he lurched over and retched on the snow.

Chapter Twenty-One

Rin ran her hand up and down Zarus's back. She did her best to ignore the sour stench. His stomach settled after the first retching, but the pain remained in his eyes. Neither said a thing, and eventually she felt his breaths calm down under her touch. The darkness misting from his hands subsided. Finally, he sighed.

"I'm sorry." His shoulders slumped and his head hung low.

Rin silently nodded. It wasn't okay. Zarus wasn't okay. She looked at the blade that he held so tightly. What was the story behind this sword—what painful memory dwelled in his mind? A small murmur in the back of her head suggested leaving the sword behind just to avoid any trouble it would bring about. Zarus caught her staring at the blade.

He struggled to his feet, swaying this way and that, only finding balance with her arm. "Once we get into the forest—"

Rin's eyes narrowed, her grip on his arm tightened. "Not without an explanation," she interrupted.

"Rin, please. We can't be out in the open too long. Once we get under the forest's cover—"

"I'm not going anywhere until you tell me what on Armiria is going on, Zarus! I mean it! You expect me to follow you when you've barely told me anything about yourself. And suddenly you have some panicked episode in the middle of nowhere and I'm just supposed to ignore it? It doesn't work like that! Friends don't work like that!" She shook her head. "How do I even know I can trust you...?" Her anger flared. A sudden icy-burn pulsed through her arms and down her fingers. The same as when she fought Tatsuo.

"Dammit, would you listen!" he roared. He advanced a step, and Rin had to stop herself from reaching for her scimitar. "I'll explain everything once we have cover! It's too dangerous to talk out here."

She watched him for a moment; watched as his hair threaded through the wind, and as the trees danced behind him. The foreign sensation in Rin's body faded. Her mind calmed. "Fine. It's a deal," she said shortly. She jabbed her hand forward to officiate the deal, but Zarus turned and walked towards the woods. Rin bit down on her irritation and followed.

Rin thought back to the time she had first felt that heat surge through her. Energy ignited in her body for that split moment, yet it disappeared so fast. Had Zarus noticed it or was it just in her head?

One thing at a time. Just focus on one thing at a time, Rin.

***

They entered the woods in silence. Rin was lost in thought, and Zarus wasn't searching for a conversation.

His hand brushed against the sword's hilt at his hip. Of all places... How did it get there? That sword should be lost forever. He had watched it disappear with—

Zarus cut off the thought. He needed to focus on the forest, on Rin; not the past.

He turned his attention to the thicket of trees. Tranquility blanketed the forest despite Rin's uneven steps—breaking twigs and stirring leaves. The breeze whistled past his ears, the thick scent of rotting wood and damp air carried by it. The natural beauty fascinated Rin; Zarus scowled at it. The lush forest only offered cover for Eretimis's loyalists to hide before they attacked. Even the slightest rustle of an animal in the foliage sent his nerves on edge. Zarus's hand subconsciously brushed against the sword again.

***

The ancient forest stretched far and wide. The musky scent of damp earth flooded Rin's nostrils, and the cool breeze refreshed her senses. Birds chirped, animals scurried underfoot, brooks sang, leaves danced, and the wind whistled.

Her hands wandered into the branches, feeling the grooves of the leaves as she walked. There was nothing like this in Aresan. It reminded her of the tales she read about the birth of the world; when Yath Ha asked their attendants, the kaetha, to add their divine wisdom to the infant land. The kaeth Mynil roamed the forests, teaching the birds songs, the deer how to run, and the foxes how to sneak. But beauty has its secrets. Animals cried in the distance. They were facing danger, and she didn't have time to stop to take in the splendor. While the rays of light poking through the canopy faded, she noticed Zarus hadn't said a word.

It was only when the mist soaked through her clothes entirely that Rin spoke up. "Are we going to stop for the night?" she yawned, damning her exhaustion. The soft forest floor was a dream compared to snow piled above her knees, but walking through the underbrush without light was a call for disaster.

Zarus searched the woods. "I can't find anywhere on the ground safe enough to sleep through the night." He walked up to one of the largest oaks Rin had ever laid eyes on. The branches dipped and raised wherever Mynil's persuasion led them. Ancient and strong. "Can you climb?" he asked.

Rin's eyes lit up. Climbing trees was one of her many pastimes at home. She didn't care that she couldn't see the top of the massive oak, just that they were finally going to sit and talk. She stretched her arms out to grab ahold of the nearest branch, but Zarus put his hand on her shoulder.

"Wait here," he said. Without another word, Zarus grabbed a branch, and pulled himself up with effortless grace.

***

Zarus climbed until the ground vanished under the maze of branches. The oak was more than stable enough to hold them for the night.

He made his way to the edge of a sturdy branch and peered over the deep-rooted forest. His eyes drew to the night sky, where the rising moon offered comfort to his weary mind. The sun's touch still laced the horizon with a splash of violet, the Lennaels standing proudly before it.

Completely spent, Zarus moved to the base of the branch and sat against the wide trunk.

The situation at hand was less than desirable, but he had to admit that it was peaceful in the mask of leaves. That was until he found his hand on the hilt at his hip. His head rang mercilessly.

Three hundred years and I still can't let you go.

Zarus sighed, looking up to the moon. "Only a little longer, then I can figure this all out..."

He gathered his will and climbed down, hoping that Rin hadn't wandered off in the five minutes he was gone. He found her sitting against the trunk, staring at her hands in deep thought. She looked up when the leaves rustled.

"Everything go well?" she asked softly. *Are you okay?*

He nodded slowly. "Don't move around too much in your sleep." He released the last branch and jumped on the ground. The canopy swallowed the moonlight. He offered to help her, but once she started climbing, Zarus realized she didn't need it. He moved to follow, but a small glint deep behind the wall of shadows caught his gaze. It took a moment—it took *effort*—but he finally settled on a gap in the brush, barely visible beneath the shade. Zarus squinted and gritted his teeth.

A pair of eyes loomed through the darkness. Eyes that watched him. Eyes that he caught only a glimpse of before they disappeared. He blinked, trying to rid himself of the exhaustion keeping him from seeing clearly in the dark. Zarus watched the bushes. He searched for a presence, even tried to smell if something was out there. Was lack of sleep finally catching up with him? There was no weather blocking his senses down here. He would know if someone was out there, he would've sensed them.

"Are you coming?" Zarus jumped at Rin's call.

There was nothing. He was just tired. Zarus grabbed a splintered branch and caught up to Rin with ease.

Chapter Twenty-Two

Rin climbed to the sturdiest branch she could find; it didn't sway in the wind too much, wasn't shedding bark, and was full of vibrant leaves. Zarus opted to take the nook of limbs slightly lower.

Rin sensed Zarus's unease. The sword, perhaps? His hand hadn't stopped grazing its hilt since he took it from her. His possessiveness over the blade was unnerving. That aside, how did the weapon even get there? It all seemed too convenient... And there was something else. Something tugged on the hairs on the back of her neck, sending a chill down her spine. There was something about the forest, about the air—

Zarus sighed. This was the moment Rin had been waiting for all evening. He focused on the sword, not deigning to look at her when he spoke.

"Out of everything that's happened recently, this is the most surprising yet," Zarus muttered. He took a deep breath. "There's too much history in this blade to tell all of it, but I'll share what concerns me." Another pause, and then he finally began. "I used to live with humans—used to live as a human—before I knew I was a demon. My childhood village accused me of murder. I was still young. They gave me an unfair trial, which provoked these powers I didn't even know

I had until then. They wouldn't listen and kept attacking until I…" Zarus broke off the thought. "That's when he first found me."

"I don't think Eretimis wanted me then. Looking back; he's the hand that fed the lies to my village, then tried to kill me after they were dead. He saw me as a threat. I was injured, but fled from him with my life and was cautious about wherever I went and whoever I met. The sudden use of my magic took a toll on my body. So many years bottled up, growing but dormant; it tore me open when I finally used it. It felt like it was destroying me. Anyone that I went to for help slammed the door in my face, or worse," he said grimly. "It was difficult to adjust; back then, I still had the slight hope humans would be reliable. Then years passed, too many years."

"I was on the verge of death… one of many times, at least. I had this power and had no idea how to control it, to where it almost killed me time after time." Something below snagged Zarus's attention amid his story. Rin's ears strained to detect what it might have been. The unease in the back of her mind still rang. He glanced at the curtain of leaves below, then resumed after he found nothing. "When I was struggling, a demon found me. He pulled me back to my feet, helped me sort everything I struggled with. We didn't belong in this world. He was in a similar situation, and we had to resort to defending ourselves from human superstition. We moved around, traveled where no one knew us, and eventually settled down in an abandoned stronghold. That's where I saw the dark mirror for the first time. My friend took an interest in it, but could never find its origin. He started asking around about it. Until one day someone appeared, offering us a place among our own people. I didn't want to at first, I fought him on every word of it, but my friend convinced me…" Rin noted the pang of sadness in his tone. "That's when I started working for Eretimis."

Zarus scowled. "He taught us how to control our magic, hone our powers, and in return, we carried out his orders. Usually assignments that were too difficult for the other soldiers. He needed demons he could trust to get the job done and eliminate threats. It was a catharsis, being the center of all that death after years of receiving the blows, but I grew numb to it after so long. My friend reveled in it." Rin swallowed a dry breath. She thought of Tatsuo's parents; her gut twisted. "But I guess we grew to be a threat, more powerful than Eretimis could handle. One day, he sent us out on a mission and one of his soldiers attacked us. He injured my friend, but not gravely. We fought back and the soldier fell, but he called for backup before he died. We were out-numbered—surrounded." His body stiffened, voice hardened. "They killed my friend. I couldn't make it to him in time, and Errogan was killed."

Rin's heart pained. It all made sense. *Zarus* made sense.

Zarus collected himself after a moment. "This was his sword," he said, shifting the blade in his grip.

"How did you escape?" Rin quietly asked.

Zarus's stare calloused as he looked toward the moon. "I remember standing over the cliff where he fell; not even a demon could survive that fall. That was all it took. I killed them. Every last one of them." A chill swept through the air from his direction. He finally forced himself to look her in the eyes. So much sorrow and grief within those crimson eyes...

"I went straight back to Eretimis's fortress in the north. Eretimis—" Zarus stumbled over his words, his teeth clenching as a spark ignited in his eyes. "He wouldn't get away with it. Not again. I fought him until he fell to the ground. I was in the Dark Tyrant's throne room, about to kill him." He breathed in and rested back into the vines growing around the tree. "I almost killed him, but something stopped me. My body froze against my will. Eretimis gained the upper hand, and forced me to flee again." Zarus practically spat out the words, his expression twisting with disdain.

"In grief, I returned to the stronghold we lived in before Eretimis found us, and there I found the mirror again. The sight of it made me sick. I tried to shatter it, but it didn't break. The mirror absorbed the magic I threw at it, and it dragged me in. I was stranded alone somewhere on Eroz for one hundred years before I could get the mirror to work again. When I finally came back to Armiria, I was in a castle on the top of a mountain and the humans there thought I was a monster. I was sick of the bloodshed. I lost my hunger for it, but the humans didn't listen and attacked. The ones who fled died in the storm." The castle. Rin swallowed hard on her breath and lowered her hand, gently placing it on his shoulder. He didn't even stir at her touch. "He fell holding *this*."

The wind howled past Rin's ears, causing the leaves to brush against her arms. *No wonder you lost it...* "Eretimis spent all that time training you just to turn around and kill you? I don't understand," she muttered.

"It was never about training us, it was about training our magic. That's all he ever wants. Power—*more* power. He stacks up his armies, racks up his pawns, and strengthens his allies so that nothing can stand as a threat against him." Eretimis found a spring of power, if that was the case. Zarus began running his fingers across the blade once more. He stared at it as if in a trance.

Rin watched Zarus. It was too convenient, all of it. He had to have known it, too. His pain couldn't blind him to *that* extent. "Zarus," she said carefully, "if your friend fell holding that blade, it couldn't have been difficult to go to the bottom of the cliffs to search for it. Clearly you recognized it, and I'm sure Eretimis would take any chance to make you tick..." She shook her head, feeling her stomach churn. How easy would it have been to plant his friend's sword in their path? Rin's head spun so violently she had to hold on to the branch beside her.

Zarus's eyes suddenly narrowed to the world below. They had walked into a trap. The hairs on the back of Rin's neck stood on edge. He neared the edge of his branch, gazing down through the canopy. "It is far too convenient, but nothing emerges from Mortality's Edge after falling into its depths." His words were tight. Without giving her a chance to respond, he began his descent.

An eerie silence replaced his voice until Rin could no longer see Zarus through the leaves.

Mortality's Edge: the ravine rumored to be the kaeth Vulyn's gateway into the afterlife. If his friend had fallen there, then that should have been the end. Yet the sword had resurfaced.

***

Zarus peered into the dark for what felt like hours. Sweat beaded his brow, sending chills along his back.

He couldn't feel a specific presence, but the forest felt wrong. Zarus quietly landed on the ground, not a rustle of leaves or shine of moonlight to be traced. There should have been a sign; a mouse scurrying, the wolves prowling miles away—*anything*—but a wall of nothing met him. Then he remembered. He'd felt a spell like this before, long, long ago. A spell that suppressed the senses of those trapped in it. Someone had cast it over the forest.

Zarus's jaw tightened, urgency swelling in his chest. He idled too long under the spell that diminished his senses to that of a human. He should have recognized it. The fact he could barely feel the wind was enough of a sign! The curses ran off his tongue. They were defenseless in the tree—*Rin* was defenseless. He needed to get to her. As soon as he reached for the lowest branch, something threw him backward.

His vision roared in shades of red. His thoughts whirled. *What happened?* His head had smacked down on the roots below. Who threw him?

Zarus snapped back into focus. He jumped to his feet, but a cool edge pressed against his throat before he could reach the tree. He opened his mouth to shout a warning, but a hand covered it. Zarus tried to glance behind, but with any slight motion, the cool edge of the blade pressed against his neck.

Before he could think of a plan, something rushed past him and up the bark of the ancient tree. Dread flooded Zarus's veins. He snarled as he slammed the back of his head into his captor's face. The grip holding him loosened, but never released. The knife sunk deeper until his blood trickled down the steel.

"Just wait, Lowwenth" a malicious voice whispered into Zarus's ear. "You'll see her in a moment." It was too subtle, too hushed. He couldn't hear them clearly enough to decipher against the spell. Above, a shriek tore through the tranquil forest. Rin crashed to the ground.

***

Rin had no time to react as the enormous oak shook. Someone shoved her, and she screamed as she smacked against the limbs. First her shoulder, then her ribs. She fell blindly through the branches. The air forced out of her lungs when she finally hit the ground. Her ears and teeth rang. The fall should have broken a bone, but from what she could tell, she only had a sprained wrist and an enormous ache in her head.

Rin pried herself off the ground and heaved a cry. She couldn't see anything through the dark, she only heard ominous laughter.

Suddenly appearing from the veil of night, someone grabbed her and held her off the ground by her hair. Her cry shattered the silence.

Tears gathered in Rin's eyes as she heard Zarus's muffled shouts. She still couldn't see him. Not until a gust of wind caught the branches overhead and moonlight peeked onto the forest floor. And just on the other side of the clearing, Zarus stood with a dagger against his throat and a hand masking his mouth.

The female that pushed her from the tree held her. "This was more effort than necessary to kill one human," she remarked unenthusiastically. Rin grabbed onto the demon's arm for dear life, her feet scrambling beneath her.

It felt like her hair was being ripped out of her skull, yet the silence stretched. Rin saw a silhouette move in the dark, and then the knife fell from Zarus's neck. Her chest knotted.

Someone as swift as the like-wraith approached.

"W-what do you want?" Rin meekly demanded. The female released her hair and let her feet touch the ground as the other demon paused his step. The darkness hid his features well, and the only thing Rin could see was that the skin on the demon's hand was as ghostly as Zarus's. Fear, pain, stress—it all watered her gut. She braced herself as the male grabbed her wrist and lifted her to eye level.

"Who are you?" was all he asked. Three simple words. Three words that Rin felt unsafe in sharing.

Why did he care who she was? She's the human traveling with Zarus! What difference did names make? Rin swallowed the spit clumping in her throat and thrashed her elbow out.

***

Zarus's heart out-raced his temper.

"Let her go!" he snarled and lunged for the demon who put a blade to his throat. He would've ripped them apart if it hadn't been for another demon behind. They yanked back his arms and forced him to his knees.

These demons were stronger than any of the others. They weren't bounty hunters; they were soldiers. But who was *he*? The one who drew blood from his throat, the one whose voice stabbed into his memories.

"Not even death will offer you peace once I get to you," Zarus seethed. Another blade threatened to cut him.

***

Rin's elbow slammed into the female's chest behind her, but the male restraining her remained unaffected.

"*Who are you?*" he repeated, his grip tightening. Tears flooded down her cheeks.

Rin kept silent. No good would come of answering. Hopefully, Zarus was already working on a plan—

She looked over and saw Zarus on his knees with a sword to his back. His calm facade was burning up.

A shattering laugh erupted from her captor's throat. He followed her stare and looked at Zarus. "Don't get your hopes up, human. He can't even help himself right now. The Shadow of Evenfall is helpless against a little spell." Light struck the bottom half of his face, revealing a bloodthirsty smirk. "Now, before I lose my patience," the demon pulled her closer to his face, "*who* and *what* are you?"

"G-go to hell!"

The male broke into a cackle. "Where did you find this one, Zarus?" The female behind her and the male holding Zarus down joined in. Rin's face burned red. "I'm surprised you haven't killed her by now." The demon suddenly released her wrist and let her crash to the ground. He sauntered back toward Zarus.

Rin pulled herself off the ground. This demon didn't see Zarus as a threat. He talked with such nonchalance. Something about him was eerily familiar. She couldn't put her finger on it.

***

The leash on Zarus's magic pulled taut.

"Don't talk like you know me," he growled. A red hot prong pushed on his thoughts. "Step out of the shadows and we'll see how far that ego stretches."

A mocking scoff. "You really haven't figured it out yet, have you?" The male circled around Zarus. "You used to be sharper than any blade in the fortress."

Wrath was an old habit, and it smothered his reason. Zarus's pulse pounded. His breath hitched. "I'll rip off your hand if you touch Rin again." The temperature in the forest plummeted. Frost grew along the dead leaves below his legs. Dark mist stirred on the forest bed.

The demon paused his step between Zarus and Rin. "So her name's Rin?"

Zarus cursed at his carelessness. "*Coward.*"

"Let's not be a hypocrite, Zarus."

***

Rin watched Zarus's expression mold into murderous intent. She pushed to her feet, but barely held back a cry when something on the ground cut into her palm. She glanced behind her and found the silver blade glistening against the moon. Zarus must have dropped it when he was captured. And suddenly, Rin's mind sprang to reality.

The sword.

Her head throbbed with nausea and dread. "Zarus," she said levelly. No one restrained her; she wasn't the threat. The shadows spreading on the ground stole the warmth from her legs, the ice splintering out of Zarus almost reached her. Grief blinded him.

Rin swallowed hard. "Some things *do* emerge." She tried to keep a stern clarity in her voice as Zarus's eyes met her own. However, everyone's eyes also shifted to her. Five pairs of eyes illuminated against the sheet of darkness.

***

"What?" Zarus growled.

'*Some things* do *emerge.*'

"That can't be." He heaved heavy breaths. "I watched him die…" A weight crushed further and further down on his chest.

"Zarus..." Everything was a blur, but somehow out of the corner of his eye, he saw Rin stand up. "Why else would this be here?" She held his friend's sword—*Errogan's* sword—with two hands.

Blood stained the edge.

Zarus looked back to the demon between them, his throat dry. He refused to believe it. Errogan *died* right before his eyes. There was no way in Ashnagz that this was him. Zarus tried to stand, but three sets of hands suddenly held him down. His thoughts burned so... so... he didn't know. His mind grew hazy.

The demon's devilish smirk dropped. He offered little more than a shrug as he walked back to Rin and swiped the sword out of her hands. "The human is smarter than she looks." With a sudden snap of his fingers, the spell lifted.

Zarus's senses returned with a jolt. He pinpointed the three demons hovering around him. He smelled Rin's blood in the air, even tasted the faintest metallic tang it left. How had he not noticed this when they first arrived in the forest? Was he that distracted by the blade? As soon as he regained the profound sense of awareness, his blood iced.

The demon's white hair repelled the darkness, his arctic blue eyes pierced through the night. The presence, the smirk, the godsdamned *scent...*

"Errogan..." Zarus whispered.

"Long time no see, Z." A bitter curve crossed Errogan's lips.

Zarus felt his chest knot. "Errogan," he addressed through his teeth, rage seeping into his voice. The shadows drifting about the glade suddenly sprung to life. A wave of thick mist crested right toward his old comrade. Errogan didn't bat an eye.

"Sorry, old friend, but I don't have time to explain." He whirled the sword around with skillful precision, spinning and catching it in a way that cut right through the dark wave. "My deadline is dawn." Errogan raised the pommel of the sword over Zarus's skull.

His eyes didn't even have time to widen before Errogan knocked them shut. The cresting darkness slowly disappeared.

***

Without the spell, clarity filled the moonlit forest. Errogan smashed the pommel into Zarus's skull. Rin watched paralyzed as his ice melted and the darkness receded. She was useless, even with a sword in her hand. The scimitar weighed down at her hip. A useless, dead weight.

Malice curved Errogan's lips as he turned to her. "Now," he offered an almost humbling gesture, "I'm supposed to kill you, but there's something I don't understand yet. You're coming with us too."

Rin felt the color drain from her face.

One male that held Zarus down cut Errogan a scathing look. "We were only supposed to bring back the traitor. Eretimis said nothing about the girl." However, the same male squealed like a pig a moment later. The scent of iron filled the air.

Errogan growled. Red dripped off the edge of the sword in his hand, the maimed demon crashing beside Zarus on the ground. "Eretimis thinks she's useless. I, on the other hand, think there's something she can offer. We all sense her presence. There's something odd about it. She'll die, but I want to see something first."

The words left his lips so easily. *She'll die.* Were all demons like that? Did they all hold such hatred and evilness in their hearts? From the moment Rin met Zarus on the top of that mountain, she'd only met demons who wanted to harm her.

Errogan neared. Morbid curiosity stared at her through crystal eyes familiarly. The hair and eyes threw her off at first, but Errogan looked remarkably like Zarus. The same sharp nose, the same cheekbones. Even a similar voice, but a different dialect. Yet Errogan carried a scar stretching from his right temple down his cheek. They even had the same murderous stare. Now Errogan's directed at her.

Maybe if she begged, she could convince them not to harm Zarus any more than they already had. Rin glanced at her friend's prostrate body sprawled on the dead leaves. He could barely fight back... But the pleas dried in her throat.

'She'll die.'

She doubted that he'd be gracious enough to make it quick. What about Zarus? What fate awaited him when he returned to Eretimis's clutches? Oh gods, oh gods. She truly thought that they were going to make it. Truly thought that she would finally meet her mother, that Zarus would be free of Eretimis, and Tatsuo... gods knew where he ran off to. Why? Why did she leave Aresan? Why did her mother have to leave all those years ago? Why was Zarus the one she had to run into?

Why!

It wasn't fair. Did the gods think this was amusing to watch? They shifted her world upside down, and now they were going to take it away. She should have been outraged, but she found herself praying.

Please, just please let my father be at peace when all of this is over.

Tears masked her cheeks, soaked her chin. It was the end. Her end.

Brace yourself, child.

She braced herself for whatever might happen, and gods, she was glad she listened to the small voice in her head that told her to do so.

Rin closed her eyes and tensed her body. With the force of a falling tree, someone's arm wrapped around her waist and plucked her off the ground. Rin dared to open her eyes, and when she did, she found a masked man holding her close as they swung through the vines hanging from forest's treetops.

She was saved, but Zarus? Zarus wasn't so lucky.

Chapter Twenty-Three

The stranger flew through the air, jumping from tree to tree while Rin held tight to his sturdy build. It had to have been ten minutes before he decided they were far enough away from Errogan and merely placed her on the ground.

The world refused to stop spinning. Or was it her head? Whatever it was, Rin sat hunched over on a damp log, trying to catch her breath and keep her stomach settled. The mossy stench wasn't helping. The stranger hadn't said a word since he'd scooped her off of the ground and saved her life.

He simply sat there, watching her behind the cloth mask.

Rin could only think of Zarus's motionless body being hauled off to gods knew where by that monster—*Errogan.*

"Is your head okay?" The stranger's words curved in the slightest accent. It was the first thing he'd said. Black cloth hid his nose, mouth, and chin.

Rin buried her eyes into her palms. "What are they going to do to Zarus?"

The man was still. "He won't die." The mask muffled his words. He glanced toward the horizon behind the trees to the rising sun. His dark brown hair tugged in the wind before it fell back to his rich bronze shoulders, his golden eyes scanning the trees.

"Why save me and not Zarus?" The words came out harsher than Rin intended.

"Zarus," the man emphasized, his voice calm and low, "can take care of himself. He's dealt with demons before, lived with them, even fought against the Dark Tyrant." Rin recalled Zarus's tale. "He can handle himself. You, on the other hand, can't. Not against demons."

A scowl covered her face, her hands balling into fists. "And how would you know that? I've stood my ground against demons and even injured a few." She didn't know why she was being so defensive. She was on the verge of exploding.

The man remained calm. "I didn't see you stand your ground against that demon, nor did I see you injure him. Quite the opposite, actually. Did you do anything besides hand him that blade?" He eyed her bruised wrist, the one Errogan had suspended her from. "How long do you think you would last in a fortress full of Eretimis and his loyalists?"

Her scowl remained in place, but she couldn't argue. "So you helped me because you were waltzing through the woods and saw me being tossed around like a bottle?"

"I heard about Eretimis's bounty and was looking for you," he said, scratching the back of his head. "I also think that you could help us."

Us? Who was *us*, and what could she do to help?

He read through her frown. "Why do you think that demon didn't kill you? There's something about you that makes you a threat to them." He leaned closer, resting one of his knees in the dirt below. "Eretimis's dealings in this world stretch further than you think, Rin. I'm working with a group of people to fight back and help those who are powerless against him. Barely anyone on Armiria knows about the destruction he's spread throughout this world for hundreds of years, and most of the few who do are too scared to do anything about it. He's already dominated half of Eroz, now he wants to enslave this world too. I can't let that happen." His tone lightened a bit. "So, will you help us stop him?"

Rin nearly spat out a laugh. She couldn't see how she fit into any of this. She failed Zarus when he needed her most, and here some stranger was telling her *she* could help him? Truly laughable. "I don't see how I can help you, er—" she paused, having no name to call him. "The only reason I got mixed up with Zarus was because I got lost trying to find my mother... that's the whole reason I started this trip and got lost and—" she felt like she was rambling, and knew she should stop, but she didn't. "I wish I could do something for you. I really do, but I'm just human. There isn't anything extraordinary about me, and as much as I want Eretimis to stop whatever it is he's doing, I just... can't." The sun cut through the brightening canopy and warmed the forest floor enough so that Rin had finally stopped shivering. Unlike the mountains she was on only hours ago, this part of the forest was actually quite nice.

The man stared at her longer than she was comfortable with. His eyes were intense with thought, and it put her on edge. "Everybody underestimates humans. I don't understand why," he mumbled. "Do you have any idea where your mother is hiding?"

Rin frowned. It seemed so long ago that she held that map in her hands. "Lilit. It's small, and not on any conventional maps, but it's on this side of the Lennaels."

His demeanor jumped at the name. "Well, *not extraordinary human*, Lilit happens to be the next village past my base, or the only village," he mused with a twinge of whimsy. "I'll make you a deal."

Her heart bounced at the thought that he might offer to take her to her mother, but then what would happen to Zarus? She couldn't just leave him to suffer at the hands of those monsters...

"If I agree to deliver you to your mother, then you agree to stop by Base and tell us everything you know about the demons you fought, and Eretimis, and Zarus. We need to gather all the information we can." It was an interesting deal, and had a feeling of hidden intent, but it was her best bet. Although...

"I accept," she said with a generous smile.

"Great, then let's get moving. It's a decent way to—"

"Under one condition," she finished.

He tilted his head in suspicion.

The statue of a stranger looked comical for the moment, and Rin had to push down the urge to laugh. "I'll tell what I know, and I warn you it's not much, but only under the condition that you promise you'll do everything in your power to help Zarus get away from Eretimis." She needed to know something was being done to get Zarus out of the mess she helped bury him in.

Silence. Was he considering, or just holding out long enough to make her back down?

"Alright, I think that's fair enough." Without any objections or add-ons, the man stood up and held out his large, callused hand to shake.

Rin examined it for a minute, unsure. "And you promise you're not lying so you can just kill me and collect the reward?" She realized how stupid asking someone if they were lying was, but his laugh eased her concern.

"I promise that I have no intentions of killing you. You're part of the world I'm trying to save," he said cheerfully, but let out an honest sigh. "I'll do everything I can to get Zarus out of there, but I can't promise he'll decide to leave when the time comes." A warning or a loophole. Rin wasn't sure.

"That," she said with a huff as she stood, "is good enough for me." She grabbed his hand and shook. A warm breeze licked up Rin's neck.

"We should go. The sooner we leave, the sooner we get to Base, and the sooner you get to Lilit."

"And what name might I address you by?" Rin asked before she followed him through a thicket of leaves.

"Just call me Feyne," he called back to her.

Caenlin for *wolf*.

"Well, Feyne, I'm Rin. It's nice to meet you."

Part Two

Ghosts

Chapter Twenty-Four

By the time the sun crawled high in the clear skies, Rin walked out of the ancient forest. The song of birds and trickle of streams bled dry the farther they walked beyond the trees and into the arid plains. The stench of moss and dirt disappeared with the kiss of mist. As far as she knew, the silent terrain stretched forever. Thin, wispy trees stalked up from the flat ground. Lazy boulders basked amid untamed yellow grasses.

Before they traveled too far from the forest's edge, Rin glanced behind one last time. A thick fog settled around the forest bed, and behind towered the Lennaels. The silver mountains glistened in the sun's radiance. It all felt like nothing more than a nightmare from this view. Rin turned around, trying to subdue her concerns for Zarus and walked until her feet were splintering.

She finally convinced Feyne to take a break once the sun was midway to setting. Complaining wasn't her favorite pastime, but neither was dehydrating. Kneeling down in the warm grass, she cupped her hands into the stream. "So what type of demon are you?" she asked through sips. "Because out of all the ones I've met, you seem... different."

"How so?" Feyne took a few handfuls of the chilled water. They walked in silence mostly until then. Whether it be wary of a demon following their tracks, or the burden of the sun, Rin didn't mind.

Feyne faced away while he pulled down the mask around his neck, pulling it back in place as he swallowed. Only his amber eyes remained visible.

"Well," Rin paused her sip, lowering her hands, "you hold yourself differently. You seem more at ease than Zarus, the soul stealer, even Tatsuo. Not to say that they weren't relaxed, but they were always... anticipating something." *Yes, that sounds right.* "Every demon I've met never stopped paying attention to every detail, always watching for some potential threat." She dried off her hands on her pants, then stood and stretched her back. "They were all fierce."

Feyne nodded. "Most demons are instinctively observant. Their intensity is hard to match, but that's only because I'm not a demon. I'm a shifter." He sat cross-legged with his hands on his knees.

Her brow furrowed. "How does that work?"

"We turn into things."

Who would have thought? Rin plopped down across from him and readied her questions. "Can you turn into anything, or are you limited to living beings?"

"We're typically limited to one creature, for the most part animals, with a few exceptions here and there. So no, we aren't as flashy as dragons and fae and demons." The flinch of his eyes hinted at a wry smile beneath the mask. "I'm one of few wolf shifters." His tone hinted with pride.

"A wolf?" she asked. "Do you have a pack?"

Feyne's stare didn't falter at the question, but his eyes hardened. "I used to, a long time ago." This was becoming too common of a tale.

Rin apologized, but he wasn't mad.

"Was it because of Eretimis?"

He shook his head. "No. It was a group of human hunters." He adjusted so his legs stretched out and his arms braced himself in the dry dirt.

Rin's eyes widened. Humans hunted down a group of shifters? "W-why?"

"Hunting shifters on Armiria was a popular sport on the eastern continent two hundred years ago. The humans on the other side of the sea are aware of the other races of the world, but they see us as supernatural. Demons started the practice of hunting shifters as trophies, and humans quickly caught on. You see, shifters are looked down on, not quite as much as humans, but most think we're nothing more than filth." He gave a shrug. "When Eretimis first attacked this world, most of the shifters in the west traveled east to escape him. Our hides were trophies. The fascination of the activity quickly died down. I think the humans finally realized what they were doing... Wolves were commonly prized." His voice trailed a little. "I was nine when my pack was hunted."

Rin was silent. Her father once told her about the old hunting traditions in Sheng Ní across the seas. They celebrated the event with festivals and ceremonies. She was told they were hunting animals. But shifters? Just nine years old, and suddenly his whole family was killed—hunted. How old had Tatsuo been? Just a child as well when his parents were taken from him. "I'm sorry," she said.

Feyne shrugged again. "Thank you. I've come to terms with it, though. After all, why would I be fighting for this world if I hadn't?" He smiled, but Rin couldn't muster it.

Zarus's words echoed in her mind. '*Why do I call them insects?*'

"Why are you fighting for this place?" she asked. "Humans hurt you. Why waste the effort?" She looked into his eyes for an answer.

They offered nothing. Only his voice answered. "Because when my sister died saving me, she said I was proof our bloodline hadn't ended." He wasn't offended, or even sad when he spoke, but his tone fell rather intensely. "I promised myself that I would do everything in my power to prevent anything like that from happening to someone else. I don't hate demons for how they hunted my kind, or even the humans for their ignorance. Mistakes can't be generalized. What I hate is that pointless violence exists. Armiria has so much to offer and so many joys; I hate seeing them wasted. When I heard what Eretimis was doing to the people of this world..." he shook his head, "I couldn't do nothing."

Feyne had all the reasons in the world to hate humanity, to hate the entirety of the demon race, but he didn't. He sought to better his world. She almost forgot about the sweat dripping down her back.

"Why are you wearing that mask? I'm starting to think your face is an eyesore." The change of topic lifted the mood of conversation.

His eyes narrowed, but Rin sensed a smile beneath. "Hm, is that so? Then maybe this eyesore won't stop for another break until we've arrived at our destination." Feyne finally stood up, and Rin realized she barely had anything to drink. She guzzled down a few more handfuls as the shifter prowled off without her.

Even as much as she tried to ignore it, Rin's thoughts flooded with guilt, knowing that Zarus was not laughing that afternoon.

Chapter Twenty-Five

Despite the pounding inside Zarus's head, his eyes peeled open. The air was thick with musk and mildew. A measly lantern lit the cellar, not even bright enough to see beyond the bars.

A fool. A useless fool is all he had been in the forest. If he couldn't keep himself from capture, how in all of Ashnagz was he to ensure Rin's safety? He never stood a chance. He didn't even know if she was dead or alive right now! *A damned fool.* Errogan was alive...

A fool.

Zarus's eyes throbbed. His mind fought consciousness. Another spell had been cast to keep his senses dull; Eretimis's spellweavers were hard at work. Perhaps they meant to dissuade his escape by blocking out what waited around each corner. Stiff and sore, he slowly sat up on the damp floor.

"I see you are finally awake."

The hairs on the back of Zarus's neck stood straight. "No thanks to you."

Eretimis sat outside the light's reach. "I was not the one who drove Errogan to such measures; that was your own fault."

"To think after all this time, I was under the impression you wanted me dead." Zarus only then felt the rawness of his throat. "But here I am, in your prison and chained to the floor like a dog. It's good to know I still pose that much of a threat." A scowl pulled his expression. "Are you so desperate for power that you're willing to risk my help again, Eretimis?" He narrowed his eyes, pinning down where that dark voice emitted.

"Whether I want you dead or alive will be decided shortly. Now that you are fully rested," Eretimis mused, his footsteps thudding in the dark, "we will see if you are worthy enough to serve me once more." The Dark Tyrant stepped into the dull light, his hair and cape blending with the shadow beyond.

Zarus's temper burned. "I'd sooner slit my throat than serve you again," he spat. The demon-smithed chains cut into his wrists as he stirred.

Malice filled the depths of Eretimis's eyes. "Now you see, Zarus," the tyrant said in a low, indifferent tone as he took a step towards the cellar door, "that will not be your decision to make after we are finished." A haughty grin plastered to his lips. He nudged the iron door, revealing it unlocked and unguarded. Zarus's eyes narrowed at the salt in his wound. His gut twisted.

Nothing short of a miracle would save him. But no matter what torture, misery, and anguish Eretimis subjected him to, Zarus refused to pray for one.

Chapter Twenty-Six

That smell... A fire? No, no, there's something else. It smells... delicious.

Rin forced her eyes open despite the desire to fall back asleep. Once the grogginess faded, her breath escaped in a gasp. The vibrant night sky displayed a tapestry of beauty. Hundreds of thousands of stars—no, more. More than she could count, more than she could ever comprehend. A conquest of light in the darkness. Some were as bright as a newly oiled torch, some dimmer than the fading gleam in Zarus's eyes. The vast skies crested from the void, to rich navy, and faint hints of violet. A familiar face in an empty part of the world. A fierce face glittered with beauty.

"Food's almost ready."

Feyne sat on the other side of the crackling fire. He kept his voice low, head angled upward at the sky.

Once night had finally fallen, Feyne agreed to take a break and let Rin rest. The heat of the day sucked out what little energy she had left, and even he blissfully fell back in the grass.

She shuffled to her feet and stretched out. Had Feyne gotten any rest since they stopped? The small campfire and rabbits roasting overtop hinted at the answer.

"How long was I out?" Rin yawned, combing a hand through her greasy hair. The temperature chilled with the sun's fall; a delightful fall evening. It could've been a peaceful night between the fire and sky if she didn't know any better. But she did know better, especially with the dirt and grime layering her skin.

"An hour or two. I was actually just about to wake you," he smiled apologetically. "I'm sorry it couldn't be longer, but we still have a ways to go. Take as much as you want. I ate already." At that, Feyne jumped to his feet. Instead of taking the flask of water offered to her, Rin couldn't stop staring. For the first time since they had met, Feyne was without his mask.

His golden irises glowed even brighter against his bronze complexion. A black tattoo lined high on his cheekbones, curving beneath each eye. His left arm also bore a tattoo; only slightly darker than his skin tone. It wrapped around his left bicep. A ring stretching down into six points connected by smooth arches. His strong jawline looked like it was chiseled from stone. As fierce as his face could have been, nothing but sincerity hung on it.

Rin stared at his arm. "Do your tattoos have any meaning?"

After too long of holding the canteen out, Feyne shrugged and tossed the flask onto the ground. "The ones under my eyes symbolize my first hunt. The one around my arm is my pack's mark. Kind of like the family crests royals have. We had it tattooed on us when we reached a certain age, but I was too young to undergo the ceremony before my pack passed. So I did it myself when I was old enough. The six points symbolize each century that my pack stayed together. Another point would have been added at the beginning of the next century for the next generation of tattoos." He started to turn around, but stopped himself midway. His smile faded.

"Rin," he said soberly, "there's something you should know." Her chest knotted against his tone. "Like I said, I'm taking you to Base so you can tell us everything you know about Eretimis and such, which is something I can't thank you enough for. Though some of my companions won't."

Rin's lips straightened. "I'm not doing this for praise."

Feyne nodded. "Even so, some of them are untrusting. It's hard to believe everything you hear. Eretimis has been more active lately, becoming more daring." He paused for a moment, if only to shrug. "I'm just warning you. Some may not welcome you." He offered another grin, and Rin accepted, whether she was pleased to hear she'd meet ridicule when they arrived or not. "Oh, and also when we get there, I'm going to prove that you are special. Despite the fact that what's-his-name didn't kill you right off the bat," he said nonchalantly, not caring to remember Errogan's name, "there's just something else about you I can't put my finger on."

Feyne's intentions were slowly becoming visible. She frowned. "How do you plan to do that?" It better not delay his end of their bargain.

"My friend will help. One of the nice ones, I promise." Mischief grew in his eyes under the pale moonlight. "But... I don't exactly know how long it will take, so be patient. And before you give me that look," he interrupted her scowl with a raised finger, "knowing what's different about you might help you avoid Eretimis in the long run. It's smart that you find out sooner than later, also..." another smirk, revealing elongated canines in his lower jaw, "it's not like you can get to your mother on your own."

And there it was. Rin groaned her reluctant agreement. It's probably what she deserved for trusting another stranger, and it could be helpful to know what caused Errogan to disobey a direct order from Eretimis. Still...

"Fine," she finally gave in. "But I've waited twelve years to see my mother, and I don't want to wait any longer. I'm starting to believe you only saved me to prove me wrong." She sighed, sitting back down and grabbing a rabbit from the fire.

"Other than the fact that you were about to be taken prisoner by Errogan who had said something was off about you? Maybe." A wink of jest flashed her way. "Something told me to help. I've learned to trust my instincts at this point." Rin considered it. She was alive and free because of his *instincts*. "Anyway, we're starting out again soon, so do whatever you need before then." It sounded more like an order than a recommendation, but clearly Feyne wasn't too pleased with their current timing. Without another word, he jumped back to his feet and walked off until Rin could no longer see him.

Chapter
Twenty-Seven

Eretimis called in two guards before taking his leave. The two demons bound Zarus's hands in front of him and escorted him through the damp dungeon into the main levels of the fortress; a female leading and a male following behind.

A spear threatened his back with any reluctance to walk. Zarus met the jagged blade with a snarl each time. *Keep it moving,* the soldier behind him would say. Only three hundred years before, Zarus was the one giving orders. His presence alone was enough to send a shiver of nervousness through the room. It wasn't until he passed by a large arrow-slit window that he stopped again. The opaque glass reached higher than he was tall and stretched wide enough for him to slip through.

He stared longer than was wise. Glass would shatter and skin would heal, but something wasn't right. Leaving him guarded by unskilled and unknowing demons was an offensive act, but having them walk him right by a window? It was too easy, too convenient. Hraesan forged chains might be impossible to break, but he was being underestimated. He kept his gaze forward as he mulled it over. That damned spear nudged his back one too many times.

"K-keep walking," the guard stuttered, needing an extra step to keep balance. The repulsive stench of liquor mixed putridly with the guard's breath.

Without an utterance of retort, Zarus kicked in the back of the female's knee in front of him, then spun around and slammed his elbow into the drunk's abdomen. The female's head smacked into the stone wall before them while the male crashed to the floor, gasping for breath. Zarus rounded behind him, placing his foot on the demon's back. He wrapped the chains restricting his hands taut around the male's throat.

The demon made the struggle for air a dance. He waved his arms around feverishly and kicked his legs. No matter how desperately he tried to dislodge Zarus, sobriety was far off. Only when the demon stopped convulsing did Zarus remove the chain around his neck. Not before snapping it. The cracking of bones echoed through the demon's armor.

Zarus drew his attention to the female guard dragging herself to her feet. The demon unsheathed her sword and charged seamlessly, but Zarus tailored his own masterpiece. He twisted out of the sword's path and caught the female's arm. He crushed it. Her shrieks were pitiful, bouncing throughout the halls.

He wanted the demon to feel every last nerve screaming beyond reason. Because for *centuries*, Zarus had remained dormant on that mountaintop. For years, he hadn't encountered another living soul. Even as he fought those useless demons collecting his bounty, he had held back. Maybe for Rin's sake, maybe because he still felt some strain of control over himself. It nearly killed him. It brought him *here*. Zarus had no reason to keep himself in check. Rin was possibly the best thing that ever happened to him because now he unleashed his wrath without restraint. And gods, did it feel good.

The demon tried to free herself, but Zarus slammed her skull on the ground. The force splintered the wooden floor below, reverberating through his arm. Her skull cracked open. Blood rushed like a fountain, iron masking Zarus's nose.

Adrenaline sizzled his blood before he remembered. *The window.* He needed to get to the window. Anyone would have heard those screams. Zarus raised his arms to shield his face as he rushed for freedom. Ten feet stood between him and his escape. Ten measly feet. Gods, how sweet thrill dulled his mind. While his thoughts cemented on breaking through that frail glass, Zarus barely heard the footsteps behind. Just in time did he throw his arms behind his head, tautening the chains around his wrists to block the nape of his neck. A sword crashed against the chain, sparking as it slid down without breaking. Thank the gods for Hraesan crafters. Zarus bared his teeth, catching a glint of white hair as he turned around.

A sardonic twist sat on Errogan's lips. "Going so soon? You've only just arrived."

Zarus lowered his arms, eyes meeting the silver steel of the blade. "You once said that sword was a useless weight in your hands." He kept his words short and his lips straight. He wouldn't fall so easily again.

Errogan rapped his fingers across the hilt. "I've grown fond of it in the last hundred years. There's something so poetic about killing humans with their own weapons. It was odd parting from it in the forest. Then you brought it back so quickly, along with the dagger. I really should be thanking you." He slid the sword into the sheath at his hip, then removed Zarus's dagger from another sheath at his thigh. "Now hurry, we're late," he said, adjusting the dagger in his hand.

Zarus opened his mouth to respond like it was the old days. Those days were a memory. He knew it the moment he laid eyes on his long-dead friend in the forest. Errogan delivered him to a fate worse than death—Eretimis. The pause allowed his old friend to send the pommel of the dagger into his spine. Zarus clenched his jaw as fire blazed up his back and seared his vision. He collapsed, then found Errogan's foot firm on his back.

"You've grown slow. Years of isolation made you weak," Errogan hissed.

Zarus pushed himself up, but Errogan's foot pressed him down. He managed a forced laugh. "Maybe I'll finally take you as a challenge."

Errogan's smirk was gone in an instant. The weight on Zarus's back pushed down, and his elbows threatened to buckle under the pressure. "I'm going to make you wish it had been you to fall off that cliff," the demon growled through his teeth. One final kick, and Errogan forced Zarus flat on the ground. Zarus suppressed a wince as his chin slammed down, making way to his feet before the demon could drag him up. The edge of the dagger met his neck right away. "Let's make sure you don't get away this time."

Zarus scoffed, but kept silent as Errogan forced him through the endless maze of the fortress. The layout was foggy in memory. He once knew every detail like it was the back of his hand—knew it and walked it daily. He had memorized every path leading in and out of the stronghold. Had he ever needed to flee when he lived here, he would have known his way out. If only life were that predictable.

He loathed the fortress. It felt like a prison even in the old days; never allowed to have a thought to yourself, always watched, never able to leave without permission. Even Errogan didn't want to leave, despite how Zarus begged him. Eretimis would have brought him back anyway. Just as he had. And now it was a prison in an entirely different way, and his closest friend held a dagger against his jugular.

Errogan pushed Zarus around the corner, and a faded red door sparked his memory. However, the iron bolts barring the door were a new installation to the lounge's entrance, and the room was unrecognizable inside. Worktables replaced the velvet sofas and chairs that he remembered. Cabinets lined the walls, full of scattered papers and notes, beakers containing mysterious substances. A bare stone table centered the room. A scent of smoke lingered in the air, a smog of herbs accompanied it. He nearly choked on the stench. As Errogan led him forward, Zarus eyed shelves stocked full of various equipment for experiments. The guards posted at each corner watched him warily.

Eretimis always had a fondness for the study of living creatures—or what it could allow him to do. He even had some hellishly good ideas that would make him even more powerful. It became clear, however, as Zarus fought each step pushing him closer to the table in the room's center, that Eretimis started acting on those ideas. Ice crept into his blood.

Errogan must have felt his reluctance to go any further, for he let loose a dry laugh and practically threw Zarus into the room. *Now.* He needed to act now. Just as a new line of blood seeped from the shallow graze on his neck, Zarus turned to attack Errogan. Yet the guards lunged from their posts and held him down.

Errogan clicked his tongue, waving a disapproving finger in his direction. "Not so fast."

Zarus gave into his instincts and fought with everything that he had to get free. It was a bloodbath. He worked one arm out of their hold and grabbed a stiletto knife from a counter. One demon screamed and covered his blinded eyes. Zarus nearly ripped off another's arm as their hand tried to wrap around his throat, and he successfully stabbed deep through the muscle in another's leg. That still left two demons, and they were by no means weak. Zarus fought to free himself, but they dragged him onto that cold table and restrained his wrists and ankles.

He seethed, he snarled, he cursed and spat on the people above him. He could not break free. Errogan swaggered over him, mercilessly looking down on his prey, enjoying every damn second of it.

He grabbed Zarus's jaw in his deathly grip, yanking his face to meet his crystal stare. "Try not to scream too loud. There are others working nearby."

Zarus would have bitten his hand right off, had someone bearing a long and thin knife not appeared beside Errogan. The demon's other hand held a beaker containing something that Zarus did not want to experience. The black, oily substance was nearly too thick to be called liquid, but the smell. The *smell* made his teeth grind. Nothing natural, nothing good. He roared in one last feeble attempt to get off that table, but Errogan slammed his head down.

Everything hazed, enough time for the knife to slice deep into Zarus's skin. Burning blood welled, and the vial poured into the laceration. It felt like Ashnagz's blackest flames engulfed his arm, spreading like wildfire as the serum coursed its way through his blood, stretching up his neck and across his chest. His teeth clamped down so fast they cracked as the agonizing sensation of burning alive consumed him. He didn't hear his screams, didn't hear anything over the raging pound of his head—a constant drum beating on and on and on. Everything but the pain burned away. Death... just maybe, this would be it. Zarus craved its sweet release.

Right before he blacked out, Zarus heard a whisper. The slightest hum in the back of his head. Words so soft, they didn't make it past his cries. He couldn't hear what the voice said over his raging pulse, nor did he want to. Right then, in that second, all Zarus Lowwenth wanted was to die.

Chapter Twenty-Eight

"**Y**ou can't be serious," Rin whispered. They both stood under the moon's grace, halted in the middle of nowhere with no shelter in sight.

Feyne's feral smile sent shivers down Rin's spine. What at all about this situation warranted a smile? "Afraid so."

"No, you're not," Rin snapped. "You're grinning like it's your birthday, for the sake of the gods!" She truly thought it would be a calm night. After all, she found the time to wash up in the stream and sit for a while as she dried off before Feyne returned. She glared at his excitement. "How do you know?"

"I can smell them," Feyne said in a hush, subtly sniffing the air. "They're far off, but someone is definitely following us."

A harrowing breeze sent a few strands of hair mingling with Rin's face. It could have been Errogan coming back to take what was stolen from him. The sheer thought almost made her knees buckle beneath her.

Oh gods oh gods oh gods.

Pointlessly, Rin brushed the hilt of her scimitar, if only to make sure it was still there at her hip. She had forgotten how to use it when Zarus was stolen from her. She had been useless. If only she had—

"Hey," Feyne said, ripping her away from guilt. "Take a deep breath. They won't get us." Rin nodded and forced herself to relax. She needed to be calm if she was going to get out of this. When she looked back at Feyne, he already pulled the black mask over the bottom half of his face. "Just follow me."

He led her into a casual stroll through the field. He kept his steps quiet, but Rin wanted to tear the skin off her face. She did her best to act like nothing was wrong and tried to focus on Feyne instead of their follower. They came to a field of boulders jutting up from the ground; towering pieces of granite that caught the moon in glittering lights—some of which were four times her height. They walked through the maze of stone for what felt like an eternity. Rin desperately attempted to distract herself with the rocks before Feyne glanced at her. His face remained hidden, but his eyes said it all.

'Get ready.'

He wrapped his hand around Rin's forearm. She was not ready for the acceleration. Feyne took off at speeds that blurred the world passing by.

Swiftly and nimbly he ran throughout the maze of granite, jerking Rin this way and that as she dangled behind. She feared they would crash into every rock in their path, but Feyne moved loosely as if he was having the time of his life. He glanced backward after dodging another jagged piece of granite.

"This guy isn't half bad!" he shouted. She barely had the strength to breathe, nonetheless, keep up with him. The world flying past turned into streaks of glittering silver. Feyne wasn't even sweating.

Just as she finally pushed herself to match his speed, Feyne came to an almost immediate stop.

He wrapped his arms around her waist, jolting her to a stop so she didn't smack into the two towering slabs of granite he pulled them behind. Rin covered her mouth before she gasped in the air.

Rin followed Feyne's gaze out to an opening in the rocky labyrinth. He panted quietly and waited. Anticipation crept into his posture as he listened to the world and sniffed at the air. Rin didn't believe that he would be happier doing anything else other than stalking his prey. Because apparently, rather than just losing their tracker, Feyne fully intended to attack them. Rin couldn't understand it.

She finally caught her breath. The air felt cool and damp between the rocks. Barely, just barely enough that she had to shut her eyes and focus, Rin heard the drum of feet. The sound was amplifying quickly.

Feyne shifted to his toes, slightly lowering his shoulders. He was ready to pounce. Rin was certain he was smiling like a madman beneath that mask.

A silhouette appeared through the clearing of the stones. Feyne lunged. Before his feet touched the ground, light flashed around his body. It nearly blinded her—hours spent in night's cover—but through her squinted eyes and shielding arms, Rin saw Feyne shift.

All at once, his nose elongated into a snout, his eyes narrowed to golden slits. Limbs thinned and narrowed at his hands and feet to form paws, and his torso reshaped. Massive claws replaced nails, and soon Rin found her attention being drawn to the long, bushy tail hovering above the ground. What landed was no longer Feyne, but a snarling wolf—only the beast was almost as large as her. What was once tanned, lean skin was now a heavy coat of brown fur. Rin was completely and utterly speechless. How could demons look down on such a magnificent being?

With the slightest graze of his feet on the soft grass, Feyne leapt forward at the figure in the dark. They didn't see the beast jump, not in time; a grunt sounded at the impact. Feyne hovered over their follower, but they kicked him off. The shifter tumbled into a boulder twice his size. Without so much as a yelp, he regained his stance and advanced. He jumped behind their stalker, vaulted off of a shard of ebony granite, then pounced. He sunk his teeth into the curve of their neck.

The agonized cry echoed off the granite, but it wasn't defeated. "Where in the Flames are you hiding Rin!" Rin's mind froze. The male summoned a handful of flames and slammed it into the side of Feyne's head.

Feyne released the male's neck with a whimper, but his teeth gleamed.

The stench of burnt hair and blood burned the back of Rin's throat. However, she saw the male's yellow-green reptilious eyes.

"Where are you, Rin?" the *narikaah* called out.

"Tatsuo!"

Chapter Twenty-Nine

Consciousness was slow to return. Zarus couldn't find the will to open his eyes, so he listened. Except there wasn't anything to listen to. No chatting of demons, no subtle drip of moisture. Just his own uneven breaths, and of course, the ringing in his ears. All Zarus could do was sigh in relief that there was nothing else to add to his grievances.

He pulled himself upright, and immediately his right arm writhed in protest. His eyes ripped open, blinded by the sconces scattered along the walls, until his focus gradually came back to him. He was in an isolated cellar, but not chained down. Zarus forced himself to sit up again. Fire ran through his blood in response. Everything ached, everything pained. Turning his neck was obliterating, especially when he willed himself to look at his arm. Bile stung the back of his throat at the sight.

A cauterized scar remained where Errogan lacerated his forearm, and from it, black veins spidered along his skin. Then his memories flashed. The guards held him to the icy table, the obsidian substance leaked into his arm, the screams echoed off of the laboratory walls—*his* screams. He remembered the complete and utter torture of having to endure that black sludge coursing through his blood until his mind couldn't handle it. The knowledge that every beat of his heart mixed the serum more into his body twisted his stomach. The throbbing in his head intensified, the ringing in his ears louder. Zarus hunched over on his knees and waited to stop retching onto the rough stone below. His life was in more danger than he ever thought.

He inched backwards and leaned against the wall. Adjusting to the constant surges of pain, Zarus slowly peeled back his sleeve on the arm that hadn't been cut open. No sign of stained veins. His left arm was unaffected by the serum for now. He had more time until his entire body felt like it was burning from the inside out. A timer for when the poison's purpose would fulfill, he assumed, and his veins were the countdown. He still had a sliver of hope left.

There weren't any windows in the cell, but it was drafty enough to fog Zarus's breath. He braced the tremble in his core and stood.

"You're certainly doing well," Errogan laughed from the darkest corner of the room. "You even managed to stay standing on your first try... that's better than we anticipated."

Zarus narrowed his stare. "Don't hide in the shadows if you have something to say, Errogan," he spat, but pain stole his voice.

"Who's hiding? Just because you can't sense me doesn't mean I'm a coward," Errogan taunted, stepping out into the lantern's glare.

Meaningless ridicule. There was no way Zarus could sense anything with these cursed spells, and Errogan knew it. "What do you want?" he asked. He bade his legs to move to the front of the cell.

"After all these years away from each other, that's the greeting I get? I'm hurt, Z," Errogan said, mocking a frown, covering his heart with his hand. The fake wince was pitiful. Zarus didn't feed the derision and instead waited for Errogan as he walked toward the cell, stopping only when the sleek bars separated them.

A sense of betrayal and loss finally settled in. Zarus attempted to push away the lingering thoughts as his chest tightened. The shadow and firelight danced in his red eyes. "*Why are you here.*" The sentence faded from question and rang as demand.

Errogan smirked. Rancor lingered in his eyes. "I'm here to check on you. See how you're holding up and whether you've died yet. And since you haven't died," his tone fell to dark amusement, "I'm here to take you to Eretimis."

He was looking for a reaction. Any flinch in Zarus's body, any twitch of his face, any flick of fear or hatred in his eyes. He was treating Zarus like a normal prisoner, intentionally or not, and Zarus wouldn't play along. He kept his face blank as he watched Errogan unlock the cellar.

The hinges groaned as the demon swung the door open. "Don't think of trying to run off again, though I doubt you'd get very far in your current state," he smiled, gesturing Zarus to move.

Zarus held back the urge to bar his teeth. His body screamed at him not to move another inch, but Errogan was uncharacteristically patient and allowed him to move at a slower pace. Zarus added to his tattered mental map of the fortress at the chance.

They walked in silence back to the higher levels of the fortress. Zarus didn't particularly want to start any conversations, but there were so many things he wanted to ask—*needed* to know. Even if Errogan was just another enemy, an obstacle to overcome in order to be free, speaking to him only made his stomach sick. Errogan betrayed him, for reasons Zarus didn't know and might never know. What about their shared history? This demon was just another who turned against him, and it didn't matter why. Not now. Even if it killed Zarus to know the person he once thought of as a—

Zarus cut off the thought. *Focus.* He glanced at the walls to keep his eyes from lingering on the demon behind. They cut into a long hallway with a wide berth, and tension instantly seized his demeanor.

One more corner. Despite Zarus's best effort to keep calm, dread weighed on him.

They finally rounded the last turn of the hall. The enormous, gothic doors that led into the throne room towered higher than ever before. Nothing good ever came of a prisoner walking into Eretimis's throne room—he would know; he had seen it all before. He gritted his teeth. The pair of guards posted in front of the regal doors regarded Errogan with due respect, but looked at Zarus in bewilderment. Not everyone had forgotten about him after all.

Zarus begged his heart to calm down and stop racing so that the serum wouldn't spread faster. Errogan nodded his head, and both guards thrusted the doors inward. An unpleasant draft met Zarus's skin.

He stared at the ivory marble lining the ground. That same marble he walked on three hundred years ago, and the same marble he bled on the night he fled. Eretimis caused that blood to shed... Eretimis sent him and Errogan on that last mission, where the demon standing behind him should have been killed. Eretimis put Rin's life in danger... all of it traced back to Eretimis. He had been so afraid of returning to where he last failed. However, as the twin doors waded open, all the fear Zarus felt walking up to this deathly chamber instantly faded to wrath.

Chapter Thirty

The doors slammed behind him. He was alone with the Dark Tyrant.

"Hello, Zarus," Eretimis called from the ebony throne.

Hello, Zarus. So casual, so welcoming. So malicious.

Zarus said nothing. He willed himself to meet the gaze of the demon before him. Three hundred years. It had been just over three hundred years since he stepped foot in this room, and he barely escaped it with his life. Nothing had changed; the ebony throne carved of stone brought from Eroz, the alabaster pillars lining the corridor, even the shadows concealing the walls. Atop the throne was the demon who controlled all of it. That would never change. Zarus struggled to calm himself. The burning of his arm intensified the more he moved. He took one more deep breath before his first step.

He tried not to break the stare held on him. His mind was dull and his thoughts short. Courtesy of the serum, without a doubt, but the predator's eyes monitoring Zarus's every step didn't help. He halted halfway to the throne. *A nightmare.* It had to have been another nightmare. Soon he would wake up and guide Rin down the mountain—

Have strength, Zarus. You are not alone in this fortress...

Zarus flinched. It felt like frigid water ran down his spine. *A voice?* It was definitely a voice he heard, and it came from his head. But different... it appeared like one of his own thoughts, leading his worry to relax. The voice rang familiar... or lack of voice. The same he heard when he blacked out in the laboratory. Words that echoed in his mind, put there by someone else. His mind was too tired, too strained to think of anything beyond the demon staring down at him right then.

Zarus dragged his focus back to Eretimis. "What is it?" he snapped.

"A warm welcome to you too, boy," Eretimis mused, head resting on his propped hand.

Zarus narrowed his eyes. He didn't give a damn about formalities. *"What did you put in my blood?"*

"Is it giving you problems?" The tyrant smiled down on him without a care for the threat in Zarus's voice.

"What does it do?" Zarus asked directly.

Eretimis waited a moment—examining, thinking. Zarus didn't hide his hindered state, but maybe it was clearer than he thought. Finally, the demon loosed a grin and said, "It is a serum that I developed recently. In the most basic terms, it removes your freewill." Eretimis flashed a grin, which never meant anything good. His voice was calm and full; he didn't bother with cautions. "By distorting the connection of your brain to your body, it allows me to control you and use your body like a puppet. Once I get into your head, you will not complete a task as simple as breathing unless I give you permission."

The weight of those words hit hard. Zarus's lips straightened, his face drained of all color. The thought of losing control over his body was terrifying enough to make the breath in his throat hitch. A puppet.

"I believe I had spoken to you about such a poison in years past, but you doubted the possibility."

Zarus slowly met Eretimis's gaze. That stare, those empty eyes—calmer than a summer day, holding all the power of Anöwe's wrath. Monster. He was a damned monster. It had to have been some twisted joke.

Breathe. Just breathe. You expected it to be bad... Just get as many answers out of him as you can right now.

Zarus took a deep breath. "If it hasn't taken full effect yet, then why am I losing control of my body now?" he asked, trying to subdue the dread in his tone. He tried to clench his fist with his poisoned arm, to no avail.

Eretimis smiled again, and Zarus fought the urge to shift beneath it. "It is a gradual process. Numbness is just a side effect of your body transitioning to the poison. It spreads through the blood, letting you feel every ounce of pain while you try to fight it off." He spoke with a hint of pride. It was one hellish development, but of course only the monstrous demon before him would think of making it—and succeed.

Zarus nodded as if he were listening to Eretimis speak of trivial matters. "How do you know it will work on me?"

"I do not know."

The words echoed in his head for a few seconds. "What?" Zarus finally forced out, his teeth baring. And at last, the dwindling flame in his chest flickered again. "If you don't know, then why waste—"

"I do not know *yet,*" the tyrant corrected, not bothering to concern himself with his prisoner's ire. Before Zarus could retort, Eretimis rose from his throne and walked down the steps of the throne's dais. He stopped an arm's length away. Without so much as a murmur, the ruler of the demons reached out and grabbed Zarus's contaminated arm. He winced as the tyrant flipped the limb over, allowing the discolored veins to show. "These will tell me."

Zarus glanced at his arm, failing to hide his ignorance—something Eretimis took great pleasure in. "If these lines continue to spread, it means your body is unable to handle my possession, for lack of a better word. It is not a regular poison, as you have probably guessed. I infused it with dark magic. It always spreads at first, however, so it seems your fate is yet to be determined."

Zarus's blood curdled. He wanted to rip his arm out of this monster's grip. "So if I can physically endure your possession, it will stop and fade away," he forced out, distracting himself.

"Yes," Eretimis said. "But only if you can endure it. Once it reaches your vital organs, it will cause them to shut down, just like your arm, and you will die." The tyrant dropped his arm and turned back to the throne. Zarus stared at Eretimis's back as he ascended the steps—a target he didn't possess the strength to strike. "The serum is convenient. If the person can sustain it, I will use them. If they are too weak, then I see who is useless and they die because of it—a rather painful death, at that."

The fear Zarus had done so well to suppress crept upon him again. *So it's become his tool, or die.* A scowl overtook his expression as he met Eretimis's malevolent smirk, and he forced his lips to straighten. Words ran dry in his throat, and even when he opened his mouth to speak, nothing came out.

"That is all you need to know for now, boy," Eretimis said, waving an uninterested hand at the doors.

Zarus leered at Eretimis until the doors were open and Errogan met his side. Without a doubt, he was listening from outside the throne room.

"Back to the cell?" the white-haired demon asked, bowing to his sovereign.

"No. Give him a regular room." Eretimis cut Zarus a cruel smile. "He is an honored guest and will be treated as such."

Zarus snarled at the taunt. He would have said something, would have tried to pry more information out of his once mentor, but Errogan grabbed his shoulder and shoved him toward the door. It took everything not to scream.

There has to be a way out of this.

Zarus glanced back one more time, but Eretimis was nowhere to be seen. That small, hushed voice replaced his own thoughts again.

Chapter Thirty-One

"Tatsuo!" Rin ran in the middle of the fight and landed right in Tatsuo's arms. "What on Armiria are you doing here?" The warmth pouring out from his neck met the bare skin of her arms. She quickly pulled back to assess the wound. Feyne had bitten deep.

"I came back for you." Relief flooded his voice as he took in the sight of her. A smile spanned across his face, but just as quickly dispersed. Guilt trickled from his words. "Zarus hit a sore spot..." he said, trailing off into shame. "I shouldn't have left you, Rin. I'm so sorry." He pulled her into another hug. She reveled in it.

"Don't worry about it," she said into his shoulder, eyes brimming with tears.

"I tracked you guys back to that forest, but it took me a while to pin you down." He shook his head. "I finally found your trail after a while, but..." he placed a gentle hand across the bite marks, "there was someone else with you." His gaze swept behind her. "Where is Zarus and who is this?"

Rin glanced over her shoulder. Feyne remained silent while Tatsuo spoke: no snarls, growls, or warnings of any kind. The shifter moved to her side. Even in this form, he was nearly as tall as her. It was clear he didn't trust Tatsuo. Most of the fur on the left side of his face was singed or completely scorched, but he appeared to be fine otherwise.

She knew firsthand what Tatsuo's fires could do and was grateful that Feyne was in better shape than she and Zarus were after they fought him.

Rin bit the inside of her cheek as she flicked her gaze back to Tatsuo. Where would she even begin? She shifted her weight on the soft grass below her feet, smelling the smoke mix with the earthy tones of the world. "Well," she hummed, "that's a good question."

***

Rin told Tatsuo everything.

A lifetime of silence passed as Tatsuo studied Rin's face, making certain she wasn't jesting. "He's gone? Someone captured him?" the *narikaah* repeated, not believing his own words. "How is that even possible? That male is one of the strongest, if not most stubborn, demons I've ever met... who has that kind of power?" He shook his head. She could barely believe the story herself.

Rin opened her mouth, but the words never came out. All she could think was how helpless Zarus had become upon seeing Errogan's face. It was horrifying. He fell to his knees, and Errogan brought him back to Eretimis. And the worst of it all? She hadn't been able to do a damn thing to save the male, hadn't even tried. Fear paralyzed her. Feyne was convinced she was *special* in some sort of way. It made her want to laugh.

"I should have been there." Rin glanced to find Tatsuo's face turned downward. "I should have been there to help him fight," he growled.

"Tatsuo," Rin whispered, "you had no way of knowing what would happen." She rubbed her thumb against the pommel of her scimitar. "Zarus pushed you to leave. I don't blame you for what happened to us and I doubt that he does, either." She wiped the tears running down her cheeks and forced her throat to clear. They couldn't do this. They couldn't blame themselves, even if it was her fault. It wouldn't solve anything. Rin dug a handkerchief from her pocket and handed it to Tatsuo. "Here," she said with a faint smile, "you're weeping worse than a willow in the wind."

The dragon snatched it quicker than she could see, but returned the grin clearly enough. "Shut up," he said, pulling her into another hug.

It warmed her soul to see Tatsuo smile, but the subtle growl that emitted from behind her said otherwise. Feyne had either grown restless, or knew they had spent too much time standing still. Tatsuo released her, and she saw a weight lifted from him in midst of the darkness.

"*Feyne*, was it?" Tatsuo asked. "You can change out of that form. I won't attack you if Rin says you're fine."

Despite the gesture, Feyne shook his head. The wolf remained.

Tatsuo raised a brow. "I said I won't attack you."

Even Rin cocked her head. *Why wasn't he changing back?*

After letting out a rather dramatic sigh, Feyne pushed himself up to all fours and prowled out of the firelight. A few moments later, he used his snout to nudge his clothes into the dim light.

"Oh," Tatsuo murmured. Before Rin could figure out what he meant, she was being spun the opposite direction by the *narikaah* and facing the open darkness of night. She glanced at Tatsuo, who also turned around. "Go ahead."

Without a chance to investigate, a blinding flash of light illuminated the rocky maze—the same flash that lit up when Feyne shifted into his fuzzy form. Her face burned red as realization struck. After a minute of clothes brushing together and buckles snapping shut, footsteps walked toward her and Tatsuo.

"Done," Feyne sighed, loosing a lazy groan. The side of his face barely burned; his singed hair took most of the damage. The delight didn't last long. Rin watched Feyne's golden eyes narrow as he focused on Tatsuo, and though his mask remained lowered, the shifter clearly didn't trust the half-demon just yet. "Now... *Tatsuo*," he said sharply. Rin couldn't tell if he was imitating the way Tatsuo had spoken to him or if he was just being an ass. "You said you got worried and came back to find Rin?" He crossed his arms and took in the entirety of Tatsuo Kurosawa. The deaf could have heard the accusation in Feyne's voice. Tatsuo refrained from answering at first, merely sizing Feyne up. The shifter was shorter than him, but his muscles were broader than Tatsuo's. Standing between the two, shifting her eyes back and forth as the beings squared each other up and down, she knew—just knew—that their arrogance was taking over.

Rin placed a hand over her eyes and rubbed her temples. "Look, can we sort this out later?" She glanced toward the sky, and though there was no sign of morning, it was bound to come sooner than later. "I mean, we have bigger things to deal with, don't we?"

Tatsuo let loose an exasperated laugh. "I suppose, but I don't think your friend will let us go anywhere unless he gets some answers."

Rin looked to Feyne, who nodded. "Answers that require us to stand out in the middle of the night with no protection?" she asked, stretching her point as far as it would go.

"Things that could endanger you, me, and all the people back at Base." The words were stiff as they came off his tongue. Her brow furrowed.

"What? Do I have to give you a bone before you trust me?" Tatsuo retorted.

The comment didn't faze the shifter. "No, that won't be necessary. See, what I really need is to know why you smell like dark oak."

Rin's face scrunched up at the absurdity. "He controls fire. Trees burn. I think he's going to smell like some trees now and then," she said in complete and utter disbelief. He won't trust him because he smells like a tree? Rin turned toward Tatsuo, but a smirk no longer sat on his lips. His eyes raged.

"What?" A thin leash was all that controlled the *narikaah*'s temper.

Rin shook her head. "What on Armiria are you talking about, Feyne?"

"I'm asking your friend why he smells like dark oak if he claims he turned around immediately and came back to find you, Rin." He shot her a glance, not irate or irritated, but stern.

Tatsuo clenched his fists at his sides. At least the *narikaah* understood what Feyne had implied. "I never said I just *turned around*. A band of demons attacked me. Not the bounty hunters that wander Armiria; they were stronger. Eretimis's soldiers." Tatsuo stood eerily still as he spoke, probably the stillest she'd ever seen him. "They kept asking me where Rin was." His gaze flicked to Rin. Guilt still swam in his eyes. "I told them to beat it, and they attacked. I killed one, but the others retreated. After I realized how stupid it was for me to leave Rin, I turned around." He took a half step forward. "If I smell like dark oak, it's because I ran into demons that came directly from the fortress, not because I'm working for the Dark Tyrant." He nearly spat out the words.

Rin could feel Tatsuo's radiating rage at Feyne's casual implication.

A warm breeze danced past the trio, carrying the lone cry of some far off animal with it. The moon dripped its grey light over the ancient terrain as the remainder of Tatsuo's fires died out.

"Dark oak," Feyne finally said, "is a tree commonly found where Eretimis established his fortress." He didn't peel his eyes off of Tatsuo as he spoke. "You see, the fortress he settled in was once a temple for

Yath Ha and the kaetha. The area was full of life and flourished from their divine presence despite being in the frozen wastes. Then Eretimis came and insulted the Divine by sieging the temple and claiming it as his own. The plants and animals withered away until the land became barren—all except for one tree. It dropped all of its leaves and the bark faded black, acquiring its name. They're only found there. Eretimis's darkness eroded and twisted the plants."

Rin shifted her weight from side to side. Fighting Eretimis's soldiers explained the scent. She had a gut feeling that she could place her life into Tatsuo's hands and remain unharmed. Instinct, Feyne would have called it. Rin rubbed her throbbing temples. The phantom fragrance of withered leaves and rotting tree suffocated her senses as her mind ran rampant.

"Rin, you know I would never do that to you," Tatsuo pleaded. The fire calmed when he looked at her.

Rin dropped his stare and ignored Feyne's as well. The decision wasn't up to her, ultimately. It was Feyne's friends, Feyne's Base, who were at risk. Did he want her opinion on the male standing at her left? Tatsuo was her friend, he fought along with her and Zarus—

Zarus—what might he be enduring right now? Her stomach twisted at the thought. She longed to break him out of Eretimis's clutches. She wished she had the power to carry him away from Eretimis, rid him of all the troubles that plagued him for years and years. Even if it meant going to the other realm he told her about. Anything to bring joy into that demon's face. But she couldn't. Not when she was still so weak. A sickening weight pressed on her chest and she wrapped her palm around the hilt of her scimitar. She hadn't unsheathed it in days.

"I would bet my life that Tatsuo isn't scheming with Eretimis," Rin said as she peered at nothing in particular. "The dark oak came from the demons who attacked him; I have no doubt." She sorted the words as she spoke, tightening her grip on the smooth hilt of the scimitar. "You're wrong to distrust him, Feyne, but this is your decision, your home and your friends. I think it would be wise to let him come with us to Base. He could offer a lot more input in your dealings against Eretimis." Tatsuo *was* against Eretimis, after all. Why not give him the opportunity to work with a larger group? Finally, she raised her gaze to the two beings she stood between.

Feyne remained unreadable, but a weight lifted off of Tatsuo's shoulders. He gave her a grateful smile as Feyne thought it over. Trust was all she could give him at this point. A warm breeze rushed by every so often, sending ginger strands to tickle her cheeks. It would have been a peaceful night had she been back in Aresan.

A loud huff brought her attention back to the world around. "Alright," Feyne said, stretching his arms upward. "If Rin thinks you're fine, then you can come." Before she could smile, the shifter held up a sharp finger. "But get one thing straight, Tatsuo: you have yet to prove that I'm making the right decision." He held up the finger until Tatsuo nodded. It was only then that Feyne let his arm fall to his side, and yawned, revealing his elongated lower canines. "Well then," he mumbled, "we still have a good distance to go, and I want to be there by tomorrow night. So follow close or you get left behind." He offered another feral grin before the shifter walked on, and then gave Rin a hard pat on the back that left her shoulder blade stinging.

"Well, that was... anticlimactic," she muttered to herself as she watched Feyne disappear. A bit of shock still rested on Tatsuo's face. Apparently he didn't expect Feyne to let him come either, but Rin was just grateful that they hadn't hurt each other too badly. Before she knew what was happening, Tatsuo wrapped his arms around her again.

"I'm really glad you're okay, Rin," he said. She hugged back, letting it last as long as it could before Feyne yelled back to them. She thought she had lost a friend forever, and he likewise. It was good to be in each other's company again. "Come on," he let her go, "let's see what this guy can offer us. I've heard rumors of a small resistance against Eretimis... Who knows, maybe it'll even help us get Zarus back." Though the topic was grim, Tatsuo didn't let it keep him from smiling as he followed into the darkness.

Rin's lips straightened. *Later.* She'd tell him later that she wasn't going to help rescue Zarus. For now... she released the tension in her chest and trekked after Feyne and Tatsuo.

Chapter Thirty-Two

For the rest of the night, they walked in a loose line—first Feyne, then Rin, and Tatsuo trailed somewhere behind. No one spoke, whether committed to walking on in silence after their altercation or lost in their own thoughts. The silence stretched long before them. Rin hardly noticed, her mind a labyrinth.

They trailed out of the rocky maze sometime before dawn, walking into the beautifully painted orange and pink sunrise. The plains turned into a gradual incline of copper hills and vibrant grass and beautiful arrays of flowers.

For a brisk hour around noon, Rin felt a cool breeze that usually only drifts off of rivers and lakes. When Feyne made it to the top of a rather damning hill, he looked back at her and Tatsuo with a beckoning smirk, then disappeared behind the peak while they made the rest of the climb. By the time Rin finally carried herself to the top, the words dried in her throat. She gaped at the shimmering lake spanning at the bottom of the hill. Crystal clear waters stretched far and wide. The quiet surface swayed back and forth in the breeze from the highlands beyond.

"Nice, isn't it?" Feyne smiled as he inhaled the remaining morning mist. Rin merely nodded as she caught her breath and stared in awe. He pointed to the distant plateau towering behind the copper-stained hills and explained they were heading for a small pass that would take them to the top of the highlands instead of the two-day trip around. When neither she nor Tatsuo protested, Feyne led them to the lakeshore, where there was already a small canoe waiting for them. Rin might not be much of a fighter, but she could keep a boat moving. The lake was a breath of fresh air compared to navigating across the small, unnamed river near Aresan.

Tatsuo and Feyne exchanged backhanded insults to each other for most of the journey, almost creating some smug system. Tatsuo would comment on how loud Feyne was walking, then Feyne would mutter he could smell the dragon's breath from a mile away. It went on for a few hours as they crossed the copper hills, and Rin stayed silent as they rambled, refusing to encourage either.

Dusk settled over the hilltops as they reached the base of the plateau, where Rin's legs burned with every step she took. Feyne led them to the hazardous trail heading up the side of the steep cliff. The shifter assumed a silence that ran questions and inquiries through Rin's head. Tampering with such a silence felt unnatural.

Their path led through areas that were almost too narrow to pass. Rin's smaller frame allowed her through without a problem, but the others were forced to move sideways between the crevices of rock. They stayed on the outside of the highlands. Feyne was noticeably tense whenever they entered a cavern that didn't allow free movement. She wondered about this for a while, about how easy it would be for someone to see them as it wasn't quite dark yet, but Feyne kept them away from the inner passes.

The stars reached the sky long before they reached the top of the plateau. Nothing but dried clumps of grass and sun baked soil sat atop it, tinting the dirt a dry gold. Barren, as everything was in the lands unclaimed by the kingdoms of this continent. No one had wanted this patch of dirt for a reason when the kingdoms were dividing lines after the peace treaties were signed five-hundred forty-one years ago. Rin started heading for the other side when Feyne spoke.

"We can rest here for a little while." His raspiness clued how long it had been since any of them had spoken. The words seemed louder than they should have in Rin's ears, but she merely stared at him with suspicious eyes. "And yes, you guys can talk now."

Tatsuo was the first to speak. "How often do demons reside in those caves?"

Demons?

"It depends," Feyne said, rolling his neck. "They rarely stir, but now and then someone wanders in when they're sent on Eretimis's trivial tasks."

"What kind of trivial tasks?" Rin asked, feeling left out, not having realized their silence was to keep unwanted visitors away.

"Mostly trying to find Base," he shrugged with a yawn, "but sometimes they do other things. Sometimes they're not even demons, they're humans or shifters or whoever else roaming in lawless lands. They use the tunnels for quick travel through the highland, but also defense. Everyone has their own ways through the maze."

"So why don't you use them?" she said, yawning herself.

"Running into a demon could lead them back to Base, and anybody else out here is just looking for trouble. It's easier. Plus," he grinned, "I like the view up here better." He glanced at the skies. Rin traced her eyes across countless stars, along each and every constellation, and the silver moon glowing above. The horizon was still a mix of faded fuchsia and violet, but the sun was out of sight.

"Where is this Base, anyway?" Tatsuo asked.

"Ahead; we should get there before sunrise."

Rin was fairly pleased to hear this, but before she let herself rest, the world beyond the plateau caught her eye—or rather, the lack of. "What's past the highlands?" she asked. The night was dark, but the moon rising in the sky gave off enough pale light to brighten the world for human eyes.

"A desert."

Rin's brow arched in disbelief. "Seriously?"

"Of course. How else would we keep Eretimis's forces away? Not even a demon could survive being lost in an uncharted desert," Feyne said with light amusement.

"He'd find a way," Tatsuo mumbled to himself as they all stared into the invisible horizon. "He always does."

"He hasn't yet," Feyne huffed, though Rin didn't think it was aimed at Tatsuo. "Passing the desert under the sun is suicide. We'll start out again in an hour, so do whatever you need to until then, but don't wander off. We're already behind schedule." With that, the shifter strode to the edge of the plateau.

Rin watched the sky for a while, but she eventually followed Feyne. He probably wanted to be alone, but Tatsuo had already laid down and closed his eyes. The flat rock stretched on forever in the dark, startling her when she reached the abrupt edge. Rin peered over, gaping at the drop into darkness.

"Beautiful, isn't it?"

Rin squinted her eyes, but to no avail. A frown reached her face. "Couldn't tell you. I have human eyes, remember?"

"And I have shifter eyes," he said, smiling at her, "I see just as well as you can right now, but that doesn't mean I can't appreciate the vastness."

She furrowed her brow. "But you're a wolf. Don't they have great night vision?"

"Yes, and I see better when I walk on all fours, but right now," he gestured to his current form, "no better than you. Unless you need spectacles, that is."

"Then why do you stay as a human so often—err... male?" If she had the ability to be something other than human, she'd sure take advantage of it.

"Because I am what I am," he hummed as he sat down and swung his legs off the edge.

"What do you mean?" She would have sat down as well, but then she made the mistake of glancing over the cliff again. She backed up a good five feet and planted behind Feyne. Gods knew what would become of her if she fell off.

Feyne leaned back on his hands and closed his eyes. "I mean, I'm a shifter, so I shift. I'm no more wolf than I am *ghren*. Some attributes of my other form carry over into this one, like my nose and ears, but I use both forms to my advantage."

"So what's the advantage of being a... *ghren* right now?"

"Well, I'm talking to you instead of barking, aren't I?" he mused. "Plus, if I were a wolf, I'd just have to keep redressing every time I needed to be a *ghren* again. And that," he yawned, "would just be exhausting." He caught her confusion before she could ask. "*Ghren* is the masculine title of this form for shifters. *Ghren* and *ghran*."

"Both forms have their uses," Rin muttered to herself. She smiled, resting her hands behind her in the dirt. "So, how many are there?" she asked, inching the slightest bit closer to him.

"Hm?"

"Base; how many of the members are there?"

He swung his legs over the far off ground as he thought. "I'd say about twenty to thirty regularly. More people are part of the group, but they come and go as they please. Base is a loose organization of unofficial alliances. The desert is where we hold our meetings and share information. As far as nonhumans, the other shifter is helping a village in Johait deal with demon raids. The only fae with us is somewhere in Melibor right now."

It was almost like a bell sounded in her head. "What are their names?" she blurted, scooching closer. "What does the shifter turn into?" Her eyes widened. She almost completely forgot about the cliff a few feet away.

Feyne grinned at her excitement. "Shayl is an eagle shifter."

Rin's heart danced at the thought. Being able to fly, letting your wings guide you wherever your heart desired... It was intoxicating to think about. "Are you close with either of them?"

"Shayl and I go back over three decades, but I don't know if you'd count Vi and I as close. We're friends, but only ever talk when she finds her way back here. We have different agendas, but I trust her not to sell me out."

Rin nodded, far too tired to pry. Instead, she fell back onto the dirt and stretched her arms behind her head. "I still can't believe there's another world out there that no one really knows about. It's crazy that something so huge would just... remain unknown, you know?" The foreign world she concocted in her head appeared behind closed eyes.

Feyne made an indistinct sound in his throat. "War will do that." Sensing the question in her silence, he went on. "A long time ago, way before me or Tatsuo, even before Eretimis took over Hraesah on Eroz, the Crimson War broke out over both realms."

Rin perked up. "Zarus mentioned that before. Demons and humans at war. What happened?"

"More than just humans and demons," Feyne nodded. "No race was safe. It lasted five hundred years, and when it was over, all relations held between the different races collapsed. For demons and fae, five hundred years is nothing; even some shifters lived to see the end of that war. It was a different story for humans; countless generations that only knew bloodshed." He recalled the tale, stretching out his arms. "The ancient Alliance that held the bonds between the five races couldn't fix things, couldn't put the remnants of a united society back together. I think that's when travel between worlds was banned. The Alliance broke apart, and knowledge of the other world faded amongst humans. Truth turned to legends and myths for you."

Rin bade an eye open as he spoke. She wondered if he was taught this as a child, or if he taught himself as he grew older. Maybe it was only after he found out what Eretimis was doing. She had so many questions at such a late hour with so little sleep... her head was ringing louder and louder.

"I wonder how much of this Zarus knew..." The words were stiff on her tongue, too hollowed.

"Far more than I could ever hope to," Feyne shrugged, "he has at least a thousand years on me, according to rumors." A soft laugh left his chest that was soothing to the ears.

"He sure didn't say much about it if that's the case," Rin muttered under her breath.

"I'd imagine... Hey, Rin?" he asked rather abruptly. "Why didn't you tell Tatsuo you're not planning to help rescue Zarus?"

The words were a punch in the gut. A silent breeze ruffled her hair. She didn't want to lie to Tatsuo about her decision; let Feyne handle the demon while she went back to the safety of Aresan. She just didn't know how to tell him. A mix of shame and fear of Feyne's reaction kept her tongue tied in her throat.

"I just..." she paused, sitting upright, "I don't know how to tell him I'm not able to help. I would only get in the way; one more person to worry about. It's not that I don't want to get him out of there, but... What could I possibly do to stand against Eretimis, or even Errogan? I'm only human." The word stung her tongue. It was pitiful to say, pitiful to think, but it was true. What did Feyne expect her to do against a demonic tyrant? She was human. No special powers, no magic flowing through her veins. Just plain human. She waited for him to say something, prayed he would just stop staring into her and make some damned comment—whether insult or comfort—but Rin felt herself shrink when his stare fell. It was a long few minutes before either of them spoke again.

"Anyway," the shifter said, pulling himself to his feet where he stood way too close to the edge of the cliff, "you should get some sleep. It'll take two hours to get to Base, and you look like you're going to pass out." A grin curved the edges of his lips, but didn't make it to his solemn eyes. A look she found difficult to sit beneath.

Rin would have protested, claiming that she was fine and wanted to learn more about the worlds, but a yawn came out when she tried to speak. She yielded to sleep rather than curiosity. When she finally returned to where Tatsuo was snoring softly, exhaustion struck her. Physical, emotional, mental weariness brushed her eyes closed. Rin could have counted the stars as she attempted to sort out her dilemmas and convince herself there was nothing she could do against a power so great, but she was only human. And humans needed more than an hour or two of sleep every two days.

Chapter Thirty-Three

She slept like a baby from the moment her eyes shut to the unpleasant moment when Feyne nudged her awake. The moon was still high in the sky. She felt far worse than before. Feyne foraged some berries from brushes, and they ate without a noise.

They left almost immediately after, each one of them making sure they left no traces behind. The trail down the cliffside was easier than the trek up. Feyne led them down a winding trail directly to the desert.

Two steps in, and Rin decided: sand was tedious. The loose grains shifted too easily under her shoes, and walking up the towering dunes made her rethink not letting Errogan capture her two days ago. Being taken back to Eretimis's fortress would at least ensure a quick death instead of having her legs fall off and dehydrate in the drylands. She didn't ever intend to step foot in a desert, and her current attire would for sure come back to bite her once the sun rose. To her relief, Feyne hadn't lied. About an hour and a half after they stepped onto the wretched sands, small shapes started forming against the dark horizon.

"There it is," the shifter said, stretching his arms out wide and inhaling the scent of the dry air. "Home sweet home." He rolled his shoulders a few times before halting. "Now, remember what I said:

everyone might not trust you." He gave Tatsuo a distinct look—not necessarily a glare. "When we get to the village, stay silent." The last part wasn't a choice, but a demand. They were in his territory now, his home. And neither she nor Tatsuo intended to disrespect his wishes to keep it safe.

"This place better be all that you're making it out to be, Snarls," Tatsuo said. He sounded disinterested in the warning, but Rin thought it might have been from the pressing exhaustions currently placed on all of them.

This is it. This was where her life would start its course to normalcy again. Rin would give them information, then go to Lilit and meet her mother, and then go back to Aresan to see her father. The long week taught her where she belonged. Not meddling in the politics of different species, or fighting demons, or even seeking adventures. Feyne would manage with Zarus, and Tatsuo would find a place at his side. The two were already warming up to each other, whether they admitted it. So she took another step toward the lackluster fate awaiting her in that small, rundown village in the distance. She accepted it, accepted that some people weren't meant to live lives run by excitement and adventures. Her father needed her, if anything else, and she promised him she'd come back. Just as she had silently promised herself she would eventually go back out in the world and learn about it, live in it, actually be part of it. Yet a cold, remorseful tune of the voice drowned the thoughts of that potential future.

Not if there is no world left to adventure in.

The ownerless voice in her head repeated those words end upon end. Things had changed, and there was no undoing what Eretimis had already maimed in her life. She didn't know it yet, wasn't even the slightest bit aware that each step she took carried her further and further away from the comforts of her *boring, peaceful* past.

On she walked.

Chapter Thirty-Four

As Zarus was escorted through the hallways, he encountered countless demons who stopped and murmured to one another. He held his eyes shut the whole time they walked, focusing solely on Errogan's crushing grip on his shoulder. Zarus spoke softly, barely a sound passing his lips.

After they walked for around ten minutes and climbed a rounded staircase, the demon finally grew tired of it. "I'll break your jaw if you don't shut it," Errogan threatened from behind. His tone was no longer amused; apparently the delight of Zarus's suffering was wearing away.

Zarus slowly opened his eyes, finding nothing but a sole door at the top of the tower they climbed. If he didn't know any better, he'd believe that this section of the fortress had remained untouched ever since he fled. That was exactly why Zarus chose this abandoned corner of the fortress when he used to live here: solitude. Errogan had tried to convince him to choose a room closer to the barracks, but Zarus had been willing to spend his nights alone if it meant he was far from the tyrant.

Errogan pulled out a skeleton key from his pocket and opened the door. The stale air within hit like a brick wall. His old friend shoved Zarus inside before he could absorb his nostalgia. He stumbled, a splintering cry slipping his control as he fell on his bad arm. Errogan slammed the door shut before he could curse him to hell. The lock clicked, and the footsteps eventually faded. Zarus was completely alone again. Or was he?

You are not alone in this fortress. Be patient and go to the dungeons.

What in all the Flames was that supposed to mean? The ownerless words echoed through Zarus's mind.

You are not alone.

He worked up the energy to scoff, but nothing came out. Zarus had spent a lifetime alone. And the dungeons? The dungeons held no hope. Who was whispering such nonsense into his head? It could be Eretimis playing tricks on him; making him hear things and giving him false hopes. Though that wasn't Eretimis's way of things. It was closer to Errogan's, and as far as Zarus knew, Errogan didn't have any such ability. Who else then? He tried to reach out to the voice and ask, but no one answered.

The mystery voice was almost enough to distract Zarus from the unbridled pain seeping into his body. He wondered if this was how it felt to be burned from the inside out, because he couldn't imagine anything worse. And he was exhausted. For once in his life, he actually wanted to sleep, but of course he couldn't. He had to find a way out of fate as a puppet.

Zarus calmed his mind enough to think. He needed to escape, but the magic thrumming from the door hinted it was sealed, and he certainly didn't have the strength to fight his way out now. Time was all he needed, even if his own was ticking away. Zarus squared his shoulders, straightened his back—with a slight wince—and closed his eyes.

His thoughts immediately bounced to doubt. *It might not have worked. It might have been a waste of strength.* He breathed in the musty air of his old quarters. Zarus slowly exhaled, crossing his legs and gently resting his hands on his knees. His eyes opened, but they were not red. Crimson bled to pale blue. He no longer looked at the walls of his room. He didn't even see out of his own eyes.

Despite everything that had happened since losing Rin, Zarus let loose a satisfied smirk. "Errogan," he mused to himself, "you really need to pay attention when your prisoner is *muttering* to himself."

Zarus watched as Errogan walked into the throne room through the demon's own eyes. Everything was as clear as if he was there himself, but the edges of the vision blurred. The spell limited Zarus from looking around, only seeing through Errogan's eyes and not directing them.

After bowing, Errogan spoke shortly. "He won't endure it." He moved to his usual spot beside the throne and leaned against one of the alabaster pillars that stretched from floor to ceiling. "It's only been a day and the godsdamn poison is smothering his entire arm. It's spreading too quickly. You should kill him now and stop wasting time."

"What was that?" Eretimis's voice pierced through Errogan's absent-minded rant like a blade through skin. Zarus felt the demon's ice-blue eyes widen. He opened his mouth to utter an excuse, but Eretimis spoke first. "Errogan," he said, the calm before the storm, "what have I told you about letting your emotions cloud your judgment?" Even Zarus squirmed beneath the Tyrant's leer a ten-minute walk away.

Foolishly, Errogan tried to plead his case again. Eretimis shed his temper and roared. "*Do not interrupt me, boy.*" The boom echoed through the empty hall like thunder in the night. Errogan's excuses fell submissive, his lips thin and tight. Zarus felt the demon sink into himself, but he was smart enough to hide it. "You and I both know we cannot risk killing him." Eretimis's voice held that silent promise of death, the kind that chilled even the most heartless bastards to the bone. "If his body submits to the serum, then he will die, but if the serum *does* work and I have reign over his power, then you know that Zarus's unlimited power is all that matters. Not your trifling grudges toward him."

Unlimited power? What is he talking about...

A few moments passed before Errogan dared to say anything. When it became clear he was smart enough to remain silent, Eretimis faced forward. Errogan's stare morphed into a scowl. Zarus felt the words scratching in the demon's throat, yearning to yell, but he didn't. Errogan was holding back, which was a seemingly new characteristic of the Moonlit Bastard. "Yes, sir." Errogan pushed the words through bared teeth.

Eretimis didn't look at Errogan when he spoke. "You and Zarus may share the same blood, boy, but it would be wise of you not to pick up his habits of insubordination. My patience does not stretch far enough for the two of you." The Dark Tyrant's words were cold and lifeless. "In the meantime, enjoy watching him suffer, and tell me what about this human girl made you disobey my orders and let her escape with air in her lungs."

Zarus's stomach crashed to the floor. He hoped—hell, he actually *prayed*—that Rin had been spared of Eretimis's interests. Maybe even the Creators had no leash on Eretimis's power, or maybe they sided with the mad demon. Maybe they just wanted to see Zarus suffer until he no longer had free will to do otherwise...

Or maybe they were on his side for once.

Rin escaped with her life. *Alive!* That damned girl was actually alive! Zarus's heart leapt. Rin Nowell, the human who smacked Eretimis right in the face by simply being alive. He shouldn't have felt so relieved, so thrilled to hear the news since Eretimis was still asking about her, but he couldn't help it.

"Alive," he whispered to himself, so quiet and hushed that he barely heard it himself. A smile curved his lip right before he realized what he had done.

Idiot! You're still connected by the spell. Keep your mind blank.

Zarus could have scowled at himself, would have too if it wasn't for the fact Errogan could feel fragments of Zarus's emotions right then. With a silent breath, Zarus forced that trembling sense of guilt and worry and joy and victory out of his mind.

Errogan looked to Eretimis, calm enough to speak as even-tempered as Zarus would have. "I sensed something when I was about to kill her. A foreign essence, different from most humans... I think she might possess some power of her own." He paced alongside the throne; enough to get his mind to work faster. It had always been a quirk of his.

"Why should I believe you when you seem to have adopted your own agenda?"

Errogan didn't squirm, didn't shift beneath that steel tone. "Because all of my actions are only to serve you, my Lord."

Eretimis's head perked, but he still leaned on the arm of the throne. "Is that so?" Sardonic poison seeped from his tongue. He sat up. "Well then, it would not hurt to look further into this human." A malicious smile formed across his face.

Errogan returned the gesture. The white-haired demon only stirred slightly as Zarus's sense of disgust brushed over him. "The girl seemed rather fond of Zarus," he mused, toying with the dagger he withdrew from a sheath at his side. "We could use that to our advantage."

The triumph drained from Zarus's heart.

Eretimis deigned silence as he mulled it over. A small spark of amusement flickered in the tyrant's eyes that mocked the dim lanterns on the walls. The room stood eerily still as Zarus and Errogan alike waited for whatever twisted idea came forth from the tyrant.

After what felt like his age doubled, Eretimis spoke. "Take a few hunters and track down this human. Bring her back here and I will see whether we can use her. Tell her we will spare Zarus's life if she agrees to our request." He paused for a moment, and then another terrifying smile marked his lips. "Find whoever is hiding her as well and annihilate them. Something tells me we will end up killing two birds with one stone…"

Errogan nodded and retreated from the room. "Your will be done, my Lord. I'll gather a team now." He was almost out the door before a thought suddenly occurred to him. He stopped in the grand entrance way, glancing over his shoulder. "If Zarus proves to be unpropitious to us," a wicked smirk pierced his expression, "may I request the honor of ending him?" The nonchalance was a final blow to Zarus's gut.

Eretimis held a tight grip on his stare before responding. "Bring me that girl, Errogan, and I will consider it."

Errogan held back his delight. Without another word, the demon faced forward and the doors slammed shut behind him.

Chapter Thirty-Five

Zarus released the spell, having heard all he needed. The magic bridging his and Errogan's minds snapped like a thread. And then he roared.

His magic unleashed. Snow and ice swarmed around his hands, smothering the corridor until dunes piled against the walls.

It all came out; his anger, his pain, his powerlessness. How stupid could he have been? He should have just left that girl stumbling in the snow alone. She would have had a better chance of surviving if he hadn't helped her. At least hypothermia was a better death than whatever Flames Eretimis had waiting for her! Rin stood no chance. She was going to die, all because he didn't turn the other way. His teeth ground against one another.

Shit. Just—shit.

Zarus's thoughts were still cloudy. His head swayed, but he forced himself to pace back and forth. He ran a shaky hand through his hair, pulling the stray raven strands out of his face.

"Rin's hopeful enough to believe their nonsense offer," he murmured to himself. "I can't… I can't let her be dragged to this hell—not because of some asinine lie." He pinched the bridge of his nose as he struggled to construct a clear thought. "Whatever underlying mystery Rin possesses, it's better left unknown." Even as he said the words,

Zarus knew it wouldn't remain a mystery for long. He had tried to figure out what he sensed about her for their first few days together. Something so depthless, something so... old. Ancient, actually. Ancient and reawakening. Her youth threw him off at first on the mountains; he thought she was one of Eretimis's scouts out to hunt him. How could a presence so ancient lie within that human? Yet subtle enough that no one noticed it until now. Rin's glowing green eyes suggested magic coursed through her veins, but there was no comfort in that idea. Zarus slaughtered countless users under Eretimis's command for having stood in his way. He murdered hundreds more because the Tyrant thought that they would eventually pose a threat. He had been sent to recover any information on human magic wielders as often as a tip about them came around—seen with his own eyes what happened to every last one of them. Even he had to look away from a few. Only ever once had someone walked away from the Dark Lord's sentence. And that being found himself stranded in a tower with a serum in his arm that could either turn him into a puppet or announce his execution.

The irony wasn't wasted.

He took as deep of a breath as his lungs would allow, but a whip of pain reverberated through his bones. Zarus crashed to his knees. His chest felt like it was caving in, collapsing into his heart and lungs. Quickly, he turned to the ice covering the wall, his reflection as clear as any mirror could provide. He slowly lifted his shirt.

The black veins had taken his shoulder, reaching for his neck and down the left side of his chest. By the looks of it, it wouldn't be long before the poison snatched his heart and lungs.

Zarus scowled and dropped his shirt. "Will I even be able to breathe when it gets there?" He glanced at the window. The corrupted sky was just as black and bleak as it always was around the fortress. He heard the faint echoes of laughter and shrieks. Hundreds and hundreds of demons lived beyond these walls, yet Zarus felt none of them. He wondered how many of them knew of Eretimis's true intentions with not only this world, but both of them. How many would believe him if he told them the tyrant lied? How many would care?

A fog settled over his mind. So thick that he could hardly remember what he was thinking until it traveled along to his vision and down his neck into his lungs, weighing down on every inch of his skin.

"D-ammit." He grabbed at his head, legs swaying as the fog reached them. Blurred stars sparked in his eyes. The entire room ran in and out of focus.

His head rattled, a constant drum as his blood pulsed like a forge. The fog of his vision stretched further and further, grabbing greedily until he couldn't see at all.

Bed. Get to the bed now.

Zarus couldn't tell if his pulse was racing or slowing as he stumbled, grabbing at the furniture to keep him from tumbling. His hands searched for his old bed, but the searing throb in his skull won. His legs failed. And then darkness swallowed him whole.

***

The metallic stench of blood roamed into his nostrils.

Zarus's arms and legs were stiff, the back of his head felt like a dagger stuck into it. He opened his eyes painfully and saw the ice and snow melted. His skull leaned on the headrest of a wooden chair near a desolate hearth. He fell hard. Yet the back of his head hadn't cracked open, nor was it still bleeding. Demon or not, he should have been dead from the fall or blood loss pooling below the chair. Maybe some twisted presence still wanted him alive. Gods needed entertainment, after all.

Errogan, the next time you show up, I swear I'll make you wish you had truly died all those years ago for putting this poison inside of—

"Errogan," Zarus whispered. He flicked his eyes to the door, as if saying his name would somehow summon the demon. The conversation he eavesdropped on replayed in his head, Eretimis's words specifically. "The same blood," Zarus repeated absently. "What in all the realms of Ashnagz was he talking about?" A stale breeze made its way through the window, smelling of old tales only the wind dared remember. "How would that even be possible?" He took a deep breath, slowly putting one foot in front of the other. Something not too deep inside of him pleaded not to walk around.

"I need answers," he sighed as he rubbed his hands over his eyes, "before I can't even ask the questions anymore." Another moment's silence for another moment's thought. "I can use Errogan for that... I just need to figure out how to get him to talk."

Impossible with your current state, you fool.

He stifled his doubts and pushed aside the uneasiness in his fractured mind. Time was running out, and he was desperate. Searching, he found himself at the bookshelf overflowing where he had left it all those centuries ago. He thought it odd Eretimis hadn't removed his belongings as he flipped through the ink stained pages of an old journal, yet his eyes widened as he landed on a page folded at the edge. His breath hitched in disbelief at what he read. A smile tugged at his lips. Zarus held firm on what shredded focus he still possessed as his mind swelled with a plan. He needed all the luck and miracles he was owed. Because something told him, deep in the darkest corners of his mind, that there would be no second chances from here on out.

Chapter Thirty-Six

Zarus paced the length of the room as he waited for Errogan to return or for the serum to hit his lungs. Whichever came first.

He couldn't sit still any longer after he decided on a plan. Doubt filled his mind, fear that somehow Errogan had already found Rin and brought her back to this fortress alive, only to be questioned and tortured until the kaeth Vulyn gave her his ultimate gift. He was certain that hadn't happened yet, because neither Eretimis nor Errogan had been around to gloat about it. Zarus couldn't tell if Eretimis was trying to make a statement about what happens to those who sympathize with humans, go against him, or if there was no statement at all. Maybe he wanted Rin dead because she was unfortunate enough to cross his path.

Just breathe. Breathe and keep your head clear. He'll come, and when he does—

Zarus nearly toppled over the chair in his way when he heard subtle footsteps walking up the tower. He quickly hauled across the room and jumped onto the bed. He brushed his eyes closed just before the doorknob clicked. "Rise and shine," Errogan growled, "I need to check on you before I leave. Get up." The order flared Zarus's temper, but he stifled it. Part of his plan. It was just part of his plan...

"Pleasant as ever, Errogan," Zarus muttered. Showing every bit of weakness that he could muster after hiding it for so long, Zarus sat up and opened his eyes. A wince or grimace, whatever would convey the pain he was feeling. It wasn't all an act.

The demon before him scoffed, "I wasn't ordered to be pleasant."

Zarus ignored the comment and focused on standing up. A draft worked past the window, carrying the faint scent of the dark oaks scattered around the fortress. As the stars cleared from his eyes, a familiar discomfort seeped in.

"Could you move any slower?" The moonlight-haired demon scowled, impatience taking hold as he walked over to his prisoner.

Zarus forced a smirk. "Your patience is as lacking as your aim, E." As hoarse as his voice was, the challenge danced within it. Errogan accepted the invitation with open arms. He gritted his teeth and advanced a step, but that was all.

Without so much as a warning, Zarus reached toward the center of the demon's chest and stabbed his nails into his flesh. The ancient Caenlin incantation he had been memorizing for the last hour flowed from his tongue like a maelstrom. Harsh and dark and irreversible—a spell older than Zarus himself.

The dark spell seized a morbid hold of Errogan and forced him still as stone. Zarus's own vision hazed as he recited; his skin turned frigid. Life and death itself were coursing through his veins rather than Eretimis's serum in those long moments. The weight of the spell, a reminder of what it was he was inflicting upon his old friend—no doubt a reminder from the human who invented the spell. Errogan couldn't break the spell's hold, but the deathly sensation was short-lived.

The dead language faded from Zarus's lips. A lightless flash consumed the room, causing both demons alike to stumble backward. The grave weight of warning sank its teeth deeper into Zarus's mind, and they both fell back when he ripped his hand free of Errogan's chest. Errogan loosed a piercing cry. The weight of the magic disappeared from the room.

"*What* was that?" Errogan demanded, unable to find the strength in his legs to stand.

Zarus couldn't even do that much. The spell took more magic than he anticipated. Energy he didn't have to spare. He focused on breathing until he finally spoke. "*Poaeian Igonen*," he said the spell's name without trembling. "No one has used the spell in centuries since the Empire of Aelius marked a map." By the time Zarus was on his feet, Errogan had been standing for twice as long.

The demon seethed, clutching where blood leaked from his chest. They stood eye to eye. "*What does it do?*" Errogan had no idea what the spell did. Good. Zarus's smile only further pissed him off.

Poaeian Igonen. A dead spell that the ancient Empire of Aelius used as a method of torturing prisoners. It was cast with an incantation resembling a priest's prayer that helped the souls of the dead find their way to Vulyn's Hand. As it's recited, the spell redirects the flow of magic in the world to tamper with the mortal body. The effects are gruesome, breaking down the victim's body from the inside out, leaving their corpse as nothing more than a hollowed shell. It was actually rather fitting, considering the serum in Zarus's veins. And it was a spell that Zarus had tried to learn four hundred years ago when he wrote the incantation down in the journal he found on the bookshelf. He had completely forgotten about it, but the ink of his notes had not faded.

The spell could be stopped, but only if the caster allowed it, and that was exactly how Zarus intended to get Errogan to help him escape. A spell of that power, however, needed a tremendous amount of strength and energy from the caster to perform. Was it any other day,

Zarus could have cast the spell without a bat of the eye, but that wasn't the case anymore. And Errogan might stay loyal to Eretimis until his very painful end. It was a gamble Zarus needed to make. This was his only shot of freedom, of saving Rin... he *needed* to take it. So he had spent two hours meditating and gathering as much energy as he could muster until Errogan returned.

"In summary," Zarus said, finishing up his spiel about the spell, "you'll die." He glanced at the door that remained open and made sure no one was out there listening. For all the strength he had collected to cast the deathly spell, he had none left to fight or even run. In a way, it was all a large bluff. Zarus had no way of knowing if he made the spell strong enough, or if it would even work. It was the first time he ever cast it, and he relearned it only in an hour. From the misery in the demon's cry when he finished the incantation, he was fairly certain Errogan was on his way to the grave—unless Zarus said otherwise.

Errogan offered no haughty remarks or feral grins. He kept his thoughtful stare on Zarus. "Why did you cast this?" he finally asked, austerely but not gravely. As though the concept of an agonizing death didn't faze him, just like it hadn't Zarus.

Zarus narrowed his eyes. "I need your help."

"Of course you do." The demon chuckled. His crystal eyes laced with amusement. "What can I do for you?"

"I want answers and out of this forsaken place."

Errogan inclined his chin and gave a lazy wave of the hand for Zarus to continue. He sat in the same chair Zarus bled on only hours before.

He took a deep breath. "How do I get this serum out of me?" *What did Eretimis mean by us having the same blood?*

"You can't," Errogan replied straight forward, crossing his arms behind his head.

A growl almost slipped Zarus's resolve. "Lies. Eretimis always has a backup plan for this type of experiment." Oh, how much he desired to make Errogan choke on his own teeth at that moment.

"No, really," the arrogant demon sighed, "you yourself can't get it out of your body. But..." he mused, holding a patient finger up to Zarus's growing scowl. "There's a way to cancel it out, and then your body will take care of the rest." He kicked his feet up and crossed them on the small table before the hearth.

If Errogan pulled his temper any further, Zarus couldn't promise that this wouldn't end in violence—exhausted or not. "And what might that be?" he ground his last nerve, holding his frustration as best as he could.

The demon clicked his tongue and waved his finger. "I don't talk for free. You need to tell me something now, Z." His smile was feral, even in the face of death. He hadn't changed a bit.

"I can tell you how much longer you have to live if you don't start talking," Zarus retorted.

"Cute," Errogan said, rolling his eyes. "I can do the same for you. Now tell me something worthwhile."

Zarus clenched and unclenched his fists at his side a few times. "*Like what.*"

Errogan narrowed his delighted eyes, and Zarus cringed for allowing a bargain of any type. "Where does this human come from?"

"I don't know." Zarus was as good a liar as Errogan to most, but...

"Convenient," Errogan sneered. "What *do* you know about her?"

Zarus pressed his lips together. Giving information away about Rin was the best way to hide the relationship that had formed between them. He would have to polish whatever bullshit he made up for it to strike as believable.

"She's a nomad from the south that was stupid enough to cross the Lennaels alone."

Errogan's disbelieving stare was sharp enough to cut. "Whatever, it's not like it matters where she's from, anyway." He thought for a moment. "Who saved her?"

A frown broke through his mask. "I have no idea," Zarus admitted, quieter than he meant.

Errogan sighed. "At least that was true, now what about—"

"Hold on," Zarus interrupted. "It's my turn. How do I get out of this fortress?" *What did Eretimis mean by us having the same blood?*

"Not enjoying the stay?" Zarus didn't deign to respond. "There are countless ways out; you know that," Errogan hummed. "It's just a matter of picking the right one."

"And that would be?"

"Depending on the time and day."

Zarus felt his hand itching to rip the smirk off Errogan's face. Rather than waste the time and energy, he instead shoved his fists far into the pockets of his pants, distancing them from the temptation to strike.

"Now, what of this third member traveling with you and the girl? Where is he?"

Zarus rose a brow. So that soul stealer ended up delivering the news to Eretimis... "Why does he matter?"

"Eretimis doesn't like dissidents," the demon smiled. "Why would some *narikaah* be excluded?"

Zarus's nostrils flared at the fact that he used to be Eretimis's follower too. Tatsuo raged somewhere off the mountains without a doubt. He was heading east when Zarus forced him away, but he could be anywhere by then.

"He was heading south the last I saw, and before you ask, I know as much about him as I do the girl. I don't care about formalities if you've bothered to remember anything about me after falling into that ravine."

Errogan just stared up at him with that smirk, a snake's sneer. "I remember you're a pisspoor liar, and I remember you refuse anyone inside that sad excuse for a heart of yours." The demon let out a disdainful chuckle as he broke their stare and veered it to the side. Errogan stood up from the chair, his chest already clotted.

"You're a damned fool to believe that," Zarus growled, taking more offense than he probably should have as he turned his back to Errogan and paced toward the open door. He didn't try to escape. He just gazed at the faded stone beyond his prison. "Here's my last question, Errogan: what happened on that cliffside three hundred years ago?" He glanced back at the snow-haired demon, eyes piercing through whatever facades they upheld. "What made you loathe me so much?"

Errogan didn't budge beneath the weight of the question. His smile deepened. Zarus's ignorance fueled him further, and the less Zarus knew, the more pleased Errogan would be. Zarus almost believed it too, had it not been for the emptiness that grew in his eyes.

Errogan hated him—despised him. Yet the hunger for death in his eyes still picked away at Zarus.

Errogan was silent. The emptiness eventually faded from his eyes, and he was a plethora of haughtiness once more. Zarus had struck something deep within the demon.

"Let's both ask questions neither of us are getting answers to: I know you haven't changed in the last three hundred years, Zarus. I know you're the same frozen demon as when I met you; I can see it in your eyes. You're empty, filled with the nothingness you've always had festering inside of you. So what vile interest stirred your head to make you decide to help a human?"

Zarus went eerily still, even against the dizziness swaying his head. A chill licked up his spine while another cool breeze rattled the small window. He had changed. He was not the same demon that foolishly joined his friend and followed a mad tyrant. Errogan had also changed. A small feathery sound tried to escape his throat, but he swallowed it. "I guess we'll never know."

"What's your decision?" Zarus pried, dragging Errogan to a different topic.

The desire to keep the conversation going was apparent in Errogan's smile, but his smirk straightened. He slowly touched the center of his chest. "How long before I'm dead?" he asked.

Zarus turned around and studied the male for a moment. "Twelve hours, give or take."

"And you'll reverse the spell if I help you?"

"I can stop the spell, but whatever damage it does before that point will remain. So I suggest you make up your mind quickly." Zarus heard faint voices in the distance. Errogan had taken too long to report back to Eretimis. "Before it's too late," he pressed, his own patience hanging on a wire.

Another moment's thought, and Errogan sighed. "Fine, it's a deal." Zarus's bewilderment smacked the calmness right off of Errogan's face. "Don't for one moment think I'm doing any of this for you. So long as you stop this spell, I'll be reasonable," Errogan sighed, rather annoyed.

Zarus wiped his surprise away. Grogginess coated his head, and that numbing fog smothered him again. He nearly doubled over when he tried to take a step.

"Do you have to be so overdramatic?" Errogan groaned. He grabbed Zarus from where he slouched onto the desk in the corner, pulled him upright with the sharpest motion, and yanked his hands behind his back.

"What are you doing?" Zarus demanded through winded breaths. The cold bite of shackles caught his wrists.

Zarus tried to yank free, but Errogan held firm until his hands were bound—leaving him defenseless.

"Calm down and start using your head for once," Errogan hissed. "Do you think all prisoners get to walk around freely?"

Swallowing his pride, Zarus stopped struggling. "Fine. Let's just... hurry." He hated how it came out as a plea, hated even more how he didn't have the energy to argue against the chains around his wrists. He was the one controlling the fate of this demon, but it didn't seem like he possessed any ounce of power in the situation unfolding.

"After you," Errogan smirked as he pushed Zarus into the doorway.

***

Despite hundreds of demons living and working in the fortress, the drafty hall remained empty. Only after the serum did the chill of the north start to bother Zarus.

The duo ran into a pair of guards at the bottom of his tower, neither of whom questioned them after seeing Errogan's fury. Zarus wondered if the guards would follow, but it seemed the demons were smart enough to stay out of Errogan's way when he was like this. The rest of the walk was a silent blur. Zarus suffered the waves of his impending doom as they stuck to the lesser used passages, sneaking away from the throne room. His head was in such a fog that he lost track of where they walked. A few demons passed them, but they were too busy with their own workload to care about him. However, the serum became excruciating. Errogan eventually held Zarus up by the back of his neck to keep him from collapsing. He hardly realized it as they walked deeper into the depths of the stronghold, but he hadn't seen another demon for a while. Errogan led him to an iron-railed staircase spiraling into darkness before Zarus could question where they were going.

As Zarus stared down into the darkness that seeped from the depths of the steps, his stomach churned. Even through the spells blocking his senses, he knew something unpleasant lurked in the depths. That hushed voice replayed in his head.

You are not alone in this fortress.

The words were a bitter lie on the lips of his mind. There was something else the voice had said. What had it been...?

He couldn't recall before being thrust forward.

Chapter Thirty-Seven

The closer they walked to the village on the brightening horizon, the more Rin realized that *village* was a kind description. Eight measly buildings lined the lackluster path. As she and her companions waltzed into Base, not a hint of life dwelled within. The derelict structures were skeletons of their former selves, run down by the unforgiving desert. No footprints marked the road, and as she stood in the middle of the desolate village, she saw none of Feyne's friends. Rin would have sooner thought Eretimis had destroyed the village rather than it being a secret headquarters hidden from his scouts.

Tatsuo caught her gaze, and they exchanged equally confused glances. The shifter continued walking ahead as if he had no care in the world. Rin shrugged and followed suit. She watched the buildings as she passed them, trying to decide what color each used to be before the sun baked the pigments right out. The crumbling structure of an aqueduct littered across various spots of the ground. At last when they came to the edge of the path, Feyne halted at a well that hadn't known the touch of water in years.

She raised her brow as he glanced back with a mischievous grin. Feyne knocked on the dried wooden beam of the well's hood three times. She heard stone sliding against stone from the bottom of the well, and then Feyne jumped in.

Tatsuo finally broke the silence. "Hm... didn't expect that," he admitted as he strode to the well and placed his taloned hands on the stone brim. He gazed down, a spark lighting in his eyes. He glanced over his shoulder to Rin, then followed their guide and jumped into the shaft without another word.

She was alone, gaping in the dim dawn of morning. Rin slowly approached the well, not sure what to expect at this point of the week, and peered down into pitch blackness.

Nothing. She saw nothing. Not Feyne or Tatsuo or anything.

"Stupid human eyes," she muttered, rubbing them with her palms. A rusty ladder sat on the inside. Shrugging, Rin hauled herself over the edge of the well, and lowered herself onto the first step. A strange breeze picked up. It gusted away from the plateau, opposite of the wind. Rin froze. She peered over the brim of the well.

Dread crept up her chest and grabbed her by the neck. No matter how long Rin searched, she saw nothing approach through the coarse dunes. She tore her gaze away from paranoia and reached down for the ladder with her foot, and left her nerves at the surface.

"Hello?" Rin called in the dark pit. It wasn't a far drop. She could still see the sky slowly fading pink above, but nothing else. She reached her arms out as far as they would extend, but the well was too wide to touch. The cool rock offered more comfort than the dry surface, but the air was moist.

"Of course they would leave me down here, alone, without any explanation as to where they jumped." Rin's ramblings were probably louder than they should have been, given Feyne's warning, but she went complaining about it to no one, for no one was with her. However, Rin's ears abruptly shuttered. The sound of rock sliding against rock thundered in the well, the same as before Feyne disappeared. Just as the grinding echo finally stopped, the dull sky of dawn was covered.

Alone. And tired. And slightly scared of what waited for her in the darkness. And tired. And maybe... not so alone? The hairs on the back of her neck stood tall.

She sighed dramatically, and all Rin could do was inhale the familiar scent of embers.

"How long are you planning to stay back there, you creep?" she demanded, a slight smugness glittering her tone.

"Until you found me," replied the *narikaah*.

"Well," she sighed, pivoting on her heels to face Tatsuo's voice, "I found you, so could you maybe light a match or something?"

"Somebody's bossy. Fear of the dark?" She heard the shift of his feet on the damp floor.

"A newfound fear of who's watching me, actually," she jested, but there was more than enough truth behind it.

Tatsuo laughed. "Fair enough." At that, he snapped and a small flame flickered at the edge of his talon. His sharp features glowed in the orange light.

"Is that little gesture required, or do you just like the dramatics?" Rin used the magical flame to examine the walls. Still no exit, still no Feyne.

"Who says it can't be both?" He turned away before she could retort, knocking on the curved wall behind him three times, just as Feyne had on the well above. "Open up, Howls, you had your fun."

Sometimes Rin wanted to flick that shifter right between his damned eyes.

The wall behind Tatsuo rumbled, rock sliding on rock. A line of light cracked through a gap in the wall behind him and grew into a doorway. Feyne's silhouette stood waiting. Rin stared through the hidden passage. A hall lined with lanterns stretched beyond. An old strip of carpet stained with dirt and sand reached the other end of the hall. Rock shaped the entire corridor. There was no breeze, but it was cooler than the well's shaft.

"Welcome to our humble Base," Feyne greeted from the doorway. Behind him stood two people—humans, by the look of it—armed to the teeth with rather shabby weapons with a close eye on Tatsuo. However, they offered a warm smile her way, and she sleepily returned it.

***

The light. That was all that she could describe. The pure, blinding, burning light shining from behind the figure standing in front of her. The figure that she could barely see against the blinding light, and certainly couldn't distinguish. Rin's eyes only burned, only flooded with tears, when she was staring directly at the figure, not the light.

It was painful. The feeling of skin melting away, bones being burnt to charred, brittle fragments under the stare of the figure. Because even if she couldn't see them, she felt those eyes press down on her, on her soul, and look right through her very being. Every intention she ever had displayed on her forehead, every deep, dark fear staining her heart. She was being read like a book. For all that she was, and all the good she knew she had inside of herself, Rin only felt shame as the nameless, voiceless watcher studied her.

She tried to peel her eyes away, but couldn't muster the strength. Staring at them... it drained her, yet enriched her. A giving and taking of life all at once. Rin could only marvel at the sheer presence of the being standing on the other side of the depthless chasm before her feet. A chasm that was as dark as a moonless night, stretching as far as the horizon on either side. Shadow itself reached out of the jagged crack in the earth. She didn't care. As long as this being was with her, Rin knew she was safe from the drop. Yet she couldn't bring herself to walk closer to the pitch black fog that seeped up from it. Even if those steps would carry her closer to the being on the other side. All Rin could do was stare in awe. She knew speech would be pointless. She was the one without power here.

Suddenly, the ground below her shook, tossing and turning her balance with each rumble. Gods knew how she kept her footing, and gods knew how she hadn't heard that noise before the quake. No, not the sound of earth tearing apart as the chasm widened, but the frantic mutterings that echoed around her. As if her ears had snapped awake to reality, Rin could hear the faintest hum of speech. She couldn't decipher what they said, she merely felt the vibrations of each syllable pronounced, of the urgency in which the being spoke.

"I can't hear you," Rin called, the words nearly inaudible. Her nerves were razor sharp. She glanced down and saw how far the earth ruptured between her and this being. The earth tore and crumbed into the abyss, the being on the other side growing farther and farther away. The light behind dimmed.

The voice continued to speak—no, not speak: yell. Scream. Feverish, manic, raving, but Rin couldn't understand what they were saying. Calm, yet anxious; they spoke slowly, yet rushed; quiet, yet roaring. Rin could have sworn that the being spoke with a thousand voices all at once. A language her ears had never come across and one no one had ever heard. Rin only understood that the being was in a hurry to speak; fear littered each word. The calmness that they possessed... Rin wasn't sure they feared for themself.

Before she knew it, a trance fell over her. So enthralled by the being that she noticed far too late that the chasm now stretched mere feet away.

The darkness clouding the cliff blotted out the being. She was alone, and even the frantic voice had faded from reality. Panic filled her thoughts. Ice flowed through her veins. She could do nothing but inhale the mist into her lungs.

She tried to run, but it was too late. Poison, that's what it was. Her legs moved like lead, her thoughts fuzzed in and out of focus.

She couldn't call for help, couldn't plead out to the being who once stood across from her, nor to the gods who she did not yet want to meet. Silent prayers were not enough to reach out of the suffocating fog, and if she uttered even the softest whisper, her throat would shatter like glass—she knew it.

Her head cleaved open. Sinister darkness replaced the blinding light, and she was not to escape it.

Rin closed her eyes. It was the same with open lids. She struggled for one more deep breath of the poison and allowed her body to go limp. This was her end. This was her fate. Death gripped her throat.

She would die alone.

***

Rin gasped for air as she jumped up from the pillow.

A thick layer of sweat drenched her skin. Her heart drummed, and Rin was certain she might very well have died if she woke a second later.

A dream. As vivid as the torches strewn about the room in which she slept, as real as the heat sneaking into the bunker known as Base. Just like her last dream.

Rin's eyes swept along the small room. She was completely alone.

She shook off the memory of the dream. Because it was only that, nothing more and nothing less. It left her feeling as empty as the bedroom around. Listening to that being physically took something out of her. She couldn't figure out what was gone. Before she let the vision eat her alive, she jumped out of bed and threw on the clothes she was given before retiring. Clothes meant for the desert. A quick fasten of her scimitar, and Rin left all thoughts of that dream in the room behind her.

Chapter Thirty-Eight

B ase was much larger than she thought a hidden bunker would be. She was more likely to get lost in the facility than she was to run into someone else and ask for directions. She passed twelve bedrooms before stumbling into an empty conference hall cluttered with maps. When she stole a peek at them and saw the lines of red ink marking where Eretimis's demons lurked, she was speechless. Feyne mentioned Eretimis was acting more daring lately; if only humanity knew how close the demon tyrant lurked to their territory in the north. Far too close for her liking. Rin finally found Feyne working in the lounge, but only after finding a freshwater cistern first.

The lounge was spacious and filled with furniture not even a farmer like herself would claim as her own. Colorful carpets and cushions drew away from the lusterless appearance, and the people inside were still smiling and laughing amongst each other. Rin thanked the gods she wasn't tall after she saw Tatsuo's head mere inches away from grazing the low ceilings. He leaned over a table beside the shifter.

"Sleep well?" Feyne greeted, patting her on the back as she met his side.

Rin pushed the memory of the dream away and lied, "Like a puppy." She looked to see what the *narikaah* and shifter were hovering over.

"A map?" Piles of maps littered the table, in fact. She studied the map of the continent with familiarity owed to her father; Nokomic spanning long in the north with the Unclaimed Lands bordering it in the west and north, Damrok in the east hovering over Melde in the center, the horn of Melibor curving in the south-west, Weslyc in the south-east, and the small island of Johait tucked in the left corner. Then she looked beside it to a map Western Nokomic and the desert were drawn on browned parchment. What most thought was an uncharted sandpit, Feyne had clearly chosen to explore thoroughly.

"*My* map. Of the desert and other places of importance." The shifter ran his fingers along the black ink. "I was just showing Fireball here exactly where we are."

Tatsuo didn't deign to comment on the nickname, but Rin knew he understood the importance of the reluctant trust, especially with how tense all the other humans grew when he stood near them. She glanced at Tatsuo. "Like what you see?"

The half-demon shrugged, not tearing his gaze from the map. "We're close to the highlands; it wouldn't take long for anyone to find us, especially if they had hunters."

Hunters. The thought of hunters tracking them down churned Rin's stomach.

"They've been over this village hundreds of times before, and not once did they suspect a thing," Feyne countered, taking a step away from both of them as he stretched. "We have a watch line set up around Base, anyway." He glanced down. "No one's getting into the village above without being noticed."

Tatsuo didn't seem convinced. He sighed, then turned to Rin. "Someone looks more comfortable." He looked at her new clothes.

"Indeed; leathers weren't made for the desert, after all." She smiled. "So, is this friend of yours still on watch duty?"

The shifter yawned as he nodded. "She should be back any minute now." Whoever Feyne intended for her to meet was stuck watching out for suspicious activity on the morning shift when they arrived. Rin wasn't looking forward to the confirmation that there was nothing remotely special about her, even if she expected it. Perhaps it would be the kick she needed to stop fantasizing about staying... She'll prove she's not the right girl to join Base, then Feyne will show her the way to her mother's village. Speaking of which...

"Hey, Feyne," she called, looking back at the map. Within the whole desert, there was only one place marked as a village, labeled as **BASE**. "Where's Lilit? I don't see it anywhere on this map..."

"That would be because it's not in the desert. Lilit's on the northern shore of the Unclaimed Lands—out of the map's reach." He busied himself reading the papers left on a table near the shambled couch.

"The northern shore..." Rin repeated, making sure she had heard correctly.

"Uh-huh," Feyne assured as he put down the sheets and started walking toward the door.

Rin felt like someone knocked her breath from her lungs. The northern shore of Armiria's Unclaimed Lands was far. Easily another week's time, given how far in the desert they were. Her head drummed. "I thought you said Lilit was the *next village past Base*, Feyne." Rin felt her hands trembling like she was back on the freezing mountain. Her head still throbbed. Not just anger... but something—something was flickering in her head. "Why didn't you mention it would take a week to get there?"

Feyne stopped under the doorway, glancing over his shoulder. "You never asked."

A scowl poisoned Rin's expression. "You could have warned me!"

"What difference would it have made?"

Oh, how she longed to punch him square between the eyes. "You deceived me."

"We would have had to stop here before we left for Lilit anyway, Rin. I didn't lie to you. I didn't force you to shake my hand."

"You didn't give me much of a choice! Go to Base or have Eretimis's demons find me and kill me. What other option did I have?" What a choice that was! Helping the world who needs it? No, Feyne only helped her because she had information he wanted. But... she owed her life to Feyne; going to meet whoever his friend was shouldn't have been a problem. Even if she escaped Errogan in the forest alone, she would have had no idea where to go from there. Hell, she'd probably have wandered into Death's Yard and died within a day. So why did it feel like he tricked her?

Feyne shook his head, a stoic apathy staring her in the eyes. "Stop blaming me for the fact you think you're useless, Rin. If you don't want to do things for yourself, then don't complain about how others do them." His words were sharp, cutting deep into her skin and down into her heart. Whatever thrummed in her head dispersed into nothing. Without giving her the chance to utter another sound, Feyne had already exited into the hall in conversation with a short woman, leaving Rin empty in a room full of curious strangers.

***

"Tatsuo, wait!" Rin yelled, trying to keep a grip on the *narikaah's* burning arm. "Stop!"

She could see the rage blazing in his eyes, the first blow he was dying to land against the shifter with his talons. Rin stood no chance of keeping Tatsuo from engaging in another fight with Feyne. He was dragging her behind him as he stormed across the lounge and into the hall. With one last desperate attempt, Rin used every ounce of strength she possessed and threw her weight down while yanking Tatsuo backward. "*Please!*"

Tatsuo whipped his eyes back to meet her; she nearly crashed into him. "He has no right to speak to you like that, Rin!" The words could have caught fire as they left his tongue.

"That doesn't matter!" she yelled. "Would you stop and think for a moment?" Rin released his arm, only then realizing how hot his skin had become. "Tatsuo, you're the first demon-kind ever allowed into Base! Don't you think it would make a better impression if you didn't try to fry their leader a few hours after being here?" Already, some people from the lounge flooded into the hallway behind. Even Rin heard the weapons clinking at their sides. "Look," she said quietly sighing, "he... he's not wrong." Her heart sank even deeper as the words left her mouth. "I need to talk to you about Zarus." She dropped her stare to the ground, to the walls, the back of her eyelids. Anywhere but Tatsuo.

The snarl disappeared from his face. "What about him?"

"Tatsuo, I'm not rescuing Zarus from the fortress." The words tried to crawl back down her throat. Rin took a deep breath and closed her eyes, even placing a gentle hand on Tatsuo's burning arm again. "I can't help you bring him back. I honestly want to, but there's nothing I can do to help. Feyne is going to take me to that village to meet my mother, and then I'm going home to Aresan where I belong. You should stay here and work with Feyne. You two are the only hope for Zarus, I can't let—"

"You're going to leave Zarus in the fortress to die?" Tatsuo interrupted. Rin opened her eyes.

"There's nothing I can—Feyne will try—"

The *narikaah* scoffed harshly. "Feyne, the one who doesn't even trust me, is going to free Zarus? When did you plan on telling me?" He ripped his arm away from her touch. "If Feyne hadn't called you out like that, would you have?"

"Tatsuo, I..." Rin struggled to speak. "I can't stand with you..."

Something flickered in the dragon's eyes that left Rin feeling hollow. A hurt that made her realize she chose the wrong words. She barely took in her next breath before Tatsuo stormed off.

Chapter Thirty-Nine

Yet again, Rin was left alone. She couldn't bear to think of the betrayal in Tatsuo's eyes when he stormed off. She hadn't meant that he was the reason she was leaving, but it was too late to explain now. And Feyne... His words pierced through her soul. She knew he was right, though. Everything he said, as far back as when they were still in the highlands. She had been pitying herself for the entire journey with Feyne and Zarus. Even when she fought against those demons—her, *a human*—she still only focused on what a burden she was to those who helped her. And all for what? Rin wasn't even sure. The weapon bound to her hip weighed down like a megaton. Thinking they helped her out of pity was an insult to all the people who saved her.

She was finished acting like that.

Rin sighed and rubbed her palms where she had held Tatsuo's arm. Any longer and his skin would have burned her. He just needed to cool off. Right now, she needed to find Feyne. What would she even say? Gods, just thinking about it made her cringe. What a great first impression to the members of Base... she wasn't even outside yet, and she still felt her cheeks burning bright red.

***

The decision not to retrieve the extra wraps to cover her face was a mistake Rin discovered the moment she stepped outside another pair of hidden doors.

She was slick with sweat within minutes of being out in the dried yellow sea. Though there was a strong wind that never stopped rushing, all it did was blow scorching sand onto her face and clothes. Even if the sun wasn't nearly at its peak, the heat was unbearable. It shone onto her face like a rain shower in spring, soaking into her skin and clothes. She prayed to Yath Ha using every one of their names that she would not burn up.

It didn't take long to find Feyne—with the help of others, of course. He was a five-minute walk outside of the rundown village, standing with two other people. A walk that Rin didn't have to make alone thanks to the generosity of a Base member named Leew—a Meliboran man with curly haired, warm skin, and dark eyes. He led her to Feyne's loud and aggressive gathering. There was a girl that looked to be a few years older than Rin with dazzling wine-red hair, and a weathered man with pink pale Damrian skin a little shorter than Feyne, who couldn't be older than fifty. Both Rin and Leew hesitated.

The weathered one was causing the ruckus. He yelled into Feyne's face, but the shifter merely looked disinterested. The girl was more concerned at what was going on, but not too worried, as if the screaming Rin heard five hundred feet away wasn't unusual. She didn't blame Leew when he suddenly remembered he had chores to do in the bunker and excused himself before they got too close. She probably would have turned back and talked to Feyne at a less hostile time, if they all didn't already look in her direction. Silence fell on everyone's tongue when she finally reached them.

Rin cleared her sandy throat before she spoke. "I can come back later if this is a bad time?" She was already turning away from Feyne and the strangers, but a wry smile stretched across the shifter's face that stopped her in her tracks. It was a dangerous thing to cross, even if not meant for her.

"Your timing couldn't have been better, Miss Nowell," he chimed. The sound of her name wrung alarm out of her chest, but the habit of secrecy didn't seem to have a place at Base. Feyne suddenly smacked the man beside him on the back in a much too friendly motion. "I was just telling Bjarkh about your situation and why it is I brought you here." The condescension was lethal, and amusement danced in his golden eyes. "But maybe he would be more accepting if he heard it from your own lips."

Fine wrinkles formed around Bjarkh's eyes when he shot Feyne a glare. Despite his age, a composed posture complimented his strong physique. "I don't give a damn what she has to say!" He waved. "It doesn't change the fact that you went against everything I said and still brought her and that *demon* to Base. *And* risked letting Eretimis's hunters follow you back. Do you have no worth for *our* lives?"

"He's a *narikaah*," Rin corrected, and it earned her a fiery leer from the old Damrian.

"The last time I looked, Bjarkh, you're not the one in charge of Base. No one is." Feyne calmly smiled at him. "Besides, those demons were too distracted by Zarus to even think about following me."

Zarus... What nightmare was he experiencing right now? Rin bit her cheek, lost to thought. The argument escalated, Bjarkh getting angrier and Feyne's contentment fueling it. Bjarkh wasn't happy that Feyne went looking for Rin and Zarus, and brought her and a half-demon back with him. He said, or rather yelled, that she and Tatsuo were a danger to Base, and that Feyne's arrogance was going to be the downfall of an already struggling organization. *Not everyone would trust me, indeed.*

While the four stood in the middle of nowhere, the girl on Feyne's right stared at her. As if looking right through Rin's physical body and down into her soul, barely blinking. The girl's eyes were magenta, bright as a rose. They were beautiful, but something otherworldly about them. Something not quite human.

Rin finally realized the silence that rang rampant. When she looked up, their stares met her. Feyne's prideful golden, the girl's cool magenta, and Bjarkh's sea green. Waiting for a response.

"I'm sorry?" Rin croaked after clearing her throat. "Could you repeat that?"

Bjarkh rolled his eyes to the moon and back, scoffing along the trek as Feyne said, "Bjarkh wants to know exactly how you got tied up with Eretimis and Zarus, and eventually me. Apparently, my version wasn't interesting enough for him to remember."

"There is a lot of risk in helping you, girl," Bjarkh grounded.

Her brows furrowed. "Isn't helping what you do…?"

Bjarkh looked like he was about to explode, but not before the other girl spoke. "It's exactly what we do here." She glared daggers at the man, then turned toward Rin with sincerity. "I agree Feyne was reckless to bring you here," she gave him half of a flat stare, the other half full of something wild Rin couldn't decipher, "but recklessness keeps the day interesting."

"See, Scarlette understands," Feyne muttered, acting as a lightning rod to Bjarkh's wrath.

Scarlette was Meldii from the looks. The hue of her almond eyes was just a fragment of her alluring nature. The left side of her head was shaved to a buzz, but the right side flowed like a waterfall, landing at her shoulder. A thin braid tied at the front of the flow. Her dark olive arms suggested a fair amount of muscle, and her winsome voice graced the air. Although the bow on her back suggested that kind smile wasn't one to be crossed. "I think we'd all appreciate it if you would explain how you ended up all the way in this corner of the Unclaimed Lands."

Rin stared at each of them before she nodded. "It's kind of a long story, one I'd prefer to explain inside where we're not so... exposed." She wiped the sweat beading down her brow. Her head was already humming from the nauseating heat. Not wanting to give any of them—mainly Bjarkh—a choice in the matter, Rin pivoted on her heels and strode back to the bunker. Thankfully, the suggestion bothered no one. They all followed, Feyne wearing a pleasantly not-so-surprised grin all too well. In fact, when he eventually moved up to her side, he was first to apologize.

"I thought you needed a push, but it was the wrong way to go about it," he said, walking up and down the loose sands far easier than she did. They all did, though Scarlette and Bjarkh chose to stay behind in their own conversation.

"You had every right to call me out," she admitted without the slightest bit of shame. "But thank you," she smiled, "and I'm not one to hold grudges, so I guess I'll forgive you."

"Well," Feyne grinned sheepishly, "you made it a little too easy."

Rin struck him in the shoulder, but chuckled. "I'm sorry that I yelled at you."

"No hard feelings," he yawned, stretching his arms into the air, then crossing them behind his head. "I deserved it anyway."

She could have left the conversation at that and figured out how she was going to explain the events of the last week, but that could wait. "I told Tatsuo I was leaving."

Feyne didn't even flick an eye. "How did that go?"

She shrugged. "Not good."

Feyne slowly nodded. He dropped his arms. "He'll come around. He would barely shut up about how much your friendship meant to him while you were sleeping. Annoying as it was, he cares about you."

"I know," her throat bobbed, "but I hurt him. More than when Zarus said he was weak." She shook her head, crossing her arms. "What if he doesn't forgive me? What if he doesn't come back?"

Feyne looked at her for a long moment before answering. "I think he'll forgive you, Rin. He's just angry. He'll come back." Ahead, the village above the bunker drew near over the golden dunes. "You shouldn't hold yourself responsible for the actions of others."

She turned toward him. "Even if I caused them?"

Feyne closed his eyes thoughtfully. "You're responsible for how you react to others, not how they react to you. You should hold yourself accountable when you hurt someone, but they made the choice on how they reacted to it." Feyne trekked through the sand like it was second nature, and Rin didn't understand how he wasn't dying of the heat. She was better off to hide from the light than bathe in it.

Rin remained silent, one thought echoing in her head. What came next?

Chapter Forty

By the time Zarus tumbled down the last iron step, blood leaked from his mouth in puddles.

Cold sweat licked a chill along his spine. He laid there, eyes struggling to remain open and wounded in too many places to keep track. Errogan's footsteps descended the staircase in a daze before Zarus felt himself dragged across the cold floor. His hands were still bound. His body was reaching its limit.

Zarus caught a half glimpse of the iron-wrought bars before the demon threw him into the cell. The white splotches from his vision finally faded after the hinges screeched closed. He didn't want to think about how far the serum had traveled by that point, but the throb in his chest was a fatal sign. Errogan finished locking the cellar door, then stared down at him.

Zarus found a twinge of strength and dragged his body to the back wall of the dungeon. Through the numbing fog seizing him, he spoke hoarsely. "You're rather relaxed for someone who shares the same fate as me."

"You're a fool," Errogan said flatly. "You must be truly desperate to think that a spell cast in your current state would kill me that easily." The demon leaned against the bars separating them.

"You'll still be dead in hours," Zarus heaved, his breaths forced. He was practically talking through his teeth. "No mortal can escape the fate of that spell, not even Eretimis himself." Bluff. And a big one. Although Zarus didn't know for sure if the Dark Tyrant would survive the death sentence he cast on Errogan, he knew that Eretimis would have stopped him before he could even utter the first line of the spell.

Whether he sensed Zarus's lie, Errogan cackled under his breath. "That may be true, Z, but I'm not like most mortals." A shadow grew around his eyes. "Blood and bone might be inside me, but it will take a lot more than some pitiful spell to break what I'm made of."

Zarus opened his mouth to question what in all the worlds Errogan spoke of. There was no arrogance in the demon's curved lips, only exhaustion. His old friend didn't give him the chance to speak. He was already at the base of the iron steps when Zarus worked up a dark mirth, stopping him in his tracks.

He struggled to pick himself off the floor, but forced himself to his feet. The chains tying back his arms sang in a cruel duet as he caught himself on the bars of the cell. "Indeed, a fool," Zarus muttered as he stumbled forward, "for ever having believed that threatening your life would work. Your useless, replaceable life that has only ever acted as a parasite toward *his liege*." He spat the words along with the blood flooding his mouth.

Errogan hesitated before placing his foot on the first step. Though the serum had robbed him of almost all his demonic abilities, Zarus saw the rough silhouette of the demon fading in and out of the shadows. Errogan turned around with lethal grace, striding back so he was eye to eye—crystal to crimson—with Zarus, only the cellar bars separating them. Deep stricken rage settled in those blue eyes.

"Laugh as much as you can, Lowwenth. Soak in each pathetic breath, appreciate the smallest creeks of these bars surrounding you.

Enjoy the godsdamned stench of death suffocating you for the sake of whatever deity stays with you in your final moments. Because shorter than you'll even have time to realize, you'll either be as dead as the care I might have once had for you... or Eretimis's puppet." His voice was little more than a whisper. For the first time he'd ever witnessed, Errogan chose not to act on the promise of death.

Zarus was truly desperate to attempt instigating such a merciful death.

Without another utterance, Errogan ascended the spiral staircase, leaving Zarus to rot. Once the steps faded into the distant fortress above, Zarus expended all of his strength. Before his legs buckled beneath him, he slowly turned around and slid down the front of the dungeon cell.

That couldn't have gone any worse.

He thought to check the black veins while his eyes still worked, but what was the point? The lines ran their course, likely reaching his heart. All Zarus had to do was wait to see his ending: death or slavery. His hopes were death. At least he did everything he could to escape besides upright spilling his own blood onto the floor. An ignorant and vacuous plan was better than no plan at all, right? That's probably what Rin would have said.

Zarus sat with his eyes closed and waited for it. Whatever *it* was. For the time being, he'd just enjoy the peace of being alone.

It wasn't until he wiped the remaining blood from the corner of his mouth that the silence broke.

Chapter Forty-One

"**B**ad day?" an unfamiliar voice asked in the depths of the darkness. The words ripped through the curtain of crude tranquility.

Clouded from judgment and concern, Zarus replied weakly. "You have no idea."

"No one has been cast down here in a while, though Errogan himself didn't personally escort any of the others. What'd you do to piss him off?"

Every demon in the fortress would get sick at the sight of Errogan, but to recognize him just by his voice? Zarus sighed, facing forward and closing his eyes. "It would be easier to list what I haven't done to end up here," he breathed, a half-smile stirring his face.

"Well, *Lowwenth*, I've never heard a single soul talk to the Moonlit Bastard like that before." He paused for a moment to laugh. As ever-so-honored as Zarus was to make a complete stranger chuckle in this dark pit of a dungeon, the chattering was getting under his skin.

"It's Zarus," he said sharply. He bit down hard as he ran a hand over his ribs. He should have prayed against a fracture. "But I assume you already know that. When did you start listening?"

"The whole time; sadly your tumble interrupted my nap. So tell me, Zarus Lowwenth," the clanking of chains echoed off the damp walls as this being took to his feet, "who is a prisoner to talk about the Dark Tyrant in such personal ways? Who are you to cast a deadly spell on the White-Cloaked Reaper in hopes of ending his life?"

Damn the heavens. Was he not allowed a moment's peace? Or was this the gods' last punishment for him?

Zarus sighed, opening his eyes and glancing back one more time. "Somebody the world will forget in the next few days, chatty stranger." A faint figure leaned against the wall of a cell, but his hands were not bound, nor his legs. "Now if you don't mind," Zarus closed his eyes, "I'd like to spend the last few hours of my freedom in silence before I turn into a godsdamned empty shell and used like a puppet." The quiet that fell afterwards nearly tricked him. Nearly. Apparently he'd have to endure the living for the rest of his time.

The being spoke, but now void of all humor, "They put the serum into you?"

Zarus's body went still. "You know about the serum?" At last, his curiosity piqued.

"I'm familiar with it," he said gravely. Zarus could turn halfway around before his body screamed in protest. The male was staring at him, his deep blue eyes piercing through the dark. "How long has it been in your blood?"

Zarus stopped to think, or attempted to. He honestly didn't know how long it had been since he arrived at the fortress. He didn't know how long it had been since he cast the spell on Errogan. A drum pounded in the back of his head as he searched through the fog. After a serum-induced migraine, Zarus finally uttered, "Three days. It couldn't have been more than three days ago," he added, hoping to sound confident in his answer, though he very well could have been wrong.

"Gods, how on Armiria are you still moving?"

Zarus shook his head the best he could. "I won't be for long." He felt his joints stiffening. "How much do you know about it?"

The being was quiet for a moment, long enough for Zarus to think he finally lost interest in the conversation. "I know all I need to..." Hesitation lingered in his answer, but Zarus didn't blame him. Trusting anyone in this corrupted fortress was suicide, whether they were Eretimis himself or a worthless prisoner. Well, maybe not worthless. Anyone that was poisoned with Eretimis's invention seemed to be worth something in the eyes of the tyrant. Zarus assumed anyone who knew about the poison could be worth a damn as well. "What matters is how far it's spread. Please tell me it's not over your heart yet."

"The last I looked, it wasn't over my heart, but I doubt it will be long before it is," Zarus grunted. Another surge of pain, another sense of his blood boiling beneath his skin. "At least I know I'll be dead soon."

Another pause.

Zarus sighed. Now he was the one carrying the conversation. "What is it?"

"You're still walking and talking after three days of having that shit in your blood, Zarus." His name. It felt like a mockery at this point. "If it hasn't crossed your heart yet..." the words lodged in his throat.

"Then an agonizing death will be a distant dream," Zarus finished. He expected nothing less with his luck, but the news still twisted his stomach. Thankfully, he didn't have the energy to panic. He adjusted the restraints cutting into his wrists, and took a moment to clear his raspy throat. "Well, stranger that won't shut up, it seems that our time together won't be long. I never even got your name."

"Genesis." The male slid down to the floor, mirroring the way Zarus sat.

"Well, Genesis, thanks for the information." Zarus searched through his head, but no demon with the name of *Genesis* came to mind. "I get the feeling they reserve this dungeon for demons who have a special hatred in Eretimis's heart" he rambled. "So what did you do to deserve such a place?"

Genesis *tsked*, but Zarus noted how he kept his voice hushed. So someone was still monitoring them down here. "You're only half right. You could say I was the first of a series of disappointing experiments." Grim pride emitted from the demon as Zarus studied him.

"So why aren't these other disappointments joining us?"

"Corpses don't make for pleasant company."

"If you're a disappointment, why are you still alive? Eretimis doesn't like reminders of his failures." Case and point: him.

"Who's to say it was Eretimis's failure?" Genesis asked, poking for his own answers.

Zarus scoffed. "Everything in this fortress is under his close watch. Experiments included, especially ones that fail."

Genesis shrugged idly. "It's hard to kill unnatural things."

Zarus rose a brow. He wasn't in the mood for guessing games. He was barely in the mood to speak at all, so he waited silently for Genesis to explain what it was he was talking about, or lose the only chance at a conversation until another disappointment rolled around.

Genesis cracked first, but not with what he thought. "It doesn't matter, Zarus." He lazily rose to his feet and paced the length of his cell. "What *does* matter is that serum inside of you."

What happened to Genesis wasn't a complete mystery. There must have been some experiment that no one else survived, and Eretimis cast him down here to rot. Survival didn't mean a thing. What somehow lived was bound to die by Eretimis's hand. It didn't explain why Genesis couldn't die, and why his scent was just short of a human and demon. It made Zarus wonder, but not enough to force a sore topic out of the male he just met. "Why does it matter? There's nothing to do about it, anyway." He leaned back against the wall, staring at the dark ceiling above.

"Well, not nothing," Genesis offered. "A white mage probably could cleanse it out of you."

Zarus rolled his eyes at the suggestion. "That would be helpful if I weren't stuck at the bottom of Eretimis's stronghold with only you to help me."

"It would also be helpful if white mages weren't extinct," Genesis countered.

The words nearly passed right over Zarus's head. "What did you say?"

Genesis's inquiry shaped his face. "Where have you been the past fifty years?"

"Avoiding Eretimis," Zarus said as blunt as he could, forcing his body to turn toward the being before him. Rin mentioned how the use of magic was dying out, but the girl never said some forms of it were *extinct*. Then again, she'd never actually seen anyone use magic until she saw his... But this? This was news. "How did an entire class of users die out in fifty years?"

Genesis's laugh was bitter. "How do you think it happened?"

The disbelief set in, but he caught his jaw from dropping. "No," he shook his head, "not even *he* could accomplish something like that. He couldn't have had the means to—the strength to." But that was all Eretimis needed. A silent challenge and an impossible task. Human users always posed a threat to the Dark Tyrant, ranging from minor inconveniences all the way to landing on Eretimis's personal hit-list, but white mages weren't the typical users. They were stronger, more resilient; rumored to be blessed directly by the gods. Alone, they had wiped out entire armies of men. Alone, they could take on demons and walk away. Powers that humans were born with—natural magic—were rare enough as it was, but finding mages who had the natural-born ability to purify was as likely as Zarus escaping the fortress alive. And Eretimis snuffed out all of them.

Genesis shrugged again. "He found the strength he needed and hunted them down like animals from what I heard." *Heard.* So he didn't even know for sure. "They either joined him, or he killed them on sight. He did that with all the users he found." Zarus took to note Genesis's disdain, slowly trying to piece together how he played into all of this. "He's the reason magic is fading from Armiria," he sighed.

It was unbelievable, though Zarus somehow knew that it wasn't a lie. Eretimis killed off an entire category of people in only half a century. Although it affected him in no way, a small part of his heart ached.

He looked for a distraction. After a quick examination of which parts of his body were completely numb, he found that some of the aching and burning faded. They weren't gone, but it wasn't as intense. Zarus didn't know whether he should have been relieved.

"Where did you hear all of this?" he asked, not thinking too hard about it. "I know that a decent amount of people in this world fear Eretimis's name, but why should I believe any of what you're saying?" Zarus took the opportunity of the numbing pain to slowly, gruellingly take to his feet. His head no longer pounded like thousands of hammers.

"One demon here used to update me about the human world when she stood guard outside my door," his roommate said. "I never actually got to see it, or do anything about it myself." He paused. "I guess she felt bad for me. That was until Errogan caught wind of what was going on, and she was labeled a *sympathizer*. Never saw her again." He started quietly walking back and forth.

Zarus expected nothing less from the fate of a demon who imprudently did favors for a prisoner. He was in the middle of wondering how Errogan made the guard pay for the sympathy that she showed Genesis when a thought occurred to him.

"Wait a minute," he interjected. "You're a human?"

"No, not exactly."

"So whatever I'm sensing about your presence isn't because of the serum messing with my head?" Zarus guessed, suddenly more interested in the topic at hand.

"You can thank Eretimis for that."

Zarus focused on what he sensed from Genesis. Not human, not demon, not anything he was familiar with. Not even an offspring of the two. Maybe it was the fact he was so close to the equivalent of death, but excitement tugged at his mind. It was hard to come across something he didn't already know, and he wasn't about to waste one of his last chances of learning something new. "Just what in the Flames are you?"

"A successful failure." Genesis's smile was anything but merciful as he watched Zarus from across the dungeon.

Chapter Forty-Two

P art demon, part human.

Genesis was a hybrid. But both parents, whoever the Nokomai might have been, were completely human.

Zarus had missed some of Eretimis's greatest conquests in the last century. The Tyrant had actually attacked Nokomic's capital of Zelenia seventy years ago to study humanity's strength. What better place to attack than the continent's largest kingdom capital. Taking it down would affect the rest of the continent, and if Eretimis ever chose another target, they'd be weaker. Although, Zarus never would have thought that Eretimis would personally go to the battlefield. Only a specific interest would have driven him to go. Such as a viable candidate for his first human test subject. He demolished the city and dragged Genesis from the ruins to the fortress. He was experimented on; his blood combined with that of a demon's until he was something between the two. A concept too problematic when Eretimis brought up such an idea over four centuries ago. A concept so dangerous that it should never have worked.

Forcing the essence of two beings into one through dark magic. Eretimis ignored all of Zarus's warnings.

Anyone, no matter what species, that underwent such an extreme procedure should have died. Painfully. The mere means Eretimis would've had to have gone to break the being down from their core and rebuild them piece by piece were incomprehensible, but even if they survived that, the side effects would be death. The aid of magic would only go so far in increasing the odds of success. And yet, Genesis stood before his eyes. Alive. Even if all the test subjects after him failed and their bodies burned in mass piles to erase Eretimis's mistakes. Even after Eretimis attacked Zelenia—the man's home—and he was the last man standing on the unsuspecting battlefield; Genesis was still alive. Even after he fought Errogan face to face, Genesis was still alive.

A successful failure indeed.

"I can't believe you fought Errogan and lived," Zarus marveled. He paced back and forth as they spoke. Quite some time had passed since Errogan left him down here, and not even a mouse squeaked on the floors above.

Genesis considered this. "I wouldn't count this as living per se. It's not like I fought Eretimis and lived." He walked the length of his cell, fidgeting with the chains he had worked off his hands years ago. "Rumor has it only one person has ever challenged the Tyrant and lived before."

A crooked smile seized Zarus's expression. "So I've heard. I'd count you as lucky, but that doesn't even seem to describe it." Zarus adjusted his arms, the chains chiming with the movement. They cut deep into his wrists. "But I don't understand why you survived the experiments. What was so different about you that you were the sole survivor?"

"I'm... I'm not sure," Genesis hesitated. He turned around and shrugged. "Eretimis never cared to mention before he threw me down here seventy years ago. Hasn't gotten around to visiting much since either."

Zarus watched Genesis's back with narrowed eyes. What a pathetic lie.

"How's your chest?" Genesis asked, jumping over the topic. Zarus didn't feel the need to press further, not unless it was of use to him, so he let out a sigh.

"Still hurts," he responded, putting his good hand over his heart, "but it's different from before. Everything is just numb now." He went to roll his shoulder, but the feeling was quickly fading from his arm, as was the ability to move it effectively. As Rin would have reminded him, the pain also numbed.

Rin. He hoped, actually *hoped*, that she was alive and hidden, but she couldn't stay hidden forever. Eretimis's hunters would find her in no time. Especially with Errogan's company. The trained trackers would catch their prey before she knew what happened. And it was all his fault.

He remained silent, remembering Rin's screams as Errogan dangled her above the ground. He still heard her pleas for help that he couldn't answer. Gods, he had been so selfish these last few days...

"Are you alright?" Genesis asked, dragging him back to reality. "This isn't just the serum, is it?"

Oh, please. "And how do you know that?" Zarus scoffed.

"Your eyes tell a sad story."

His eyes? He could have rolled those eyes if he wasn't going numb. "No. This is not just the serum," Zarus snapped.

Genesis was his best bet. Even though Zarus knew the hybrid was still keeping something from him. He told Genesis vaguely about what happened. About how he was on Eretimis's radar and he lived alone in the Lennaels for two hundred years. How Eretimis eventually found him and Errogan dragged him here. He left out the bit regarding Rin, and believing Errogan was dead. He still didn't want this man to know exactly who he was, else Genesis might refuse him even the slightest bit of aid. He didn't leave out that someone's life was still in danger because of him. And he didn't forget to mention that if anything else, he owed it to that person to save her.

Genesis kept quiet. Absorbing the information, but Zarus saw contemplation brewing in the kid's eyes. "How well can you see?"

Zarus blinked a few times at the question. Not quite what he was expecting. "Decently," he grunted, finding something to focus on.

Genesis walked up to the cell wall closest to Zarus and met his stare between the bars. "Look at your arm and see how far back the black veins have receded."

"Receded?" Zarus repeated.

"Yes," Genesis pressed, "how much have the veins faded?" His urgency smacked Zarus in the face. "Hurry and look."

Zarus stared at Genesis, but after no further explanation, he relented. He moved toward the staircase where the room was brightest and somehow lifted the edge of his shirt with hands still bound back. Once his eyes adjusted, Zarus let out a curious grunt. "What the hell?" He attempted to blink away the error in his eyes. He let his shirt fall back into place, then looked to where his left sleeve was rolled. It made no sense.

"Well?" Genesis called. "How far back are they?"

Zarus couldn't look away from the veins. "They... they're all the way back to my shoulder..." Eretimis didn't mention this could happen. Zarus glanced back to Genesis. He wiped the awe from his tone, keeping that rising unease stifled. "What does this mean?"

Genesis sighed. "That means... that you have one more day left controlling your own body, if you're lucky." He wrapped his hands around the back of his neck and paced in thought.

A sound caught in Zarus's throat that could have been a scoff. It was a sick, sick joke made up by those almighty gods. He shook his head, wishing he could have rubbed the palm of his hands against his eyes.

Of course, he knew he didn't have long left. Of course he knew that this was going to happen, but every time he heard the words aloud, it chipped a little more of his soul away. "Is that why the feeling in my arm is disappearing?"

Genesis didn't answer for a few seconds. "Once the lines draw back to the incision point, you're done. Your arm is numbing because the serum is working." Which made sense. If the veins spreading to his heart and lungs meant death, then drawing back meant his body accepted the poison. Genesis sighed. At least someone didn't want him dead.

Zarus inhaled deep, soaked in the air of his own will. "Well, if I'm fated to live my last moments of freedom in a bleak and damp dungeon, then at least it was with someone who didn't make me want to rip my ears off." He held his breath and waited.

"Look, Zarus," Genesis said carefully, "I know there's an antidote kept in the fortress." And so he sat up and waited as the words scratched Genesis's throat. "And I can get you there, but only if a guard makes his rounds today, which is unlikely seeing as they haven't come around already."

Compassion was a tool sharper than steel.

"How would you be able to do that?" Zarus asked.

"I won't say."

"And why is that?"

"Because," Genesis bit harshly, "I don't trust you, Zarus Lowwenth. I'm not yet willing to tell you all there is about me, just as you won't tell me. However, we can help one another with more than just distractions from our impending doom. I can get you to the antidote, but only if you help me escape from this hell. I don't know the layout of this labyrinth, and I have a hunch *you* do."

Zarus paced around his cell like a predator circling prey. "Escape is one thing. Keeping away from here is another." He paused, letting his indecision pick away at Genesis. "If I refuse?"

"Then you'll become Eretimis's puppet." Blunt, to the point, with a hint of indifference to Zarus's fate. Too much indifference for giving out the information so easily.

"And you'll stay down here for the rest of your life, and we'll both be as good as dead," Zarus reminded.

Genesis swallowed. His chin dipped down, but he didn't drop his stare. "So what do you say, Lowwenth?"

You are not alone in this fortress.

Zarus smiled. "If you're truly confident you can get me out of this cell, then it's a deal," he said and turned his attention to the stairs. "Allow me to guide a guard down here." Frost started stretching along the walls.

***

If the sudden outburst of magic didn't summon the guard rushing down the stairs, then the incessant arguing did. The demon ran down so quickly, he nearly lost his footing on the ice sheeting the iron steps. The lantern swinging back and forth in the guard's hand blinded Zarus. Being in the darkness for so long took its toll. After the sting of his eyes dulled, he and Genesis exchanged quick glances.

As he suspected, Genesis was too young for his life to have ended so early, but not young enough for Zarus to appear that much older. His unkempt hair wasn't as dark as Zarus's, and his sapphire eyes cut through the shadow with ease. His skin was tan by no definition after being out of the sun's touch for so long. Otherwise, he looked like any man trapped in a dungeon for seventy years should have—covered in old bandages and filth. Another life wasted.

"Once I get free of these chains, I'm going to cut that tongue out, kid," Zarus maliciously promised, not bothering to glance at the guard.

"I'd like to see you try, Lowwenth," Genesis waved off the threat with a lazy hand. "You can barely stand straight." The act rolled off his tongue like second nature. Cold and arrogant. He slowly wrapped his fingers around two of the bars and rested his head between them. "You can't even keep yourself from tripping down a few stairs. How do you plan to hold your hand up long enough to cut off my tongue?"

"It'll be worth the effort wasted," Zarus hissed.

"Both of you shut up!" the guard barked from the stairs, setting down the lantern. He walked toward Zarus and gazed at the tendrils of ice that all drew back to him. The demon failed to hide the surprise in his eyes. Apparently, word was out that he should be as good as dead. The guard didn't know what was about to be unleashed on him.

Zarus didn't back away from the bars as the guard so meekly commanded him to do with his sword. In fact, the demon did little to hide his fear as Zarus glowered, and instead quickly turned toward Genesis's cell.

Genesis had asked for only silence. Zarus had his doubts, but he also had only one day left. So Zarus stood back and waited for Genesis to reveal the last card up his sleeve.

The guard barely regarded Genesis before he slammed the pommel of his blade into the prisoner's forehead. Genesis crashed down to the floor without so much as a grunt.

Contempt rotted the guard's words. "Even as a prisoner, that male is worth more than you'll ever live to be. I'd watch what you say about him."

Genesis offered a sly grin, creeping to his feet as he wiped away the trickle of blood from his brow. Zarus had to hand it to him: a hit to the head like that should have kept him down. "My apologies. I didn't realize you demons held worth to anything other than your hideous selves." Smoke practically blew out of the guard's ears as Genesis wrapped his hands around the bars again. Face to face with the demon; a placid grin still on his lips that poisoned the latter's temper.

"Let's see how long that smile lasts after I'm through with you," the guard spat. Acting without a second thought, he crushed the iron lock on the cell with his gauntleted hands—the notorious demonic strength and temper shining bright as day. All the while, Genesis stood patient. He had no weapon that Zarus could see.

The guard lunged for Genesis's throat. Zarus's heart sank. That was it; Genesis would be dead in a moment and his chance of escape gone. Genesis dodged the demon's attack faster than any human should have been capable of. He was no longer human, and the guard's momentum carried him face first into the stone wall behind.

The dark blood from the guard's shattered nose splattered all over the stone. His cries shook the walls. Zarus watched with predator's intensity, not wanting to miss a thing. He searched for Genesis's intent. Because as of right then, Zarus still found himself behind locked doors.

The guard's whimpers grew to growls. Genesis didn't lift a finger while the demon reached for the weapon at his side. He aimed the dagger with trained precision as he rushed for Genesis's throat. Genesis didn't just jump out of the way this time. He grabbed onto the guard's shoulders and vaulted over him, landing steadily on his feet. Without giving his assailant a chance to counter, Genesis pivoted around and grabbed the demon's temples between his hands. Zarus furrowed his brow, but then he saw the golden aura that emitted from Genesis's hands.

The guard struggled for a heartbeat, but he suddenly fell as still as the dead. It was like a veil fell over his instinct to fight. All the while, Genesis kept a firm hold on the demon's temples, the magic aura glowing on his hands like a torch. The guard's arms slung at his sides, his face submitting ashen and blank. Concentration replaced Genesis's amusement.

Zarus watched the hypnotized guard. What captured his interest the most was the sudden gold that replaced Genesis's sapphire eyes; matching the color of his hands. More time passed, and it became clear Genesis was taking an enormous gamble in using magic that he did not have full control over. Before Zarus could think of another plan if the hybrid's magical grip failed, Genesis took a deep breath. As if the phantom hands holding the guard had been released, the demon relaxed, his face softening with sympathy.

Mages weren't bound by the same laws of magic that tied human users. Their power wasn't taught to them through books, they were born with it. Lived with it every moment of every day, not just when they conjured it through incantations. Suddenly, Genesis's peculiar story explained itself.

The demon led Genesis out of his cage and busted the lock of Zarus's cell afterward. The hybrid made sure he was close enough to the guard so his power reigned strong. Zarus was speechless. Genesis's plan had succeeded. The man chanced his and Zarus's lives on his shaky magic and won.

The sentinel whispered softly, "No one deserves such a fate." But the inner conflict of Genesis's *influence* warring against his own will was clear; his body trembled.

Zarus walked out of his small cell feeling a dulled sense of relief. He was a step closer to escape. He caught glimpse of the sweat beading down Genesis's face. Whatever subdued the demon would not last long.

The leash controlling the guard snapped just as Zarus's shackles hit the ground.

There was a moment where the guard did nothing. Breathing in the air and blinking away the feeling of Genesis's magic. Then the forced expression of sympathy receded into a snarl. The demon saw the two prisoners outside of their cells. His hands reached for the two fighting knives strapped to his legs, his mouth opening to shout for backup. Zarus lunged forward. He grabbed the demon's neck in one hand and violently twisted his head in the other. The demon crashed to the floor, dead. Zarus stripped the demon of his weapons, then finally glanced at Genesis. The man could barely stand on his own.

"Is this the first time you used magic in a while?" he asked.

Genesis was bent over and leaning on the empty cell, but he slowly nodded. Sweat beaded down his temple. They didn't have the time to regain energy.

Zarus took a deep breath, willing his impatience at bay. "Word of advice," he called, already ascending the staircase, "don't rely on magic to save you if it's going to kill you in the process."

Part Three

Eclipsed

Chapter Forty-Three

R in twirled her thumbs beneath the table, not entirely sure what else to say.

She explained everything. The mountain. Zarus. Eretimis's unannounced arrival. Tatsuo. Errogan. Everything and everyone she'd met over the last week. Bjarkh's mood lightened remarkably since they stood in the open desert, and he even listened intently to her encounter with Errogan.

"How foolish are you to wander into the Lennaels alone?" Bjarkh's gravelly voice spurted, as if his restraint to ask wore thin.

Scarlette shot him an unapproving look, but Rin smiled.

"Quite," she said pleasantly, "but instead of getting hung up on the unimportant, why don't we stick to what matters, Bjarkh?" Rin's heart thudded uncontrollably in her chest. She didn't believe there was any other way of dealing with Bjarkh. Feyne assured her beforehand that he means well, that he's a decent person *way* deep down when you get to know him. However, it sounded like he tried to convince himself more than her.

"Agreed," Scarlette laughed. "I don't think we have anything to worry about. She just got tied up in the wrong battles." She smiled at Rin, then stood up from the table. "Now if you two don't mind, Rin and I have business to attend to."

The smile instantly faded from Rin's face. Scarlette turned out to be Feyne's friend that would decipher what everyone sensed about her.

Feyne caught on to her dread and put a firm hand on her shoulder. "Don't worry," he whispered, though loud enough for everyone else to hear, "she doesn't bite hard." He grinned right before one of Scarlette's hands smacked the back of his head.

"Shall we?" The wine-haired girl offered Rin a friendly hand, but Rin caught the sound of Bjarkh's scoff before she accepted.

"Don't waste your talents, Scar. She's just a witless human who almost died on a mountain. You won't find anything important in her." Bjarkh marched out of the conference room and slammed the door shut.

She sighed. She had heard much worse from people back in Aresan. They were just words from a stranger. She wished Feyne had the same idea in his fuming head. He stormed right after Bjarkh. Thankfully, Scarlette put her hand on the shifter's arm and stopped him.

"His daughter's condition is worsening," she whispered.

"That's an excuse," Feyne huffed, but he met Scarlette's stare.

Rin marveled at the silent conversation in their eyes. It was as if they'd studied each other long enough, hard enough, that words were no longer necessary. It was Scarlette's calmness that convinced Feyne to calm down. Her hand slid into his.

"He doesn't understand what he's on about, Rin," Feyne muttered, turning to her with tired eyes.

She shrugged, allowing the remark to brush away. Rin looked him up and down once over. He looked like hell, and he knew exactly what she was thinking.

"I know." He wiped a hand over his face, across the black tattoos around his eyes. "Figure out whatever you need to know. I'll catch up with both of you later on." After a nod from both of them, Feyne squeezed Scarlette's hand, then slipped out of the room. The girl smiled at her with some kind of wicked curiosity.

"He'll be fine once he sleeps," Scarlette said softly. "He has a lot on his mind right now." And for a faint moment, that smile faltered.

"I hope so," Rin mumbled as she looked toward the door. What else was wearing him down to such exhaustion?

"So," Scarlette said, a sudden cheer to her tone. "Where would you prefer to start?" Her stare found Rin's and snorted at the uncertainty within.

"Wherever is more private," Rin shrugged. She didn't even know what it was they were doing. Feyne failed to mention just how Scarlette was going to determine what she was.

The girl grinned. "My room it is then." She strode out of the door without another word. Rin rushed behind to follow.

While walking through the dormitory wings, Rin finally asked where the underground bunker came from. Scarlette told her that when Feyne was searching the desert for demons and humans causing trouble many years ago, he came across the abandoned village. When he explored it, he found a hidden door in one of the broken buildings leading to an enormous complex below ground. No one knows who used to live here, why they had a secret village underground, or why it was destroyed. Feyne took the thick layer of dust as permission to move in.

They passed a few people on the way—Leew was glad to see Rin made it back safely—all who greeted them warmly. Much to her surprise, Rin also caught glimpse of Bjarkh in one room, except he wasn't shouting and glowering. The old man was genuinely smiling while he looked over the shoulder of a young southern woman named Urlae.

"When did Feyne recruit all these people?" Rin asked as they rounded a corner. All the corridors and doors looked the same. She was positive she'd get lost within five minutes of trying to navigate Base. In fact, it was a shock she found the lounge room so quickly earlier.

Scarlette thoughtfully swayed her head side to side. "*Recruit* is stretching it a little. Base wasn't the exact name of this place when he first *recruited* someone other than himself to take action against Eretimis."

"Then when did people start joining?"

The girl smiled. "After he and I met. Feyne and I asked others for help, or rather I convinced him that others would be useful." Scarlette reached the second to last door of the hall and lightly rested her hand on the handle. "Before he found me, Yreyshin was just a lost dog searching for needles in haystacks spanning the continent." An utterly amused grin stretched across her lips as she cracked up at her own joke. The old doorknob hissed like a desert asp as Scarlette twisted it and walked into the bedroom.

"You two look like you've known each other for decades." Rin recalled the chemistry that emitted from the duo. "You understand one another without speaking a word." She stepped into the lightless room after the woman, slowly feeling around the floor with her feet so as not to trip. Thankfully, Scarlette pulled a match out and lit a candle.

"You noticed that, huh?" She moved toward the desk in the corner and sat down on the creaky chair beside it. Rather than cleaning the room, Scarlette had at some point cleared a walkway so she wouldn't trip and break her neck on the wreckage. "He and I have been friends for years now. It just sort of developed in the midst of getting to know him and trusting him to watch my back during raids." She busied her hands by picking up the mess. Clothes, old dishes, stacks of papers.

"If you say," Rin hummed, "but I don't know anyone else who understands their friends like that."

Scarlette's cheeks stained red. "So Aresan, huh? Where does that lie on the map?"

Rin got the general idea of where everything was supposed to go and helped clean, if only to postpone the inevitable. "Just by the northeastern Lennaels, although I doubt it's on any of your maps," Rin laughed. "It's right in the middle of who-knows-where."

"Small town?"

"Tiny village," she corrected, tossing a stale shirt toward a hamper lost in clutter. "I can list every resident by name and give you their eye color, tell you how many goats Mr. Somroy cares for, list off birthdays, and what everyone is doing at this time of day. Any out-of-town visitors usually limit their time in Aresan to the annual market day."

"What's the annual market day?" Scarlette asked, filing the last hectic stack of papers into an organized pile on the desk. "Sounds like an excellent opportunity to study people."

Study people?

Rin paused. "A day when the merchants kind enough to travel that far west come to town and sell their wares." She tightened her grip on the pillow she was straightening out on the bed. The last market day was only two months ago. Not even into this year's winter yet, and those sniveling merchant eyes looked at her like she was dirt on the road. "It's only fun if you have money to dump on their junk," Rin continued on, resuming her work. "If not, then they treat you like waste." Scarlette remained silent long enough that Rin glanced back and made sure she was still there in the room. "Everything alright?"

The girl nodded, her taut stare holding firm on Rin's back. "People can be harsh."

Rin shrugged. "People will be as unpredictable as people can be. It's not worth fretting over," she smiled, finishing her side of the room. "Da taught me that ultimately, I'm the only one who has control over my feelings. Plus, it's hard to see what's ahead when your chin's so far down." She smiled, wondering what her father was doing at that moment. "Also taught me how to toss oats beneath the merchant stands when goats were nearby and watch the chaos unfold."

Scarlette's tight expression loosed a bellied laugh. "Your dad sounds like a respectable man." She threw the last piece of trash into the bin beside the desk. Face to face with Rin, she slid around in her seat, now sitting backwards on the wooden frame.

Rin's smile widened. "He really is." The thought of her father weighed down on her heart. Any other day, he would be stretching out before the hearth, studying one of his textbooks after a long day's work outside. He didn't even know where she was. To him, she was dead as much as she was alive. She'd have to write him, explaining everything that had happened. Before she left for Lilit, maybe.

"So," she hummed, rapping a finger along the bed frame, "don't get around to cleaning often?"

Scarlette's nose wrinkled. "No, I really don't. When I'm not working with Feyne or on patrol, I'm usually dealing with some other project, have my face shoved in old scrolls, or sleeping. But," she stretched, tilting forward on the creaky chair so she was balancing on the two front legs, "I figured that you'd appreciate it if it was clean." Rin nearly squirmed under her studious stare. "Plus, you don't seem all too thrilled to learn about yourself."

"That obvious, huh?"

The girl nodded. "You know, Rin, you don't have to do this. Feyne may act like a fae, but he can't make you do something just because you made a deal. Whatever reason he has, it doesn't overrule your feelings." She set the chair back on all four legs, resting her head on her arms lazily folded atop the back of the frame. "He can be a bit of an overbearing prick sometimes. The choice is yours."

"I know," Rin muttered, not letting herself think too much about the temptation, "but if I learn what's different about me, then the better prepared I can be when running from Eretimis." Even hinting that there was a threat upon her life cast a shadow over the conversation. She tried to force out a smile, but her lips could barely manage anything. "I do have a question though..." Rin tapped her feet on the floor and sat on the bed. "How are you going to find what we're looking for? Feyne never explained it," Rin said, trying not to sound scared.

"Simple, I'm going to offer you as a blood sacrifice and leave you for judgment under the kaeth Lhaerem's watch."

Rin blinked once, twice. Her mouth opened, then closed, then opened once more. "Come again?" A dull hum sounded in her head.

Scarlette straightened in the chair, a smirk breaking her deadpan stare. "Sorry, couldn't resist," she laughed, dancing her long nails along the side of the frame. "I'm going to read your aura."

Rin's mouth did not close. "My aura..." she repeated, but Scarlette nodded in confirmation. "And just how on Armiria are you going to do that, Scarlette? Are you a user?" She honestly didn't know why she was so shocked. She'd believe anything at this point if the right person told her.

Scarlette was still laughing. "Call me Scar," she corrected, "and no, I have no magic, but it's a fairly simple process, though difficult to explain. Basically, I learned how to look past the obvious, and find the more specific details about people." She realized how vague and lacking her explanation was rather quickly, Rin's blank expression enough of a hint, and decided the long version would be easier to understand. "Look, Rin, I don't have a trace of magic in my blood, but I discovered a technique that was used centuries ago by humans who wanted a fast way to identify friend from foe. They looked beyond the physical and saw each other in a simpler way. Personally, I believe that this technique was an answered prayer from the gods during the Crimson War., but it didn't say how it was developed."

"What didn't say?" Rin asked, keeping up with the story.

"The scroll I found that taught this to me."

"And where did you find this scroll?"

"In the ruins of an ancient civilization's library."

Rin blinked again. "Why, of course. I haven't been there recently. Has much changed?"

"The upkeep went way downhill in recent centuries since it burned to the ground." Scarlette practically drank Rin's sarcasm. "Oh, the life of a scholar. Anyway, in order to tap into this power, a series of barriers in the mind need to be crossed. Which, let me tell you," she rolled her eyes, "was a colossal pain to do without any advice other than a centuries old scrap of paper written in a dialect of Weslyte used three hundred years ago. Then you have to do a certain meditation that initiates the ability." Scarlette shrugged, losing interest in her explanation. "I would let you read the scroll for yourself, but I left it in the library when I continued my travels. It wasn't mine to take. I tried to go back a few years later, but I couldn't find the city again. It was almost like it was never in Weslyc to begin with," she joked, talking like it was some campfire ghost story.

"So, how skilled are you?" Rin leaned in, intrigued by the fact any ole human could master the trick.

"Auras are tricky. They have different parts, and the further down you go into the layers, the more detailed they get. The scroll said that some people who mastered the ability could see how old the beings they examined were. I, on the other end," she waved her hand at herself, "can look just into the first few layers of humans. I can tell you what species you are, the general part of the world you're from, and what type of magic you possess, if any. Auras differ depending on the species, so I'm really only useful when it comes to reading humans. Beyond that is information I can't understand without multiple information pools to analyze, since the scroll was written after the other species fell into myth. I have a hunch that the second layer of a demon's aura reveals if they're a pureblood." She ran her hand through the side of her head that wasn't shaved down. "Once you learn this ability, you're marked for it," she gestured to her eyes, "so the gods know who took the time to appreciate their gift, I guess."

Rin scratched the back of her head. Feyne no doubt knew all this, and had learned all about it when he and Scarlette met. What was he planning to achieve from Scarlette reading her aura? "I'm very interested to see that in action," she smiled sheepishly. "Do I have to do anything for you to start?" Rin decided it was best for her to make herself comfortable, so she picked up her legs and sat with them crossed on the edge of the bed.

"No," Scarlette said, "just give me a moment."

Scarlette immediately fell silent, closed her god-touched eyes, and sat with her legs crossed and hands resting on her knees. Her back was straight as an arrow. She was meditating while sitting backwards on the chair within seconds.

Half a minute had passed before Scarlette slowly opened her eyes. And when she did, Rin's brow furrowed. "That's it?" Scarlette's features didn't change at all.

Scarlette nodded, concentration holding her tongue. Everything about the girl was the same as it was a minute ago. Scarlette gazed at Rin with her post-meditative eyes, and only then did Rin understand. There was no physical change in reading auras because it was not magic.

The scholar looked through Rin with her magenta eyes, landing at her core. Two minutes passed before Scarlette's eyes finally closed. When they opened, that far-offness was replaced by skepticism.

"What is it?" Rin asked, mirroring Scarlette's deepening frown.

She opened her mouth, but nothing came out, not even a sigh. "Good news and bad news."

Rin raised her brow. "What's the good news?"

"I can confidently confirm you are a human," the girl offered with a meek shrug.

"And the bad news?"

"I couldn't tell you beyond that."

Chapter Forty-Four

Rin shifted her eyes about Feyne's room while Scarlette delicately woke the shifter from his sleep. The wolf opened his eyes, smiled at the redhead, and groggily rose from his bed. Then Scarlette explained.

She spoke to the shifter quietly at first, hushed so only he heard as Rin stood on the other side of the room. It was not a large space, but unlike Scarlette's room, it was spotless. The tribal decorations on the walls no doubt signified his late pack. Her eyes landed on a table no bigger than a footstool, a weathered mat underneath. Two unlit candles sat on top of it, a small white cup in between with six black sticks protruding from the brim. Each stick was singed, burned low. Laid before the cup was a thin line of sand. Etched into the wall above the shrine was a thick horizontal line with six points dripping down, connected by arches—resembling what Feyne's tattoo would look like if it was straightened out.

The shifter's voice rose from a whisper, and Rin tore her eyes away from his family shrine.

"What do you mean you've never seen someone like her before?" Feyne yawned, pulling his shirt over his body.

"I mean that I have never read an aura like hers before. She's human, she's from Nokomic, but I don't know her magic wielding status."

Scarlette tapped a finger against the side of Feyne's bed frame as she spoke, then shrugged. "There are a lot of magic types out there, but I've seen a decent amount. Rin doesn't match any of them."

"Not even a little?" Feyne stretched and rose from the bed.

"Wouldn't matter if she did," Scarlette reminded. "Even the slightest difference of pigment in an aura could mean she's a different species." Feyne only grunted at this, continuing to walk the room back and forth.

"Maybe I'm just deformed?" Rin suggested, feeling what was left of the day's heat suffocate the room. They must have been close to another of the bunker's entrances.

"The magic layer would remain unchanged either way," Scarlette muttered aloud as she chewed on her thumbnail. She sat on Feyne's bed. Both she and Rin looked to Feyne, who now leaned against the closed door.

"Thoughts?" Rin inquired. The silence that accompanied the heat made her head buzz.

Feyne weighed his words and took a seat on the edge of his bed next to Scarlette. "That depends," he shrugged. "You carried out your end of the deal, and I've kept you from Lilit long enough." Rin took in a deep breath, scrunching the loose fabric of her clothes in her fingers. "So I'll take you there..." he paused for a moment, "if you still want that."

Rin sunk into herself. Damn him for sensing her desire to stay. He smirked, and she couldn't help but huff. "Am I really that transparent?"

He shrugged again, a lazy grin forming. "I'm even better at reading people than Scar is."

Scarlette outright laughed and flicked the shifter on the nose. "What *Yreyshin* is trying to say," she gave him a sidelong glance as the side of his lip twitched at the name, "is that there's room for you here. We can tell you're thinking about staying. So what do you think?"

A smile grew across Rin's face as she let herself consider saying yes. Adventure, travel, unknown places and people—*helping* people. It was what she always wanted, maybe even needed. But... a frown replaced joy. "I want to stay," she explained, chewing the inside of her cheek. "There is nothing going for me in Aresan. I don't want to farm for the rest of my life, and I can't stand the thought of having an entire world out there and not having seen it. And I owe it to Zarus to help get him out of that hell... but I still have loose ends I need to tie up before I can commit to anything." She met both the human's and shifter's stare, realizing she was dragging on. "Finding my mother was just an excuse to see some of the world. To be honest, I don't think I ever expected to find her in Lilit. I've felt so helpless this entire week, and I thought that maybe if I had other matters to attend to, I wouldn't have to face that feeling. However, after seeing what you guys do here, how you help the people that are caught in the havoc Eretimis wreaks all over the world, I can't keep ignoring it. I think I have a place here. I can help others who feel powerless with the power I've found. However, I need to talk to my dad. I need to tell him that I'll be leaving home in person." Rin's mouth was dry. She'd definitely need to get used to living in a desert. Feyne suddenly rose to his feet and walked to where she sat.

"I completely agree." He put his hand on her shoulder. "Just know that you have a place here, whether you wait a few weeks or a few years to take it."

Rin smiled at him. To think she set out on this journey with not a clue of what she wanted. Look where she was now.

"So what else did you plan?" she asked. The shifter rose a brow. She smirked wickedly at him. "You think you're the only one who picks up on things?" A sly grin followed. "Look, I said I don't want to join Base right this second. However, I'm still curious why Scar has never seen an aura like mine before. So what plan did you make up to figure it out?"

Both Scarlette and Feyne stared at her for a moment. "Like I said, humans need more credit than they're given," he muttered while he wiped the bottom of his face. Aloud, "I know someone else who might help if you're interested." She dipped her chin, wordlessly urging him on. "Luna. She lives in the caves we passed in the highlands only a half day's journey away."

Rin weighed the offer. Of course she wanted to go, but a day and a half could easily go wrong. She flicked her emerald eyes to Feyne. "When would we leave?"

"As soon as we can, I'd assume," he shrugged. "Is that alright?"

"Actually," she considered. Right away was too soon. Rin needed to at least wait a day. To give Tatsuo more time to return. "Can we leave tomorrow? If I try to make another trip across the desert with no sleep, I very well might die out there."

Feyne yawned himself. She really felt bad about waking him so abruptly, especially if she was going to stay another day. "As long as you don't mind waiting, then that's fine." He ran his fingers through his dark hair, combing the strands out of his face for a moment. "To better the chances of surviving, I suggest we travel at night again."

Rin grinned. "I wouldn't walk out any of these doors any other way."

Scarlette's graceless snort intertwined with her laugh. She slowly stood. "Since you're here for the night, you can bunk with me. You look a little too tired to find your room on your own again."

Rin's face might have burned red at the jest, but the exhaustion stole her care. She didn't want to be by herself tonight. "If you don't mind, I'd really appreciate it," she smiled, eyelids growing heavier by the second.

Feyne—beyond the point of talking—eventually growled at Scarlette and Rin for keeping him awake, to which the girls bid the shifter farewell and went back to Scarlette's bedroom. They chatted long into the night. Rin learned a fair share about the past-enriched, well-versed Scarlette Draelin lying on the opposite side of the bed. She even decided the girl might have been a little mad in the head. She wasn't sure if she had ever talked so much about herself in one sitting.

That was until Scarlette blew out the candles in the room one by one, and Rin remembered why she was dreading shutting her eyes. She only hoped the foul feeling in her chest didn't mean another dream like last night.

Chapter Forty-Five

Irritation twisted Zarus's expression. It was foolish of Genesis to risk their escape on the hunch he could control his powers. And Zarus wouldn't congratulate a fool for damning luck.

When they ran into a demon, they snuck through the shadows. Zarus guided them through the labyrinth of the fortress, calling forth his memory from three hundred years ago and hoping that nothing had changed since. Just as he feared, the numbness consuming his body traveled further. It became tedious work to recall which paths to take. The thick fog of pain dissipated, but a numbing chill replaced it. Zarus needed to find something to focus on before he passed out, so he finally spoke. "What's the story behind that bandage?"

Genesis glanced at his left arm, wrapped from wrist to sleeve. He replied, but there was distrust in his eyes. "Eretimis. After he learned I was a user and that's why none of the other experiments worked, he wasn't pleased." He rubbed the filthy cloth with his thumb. "It never healed."

Zarus stopped his hand from reaching for the scar above his heart. Or the permanent marks stretching across his back from countless whips. Or the mangled skin of his left shoulder. Any of the injuries inflicted by Eretimis's rage. Whatever Genesis classified himself as, man or demon or whatever, he had strength in him.

He weighed his words carefully while gazing at the bandage. "Scars will always be a part of us, but I can try to heal that one once we're safe."

Genesis nodded, but adjusted his arm so it was out of Zarus's sight. So little trust between each other, but he still smiled. "The offer doesn't go unappreciated, Lowwenth, but this bandage will be gone shortly."

Before Zarus questioned Genesis, he spotted two shadows approaching around the corner. He used his weakened magic and conjured a misty darkness that blended him and the hybrid into the shadows on the walls. Zarus tuned in to what sounded like a female speaking as they came into view.

"I don't believe you."

"I'm telling you, it's true."

"There's no way in Ashnagz that the boss is bringing her here. She's running his forces back in Eroz."

The second demon—a male, young and lively—chatted away, his voice bouncing wall to wall. "I'm telling you, I heard the hunters talking about it in the dining hall. Nessriq is coming to Armiria to help things around here."

Who is Nessriq?

Zarus couldn't recall the name. He wouldn't have been taken aback by it if not for the fact someone who started serving Eretimis only three hundred years ago at most was running the entirety of his forces on the home world to the demons. The thoughts made his head stir. Or maybe it was the serum.

"You're full of Flames n' Soot. What need does our Lord have of her? We have Errogan keeping things in check around here," the female countered.

The male shrugged. "I thought so too, but if he's bringing in both of his hands, right and left, it makes you wonder what he's up to. Maybe we're finally gonna do more than sit on our asses all day. I mean, when's the last time any of us did something of importance—"

The female stopped dead in her tracks. Her hand flew to cover the boy's mouth. She tried to contain the sheer terror consuming her words, but only did so well. "Careful how you speak, Rone, or you'll pay for that loose tongue." After a quick glance down both sides of the hallway, the female lowered her arm and squared her shoulders. She spoke low and stern. "I know you're new here, but that is no excuse to defile the strategies of our Dark Lord, especially in his domain." She leaned in and whispered low. "You never know who might be listening." The male tried to apologize, but she didn't give him the opportunity before she led them down the hall.

Zarus stayed in the veil of his magic until the footsteps faded into the distance. He was still processing what he overheard when Genesis shifted beside him.

"We need to keep going," he said, looking hard and long at the cloak of darkness over their shoulders. It had been the only reason the guards didn't sense them.

Zarus took one more moment to finish his thought before he acknowledged the warning. "I know," he said shortly, dispersing his shadow magic and leading the way to where he first felt death moving through his veins.

***

The laboratory was finally in sight. The door that would save him from a horrendous fate. The numbness reached further over his mind, suffocating as much of his will as it could. The time for caution ran out. Even Genesis stood restlessly behind him. One deep breath of the air, and Zarus forced his legs across the hall.

Zarus hadn't dared to hope until this point. Hope blinded, and he needed clarity to be free of this corrupted fortress run by a corrupted demon. Now he wasn't basing his hope off of Errogan. And that hopeful spark didn't fade when he found the door to the laboratory locked. Not even when he grabbed onto the handle and poured every ounce of frost and darkness he had left onto it. The handle snapped off like a dead branch.

Genesis walked into the laboratory while Zarus gasped for breath, glaring at the hypocrisy.

"Sit down on that table before you pass out," Genesis sighed as he searched through countless cabinets and racks. Unbalance seized hold of his gait as well.

"Watch it," Zarus growled, holding his hand against his forehead as he closed the door behind him. His blood still decorated the stone table. "Just get that godsdamned antidote before someone shows up."

For a moment, only the sound of clinking bottles and Genesis rummaging through the cabinets filled the room. "You know, if you got rid of that attitude, I might tolerate your bitter ass long enough to be friends," the hybrid retorted, finally pulling a glass vial out from a cabinet on the far side of the room.

"All of my friends end up trying to kill me," Zarus grumbled as he slouched on the table. His head spun endlessly.

"I don't blame them." Genesis said nothing more of it. "Let's see that arm." Zarus opened his eyes to find Genesis standing over him. He held a bottle of translucent green liquid in one hand, and a thin surgical knife and cloth in the other. He grunted his discomfort as he rolled his sleeve back. The discolored veins had raced down his arm, nearly back to the cauterized wound. Less than an hour from disappearing. "Now see how lucky you are to have run into me?" Genesis jested, though even he couldn't drum up the effort to smirk as he popped the cork out of the vial.

Zarus faked a laugh, letting his heavy gaze slide to the ceiling. "Just get it over with so we can hold hands on our merry escape."

Genesis didn't argue. After a moment of staring at the vial of serum, the hybrid gently grabbed Zarus's forearm and sucked in a deep breath. Zarus braced himself as Genesis dug the knife into his arm, reopening the wound. As blood welled onto the table, Genesis poured the green liquid into the wound, then pressed the cloth over it.

Zarus bit down on a yowl so hard his teeth could have shattered. Searing pain laced his arm. Then it stopped. It was a wave of cool water rushing through his head. Zarus finally released the tension in his body. Genesis handed over the vial and told him to drink half. Zarus sat upright with a sudden sense of clarity to his head, like the veil covering his senses had burned to ash. He drank half of the antidote, the metallic taste burning his throat. Even after mere seconds, he felt like he had died and risen back to life. He looked at Genesis with clear eyes for the first time, and the sight was better with clouded senses.

Part of Genesis was lost in the countless years of solitude and torture. His sapphire eyes were hollowed, his famished face bled dry of all life.

Without the serum clotting his mind, Zarus realized he had not eaten a single thing since being dragged to this forsaken place. His stomach yearned for food, but he couldn't afford to search for it. Instead, his gaze fell to the edge of the table. "What of the rest of it?" he asked, pushing back onto his feet—feet that held him upright without the hazard of giving out beneath his weight.

Genesis glanced down at the vial, and something sparked in his eyes. Without saying another word, he picked up the bottle and downed the rest of the antidote. "That," he said, grimacing against the unnatural taste, "would be for me."

Zarus could have cursed himself for not having figured it out earlier. The hybrid slowly unraveled the bandage around his left arm, and Zarus's jaw clenched at the sight. He thought his own arm was bad after the serum tarnished it; that was nothing. He felt like a whining child compared to what Genesis had to deal with for over half a century.

Mutilated was a delicate way of putting it. His veins still contained the control serum after so many years, tinting them an inky black, just as Zarus's were. That's where the similarities ended. The skin from Genesis's forearm to his shoulder was a bleak grey; cracked and dried to the point his flesh resembled patchy scales. Eretimis didn't gain control when he poisoned Genesis. The hybrid's body tried to reject the foreign substance until he died, yet with the unnatural resilience Eretimis twisted into his body, Genesis didn't die. He suffered a far worse fate.

"Disgusting, isn't it?" Genesis's face contorted as he looked at it. "I was surprised to see how much my body fought back after it rejected the serum; the experiment's side effects could only do so much though."

Zarus's blood chilled at the thought. "I take it you're right handed?" Only then did it occur to him that the antidote might take longer to work on Genesis.

Genesis nodded and walked toward the door. "I'm hoping it's only a temporary side effect."

Zarus stared calculating eyes between Genesis's shoulder blades. Now. Now would have been the time to do it, to ensure that he would escape from the fortress free of drawbacks. Quick and easy, and Genesis would have been none the wiser. However, Zarus found himself unwilling to bend to the demand. Not that he couldn't, he just... wouldn't. He would have, had this been a year ago, six months ago. Even eight days ago. Now? He wouldn't kill Genesis. Not the man who saved him. Zarus threw away the cruel thought and forced his legs to move after the hybrid peering out the door. "Let's hope."

Chapter Forty-Six

The night was long and without rest. Every time Rin closed her eyes, some little sound echoed throughout Base and sent an alarm blaring in her head to prepare herself. Her wandering mind didn't ease her worries. It would suddenly show her a picture of a dark shadowy being breaking down the door. Not by the will of physical strength, oh no. Its sheer presence crumbled the wood panels into dust. Rin stifled the urge to jump at every meaningless noise, if only to not wake Scarlette.

The rest of the day was no better. Scarlette was out on surveillance again, Feyne was out of his room by the time Rin made her way over, and no one had seen where he ran off to. Everyone else seemed to be indulged in something of their own while she sat there, waiting for the clock to tick. It was only Bjarkh who paid a moment of attention to her in the hall. And though she didn't believe it possible, the man was rather cheery compared to normal.

"Something finally cured your scowl?" Rin grumbled with a furrowed brow as the man rammed into her shoulder as he passed instead of moving around her.

He almost didn't deign to respond, but Bjarkh couldn't resist the twitch of his lips. "Just the thought of embarking on a new mission, Miss Nowell." His teal eyes stared down at her, and Rin felt the urge to back away. It seemed the man had warmed up to her since their first meeting. Some of that kindness Feyne promised poking through, but his intensity alarmed her. Scarlette mentioned he used to be a captain in Damrok's military, joining Base's efforts after retirement to find advancements in medicine for those in need in Armiria. He hadn't exactly been unpleasant to her. He walked along without another comment, not bothering with a goodbye. Bjarkh was a man of few words and a one-track mind. She could only assume the Damrian army was responsible. Feyne vouched for him. Perhaps she was just jumpy today.

Rin waited the rest of the day. For whatever was around every corner to get her, or for someone to come back and talk to her. She resented the thought of going outside to find someone in the unbearable heat, but she felt she needed to. Because the more time she spent alone, the closer to the edge she got. Rin finally made her way back to her room. One touch of the pillow beneath her head was all it took.

***

"Rin. Rin, wake up."

Groggily, she opened her eyes and followed the hand shaking her arm up to the shifter.

Feyne sat on the edge of her bed, trying his best not to startle her. Maybe word of her recent demeanor had spread. Maybe he was just being kind as usual. What mattered was the fact Feyne was covered in specs of sand and waking her up.

She took a deep breath. "Do I have to?" The shifter smiled at her, but Rin saw the austerity within. "What's wrong?" she asked, propping herself up with one elbow.

He shook his head, but the smile remained. "Nothing." Without giving her a chance to respond, Feyne was walking toward the door.

With little else to account, Rin fastened her boots, grabbed her scimitar, and headed out the door.

There was still no sign of the fiery *narikaah* when she caught up with Feyne in the lounge. He was talking briefly with the girl named Urlae, but even then, the shifter didn't seem like his usual self. He was distant and unapproachable.

They took longer to leave than Rin expected. Feyne seemed to keep forgetting something just before they left, whether it be assigning tomorrow's watch-duty or grabbing more rations. Something deep within told her to stay. Though she might have been mistaken, Feyne's surprise delays led her to believe something was stirring the need to stay within him as well. She didn't voice this anxiety. It would only delay their journey and back up everyone's schedule. They walked out of Base without an utterance. Feyne shifted into a wolf on the surface before she convinced herself to suggest staying another day. He left her to pick up his clothes and prowled ahead. Whatever was bothering him, Feyne had no wishes to speak about it. Rin gazed back at the dilapidated village only once. She didn't dare look back again until it was far from sight.

She found the desert much more enjoyable at night. The cold air nipped, but it was nothing compared to the icy pierce on the Lennaels. She was fairly comfortable since Scarlette gifted her with some warmer clothes. The Wolf of the Desert moved along the dunes with no inkling of slowing.

Rin judged just over an hour had passed since they left Base. Worry ate at the back of her mind. She felt the words bubbling up about her paranoia, about the dream she had. Feyne trekked fast ahead. Rin lowered her gaze to the loose ground below. She opened her mouth, but didn't know how to explain it.

Apparently, her sigh was more audible than she thought. Feyne glanced back to her, his amber eyes concerned.

"I have a bad feeling," she admitted.

He looked at her in silence.

The wolf halted. Feyne's eyes were level with her own, his giant nose prodding her to continue. She never realized how massive the beast was.

"It's just a dream I had." Feyne's eyes widened so large that Rin thought they might pop out. He hastily nodded, snorting urgency.

Rin turned her head away and focused on the horizon. She hesitated, not wishing to upset him. Her next breath hadn't left her lungs before a light as bright as the stars above flashed from the corner of her eye.

"What was the dream?" Feyne grounded.

"Feyne, what are you thinking!" Rin shouted, averting her eyes even further away from the bare *ghren*. "You're going to get sick out here like that!"

He didn't care about his nudity in the middle of the moon-licked desert. He took another step forward, to which Rin took one back. "The dream, Rin! What was your dream about?"

Rin felt the redness of her face saturate. She took a deep breath, suddenly feeling as though she and the shifter became a little too close too quickly.

Rin told him about the light that made it near impossible to see, the watchful being that brought tears to her eyes, the chasm that spewed dark poison into her lungs. The fear. She still felt the fog flooding into her throat. Felt herself dying. It made her nauseated. And she wasn't the only one. The more she described what happened in the hellish nightmare, the more Feyne looked like he was going to be sick.

Rin's stomach roiled. The last time she saw that expression was when Zarus looked at Errogan. A frigid gust of wind blew the sand over her shoes when Feyne's mouth finally opened. The terror in his eyes said it all. "We need to run. *Fast.*"

Feyne turned around and sprinted toward Base, shifting mid-stride. He did not wait for her. A new fear stole her mind, and with it, Rin found she ran across the desert in step with the wolf.

The cool night air bit her lungs, but Rin did not allow herself to stop.

They ran the exact path they came from—footprints barely wiped away by the wind. Rin kept her focus on the wolf running ahead and nothing else. She didn't let herself wonder of the horror in Feyne's eyes.

A harsh drumming welled deep in her head as she leapt over a hill in the sand, snapping her jaw down on impact. It was all too convenient. Her dream, the paranoia clawing at her all morning. It had to mean something.

Smoke suffocated her nostrils, filled her eyes.

No.

She hissed her clouded breath when she saw the last dune before Base. She bit down, forcing her legs to surge up the hill. Feyne did the same.

Ten feet. Ten more feet and they would be at the top and she'd see that there was nothing to worry about. There had to be nothing.

Please.

It was going to be okay. It was all going to be okay. Rin balled her fists so tight her nails cut into her skin.

Please gods, spare them.

The human and the shifter finally reached the top of the dune, and Rin felt a wave of nausea overcome her. It didn't matter. There were souls who would never feel a damn thing again.

Chapter Forty-Seven

Rin sprinted down the hill into the burning desert. Smoke and ash clouded her vision, and Feyne was nowhere to be found. Death was all around her. Death of the members of Base. Death of the innocents that got caught up in the fires. Death of the hope of becoming closer to the people who once lived here. She hadn't even reached the village yet... Rin held back the burning tears that gathered in her eyes. *There will be a time to mourn,* she told herself as she checked the next body, *but now you need to help them.*

Every body she found was cold, stiff, but none were burnt. Even those covered in flames were untouched by it until recently. She tried to push the fact that she knew these people down as far as it would go each time she dragged herself to another face. Some of them she couldn't even reach, the fire's consumption too ravenous. She said a quick prayer for everyone she came across. Every single one.

"Is anybody still alive!" Rin called as loud as she could. Her voice was so small, so useless in the thick smog that eclipsed the stars. No matter how many times she yelled, no one answered.

Think. Think!

She wiped the sweat and ash from her brow. Even the wrap she held over her mouth couldn't stand against the toxic smoke.

"How?" Rin looked at the destruction. She stood in the center of the village, the crumbled buildings now black with char. The smoke cast sinister shadows upon everything.

Stop it! Rin yelled at herself when she felt that first chip of hope wither away. *Get it together, there still might be survivors.*

She forced herself forward. The bunker, that's where she would try next. There had to be people down there, safe from the death that loitered on the surface. Safe and figuring out a way to put out the fires against the wind aiding its spread. The well. It was the closest door, just at the edge of the strip. Rin ran.

Just as she made it past the last crumbled wall and the shape of the well appeared through the smoke, she skidded to a stop. Her breath caught in her throat.

Debris buried the well. Rubble from the village, packed with gritty mud from the sand—ton after ton of sand—and rocks. Placed to keep something out, or worse yet, in. She whispered to the gods, horror on her tongue.

Rin sprinted to the next entrance where she and Feyne had exited earlier that night, and found her prayers unanswered. No matter which way she tried to go, which hidden door she sought, all the bunker entrances bathed in flames. Every damn one. Rin trembled. Nothing would be left to save after the fire went out.

Rin's stomach churned, her heart raced, her breath hitched.

This isn't happening. This can't be happening.

Every time she blinked, wiping her eyes with her soot-covered hands, she still found the fires to be very real, the sweat flooding into her eyes very real, and the burning of her skin very very real. The nausea beating against her stomach worsened.

No, no, no.

Rin shook her head, as if denying it would make it all untrue. She backed away, trying to convince herself of the reality unfolding around her. It all happened so quickly. Even when her tears swelled, even when her foot caught on something behind her and she toppled over.

Rin looked beside her. "Leew?" she asked, a faint wither of hope searching for any answer. She received no such thing. The man remained on his back, sword in his bloodied hand. Tenderly, she placed her hands on his chest. Warmth embraced them. Rin glanced at her hands and instantly looked away from the gash reaching along his torso. She couldn't convince herself to move. She stared at her hands, at the crimson and ash covering her skin.

A sobbing cry finally escaped as she pulled herself from the corpse. She forced herself to turn away, holding her legs up to her chest. She was outside of the village. The fire wasn't as thick, nor the smoke that made her cough endlessly through the tears.

"How?" Rin cried again. She looked up at the stars that were just barely visible. How in the world could this all have happened so quickly? How could all the entrances be closed off?

"We're going to find out."

Rin felt like she should have jumped, but she didn't. She glanced back to the clothed shifter, standing over her like a tower that reached into the heavens. She didn't even notice she dropped the satchel holding his clothes.

His voice was raw from the smoke, his ashen face streamed where his own tears had fallen. The fierce shadows cast by the fire danced grimly on Feyne's face. He offered his hand to her, his stare heavy. Where was Scarlette?

Rin would find no answer sitting here. She grasped Feyne's hand.

She hesitated, but found the will to ask, "Did... did you find any—"

"No." Feyne held his stare forward. She slowly nodded, taking a deep breath, and followed him away from the village.

Rin took one last glance at Leew. She asked the gods to lead Vulyn to his soul and give safe passage to Ashnagz. There, he would rest in peace.

Rin ran after Feyne before she lost him in the night. The desert seemed so quiet compared to the commotion of the fire. When she finally caught up to him out of the fire's light, she heard the faintest voices far ahead.

"Who is that?" she asked, but he shook his head. Rin rested her hand on her scimitar.

Feyne led them to the conversation taking place. They halted in the shadows, listening closely.

"Did you find them?" a male asked.

The second voice, feminine, answered. "They weren't in the bunker. The scouts sent into the village never came back either." The voice purred, amused by the whole situation. "Which could only mean one thing."

The first laughed. "This one was actually telling the truth, after all." Rin heard a thunk, followed by a cry. "It would insult the Mighty to infer that your organization was any form of challenge. But I say, killing you will give me more than enough pleasure after the trouble you and that pathetic bow have caused me."

Rin's chest burned. She jolted forward without a thought. She didn't know who was at the mercy of this murderer, but it didn't matter. Too many had died. As soon as her foot made it a step, a tower of pale blue flames erupted. So scalding she felt as though her bones crackled with the heat, and so bright it brought both she and Feyne into the light. The owner of the voice jumped out of its way just in time, the light allowing Rin to see the scene.

"Do not," Tatsuo heaved, "forget who it was that singed your legendary hunters to ash, you bastards." His voice was a hiss of pain, but the taunt was so clear that Rin could pin it through the night.

She almost loosed a cry. He came back. She looked behind to ask Feyne what their plan was, but he was gone.

Two people, there were two people still alive. Tatsuo was one of them. The other?

"Oh, don't worry, Kurosawa," said the male, "I haven't forgotten about you." Rin squinted through the dark. Tatsuo's body sprawled in the sand, unable to get to his feet. "But you're not going anywhere. After all, you were stupid enough to jump in front of the steel meant for the human."

"If you really want to play, *dragon-breed*," the female demon mocked, "then you'll have to wait. You don't have the answers we need."

Tatsuo scoffed, "And you think the human does? What could she possibly know that two thick headed demons don't already?" He was trying to draw them away, Rin realized. Bring them toward him, even if his wounds kept him on the ground. It worked. The male took a step toward Tatsuo, but stopped there.

The male demon chuckled, opened his thin lips, apt to shut down Tatsuo's retorts, but he wasn't given the chance. Faster than he could react, an arrow shot through his skull from below. He fell to the ground faster than it took Rin to recognize the bow.

"You bitch!" seethed the female, pivoting on her heels to charge at the magenta-eyed archer who was climbing off the ground.

"Maybe you shouldn't have taken your eyes off of me, a mere human," Scarlette spat as she drew out another arrow and fired it just as the demon leapt for her.

The female wailed as the arrow pinned into her leg. She fell to the ground, though picked her bulky self up in an instant. "Just tell us where the girl is, and we'll be off." She pulled out the arrow like it was a splinter. "It's as easy as that!"

"But it isn't," Scarlette reasoned, another arrow in hand, "because you've killed off all who know where she went. I'm the only one left, and I'd rather accept death than help you."

The demon walked on her leg like nothing was wrong, the ugliest smirk curling on her face. "Then death you shall have." The female withdrew a hatchet strapped to her back, tossing it back and forth between her hands like it was a child's toy rather than an instrument of death. Before Rin ran between them, a ring of fire circled the arrogant demon. Rin glanced at Tatsuo; he stumbled on his feet, keeping his weight leaned against his spear. Blood soaked his tunic, right where Zarus had once injured him.

The demon glared at the *narikaah*. "You expect to delay her death when you can't even stand straight?" she sneered.

A morbid chuckle left Tatsuo's lips. His arm held firm to his wound. "No, but I can distract your shrill ass."

The demon's smirk straightened. She whipped her head around to Scarlette to find the girl hadn't moved. Instead, a wolf pounced through the flames and tackled the demon from behind. They flew through the other side of the fiery ring, the demon landing hard and shrieking as something snapped. The beast sank his teeth into her neck. Snarling, growling, tearing; Feyne unleashed his wrath.

Tatsuo had used his fire to cover the flash of Feyne's shift. It was brilliant.

The demon screamed, her blood pouring onto the sands below. Rin couldn't tear her eyes off of Feyne. A shiver crawled up her spine as she watched the mellow-mannered shifter rip through sinew and muscle.

It was only when the female was a mess of shredded skin and bone that Scarlette limped over to the wolf; a gash poured blood from her thigh. She placed a gentle hand on the shifter's back. Feyne's eyes released the fury fueling him, and let the demon's remains fall from his teeth.

"It's over," Scarlette said quietly.

Rin noticed the blood still pouring from her leg. Tatsuo's wound was fresh as well. Rin made her way into the firelight, where a brief and relieved smile laced Tatsuo's tired lips. She sighed, deciding where to help first, when an all too familiar voice mused.

"How touching."

Rin nearly crashed to the ground.

***

Rin froze. She stared at the dark veil behind Tatsuo. Her body trembled uncontrollably.

Everyone felt it. Feyne's hackles raised, Scarlette nocked an arrow, and Tatsuo already had fire dancing on his fingers. Rin couldn't force herself to budge. They readied themselves, but not nearly enough.

"Nothing to say, even after you left my best hunter a pile of carnage? Pity." Rin caught the stir of shadows straight ahead just before Errogan stepped into the fire's gleam, leaving his pale blue eyes a sinister shade of blood orange through the fire. "I have to admit, for a bunch of animals rummaging through this wasteland, I'm pleasantly surprised that you took down my demons. I hand-picked them all just for this hunt."

Errogan. She should have known that he would find her. Rin wanted to close her eyes, to make it all disappear, but she knew taking her eyes off of this demon was certain demise. He took no interest in the others. Only her. It was like staring into the eyes of a serpent. His monstrous grin said it all. However, there were others with her this time. Tatsuo, Feyne, Scarlette. He had no more demons behind him.

Rin forced herself to swallow the silence holding her tongue. "You should have stayed in the north." She begged her face to remain neutral against her fear.

His devilish smirk deepened. "Apologies for keeping you waiting, but I had other things I needed to take care of before I went out. Should I give Zarus your regards?"

The name was a blow to the stomach. Only the malice of this demon kept Rin grounded in her resolve.

Her grip tightened around the scimitar's hilt. "What did you do to him?" Rin demanded.

He picked up on her temper. "Nothing I haven't wanted to do for years."

Rin gritted her teeth, the anger and fear and guilt building inside. Something deep within her started taking control of her good sense. Feyne moved in her path, and the feeling faded. Soon Scarlette was whispering in her ear from behind.

"He's still alive," she reminded, "he's too valuable to kill." Though it wasn't very reassuring, Rin found the words cleared her head.

Few things remain undetected by the ears of a demon. "Death is a mercy compared to what he's going through, human," Errogan said, his hands falling at his sides, deathly close to the daggers that hung there.

Rin focused on his face rather than the weapons. They were only decorations. Errogan never slid his hand over the daggers, never went to draw the silver sword at his back—the sword that sealed Zarus's capture. He didn't need to. They were there to draw fear out. He didn't need any of them to tear someone apart. The exact opposite of Zarus. He was ruthless, and apathetic, and a monster in his own right, but not a sadist like Errogan. Maybe, just maybe, Errogan would be forced to draw out one of those weapons standing against two humans, a *narikaah*, and a shifter.

One against four. It would be difficult, but they could do it. Before Rin could speak, the female demon stirred in the corner of her eye. Rin nearly let her attention slip off of Errogan, but caught herself.

The resilient female made her way toward Errogan amid the bloody mess of her remains. "Please, sir," she begged while her throat spilled, "please, I wish to aid you. Allow m—," a wet gasp for breath, "—e to help you remove these v-vermin from Armiria..." Rin wanted to look away. The female could barely drag herself. Ribbons of muscle, ligaments, and veins lay exposed in the sodden sand. "Please heal me, sir. Allow me to make up for that which I have failed."

Errogan barely glanced at the female begging for life at his feet. He finally knelt down to the pleading demon and placed a scarred hand on her bleeding shoulder. He smiled at her kindly, but Rin knew not to trust such a smile.

"P-please, sir, I will kill them in the name of our Lord Eretimis."

"Now there." He spoke softly, softer than Rin ever believed the monster could sound. His words grew malevolent. "Why, in the name of those gods you ought to be praying to right now, would I ever stain my Liege's name by worthless scum like you?" The female caught on after it was too late. Errogan slid his hand off of her shoulder and over the exposed tissue above her heart.

Rin averted her eyes. The screech that emitted from the female would haunt her for years to come. When she finally found her gaze trailing back toward Errogan, his hand was dripping red, a lifeless heart in the sand below. Death by Feyne's means would have been kinder.

"You're a monster," Scarlette whispered, her cheeks ashen.

Errogan shrugged, unfazed that he wore someone's blood as a glove. "That may be true," he said, returning his attention to Rin. "But it won't matter in a few moments, will it?" The faintest smirk curved his lips, a smirk Rin had witnessed once before. Her mouth opened to shout a warning. She wasn't fast enough. Errogan disappeared from her vision. And when he reappeared? He stood behind them, liquid shadows seeping from his hand.

Scarlette hit the ground.

Chapter Forty-Eight

Zarus marveled at the newfound clarity of his senses. He heard the murmurs of demons in distant halls and saw colors in the carpets and curtains he hadn't ever noticed. He smelled the stale, dry fragrances of the ancient building. Things he hadn't felt in so many years after numbing himself to the world finally started coming back to him. He never realized how much he missed it all until the antidote laced his veins. Genesis walked prouder too. His arm still looked mutilated, his face ashen and hollowed, but Zarus could see a lively flame back in his eyes as he strode through the dark halls.

They descended through an empty staircase once used as a passage for servants. Zarus had discovered the pass tucked behind the walls of the stronghold while roaming one long ago day, and favored it for its solitude. The bare stone did little to fight off the cold, even if there wasn't a window in sight.

Dust muted Genesis's step as he spoke. "Just so we're both on the same page: where exactly are we going?" Both of them had eased their efforts to stay hidden over the second half of their journey. They walked in the center of the narrow pass and hadn't run into anyone since they left the lab.

"What? You don't trust that I'll get us out of here?" Feigning confidence helped to ease Zarus's stress. He slowed to look around each turn in the walls. The servants' passageways led through countless stone stairwells, eventually leading to a straightaway in the very depths of the fortress. A stream ran along the whole pass, stretching along the entire length of the stronghold, where a multitude of doors and halls directed to different areas. Perfect for servants to travel through, and perfect for prisoners to sneak out.

Genesis glanced into the pitch black passageway they passed. "What happened to your pisspoor mood? It wasn't too long ago that you were still threatening me."

Zarus halted. They stood on a landing where the stairs paused, the icy dark hugging around his body. The chill was growing harsher with every level they descended. "The servants use these passages to traverse the fortress," he said as the silent stairwell resonated the trampling of the foot traffic many levels above them. "But it's a maze of underground tunnels that leads to an exit at the very bottom." He took a moment to examine the archways leading down two different paths before him. There was no sign where either led; only memory prevented the servants from losing their way. He waited until a frigid draft reached from the right pass. "That's where we take our leave."

Genesis nodded, though a shadow of concern veiled his expression. "And we won't have to worry about running into any of these servants?"

"Not if we're careful." Zarus glanced back at the hybrid. Another faint draft pulled a few strands of his dark hair as he passed under the arch. "And I suggest you prepare to attack if we meet any. Soldier or not, Eretimis's servants are radical and loyal, and they will not hesitate to announce our presence to the whole fortress if we give out mercies." He heard Genesis's footsteps stop.

A pregnant pause filled the air, and Zarus wished he had the means to choke it out. "But they're servants. Aren't they unarmed? Defenseless?"

Zarus paused his own step. Maybe some sense of Genesis's humanity survived after seventy years of imprisonment. Humanity had little use amongst demons. He really had no desire to tear that rare sense away from Genesis, but for his own good, Zarus said, "They could consider us the same, although they still wouldn't hesitate. Not everyone has the same compassion as you."

Genesis spared no time to retort. "Yet here you are, a demon, leading me to freedom," he muttered, but Zarus simply started walking again.

"A demon with motives of his own," Zarus reminded. He kept his eyes on the stark darkness ahead.

Genesis did his worst to not scoff. Zarus bit down on his temper and tried to remember the last time someone outside of the last week spoke to him without fear.

The further they descended, the cooler the air became and the thicker the dust grew on the floors. Even the workers had little use for these freezing sublevels, and Zarus had only discovered them through boredom and the need for quietude nearly half a millennium ago. Though he sensed Genesis's growing suspicion.

Who are you? Zarus could practically hear the question.

Who was he to direct Errogan so casually, the demon only second to the Dark Tyrant in the fortress's hierarchy? Who was he to have landed on Eretimis's personal radar, and risk the control serum? Who was he to know every insignificant detail of the fortress—the layout, the ranks, the names, the systems—and walk through it with such recognition?

Though the technical answer was easily explained, Zarus wasn't certain of its truth anymore. Once-student, once-apprentice, once-subordinate. None of it seemed as fitting as the title of *slave*. Serve Eretimis, or die. He might have learned from the malicious demon, but he didn't have a choice. He preferred if he didn't have to dissect the details of it to Genesis, especially not when the fortress was so close to being behind him. Zarus avoided Genesis's stare as he walked down from the last step of the stairwell and onto the stone of the straightaway. The last push to freedom.

The corridor's high domed ceilings threw back the echoes of a whisper. His breath clouded with every exhale. Everything was stone, from the floor beneath their quick feet to the bottom of the shallow mote streaming beside them.

Close as they were, they were not free yet. And would not be for a while. Zarus stepped onto the path before him and made use of the dry torch on the wall with a quick spell. The fire's glare didn't even reach the other side of the corridor.

"No one really comes down here?" Genesis asked, taking in the vault's grandness as they walked through the emptiness.

"The dust is enough of a hint." Zarus held the light out further. Despite the filth and desolation, hundreds of years of use had worn the walkway beneath Zarus's feet before Eretimis claimed the building as his stronghold in Armiria. So long ago, the world didn't remember such a time. Barely anyone even remembered that it was a temple before a fortress.

"Seems like a waste," Genesis muttered, stepping over a cleft on the floor. "There's a lot of space here, even just for storage."

Zarus shrugged, letting his gaze slip to the walls. "There's not much use for a chamber like this, especially with the stream. Anything stored here would freeze." It was only then that he wondered what the use of this space was before Eretimis overpowered the priests that lived in the temple.

A draft as glacial as the air outside rushed through the tunnel. He didn't let himself think of whether his new companion could survive the hazardous journey through the ice lands. The Lennaels were a hill of dusted snow compared to what lay ahead of them, half-demon or not. Zarus wished that they would have had the time to find supplies before they made their way down. Perhaps the trip would be more problematic than he thought. After all, when he first made this escape plan, it had been a few hundred years ago, and included only himself. Zarus's eyes narrowed, a new idea brewing in his head, should the situation turn dire. He never even cast that spell before due to the dangers, but he might as a last resort...

He had hoped the conversation would end there and they could continue on in silence, but Zarus caught Genesis staring intensely at the walls. The grimy structure had cracked as it shifted with time. He waved the torchlight, only then noticing the grid of plaques covering the entire wall. A veil fell over his mind—a thanatoid weight that slithered along his spine. It made his senses go wild. It screamed at him to flee.

"Do you feel that too?" Genesis asked, studying the stone.

Zarus took a step back and examined the plaques. Along the wall were a few arched doors a little way ahead. Narrow, the openings in the chamber looked more like a window than a doorway, but Zarus still moved toward one. A gust of air shuddered his skin when he stood below the archway.

The torch lit the small chamber. White marble crafted the walls. It was empty, save for a geometric altar in the center carved from the same material. Delicate grey plating highlighted its shining surface, seven feet long. A figurine plated into the wall rested above the piece, depicting a masculine figure offering his upturned hands toward the marble box. A far off voice ushered Zarus to leave. He had no reason to linger. Yet he didn't stop staring at the statue. When he finally glanced at Genesis, fear was palpable in his radiant eyes.

"What?" Zarus asked. He narrowed his eyes and took another step toward the stand. He wanted to find what sinister entity filled the room, but a trembling hand tugged on him.

"Stop," Genesis said in a hushing breath, pulling Zarus's shoulder. "We shouldn't—" he tripped over himself, "...we *shouldn't* be here. We should have never come down here," Genesis whispered, backing out from under the arched doorway.

Zarus raised a brow, but he still walked to the stand. A flare of pain flowed through his joints with every step. Another shiver crept down his spine. He pressed to the top of the stand.

Carved in fine letters read a small script in a Caenlin dialect so old, Zarus took a moment to search for the translation.

Priestess High of the 89th Generation
May the Hands of Vulyn Guide You to Rest
And the Light of Twin Eyes Give You Peace

Below the inscription was a date that predated the calendar reset by over three thousand years.

A crypt. The entire chamber from front to back was a crypt. Created as burial grounds for the inhabitants of a temple for the Divine, and now corrupted into a fortress for a tyrannical monster. Zarus could barely breathe as he stared at the sarcophagus. Genesis was right: they shouldn't be down here among thousands of resting souls, disturbing the dead and the entity that watched over them.

He forced himself to leave the tomb within the crypt and file back in line with Genesis. Countless graves surrounded them along the walls. They were unwelcome there, both of them; it was no wonder why this area of the fortress was abandoned. Vulyn himself was keeping everyone out of these halls. The deity's warnings not to overstay their welcome were clear as day. The thought made Zarus's head pound.

Vulyn the Balanced granted Zarus passage through this catacomb. It made his stomach twist. This macabre vault made sense. The ancient priests that built the temple constructed each section to honor the gods and their helpers—the kaetha. This area must have been crafted for Vulyn, watcher of the dead, so that he could give the souls a safe path to Ashnagz.

Zarus closed his eyes, pinching the bridge of his nose as he thought. He hated the idea of the kaeth helping him, but he needed it.

Although the deity's overwhelming presence was hard to ignore now that he realized what it was—*who* it was—he tried to focus on the water coursing behind to help clear his head. Genesis was still speechless. As shock faded, reality struck. It wouldn't be long before Eretimis tracked them down. Zarus forced his hands to stop shaking.

"I suggest we move on before we stir something in the shadows," he whispered. So many graves. So many dead. Even Zarus didn't want to tarry.

Genesis nodded. Zarus squared his shoulders and began walking. He wouldn't allow Vulyn the Balanced to give him any more warnings. Whatever the kaeth's reasoning for generosity, Zarus didn't wish to figure it out.

Both he and Genesis picked up their pace. All Zarus wanted was quiet, so he could make sure they both got out of Eretimis's citadel alive. His mind swarmed so badly that it was hard to focus. He had dealt with such dread thousands of times before. Genesis, however, did not find solace in silence, but held his tongue. Zarus was content to let the silence reign, only until he glanced back to Genesis, and saw the pent up dam of pain. A state Zarus knew until Rin waltzed into the Lennaels and set his life in motion once more.

"Where do you plan to go?" Zarus invited. Genesis didn't even look up. Perhaps it was the wrong thing to say? Genesis's life was no business of his. He was just about to pretend Genesis hadn't heard him when he answered.

"Nokomic," Genesis finally said, "back to where my life paused." Zarus couldn't tell whether it was disdain or anguish that coated his words. "I had family in Zelenia when I lived there. I know..." he paused, "I know they're most likely gone by now, and whatever kin I have left won't know who I am, but I still need to see them. Pay my respects to those who have passed. I need to see my home one more time."

Definitely the wrong thing to ask.

"What about you?" Genesis inquired, a little more sentiment to his tone. "Where are you going?"

For a moment, Zarus honestly couldn't bring an answer to his lips, not even his head. There was nowhere he had thought of yet, nowhere he was sure that Eretimis wouldn't eventually get to him. Slowly, he exhaled a silent breath. He didn't have anywhere to go, just someone. "I have to track someone down." He had to find Rin before Eretimis got to her. The thought alone had Zarus gritting his teeth.

"Someone who knows where you are?"

Zarus didn't answer. Something piqued his senses. He glanced across the moat and saw nothing through the darkness. He could have sworn he felt something shift. Vulyn's patience must have been wearing thin. Zarus answered, watching the left walkway. "I need to tell her I'm alive and make sure she's safe."

"Does Eretimis pose a threat to her as well?"

"Yes." Zarus said shortly, guilt pressing down upon his chest. He fought to keep his face neutral. "She's being hunted by him because of my foolishness."

Genesis now walked at Zarus's side. Once again, Zarus saw that gods-forsaken question lingering in his bright eyes. All Genesis said was, "I pray the hunt is in vain."

Another shadow sauntered in the darkness, and this time Genesis noticed too. Nothing came forward. There was nothing in the entire chamber that Zarus could sense.

Zarus refrained from letting his nerves get the best of him. Anything could have crawled into here over the decades. Although... he knew it to not be true. It was the same false hope that got him captured. Plants and animals were scarce in these lands since Eretimis moved in. Even the dark oaks just barely clung to life.

The two exchanged looks. It wasn't much farther until the exit. Whatever was following them would either try to stop them, or it was only a scout to say which way the absconders went. If Zarus and Genesis made it to the gate at the end of the crypt fast enough...

Zarus quickened their pace. "I don't know how she escaped Errogan," he muttered, "but I overheard that someone is keeping her hidden." Something, it was at least something to keep his mind at ease. "Though where at, I haven't the slightest clue."

"Wait a minute," Genesis interrupted, shaking his head. "*Errogan* was sent after her?" The disbelief in his tone screamed volumes. "You told me earlier he's the one who brought you here..."

Zarus took in a deep breath, cursing himself for speaking so mindlessly. "Yes." The answer was tighter than a bow string.

Genesis let out a sharp sigh. "You and I both know Errogan doesn't simply go out collecting any prisoner for Eretimis. It isn't worth his time."

An iron gate appeared around the final bend in the stream. Zarus hoped it would distract Genesis.

Please don't ask, Genesis. His chest tightened, dread drilling in his head. He just began to enjoy Genesis's company.

"Zarus Lowwenth," Genesis said in a low tone, "who are you?"

He knew the question would surface eventually, but Zarus still winced at it. What would Genesis's reaction be to the answer? A frigid gust of wind slammed into the front of his body.

Zarus almost looked away from Genesis to search for the gate, but the gust didn't come from the end of the hall. He narrowed his eyes. The silent urges of Vulyn upon his senses abruptly yelled louder. It was too late. Zarus stiffened.

"Now, Zarus, why not tell the boy who you are?" Finely tuned, and yet so shrill. The voice spoke from right in front of the black iron gate.

"Or," a second voice mused, tilting her head to the side, "are you afraid of what will happen when he hears you were Eretimis's lapdog?"

Zarus slowly turned around. When the familiar faces of the females smiled malice at him in unison, he knew he would not be seeing Rin Nowell for some time. If ever again.

Chapter Forty-Nine

R in shivered against the sweat running down her back. It was unbearable. She wanted to huddle for some small ounce of warmth left in her body, but even if she looked, she knew she would find no such thing. Not when her hands were trying to keep the life inside her friend.

She held back the tightening in her throat. This was no time for tears. She needed to focus. To think. No matter how hard she tried to stop the bleeding or figure out how to sew together the tear of flesh and muscle between Scarlette's breasts, Rin only found her eyes drawing back to her own trembling hands. The shadows around beckoned her. All emitting from the demon who caused it.

Errogan didn't give them the time to react to the tendril of darkness that pierced through Scarlette, no time to react when he charged faster than Rin could see.

Scarlette—she had fallen right down. No dramatics, just... down. The shadow magic that Errogan struck her with was fatal. Even if Feyne kept the demon distracted long enough to give Rin more time to think, she doubted Scarlette's clock would be so generous.

Feyne had acted the quickest out of all of them. So quick to lunge for the cunning demon, yet so reckless. Tatsuo was the only reason he survived so long with that blinding rage. The *narikaah* joined Feyne without a second thought. He fought beside the shifter, not with him. All sense of reason vanished in Feyne's head. Tatsuo covered the shifter who attacked so recklessly. Alas, the dragon could only watch two backs for so long against an opponent like Errogan. He paid for Feyne's lack of control. The open wound didn't help.

Tatsuo fell almost as fast as Scarlette. He was too far for Rin to reach, but she knew a *narikaah* had better luck of surviving a blow than the human she held. It had her cursing herself, and the Divine Beings, and the male responsible, but Rin held her restraint in check as she prayed for the dragon.

Rin turned her focus back to slowing the blood. Scarlette's face grew paler by the minute, her hands colder, her movements fewer. Rin grit her teeth.

She looked to where Tatsuo laid on his back. His chest rose in short, abrupt gasps. And yet, Rin could see he still reached for his spear.

Feyne's snarls pulled on her attention. No more the calm, smiling *ghren*. Not even when the shadow tore into his body. Back and forth he lunged, teeth snarling and claws reaching. Errogan toyed with the crazed shifter. Feyne knew it, too. Blood lust laced his eyes, wearing bared teeth like a mask. Soon exhaustion crept upon the shifter. Deep choking breaths plagued him as he jumped in front of Rin and Scarlette, a wall guarding them from the demon approaching one step at a time.

"Tired so soon?" Errogan called out, lifting his arms in a taunting gesture. "Pity, I was looking forward to a decent fight." The demon sighed and shrugged. "That's what I get for putting faith into a shifter."

Rin felt Scarlette's nails dig into her arm as Feyne emitted a low, foul growl.

How on Armiria could Zarus have ever been friends with this monster?

Her stomach churned to think that Zarus might have once been like this. Reveling in the ruins of Eretimis's commands. Her spine chilled to think of what destruction the two could cast together. Two demons, opposite sides of the same coin.

"And you, Kurosawa, stop struggling. You'll only make it worse at this point." The demon didn't have to look behind to see Tatsuo had crawled to his knees. A river of deep red flowed out of his tunic, blood streamed down the sides of his mouth.

Tatsuo coughed. "Keep your morbid care away from me, you bastard." He spat red in the demon's direction.

Rin didn't get it. Errogan landed his strike precisely where it would keep Tatsuo alive, but as good as dead.

Errogan read the question in her eyes. "You see, Nowell," he addressed her, and only her. She was his audience. Everyone else was just spectating. "I planned on sharing some generosity with the half-demon. Something that would give closure. After all, wouldn't he want to die the same way his parents had?"

Tatsuo froze. He rested on his knees, leaning his weight onto the shaft of the spear that he had planted in the ground. Not a hair flew in the wind, nor a bead of sweat dripped down his forehead. His face was ashen, carved from stone. Tatsuo Kurosawa didn't even blink. The question had finally been answered. A question that was no better than a rope around his neck, that had sent him hunting down the wrong person on an oath of revenge. Rin could see the face that tricked Tatsuo. In a mask of flames and ash, Errogan could easily be mistaken for Zarus.

Rin couldn't read Tatsuo's expression. His face was as desolate as the desert they stood within. Delight dripped from Errogan's very essence. It was all a game. One that the demon had spent centuries playing. A game whose only purpose was to force the players to see how powerless they truly were. He cut into their weaknesses. Struck where he saw they were most vulnerable. For Feyne, it was Scarlette. Tatsuo's parents were his liability. And Rin? The more he tore into her friends, the more strife and agony he caused them, the more she cracked underneath it all. Errogan planned to use each of her friends to torture her.

Rin glanced at Tatsuo. His hands clenched the spear so tightly that his talons had cut into his palms. "Liar..." the dragon seethed through blood soaked teeth. "You damned liar!" Tatsuo's braid fell over his shoulder as he dropped his stare to the ground, to the iron-stench pooling below. Another cough, another red stain in the sand.

Rin gritted her teeth. He needed help, and she couldn't give it to him. Her heart drummed; her head screamed. She couldn't leave Scarlette...

A cruel laugh slipped through Errogan's lips. "Denying it won't save you," he scoffed. His crystal gaze drifted over his shoulder to the bloodied dragon. "I only wish I would have had the wits back then to know a dragon-born wouldn't have died by the fire they created."

When Tatsuo finally raised his fiery stare, his reptilian eyes fell between her and their enemy, where Feyne was locking in his hind legs. His stare dropped to the spear in his hands.

It was with regret that he looked upon the weapon. Tatsuo would not be the one to avenge his parents, to call for the payment of a murderer. His insides were barely holding inside.

With one last shake of his head, Tatsuo at last parted his lips, fangs bared and not ready to give in. He knew what he needed to do. Rendered or not, the storm was fast approaching. "Death doesn't seem like enough for all the pain you've caused, Errogan."

Errogan raised his eyebrows, the very thought a whimsical idea to him. He turned toward Tatsuo. "I could say the same to you, Tatsuo Kurosawa. Do you know the punishment issued for even half of the treasonous acts you've committed? That your parents committed? I'm ordered to bring most demons back before my Lord and live out their punishments as an example to the rest. And let me tell you," his voice fell flat of all mirth, "Eretimis doesn't take lightly to traitors. Your parents? They got off easy." Like a flame striking in the dark, the demon's words summoned a burning rage deep within Tatsuo's eyes. Errogan didn't think twice of it. "I've seen the mightiest broken down to a husk for a third of what Hiromitsu and Nariko Kurosawa did to deny and threaten my Lord." Errogan scoffed, looking Tatsuo up and down. "Death is far from what you deserve. Do not plague me with your self-righteous proclamations when you have no ground to stand upon."

Rin didn't understand how Tatsuo restrained himself while Feyne hadn't yet attacked Errogan.

At last the wind picked up, and with it the scent of ash and ember flew. "Nothing more to say?" Errogan asked as the muscles in Tatsuo's jaw held taut, his formidable stare like so. "Good. Because I'm tired of your pitiful vengeance."

The silence that followed could challenge the weight of the mountains. Rin glanced at Feyne, who had not moved an inch. Scarlette wore the same confusion and made to sit up. Her stare was too cloudy, too far off in the moments she looked at Errogan with glassy eyes. Rin's hand stopped the movement. Scarlette whispered something so faint, it was inaudible. It was only when those still eyes drifted to her did Rin lower her ear to Scarlette's mouth. She wasn't able to hear what her friend was muttering so feverishly. Errogan had barely turned back to face her, then the shifter lunged.

The drum roared in her head. It was so loud that she couldn't keep up with the attack. A spilling of blood, muffled shouts... Rin wasn't sure what led to Feyne yelping and falling to the ground. Nor did she know when Scarlette's grip loosened, releasing so that there was nothing holding Rin's back. Or when Tatsuo had fallen prostrate and limp, or how the head of the dragon's spear ended up through Errogan's side. It was a rush of events that the ringing in her head blocked out. Whatever happened, Rin soon realized it didn't matter. As she glanced around at her fallen friends, a line of tears creased her eyes. Her blood burned. Not icing over, but burning endlessly beneath her skin, racing the heat throughout her body.

She heard a heavy *thud*. Errogan threw Tatsuo's spear into the sand. His wicked smile returned as he looked at her. One step. Then another.

Her legs froze.

One last step. His crystal eyes looked down upon her. The smirk deepened. "Finally," Rin heard him muse, though it sounded as far off as a fading echo. "There's no one left to hide behind now, no one to drag you away." Her body quaked, a tear streaming down to her chin.

Rin swallowed a hard breath as she stared into the demon who had dropped to one knee, now eye level with her.

"It's just the two of us, Rin Nowell. How it was meant to be."

***

Zarus hadn't felt that murky presence for centuries.

The frozen wastelands poured into the chamber through the gate, wind dancing the hairs on edge along Zarus's skin. All he could do was stare down at the twin sisters blocking his path to freedom. He attempted to keep his face neutral, but hope lingered on his tongue.

Those wild smiles stared right back at him, a promise of wickedness dancing within. He couldn't bring himself to focus.

He leered at the Wraith Twins.

"Zarus?" Genesis placed a hand on his shoulder. It was with that touch he barely felt that he found himself grounded, remembering what he and Genesis were less than one hundred feet away from doing.

You couldn't have warned me about this, *you damn kaeth?* he seethed at the uselessness of the Divine.

Zarus spoke coldly. "Raia, Tesyl. I see you two have crawled out of Ashnagz's Pits again." He took a step forward so that Genesis was behind him. "Bending over backwards for Eretimis, I assume?"

The sister on the left gave a crooked smile. Raia, the eldest. "Here I was, afraid Eretimis finally broke that voice out of you, Zar-Zar." She flipped her black curtain of curls behind her shoulder as she snickered. "It's good to know you're not completely hollow yet."

Zarus almost let his temper slip. Almost.

"It's going to take more than a pathetic attempt of servitude to keep me down, Raia," he retorted, forcing a half smile to crack his straight lips. The falsehood slid through his teeth like grease. He lifted his chin. "Tell me, has Eretimis sent you to retrieve us already?" Zarus glanced at the younger of the twins, Tesyl, who met him with an equally twisted grin. A quiet smile that sent a shiver up Zarus's spine. If the Wraith Twins—as they had become known throughout both worlds—were a wildfire, Raia acted as the unyielding flame burning all in its wake, while Tesyl played the role of the patient smoke who snuffed out any survivors.

"You forget we do what we please, Lowwenth," the younger mused, the straight brown hair cut to her shoulders flitting through the wind. "Eretimis does not hold us by the same leash he holds you."

He felt his nostrils flare.

Zarus bit down on the curses piling on his tongue, forcing his stare to remain on the twins as Genesis looked to him. "Not sworn to him, but whores idling at his feet," he said flatly. They were foolish. Eretimis doesn't hold his allies in high regard, even his oldest accomplices. For someone who wanted control over everything himself, allies were little more than clocks counting down. Eretimis did not share power.

Zarus sized up both of the twins. Neither carried weapons in the past, so Zarus supposed there were no blades hiding beneath their clothes now. "If not for him, then why do you feel the need to pester us with your presence?"

Keep them talking and think of something that will ensure you and Genesis get out.

It was Raia who laughed, shrill and condescending, her dark eyes sparking with short-lived amusement. "We may not serve him, but we won't let one of his prize prisoners slip through the back door."

Zarus nearly smirked. The sisters who demolished civilizations for fun were afraid of the Dark Tyrant.

"And who knows," Tesyl joined in, shrugging her lean shoulders, "it might be well worth our effort just to see what punishment Errogan receives for casting you in that dungeon." The smile she flashed was anything but pleasant. If the twins were once graced with beauty in their prolonged lives, years of dabbling in dark magics had worn it thin. They appeared in their prime; young yet ridden with age. Timeless. Their depthless eyes hollow, sunken, their skin faded to the faintest grey. Even their bodies morphed. No longer were their forms shaped with curves and muscle, but sharp and skeletal. Guided by the very bone beneath their tainted skin, it looked as if they had both stared death in the face and spat in it. Dark magic worked on their physical selves as the passing of time worked on the rest of the world, except it was that very forbidden darkness that strengthened them in matters one might see more desirable. The very matters that had Zarus gritting his teeth as he scrambled for a way out of the encounter.

The mention of Errogan brought forth the remembrance of who the demon hunted down.

"If you're going to bring us back to the Dark Eyesore, what are you waiting for?" Genesis asked, stepping up to Zarus's side. The hybrid appeared paler. Even if Genesis suspected their threat by the way Zarus froze, to budge into a conversation with these females was foolish.

Raia slid her imperious eyes to the hybrid.

Genesis should have kept his mouth shut. Whatever luck he had controlling his magic in that dungeon would be of no use here. Genesis held his ground without so much as a flinch when the smirking Tesyl took a step closer to them.

"Look, Raia, the child speaks as well," she crooned. She crooked her head and slowly paced in front of the gate. The fitted leathers she wore kept her movements mute with each step.

Raia followed suit, pacing the opposite of her sister, taking slow, menacing strides with her hands folded behind her back. "Appears so," she purred sweetly, closing her eyes as if in bliss. "Eretimis must be losing his edge, sister. To spend so many years trapped beneath his enemy's home—"

"And still have the will to think, to speak—" Tesyl crooned as they passed each other, her tone harsher than before. Another shrill gust of wind ripped through the gate.

"It's a miracle he can speak at all!" The eldest's cackle bounced off of the crypt's walls.

"Unfortunate man, stranded and forgotten."

"Pitiful human, mutilated and cast away."

The twins spoke using the same tone, the same condescending amusement that guided their extravagant steps as they told Genesis's tale.

"Useless hybrid, infected and laid to waste."

It was impossible to tell which one spoke, or if their voices simply sang their savage song in unison. A constant echo of the other.

"Miserable husk, longing for the remembrance of warmth."

Zarus peered at his companion. Genesis froze. Listening to the twin's ruthless ode drained him. He fell into their trap. And then Zarus saw his opening.

Discreetly, he placed his hand behind his back. The weight of the entire storm raging outside suddenly stacked on his shoulders. He trembled under the pressure of the magic, waiting until he was certain every snowflake and shredding wind had tamed in the dome of magic he conjured outside. Zarus clenched his jaw and struggled to keep his hand conducting the storm relaxed. A maestro of the chaos. He trembled under the tension.

His magic raged within his soul, yet Zarus's body stilled. The sisters in front of him fell into shadow, their voices fading into distance as he concentrated, and even Genesis's presence dulled. He used every split second given to him.

He grabbed more magic. And more. And more. Until Genesis realized something was brewing beside him, and Zarus could feel the weight of the power spilling over the grasp of his control. Zarus heard that small, distant voice speak in the back of his mind.

Too long...

Too long.

The weight of the magic he held hit him like a megaton.

"Oh, Zarus?" He saw Raia's lips move, although her voice didn't quite sound real beneath the might of the magic. Her smile was as real as the alarm that flooded his head. He cursed himself to Ashnagz and back.

"Whatever could be wrong, dear?" Tesyl purred. They both turned to face him and smiled as an unnatural current stirred at their feet.

Too late.

The magic that the Wraith Twins summoned was devastating. Worse than what Zarus planned to do to them. It avalanched toward him and Genesis. Zarus cursed at their distraction, summoning forth three hundred years' worth of rage. His throat acted on its own, releasing a bellowing cry—so loud, so vicious—that the entire chamber shook.

Yes, the Wraith Twin's attack was terrible. However, Zarus's had been catastrophic, and thrice as worse. It also struck from behind.

Chapter Fifty

Rin could hardly breathe. Death incarnate knelt right in front of her.

Scarlette was still in her arms, limp and near lifeless. Tatsuo was unconscious. Feyne was awake, but little more than that.

Errogan stared at her, silent and waiting. After all, she spoke so boldly to him earlier. Staring into his hateful eyes was unbearable.

Her head spun endlessly, but Rin opened her mouth. "W-what do you want from me?" she said coarsely. Her head shook, her heart raced. "What did I do to deserve *any* of this!"

What personal grudge did Eretimis have against her? Was it truly because she somehow thawed his once-student's frozen heart? Rin balled her fists, releasing Scarlette's stiff fingers. "Monster," she ground out with every ounce of hate she had been ignoring since the day she hid for her life in that castle on the mountain. *"Monster."*

Errogan watched her silently for a moment. "Who's to say what a monster is?" he challenged, leaning ever so closer that Rin felt his warm breath against the chill of the desert night. "If you ask me, I'd say it's all relative. The victim, the monster; the good and the bad. It all depends on which angle you look from. In the end, it doesn't matter." He spoke so quietly. "I'm the one that determines what happens from here on out, aren't I? So call me a monster, or whatever you will, because it's only wasting your breath, Rin. If I were you, seeing all this red staining the sand around me, the iron-stench so thick it burns, I wouldn't waste my breath on semantics."

The air hitched in her throat. His words were poisonous. She almost lost the sense of clarity in her head with this demon standing so close. When she finally acknowledged the need to confront what was in front of her, she felt it surge again. She was the only one who could help herself.

Rin bit down on the tremble shaking her body. "I disagree," she said with surprising resolve. "I know a bastard when I see one."

Errogan's expression fell short of amusement, a deathly promise flaring in his eyes. She forced herself to be calm. Rin didn't know what ran through her; what urged her to stand her ground, what screamed at her to win. It felt like fire's blaze and ice's nip all at once.

When she was certain Errogan was going to rip her limb from limb, the muscles in his jaw relaxed. He smiled, which was even more offsetting. "Finally found a backbone, I see," he muttered, glancing toward the wind. "Let me just get to the point here," Errogan said aloud, bringing his stony stare back to her. "I have a deal to offer you, Rin Nowell, one that my Lord Eretimis himself asked me to deliver."

The demon reached out his bloodstained hand to her cheek, softly wiping away one of her old tears. Only when he slid his hand to her jaw, violently turning her head to the side, did she remember the blade strapped to her belt. He leaned in to her so his lips were mere inches away from her ear. She heard his chilling voice so close and clear. The fire-ice spread out from the back of her head in another wave.

Errogan finished giving the offer that the Dark Tyrant himself sent to her, an offer so desperate yet so impossible. The pounding in her head raged. Those crystal eyes had come far too close.

Even Rin impressed herself at how fast she slashed into Errogan's chest.

***

Two forces of magic crashed down upon the crypt. It shook the fortress. The ground upturned, pieces of the high ceiling cracked and crashed down. Falling debris shattered the frozen stream. The dark blast was a stone to Zarus's skull, disconnecting the reach of his senses from reality.

His thoughts were distant and swimming.

For all he knew, the wraiths were already dragging him to the throne room. His darkness and ice struck their grey swarm just before he fell. The storm he directed hit Raia and Tesyl like a maelstrom of chaos. Something else mixed with his shadow magic. The misty darkness he conjured infused with deep red hues. Whatever it had been, the attack knocked the Wraith Twins off their guard.

The effects of their dark veil finally wore thin. Zarus heard the rushing water. He felt the icy current flowing around him, numbing his limbs. Then smelled the archaic dust falling down, the iron scent settled around his nose. Zarus opened his eyes and found Genesis hovered over him; his hands pressed against Zarus's temples, emitting a violet aura. His eyes, once blue, now matched the hue of his magic.

"So what exactly does your magic do?" Zarus muttered as he slowly touched the blood leaking from his nostril, dragging himself out of the water.

"Which one?" Genesis asked. The violet tones faded from his stare and arms as he backed away. "I can manipulate emotions," he sighed, standing up. "The extent of that control varies from person to person, like you saw in the dungeon." His eyes, once more sapphire, trailed over to the gate. Where iron wrought bars once barricaded the exit now existed a gaping hole in the stone wall. All because of Zarus's magic. Genesis let out a low whistle.

"And the other power?" Zarus pressed, trying to shove down the buzz that still laced his thoughts as he stood.

"Summoning," Genesis said quietly.

A black mage.

Genesis gestured to the fallen debris where Raia and Tesyl stood mere minutes ago. "Do you think they're—"

"No," Zarus interrupted. He stared at the rubble of the crypt. Nothing so much as shifted in the wind, but their presence remained. He wiped his bloody nose and pushed out the rest of the buzz from the dark magic.

"I really wonder where you get all these erratic bursts of power, Zar-Zar."

The hairs on the back of his neck stood straight, his blood chilled against the wind blowing into the crypt. Zarus pinned down Raia as she stepped out behind a chunk of fallen ceiling.

"That little show was quite impressive." Tesyl joined her sister's side. "Were you aware you possessed the Fallen's Mark? Because we, for two, are quite interested in learning where it came from. Not just any pureblood demon can summon the power of the Fallen Kaeth."

The Fallen's Mark? Did they mean the deep red burst in his magic? Zarus kept silent. Steadily, he handed the fighting knives he pillaged off the guard in the dungeon to Genesis. "Their black magic will suck away your energy and turn it into their own if they touch you. Aim deep and stay out of my way."

Zarus didn't give the Wraith Twins another chance to play him as a fool. He worked up enough ice to freeze the oceans, and charged.

He aimed for Raia's heart, ice covering the entirety of his hand like a clawed gauntlet. His finger grazed the wraith's clavicle, but she pulled back and caught his wrist in her bony grip.

Her shrill voice sounded like death in his ear. "There was a time when Eretimis would have had our heads for landing a single scratch on you, Zarus Lowwenth," she hissed. He bared his teeth into a snarl, failing to free his arm. "Probably still would, too."

"But given the circumstances," Tesyl chimed, appearing at his opposite side. He covered his other arm in a thick layer of ice before she grabbed it. "I think he'll understand a few crushed bones."

His bones creaked beneath their grips.

Zarus gritted his teeth. "Don't flatter yourselves." It was little more than a flash in the corner of his eye. Genesis's dagger whistled past his ear and pierced into Tesyl's forearm. The wraith's screech offered Zarus the opportunity to pull away from the distracted twins.

"Well, look at that, Raia," seethed Tesyl, yanking the steel out of her arm. Even her blood was oily grey—like all the saturation had drained away. "The child has toys."

"Indeed," her sister replied, taking hold of Tesyl's wounded arm. The sinister smile stayed ever still on both of the sister's lips.

The blood spilling from Tesyl's arm sizzled under Raia's touch. When she pulled her arm away, the hole leading straight to the other side remained, but it calloused over on the inside. "Most would say children shouldn't play with such toys." Tesyl searched for any flaw in the grim magic used to patch the wound—because dark magic never *healed*, it only stole from another source. After all seemed to satisfy, the younger sister straightened the leather tunic clinging to her body and faced Genesis with a wicked grin. "However, we're not so strict."

If steel was what Genesis attacked with, then with steel he defended. Tesyl's pulse of wicked magic ravaged the debris, and when it was over, the female was inches away from him. Genesis ducked below the blow with a breath to spare and countered her. He lowered to his heels, then sprung up with both daggers ready to sweep Tesyl's head off.

Raia shifted to aid her sister, but a wall of ice sprung up from the ground in the twin's path. Raia avoided impalement, but Zarus earned a noteworthy flare of the wraith's temper.

Zarus against Raia, and Genesis against Tesyl. He hoped they would end this fight before someone heard the commotion below the fortress.

Zarus crossed his arms before his chest, a shield of ice blocking the manipulations of Raia's blood. He intended to push her toward the gaping hole in the chamber, and stay alive doing so. The weather might slow her down. They moved and jumped, dodged and charged, but Zarus saw progress. It took ice, a lot of ice, and nearly every style of the hand to hand combat he had ever received from Eretimis, but he pushed Raia back and prevented her from gaining ground. The sisters certainly fought better side by side. However, the sweat rippling down his body kept him from celebrating.

"You're not getting tired, are you, Zarus? We've only just begun, dear. You've barely even hit me!" Raia cackled.

Zarus couldn't touch her without his energy stolen. He had to rely solely on his magic to defend him.

"And I thought you were supposed to be a challenge," Zarus taunted. He had to keep her talking, keep her distracted and think of a plan. The exhaustion in his limbs and the heat of his body mixing with the glacial air made his head spin.

Raia glanced behind Zarus, a slight frown on her face. "I have always wondered what it would be like to fight you, but I think Tesyl is getting all the fun," she sighed. "We've never played with that one before. And I greatly wish he'll still be alive once I'm done with you.

My dear sister looks like she's having such a good time, don't you think, Zarus?"

Zarus refused to look back, refused to take his eyes off of the wildfire before him, but he saw Tesyl jump back into his peripherals. Genesis maneuvered around the wraith, his blades slashing through the air. The eldest's eyes danced, paying heed to every movement.

Another bead of sweat ran down his brow. While Raia glued her attention to Genesis, Zarus delved deep into his well of magic. He crafted a dome of ice around the distracted wraith and imploded the magic into a pile of shards on top of her.

Frost clouded the air like dust. The shattered debris was enough to kill, yet Raia stirred. Zarus grabbed her throat with an ice-covered hand before she stood. "Think twice before taking your eyes off of me, Raia," he growled. Even as the female sputtered out a wet laugh, Zarus's frozen hand tightened to crush her.

"I ne-ver t-took you as the j-calous type," Raia sneered through choking gasps, her grin stained by the grey sludge she called blood. The Wraith Twins never surrendered. Faster than he realized, Raia reached her sharpened nails for him. A shield of ice crystallized in front of his chest just before the force of a battering ram slammed into him. The collision of her magic launched him back, and Raia was out of the ice he crafted before he stopped. Bleeding and injured, but the wraith had already patched up the lesions with her parasitic magic.

Keep them separated, Zarus reminded himself, finding balance and glancing where Genesis fought. Against all odds, the hybrid was still standing his ground. He worked with agility great enough to evade her attacks, and it didn't take long to figure he had been trained for battle in his life. Zarus hoped that training would be enough to keep the kid alive.

Zarus flicked his eyes back to Raia. Her wounds might have sealed, but a raw red handprint remained frostbitten on her skin. Carefully, he stood up, his chest throbbing where the blow landed as she spoke. "Such power, yet it still crumbles without purpose." Her dark, depthless eyes swept back to him. "You fit in better with the humans, Zarus."

His teeth flashed broadly in a snarl. Raia conducted another wave of chilling dark magic. It shattered the remnants of the ice dome to dust, and nearly took off his head before he crouched below the lethal gust.

The wave nearly crashed into Genesis too before he dove out of the way. "Dammit, Zarus!" the hybrid grounded across the crypt. "Break her neck for the sake of the gods!"

Raia let out a shrill laugh. She offered a foul smile, the darkness in her eyes thick as wax. "It's not every day a prodigy killer gets support from a throneless prince," she sang as she flung her arms in another theatrical gesture.

"What on Amiria are you talking about?" Zarus groaned.

"What?" Raia remarked. She gestured to Genesis on the other side of the moat. "He didn't mention it? Everyone in the fortress knows his woeful tale."

"The prince with no throne, the heir with nothing to claim." Tesyl hummed, sliding her greasy stare back to Genesis. "It's quite amusing how he continues to fight for his freedom."

Genesis threw a dagger at Tesyl's forehead. His aim was dead accurate, but she disappeared into a lightless fog just before the blade struck her skull. She reappeared at her sister's side before the dagger clattered to the ground. "How do you know about that?" the hybrid seethed.

"It's not much of a secret, dear," Raia tuned in, shrugging her bony shoulders. "You never had a chance of escaping, anyway. Neither of you did." She grinned at Zarus, but he kept his curious stare on Genesis.

"You will not stop us from seeing our freedom." Zarus walked through the debris until he stood by Genesis's side.

"But Zarus, the question still stands whether you make it out alive," Tesyl said.

Raia turned her cunning stare toward Genesis. He was still fuming from their mockery.

"Where will you go, Your Highness? You have no home left."

"No power."

Their voices fazed together, their sadistic duet ever playing.

"The poor prince turned mutant, alone and kingdomless."

"Heir of Nokomic," the sisters mused together, singing their torment in Genesis's direction, "where will you flee when all that's left of your title is death and ruin?"

Nokomic?

The wind tugged at their clothes, sending a chill down his spine and raven strands into his face. He let his gaze slip beside him, where he found the wrath of Genesis as intense as a fire in the night.

Chapter Fifty-One

It's not true. He's lying, he's a damned liar, *Rin.* Her mind ran wild, Errogan's vile words still echoing through her head. *It's impossible. 'Agree to come to the fortress, and Zarus will be freed.'*

There was no way in either realm that Eretimis would trade Zarus's imprisonment for her own, Rin knew. Her strangling grip tightened around her scimitar. Her hesitation granted Errogan enough time to compose himself.

"So, what do you say, Rin? Do we have a deal?" He managed a smirk to hide his pain. She cut him deeper than she thought.

Her lips moved without her permission. "You're mad!" she forced out. "There is no reason for Eretimis to offer such a trade. There's nothing for him to gain if I take Zarus's place." It wasn't that she didn't want to. She'd give anything to get Zarus out of the fortress, even her own freedom. It couldn't be real. It couldn't be that simple.

Errogan took a step closer to her, an urgent reminder to run.

He shrugged, the leather of his jacket reflecting the light of the falling moon. "That might be so, but I tell you truthfully," he held up a finger in her direction, "my liege rarely makes bargains to trade one of his most prized prisoners for lowly commoners, nor does he make those decisions lightly." He dropped his hand to his side, taking another step—a step that had Rin clenching her jaw. "He sees some value in you. I'd be a fool to say I didn't agree."

Whatever Feyne sensed in her, whatever Scarlette couldn't decipher, it was nothing of importance. How could it be when she was just a human? This whole *deal* was dangerous. It came from the Dark Tyrant and was likely to end in her own death. But...

Errogan scoffed. "You're going to let him suffer in Eretimis's hands while I give you the key to his release after everything that demon did for you?" His eyes shone like gems in the dark. They pierced through the shadows and embedded shame deep into her core. "We never would have found him had you not slowed him down. We wouldn't have stood a chance against him if he didn't have to watch over you like a lost child. Truly, Nowell," he spoke her name with such disdain, "are you *that* selfish?"

"N-no," she stammered, her hands lowering the scimitar so slowly she didn't realize it hung at her side. Why on Armiria should she trust Errogan's word? The word of a liar and a murderer. What if he was telling the truth? Was she willing to risk Zarus's freedom so that she could walk the world in his stead? Who was to even say she would walk away after this?

"What will it be, Rin?" The demon raised his arms in an open, welcoming gesture, but the ill intent twisting his smile offered her enough wisdom to take a step back. "I don't have time to wait around all day." Nor did they, she realized, looking to the ground behind him where Scarlette's stiff body lay.

"I," she tried to say, but the words lodged in her throat. Her knuckles drained white as she tightened her fists. "Zarus will be released? Forever?"

A nod. His impatience was growing.

Rin hated it. Despised it. The fact she dug herself into this hole so steep that she could feel her hands bleed trying to climb out. And this demon was the only one who could offer her a ladder. What would her father think when she never returned home? Feyne should be able to track him down and tell the man who raised her what happened. What would he say? She glanced toward the nearly slain shifter, but the only thing moving was his fur in the wind.

How many times now had she believed it was the end?

The hilt of the scimitar slid out of her hand and *thunked* into the cool sand. She forced herself to look up, forced her stare to strike Errogan's. Rin was about to trade her life for another when she heard the faintest whimper. Feyne trying to dissuade her. He was trying to make her see reason. He couldn't, not while he was stuck in this form without the energy to shift into a *ghren*.

Rin heard Errogan's condescending chuckle. She felt nothing good would come of this agreement; nothing that would help her *or* Zarus. She had to take that risk. She kept her stare on the cold eyes of the being who delighted in her suffering. This monster would sentence her to a life of pain upon entering Eretimis's fortress. Errogan sensed where her mind headed and raised his brows. Rin felt light-headed.

This is the right thing to do.

"I will never understand how Zarus was ever friends with someone like you," she said flatly.

Errogan said, "It won't matter in a moment, Nowell." His haughty smile had Rin dipping her chin.

A sudden gust of wind rushed past her toward Errogan. It was time to go. She knew that going with this demon meant something worse than death.

She took a single step toward him, but suddenly his entire de-meanor tensed. Out of nowhere, a dagger whistled through the air, but Errogan caught it pressed between his hands before it reached his skull.

***

'Heir of Nokomic.'

The words echoed through Zarus's head.

Prince of the oldest kingdom on this continent.

Suddenly, it made sense.

Zarus clenched his jaw and wrapped his fists tight at his sides. Seventy years inside hell, away from his kingdom. Seventy years was more than enough to draw out the anger seeping from Genesis. No wonder he was reckless enough to bargain with a stranger. The royal prince refused to look at him. He fixed his stare on the jagged hole in the wall just past the Wraith Twins.

A lattice of frost stretched up Zarus's hand, urging him to fight, but he couldn't look away. Confusion overtook him. A crowned prince should have been well protected by the strongest army of the continent. Did Eretimis truly level a city full of such skilled soldiers in a single battle? Zarus and Errogan certainly had their fair share of victories. But the Dark Tyrant took out *Zelenia*.

"Zarus, dear," Raia shouted from across the room, her arms outstretched toward him in a mask of sincerity. He narrowed his stare. "Don't leave your jaw open for so long. It's not becoming. Besides, darling, that little tidbit isn't nearly the best surprise of the night." The smile that she flashed told Zarus all he needed to know. For it was when Raia showed her wicked amusement that he realized that she stood alone. Genesis noticed as well; both he and Zarus jolted from their shock, shifting to cover one another's blindside. Grey shadows swayed before him. Her body formed from the darkness. Zarus stabbed his spiked gauntlet of ice where Tesyl manifested. Rather than lurch over at the hole seeping black blood in her chest, she grabbed his arm and pulled him close. A cold darkness consumed the reach of his mind, thick enough to block out the presence of Genesis behind him. The only thing Zarus could be certain of was Tesyl's lifeless, draining touch on his chest, and the overbearing depletion of the energy he regained from the antidote.

"You see, Lowwenth," he distantly heard Tesyl say, "in all the years that you've known us, you've never felt the effects of the power Raia and I possess." He remained linked to her dark, depthless stare as she retracted her hand from his chest. All at once, the world snapped back into motion. By the time Zarus regained his composure, Genesis had thrown a dagger at Tesyl before she disappeared into shadows again.

"Aren't you tired of hiding behind tricks?" Genesis growled at the Wraith Twins.

No. They aren't. Zarus wanted to voice his thoughts but didn't... couldn't. He couldn't force his thoughts to focus on a single matter.

The ice on his hand was gone. His magic had been sucked dry. The whole crypt spun. Even squeezing his eyes shut couldn't shake the sensation of the floor tipping out from underneath him. He toppled over. The pale stone smacked into his cheek.

Genesis's hand suddenly propped up Zarus's head. A relentless slew of curses ran off the hybrid's lips. Both twins approached, smiling like the mad hags they were. They were saying something vile. He was sure of it. Yet the swaying of his head got in the way, and in his foggy state he couldn't make it out.

It is not yet your time, child.

That damned voice still spoke to him under the layers of exhaust and toil.

He cursed. It was too late for him. Whatever Tesyl had done, whatever dark magic she possessed, it left him drained. He felt so tired and weak. Even if he escaped, he'd be in no state to find Rin in time before Errogan. With a surge of desperation, Zarus grabbed Genesis's shirt. He knew it was near impossible, knew that he barely had the magic left to remember what Rin's presence felt like. With his free hand, Zarus drew out a symbol in the air.

He had never cast this spell before. Four hundred years of failure paved the way to where he laid wrestling with the precise magic. Now he needed what he stole from Eretimis's study all those years ago—a spell to open portals. With one last whisper in his head, the air stirred.

Remember the strength of her soul.

Two lines rising and falling, curving about one another as a typhoon, circled by a ring: Armiria's official emblem. It appeared in the air as if his finger had dipped in ink. Upon his last etch of the symbol, the air thrummed around the translucent lines. He yanked Genesis down to hear him. Zarus's words slurred, and the hybrid quickly pulled back and looked at him as though he spoke in tongues. Before Genesis could say anything else, before consciousness slipped his grasp, Zarus forced his arm to swipe through the emblem. It was when the portal's maw sprung forth from the symbol that urgency tensed Raia and Tesyl beyond sadistic mirth. They nearly jumped from where they stood to grab him and Genesis. Too slow. They realized all too late that Zarus had learned the hidden art of opening portals.

The gateway was little more than a slim window. A pale blue rim of energy lined the jagged tear in the air which led out of the fortress and into freedom. The magical doorway pulled on him like a magnet. He longed for it, but knew better. He wasn't of use now, to himself or Rin. He took in one last view of the night sky through the serrated portal, and then slid his eyes to Genesis's confused stare.

"Save her." Zarus commanded through bared teeth.

Just before Raia's skeletal hand wrapped around Genesis's neck, Zarus shoved the prince into the gateway. Before either twin could dive in and follow, he swiped his hand across the symbol embedded into the center of the portal. The magic vanished; any trace of the portal disappeared into thin air.

The back of Zarus's head hit the ground hard. The impact shuttered through his skull and reverberated down his spine until he felt the shock in his toes. He didn't care. Although he no longer possessed the magic needed to escape, Zarus knew one thing for sure: Genesis would repay the life debt he created. It settled his mind, even as his eyes fluttered shut. Even when he saw two hazy figures look down on him, neither of which held the same bloodthirsty excitement they had moments ago. Zarus smiled at Tesyl's lethally hidden rage and Raia's fiery wrath. He had won. Holding onto consciousness for as long as he could, Zarus now welcomed the frigid winds. He took in the numbing chill until his lungs burned.

"Foolish boy," Tesyl's voice spat from above. "Saving that human instead of himself."

"I'm sure Eretimis will understand when you explain." His laugh was weak but rich as he stared into the empty eyes of the Wraith Twins. He tried to rub his temples as they throbbed under the blanket of fatigue, but his arms had grown far too heavy. Raia had had enough of his company. He was still smiling when her foot bashed into his head and darkness consumed him.

***

Errogan looked at the blade thrown at him. Surprise washed over his face. And then confusion settled with it.

Where in Armiria did that come from?

A sliver of hope cleaved open her chest to think another member of Base had survived. She looked over Errogan's shoulder and saw a silhouette in the night. Suddenly, someone spoke.

The voice was hoarse and raw, yet unfamiliar. "Don't accept an invitation to hell, Rin. Zarus is going to suffer either way." With each use of her name, she cringed. He spoke as if they were old friends. A deep concern swept over regarding who this new shadow dweller might be.

Still facing Rin, Errogan spoke casually to the newcomer behind him. "What's a pisspoor excuse for a human like yourself doing here, Genesis Masquarem? It's one hell of a bad time to stop by after escaping the fortress." Errogan scoffed. He acted unfazed by Genesis's arrival, but Rin saw the panic writhing in his crystal eyes. His expression turned grim, and Errogan stilled; listening, expecting, waiting. Waiting for what, Rin wondered.

"The fortress?" Rin repeated aloud by accident. Errogan's straight lips curved into a smirk once more. His entire demeanor relaxed, as if whatever he was anxious about was no longer a threat.

"Yes, the fortress in which our deal involves," he said coldly, tossing the dagger aside. "It seems the sentinels let one of Eretimis's honored guests slip away." He moved toward her. "I suppose I'll just have to see that both of you make it there safely, right, Rin?"

'Zarus is going to suffer either way.'

The words sounded in her head until the demon was standing beside her. Only then did she hear that voice in the back of her head again. With it, the rippling pools of her guilt vanished.

The duplicate speaks lies, child. Fight your way out of this alongside the prince.

Rin jumped back on her heels, kicking up sand as she tried to build some distance between herself and Errogan. "Get away from me!" she yelled, as her eyes darted to the ground. Her blade. Where had she dropped her blade? Before she could find even a glimmer of the ruby handle, Rin felt her body jolt backward. Errogan grabbed her wrist.

"Are you sure you want to do that?" Errogan asked, yanking her face to his, catching her other wrist at the same time. "Bargains like this don't come around too often, Rin. It'd be a shame to waste such a solution to your friend's suffering." His words were cruel. The more Rin saw the blood-thirst storming beneath the flashy exterior, the clearer she saw through his manipulation.

She couldn't pull away from him. She was terrified. Scared dry as the feral monster pulled her mere inches away, lifting his hand as if he was drawing something with it. A sinister smile grew across his face.

Fear transformed into a fire that spread through her core. "No, they don't, but I assure you, Errogan, bargains and deals won't be anywhere close to your concern when you show up to the fortress empty hand-ed." Rin mustered a smile. A smile that told him all he needed to know. Well, not all. It did nothing to warn him about Genesis's approach from behind.

Errogan's eyes widened as two scarred hands grabbed his shoulders and jerked him backwards. His grip on Rin didn't break. A flare of pain sprouted up her arms. Genesis rounded between them and re-leased Errogan's hellish grip.

Rin caught her balance. "Thanks," she whispered, forcing a stiff smile at the newcomer. She looked up at him, at his blackish brown hair and sapphire eyes. The man, Genesis Masquarem, looked like he had just walked out of the Flames of Ashnagz itself. His sunken cheeks told the tale of his days in the fortress, and the deep inhales of his swaying body spoke volumes of his escape. Yet a brief grin twitched his lip.

"I have to say, Masquarem," Errogan seethed, rolling his shoulder. "I'm curious how your power developed over the years. Eretimis never let you out; never let you do anything with your newfound strength." The demon let out a sharp exhale, humor hidden somewhere within. "Your body adapted well for being cramped in that dungeon for so long. It seems you're finally worth my time. But honestly," he continued, shaking his head in the night's breeze, "could someone please explain just what it is about this damn girl that seems to snatch everyone's favor? For the love of whatever those gods you pray to are worth, there is no way that you two know each other! Certainly, Zarus couldn't have known her for very long, and she still had him crawling at her feet along with everyone else she's met!" His words morphed into a bitter laugh.

"Maybe you should try being pleasant sometime so people want to be around you too, Errogan," Genesis scoffed. Errogan's smile cut short. A river of shadows appeared in his hands. Rin looked past Errogan. She heard something dragging through the dunes.

"Feyne?" She watched the wolf inch toward Scarlette. "Feyne, stay still," she urged the shifter, but he did not listen, his breaths heavy and forced.

Even though Scarlette laid on the far side of Errogan, Feyne was determined to make it to her. Rin's chest tightened.

"You honestly don't understand, Wolf." Errogan sighed, glancing at Scarlette. "She's going to die either way. We have no use for that girl. Save your effort because Eretimis hasn't lost interest in the lowly shifter leading the rebellions against him. We've heard so many things about you, Yreyshin Wuflan. It would be a waste to kill you without question."

Rin forced herself to take hold. "I know better than to waste my breath asking for some shred of mercy on behalf of that girl," she grounded, shaking her head. The demon only smiled in response. "But you know, Errogan, I've found one major difference between you and Zarus."

His brows arched in interest. "I could give you a thousand reasons, Nowell, but humor me and make it a thousand and one."

Rin pressed her lips together, holding in the urge to scream at the monster who dared act smug after what he had done. "Zarus never crowed so mindlessly."

The demon's eyes raged. "Funny," he hissed, "very funny. Though seeing all the distractions that this is causing," he turned away from her and Genesis, walking where Scarlette's unconscious body lay, "why don't I get rid of her once and for all? Then I'd have your undivided attention." He drew a dagger from his hip. Feyne growled as Errogan leaned over, but he was in no state to do anything. Neither was the man beside her, whether he had just possessed enough strength to break Errogan's grip or not.

Rin's heart raced. A hum pounded against her skull. She had had enough; enough of their demonic destruction. Enough of Errogan throwing around her friends. The fire spread from her chest to her veins until it consumed her entire body. Until the humming in her head became a cry of war.

"Enough!" she erupted.

Errogan already had the knife to Scarlette's throat when Rin rammed into him. She hit him square in his back with breathtaking force, knocking them both over. However, while it took Rin's head a moment to stop stirring, Errogan shoved her off and jumped to his feet.

Rin barely saw the shift of Errogan's shadow in time, barely flipped onto her back and out of the way.

Chapter Fifty-Two

R in's breaths were as heavy as lead, but her eyes remained diligent. The demon adjusted his grip on the sword grazing her arm. The blade had come so close to slicing her in half. Sweat laced her body.

"So," Errogan muttered from where he towered above her, "you choose the difficult route." A sneer twisted his lips in wicked delight. "Good. I think I'll enjoy it this way after all the trouble you've caused me, Rin Nowell." He heaved the blade out of the earth, sand flying as he went for the kill.

That was the moment she waited for.

The sword raised in the air, however, Rin slammed her heels into Errogan's upper leg, deep into the muscle. He lurched at the impact, biting down as hard as he could on his cry. The sword swung down, but landed nowhere near her.

Rin got to her feet with barely a moment to breathe. Errogan advanced faster than she could block, his shadow-engulfed hand grabbing for her throat. Just when she prepared herself for the menacing touch of the demon, Genesis leapt in front of her.

Genesis wielded two daggers, intent to kill. One sliced at Errogan's throat, the second aimed for his heart. The blades missed their targets, but rage spanned Errogan's face. The dagger in Genesis's hand caught her eye.

It was the dagger that had been thrown at Errogan's head. The dagger the demon tossed into the sands. It acted as a guard in Genesis's hand, held to defend his throat while the second blade defended his torso. Genesis had not walked to pick it up since. Rin was certain of that, for she had also kept her eye on the newcomer.

A venomous laugh spat out of Errogan's mouth. "Summoning won't save you, Masquarem."

Summoning? Rin wasn't certain she heard him right.

His laugh turned hideous. "Nothing short of the Divine will get you out of this alive."

Genesis clenched his jaw. "What ever happened to safe passage back to the fortress?"

Errogan sighed. "It's dawning on me that three bodies will be too much of a hassle to carry since the shifter shredded the usefulness out of my second in command. Besides," he sneered, "you're looking less for wear. Whatever you did to escape, however you managed it, it wasted you. You're not strong enough to keep using your magic."

Rin's eyes slid to the back of Genesis's head. Even if he stiffened, he held strong. "Don't write this off as a victory yet." The challenge between the two was thick as smoke, smoke that Rin could still smell even this far away from the demolished Base. Genesis was confident, not fearless. Rin saw the slight tremble in his hands, but the man looked the demon in the eye and spoke boldly. He was certain of his chances.

Genesis suddenly lifted his open palm in the air, an allure of navy and violet aura wisping around his hand. The magic was night and day compared to Errogan's dark power. The aura faded from the air, and with its departure, Rin's scimitar rested in his hand.

Genesis tossed the blade into Rin's hands without so much as a glance.

"Piece of advice," Genesis murmured when she met his side, "move in as close as you can get."

Rin nearly balked. "You've got to be kidding me." Advice for getting killed.

"That blade is better slicing at a close range. Use your small size, get in close, and slash deep." He didn't look at her as he spoke.

"I've never received formal training."

"I'd think this was the first time you've ever held it." Though Genesis offered her a faint grin, it didn't cover up the doubt carved into his face.

Genesis rushed Errogan without another word, wielding his daggers in a deathly dance that the demon joined without hesitation. Rin took one last breath, then jumped in.

When Rin and Genesis fought against Errogan, they stood side by side. They teamed against the Moonlit Bastard. Whenever Genesis advanced, Rin whorled around and attacked from behind. If Rin had grown too bold, Genesis was right there to counter in her stead. When one fell, the other worked to catch them. Rin found every slash of her blade struck the hum in the back of her head. So deep in her mind, so dark and untouched, that the entire sensation felt anew. Awakened. It raged with every decision, every wink of thought that saved her head from Errogan's darkness. It always rounded back to that hum. She pivoted on her heels, springing up to her legs and avoiding the shadowy current.

Errogan scoffed. "You're handier with a blade than I would have imagined, Nowell." He regained his stance, knocking Genesis's hand down with his elbow. Neither she nor Genesis landed a hit. "I suppose you'd have to learn fast dealing with Zarus's failures firsthand."

Rin pushed down on the ire burning in her chest. "Zarus's only failure was associating with you," she growled, mindlessly taking a step closer to Errogan. A step that nearly took off her head, for he sliced a shadow-engulfed blade at her neck. Genesis pulled her out of the way just in time, but he wasn't so lucky.

The demon's knuckle met Genesis's face and threw him down into the sandy sea.

"Even *you're* protecting her now?" Errogan called, spinning his blade into its sheath. "I thought you were the one who pulled the poor girl into this fight?"

Blood trickled from Genesis's head. Bruises formed along his jawline. Yet he still tried to stand.

Rin's chest caved. Slowly, her gaze slid off of Genesis and to the stars overhead. Stars that started fading as sunrise crept closer and closer.

They couldn't have died for nothing.

"Do you now understand?" Errogan's voice cut through her thoughts like a sword through water. He began waltzing toward Genesis, who slowly rose to his knees. "Nothing you can do, no amount of people you go through, will stop me from completing my task." No smirk sat on his lips, no haughtiness to his tone. With eyes so cold and stoic that she was reminded of Zarus, he tried to make her understand how powerless she was. The knife he held against Genesis's throat was *her* fault. And for a moment, just a single moment, Rin almost fed into it.

Her fists balled at her sides. "The only one who pushed me into this fight was myself," Rin said too quietly through her teeth, planting her feet solidly on the shifty ground. She closed her eyes, unable to think of anything but the balled up hum blaring in the back of her head. She could barely keep her body from shaking against it. "No one else but myself, Errogan." How very tempting it was to listen to that siren. Like a mermaid's song, the path less traveled, the promise of adventure.

"And I am the only one who decides when I'm finished fighting." She forced her voice to be heard. The hum screamed at her like a wild beast.

How many more people will you let fall in your stead? Genesis, Feyne, Tatsuo, Scarlette, Urlae, Leew. Zarus.

Rin felt the overwhelming cry in her head, the tug and pull of it on her body, and gave in.

She dove headfirst into the hum's ravaging current. Rin's heartbeat for the first time. She gazed upon the world with its endless beauties and horrors so clearly that she questioned whether she had truly ever *looked* at it her entire life. It was like falling into the sea. Deeper and deeper and deeper. The hairs on her arms and neck stood on edge. The sea was dark and cool and untouched. Unused. Rin fell so deep that she dug her nails into her palms to drag herself back. She opened her eyes.

"You," she said to Errogan, the words soft as a warm kiss of air on her lips. "You will not lay another finger on any of them." The power swarmed around herself. Around her head and heart and arms and legs. A current of white light waiting to be conducted.

She collected every ounce of magic that she fell into and poured it into the torrent that swarmed around her. It manifested as white tendrils that waved and slashed from her body, flowing in every direction around. Bright, blinding, cleansing. The light fought off the darkness, found every crack and crevice the shadows scurried in to hide. It was a wave of light, hitting everything that it crossed. No one moved against the force of the magic.

It felt like being reborn. She stared in Errogan's direction, although she couldn't focus on one thing while using it. Without a flinch of her muscles, the wave rushed toward him.

Errogan, the high and mighty demon who snuffed out his enemies and ripped them to shreds, could not muster his strength against her power. She saw his bared teeth, the straining veins in his temples and taut cords of his neck as the light washed away every drop of the darkness he fought to summon.

"Y-you think," Errogan grounded as a thin line of blood ran down the side of his mouth, "that a little light is going to stop me?" Each word was an effort, every syllable a strain.

She narrowed her shining eyes and held her chin higher. The flow of magic strengthened. Errogan forced his heels into the sand, another growl rumbling deep in his throat.

It was draining; it was revitalizing; it was suffocating. A force so great that Rin quaked beneath the pressure of it, but the magic did not ebb. The exquisite power roared over her commands of controlling it like she had become the hum.

She was still pushing back Errogan, burning up his very being with her light, when someone shifted beneath him.

Genesis stumbled to his feet. The wave staggered his every move, threatening to knock him down. She opened her eyes and only then truly saw what she had been doing. Her breath hitched.

Errogan was on his knees, the light blanching his moon-soaked hair ghostly. His head struggled to stay up, his eyes glassy and raw. It was wearing him thin, drying him up. And if it was doing such things to the demon, then surely, *surely*, it was tearing her friends apart as well.

Stop. Rin gritted her teeth together, tried and failed to ball her hands. Her throat withered. The magic was too much.

Stop, dammit! You're hurting them! You're hurting them all!

Something streamed down the side of her face. Was she crying? She couldn't tell.

Genesis tumbled down.

Too much. It was too much.

Stop it, Rin. Turn it off!

Panic overcame her and took the air out of her lungs. Her knees threatened to buckle. The light was a mind of its own; nothing without her, but not hers to control.

Errogan's head lowered. Rin knew what her light was doing to him; to all of them. No matter the hatred she held, would she kill everyone for it? She glanced at Genesis.

The world spun; the air turned to lead. Rin's body quaked and her magic raged.

Rin scowled at the power. Another force would not control her. She would not cower again.

"Enough!" Rin screamed, her voice a shrill cry among the sea's ruthless waves. Her command struck into the magic's core. The waves froze. The entire ocean fell still, not even her breath shaking its form. Then, in the blink of an eye, the ocean suddenly whipped into motion. The light rushed back toward Rin so fast she thought she was going to drown. It hit like a stone wall. She yelped and crashed to her knees, clutching the center of her chest as the world bathed in the lightless morning once more.

Rin gasped as if it was her first breath of life until her body finally stopped quaking and her head cooled enough to see the boots standing before her.

Errogan sucked in heavy, greedy gasps to match her own. "That was quite a show," he rasped, his voice raw enough to bleed. "You might have even killed them all for me had you not controlled yourself."

Errogan stared down into her eyes as if they were an object so foreign, not even he had come across it in all his travels. "You're not at all what I expected, Rin, and it excites me to say that the surprise was pleasant. Now you're drained, and as I've said, there's nowhere else to run—"

The blur of a silhouette lunged for the demon. Errogan stepped back just in time, but he could do nothing to hide his shock before Rin was up on her feet. The snarling growl had her throat hitching a sob. Feyne circled Errogan, his snarling jaw snapping—however apparent his limp had been. Errogan's fury slid to Rin, but as she raised her weapon, a wall of blistering flames rose and lit the darkness between her and the demon. Tatsuo slowly made his way behind her. He still held his abdomen with one arm and rested his weight on his spear, but he was walking. Rin had to hold back her cry as the *narikaah* met her side.

The flames forced Errogan another step back. His face was white hot with rage once the wall dissipated. "*How*?" He ducked below a dagger thrust toward his head before he could attack. Genesis pushed Errogan back even further.

Feyne circled, Tatsuo by her side, and Genesis not far. All of them walking. All of them breathing. Rin's heart could have leapt with joy. Errogan did not share the same delight.

The demon's eyes shifted between the beings and then back to her. There they lingered until the shadow of understanding veiled his shock. Errogan's expression filled with something between fury and dread. Not a single cut or bruise remained on any of them. His teeth gritted, his voice thundered. "You're a godsdamned white mage!" He snarled as the faintest glimmers of morning peeked over the horizon in the west.

Errogan rushed forward, heedless of form. Guided by the remnant call of the hum, Rin tightened her grip around the scimitar in her hand, and cut into his chest. The demon's blood splashed onto her hands.

"Do not," Rin panted through her teeth, "lay a damn hand on me ever again." She clenched her teeth, but her rage staggered at the sight before her.

Errogan landed on his back beside his sword. Rin gaped at his blanched face that nearly matched his hair. The hollow sheen of his sunken eyes, lips cracked dry.

She had done that to him. He grabbed the hilt of his blade, but Rin jumped onto the demon. Dodging a slice of the sword, she swung down her scimitar onto his wrist, striking true. His sword thudded to the ground with a spray of crimson, and Rin fought to dig her blade into his throat. She pushed her weight against his strength, the edge of the scimitar barely pressing against his neck. Someone shifted behind her, but Errogan summoned the scrap of his darkness that survived her light and formed a dome of liquid shadows around them. Rin pressed down harder, but Errogan's strength tried to work her off of him.

Her friends fought against the barrier, but the demon poured his will into the fracturing barrier. Rin gritted her teeth. Errogan refused to give in. For the quickest moment, a shadow befell his eyes. A desire for the death Rin could give him. His face turned grim; in such a way it looked as if it was Zarus who fought for his life below her, rather than the feral-smiled demon. They had the same cheekbones, the same nose and lips. It was in that vision of Zarus that went unseen by the others trapped outside that Rin stopped pushing down. Errogan shoved her away.

The dome melted as the demon sat upward, drinking the air into his winded lungs. Feyne, Tatsuo, and Genesis rushed forward to tear Errogan apart, but Rin held up her hand.

"Stop!" she shouted so loud it shook the sands below. Everyone froze at her command.

"Rin," pressed Tatsuo. He angled the tip of his father's spear at Errogan's heart, but Rin kept her hand held up.

Her voice was calm. "Don't do Eretimis's work for him."

Errogan kept his stare on her, something like animosity flickering in his gaze. Her mind raced back to the want for death in his eyes. She wasn't sure what to make of it. For a moment, no one spoke. The muscles in the demon's jaw clench, his eyes surveying the scene before him. Errogan finally swallowed a hard breath, then rose to his feet with silver sword in hand.

"Where do you think you're going?" Genesis asked, sharper than the steel he wielded.

Errogan scowled, his voice tired. "I know the odds when I see them, Masquarem, and you have better things to focus on." He glanced at Tatsuo's stomach, Feyne's blood, then back to Rin. A hollow smirk spread across his face. "Don't rely on that light next time we meet."

"The next time we meet will be your last breath," Tatsuo seethed from her side. Errogan regarded the *narikaah* and all the others with narrowed eyes before returning to her.

Rin watched him soberly. "Don't keep your master waiting."

Errogan stared. The side of his lip twitched as if he almost lost grip of his grin, but he said nothing more—his skin blanched and magic still struggling to flicker after her light. He then drew a strange symbol in the air as though his finger was dipped in ink, followed by the appearance of a blue-rimmed window floating above the ground. He stepped through without looking back. The window closed.

The sun peered over the horizon. Rin realized how exhausted she was, and the world flipped on its side.

Chapter Fifty-Three

Rin felt the cool sand against her face, the heat of the hands pulling her off of the ground, and the warm kiss of the sun. What she did not feel was the pounding hum in the back of her head. Where it once raged like a storm throughout her soul, her mind now sat quiet.

"*Rin!*"

Her head ached. And her body. Worse than a bad day in the fields with her father.

"*Rin!*"

Lying on the ground and letting the world spin without her would do no good. Every joint and muscle in her body protested, but Rin lifted to her elbows, and found whatever voice remained in her. "I'm okay," she croaked, not very confident in her answer. "I'm okay." When she finally took the time to split open her eyes and look around, Tatsuo knelt at her side—frantic as could be—while Genesis hovered above curiously. She could have sworn the man's fingertips were stained violet before she blinked and it faded away.

Tatsuo's arms swung around her. The comfort of a friend's embrace felt nice, but the tighter he held her, the more Rin understood his gesture wasn't just joy that they were both still alive.

"I'm sorry," the dragon whispered in her ear, "I'm so, so sorry."

His storming off had been the furthest thing from her mind. She locked her arms around him, settled her head onto his shoulder. "Tatsuo, look, I don't want to go back home just yet. I don't even know if I—"

Tatsuo let go. "Stop. Just stop." She paused. "I misunderstood you. I was stupid and rash. The thought of you leaving for good... hurts. You're the only person I've got left, Rin." He shook his head again. "But that's not your problem. Please," he finally pulled his slitted pupils back to her, "please forgive me."

Rin's mouth dried, but only for a second. "I was never mad at you to begin with," she offered a half smile. She nudged his shoulder with her fist, and at long last his expression eased, as did something in her chest. "Besides, I'm not running home anymore, at least not until I figure some things out." Her eyes fell to her hands.

"Like what on Armiria that was?" Tatsuo asked with caution for her sake.

"Like what on Armiria that was..." she nodded, eyes falling back to the dragon's abdomen.

They both stared at Tatsuo's tattered tunic. White mage. The world of magic was still so new to her, she barely knew anything about it. What did the title mean? The name Errogan spat rang through her head like an echo in the abyss until whatever was shielding the sun from her eyes moved and the light blinded her.

"And what about you?" Rin asked sharper than she intended, hissing against the morning light. "Where do you tie into all of this?" She stood, angling herself so Genesis blocked the sun again. He waited to speak until she helped Tatsuo to his feet—whatever she did to heal him, it did not close the dragon's wounds all the way. Rin bet Feyne's gashes hadn't closed over either.

Genesis scratched the back of his head. In the sun, Rin could clearly see that even the shadow of captivity couldn't hide the beauty of the man's eyes. Shining even brighter and deeper now in the light.

"Well..." he mumbled. Genesis Masquarem shared the story of how he became acquainted with a demon named Zarus Lowwenth, and the even more unbelievable details of his escape from the fortress. Rin's throat dried up. Talking of serums and crashing down iron stairs and frozen dungeons and crypts hidden beneath the Dark Tyrant's fortress. By the end, the end that Rin was so filled with dread that her stomach clenched, her lips hung apart as she searched for something to say.

"Then he yanked me down," Genesis explained, "and said, '*Find her. Find Rin Nowell and protect her. Save her.*' I thought he was hit one too many times. Not even the Wraith Twins realized he was drawing up a portal." Genesis dropped his gaze to nothing in particular. "The next thing I know, I'm suddenly lying in a desert staring at the stars." He was silent for a moment, but sighed. "We never stood a chance against those sisters."

Rin closed her eyes, letting out the shred of fallen hope she clung to. "So Eretimis still has him." She knew it was foolish, but she prayed that Zarus also escaped after seeing the dread in Errogan's face when he saw Genesis.

"How did Zarus know to send you here?" Tatsuo asked.

Genesis shook his head. "Your guess is as good as mine. I only found you because I saw the fire and followed the trail in the sand to help whatever survivors there might have been." He looked back toward Base, where Rin saw smoke was still rising. "When I got here, I recognized his voice and heard Errogan say your name." He shrugged. "It played out sooner than I thought, but I figured you were the same Rin that Zarus told me to help."

Rin shut her eyes and ran a hand through her hair. Then the question welled that she couldn't keep silent any longer. "What happened at Base?" She looked at Tatsuo. He was there fighting before she and Feyne arrived. "How did any of this even happen?"

The dragon looked down, knowing all too well the question was looming. He shifted his weight on the spear. "I—" he shook his head, squeezed his eyes closed. "I don't know. It was a bloodbath when I came back. Those demons, they tore through everyone." The faces, the bodies, the eternal cries of pain on them. She had seen them. Tatsuo *heard* them. "The bunker was already burning when I got there," his voice flattened, refusing to break. "I wanted to fight with the ones outside and kill the demons, but I was the only one who could go into the fire. I had to find anyone down there who was alive. I searched, but there were no survivors." His words turned harsh. Tatsuo's grip choked the metal of his spear. Rin placed a hand on his. "When I came back out, there was no one left."

Something rolled down her cheek. Rin finally took a moment and looked at Tatsuo's face. She took in the ash and soot that grimed his skin; at the sweat that had dripped streams through it, at the blood that washed it away. "Tatsuo..." she whispered.

"The demons were gone, too. I tracked them down and found Scarlette fending off both." That's right, Scarlette had been on night watch. She must have warned everyone. "I joined her, and you showed up not long after." Tatsuo finally lifted his head, and Rin saw nothing but festering guilt.

"I should have never left," Feyne breathed. "I should have been here."

Rin looked behind at the ghren clutching Scarlette's body to his chest. The gashes carved by Errogan hadn't closed all the way. She watched the bare shifter hold on to the girl in his arms.

So you could end up dead like the rest? Had they been there when the assault began, Rin was certain she would not be standing here to see the sunrise. Feyne as well. He didn't see it that way.

"How many were trapped inside?" Feyne asked.

Tatsuo stayed silent, pressing his lips thin together. The struggle in his expression was clear as day. "...I'm not sure—"

"Don't lie to me!" Feyne lashed, whipping his head back as he barked. "*How many did you find trapped in the fire?*" Rin saw the full stain of Scarlette's blood on the shifter's chest. She quickly looked at Tatsuo. The muscles in the dragon's jaw tensed.

"Seventeen."

The word was a stab in the heart. Rin winced at the sound of it. Seventeen lives locked underground, left to burn to death. She could hardly bring herself to think it true. Upon hearing the number, something escaped from inside Feyne entirely. His eyes emptied.

"What about all the exits?" Rin uttered. "What about the hidden passes? Every one of them knew how to get out! They had to have escaped somehow!" Rin shook her head. "Why didn't they leave?" It was little more than a whimper leaving her lips. Tatsuo barely brought himself to glance at her. She then remembered how the exits and entrances were stoned shut and buried in sand. It was impossible! No one, not even those demons, could have found every hidden passage into the bunker. Nausea hit her like a carriage. "How did this happen?" she pleaded to no one but Yath Ha.

Feyne spoke bitterly. "A traitor." Rin's chest tightened. He shook his head.

Tatsuo forced the emotion from his voice. "I couldn't identify them all by features." The words cut short in his throat for a second. "Some I only knew by scent... Bjarkh," he had to pause for a moment while he found his voice, "Bjarkh was one of them. I only made it in by breaking down one structure blocking a door. It was burning... no one else could have made it through."

Rin closed her eyes again, dreaming of a world where none of this happened.

Genesis was the first to voice what everyone was thinking. "What now?"

Nothing came to Rin's mind, only tears in her eyes. The thought of figuring out how to work past this felt like she was being sucked deep into the depths of the sands. She would not allow that feeling to overtake. Because they had to do something. Scarlette couldn't have died for nothing. None of them.

With a wipe of her tears, she started talking. "Your friend. The one we were going to meet, Feyne. Can she help us?" They were too far from Aresan to get her father's help, and even then, she didn't want to bring any chance of harm home. Seeking aid from someone she had never met was a risk, but there was nothing else to do.

Feyne barely acknowledged the question. He merely dipped his chin into a slow nod as he cradled Scarlette, knowing what they all kept unsaid. She was the only one untouched by Rin's magic.

Chapter Fifty-Four

Rin wished she could forget the awkward shuffling and attempts to find supplies while Feyne said goodbye to his beloved. They didn't have time to bury her in a grave. Not with Errogan on his way back to Eretimis. Besides, none of them wished to prevent Vulyn's Hand from guiding the souls to their rightful places.

The dry sea simmered, stinging her face as the wind carried the sand. Rin saw nothing for miles on end. The sun crept higher and higher in the pale sky as blisters formed on the pads of her feet. Her thoughts buzzed like flies. Wasteland, indeed. None of that mattered—not the lack of food since yesterday evening, her sandpaper dry tongue, or trudging up and down endless dunes as the sun mocked them. Not when she turned back and saw smoke puffing in the sky. Especially not when she looked back and saw nothing along the sizzling horizon.

The silence was numbing. She felt lost, stuck, empty. She couldn't do a damn thing about it. What was Feyne feeling? Everything he built up from the ground was nothing but ash in the winds now. Everyone he met. However, Rin needed to talk to him alone. It was only when everyone took a moment to breathe after reaching the bottom slopes of the highlands did they all agree to rest before their ascent.

Tatsuo went off in search of water, and Genesis opted to find a shadow of his own to cool off in. Rin could only assume it was midday as she glanced at everyone's shadows. It didn't take her long to become accustomed to the silence. The difficulty was forcing her voice to break through the thick layer of sand coating her throat.

She found the shifter resting behind a slope of rocky outcrop. It offered a small pocket of shade against the beating sun.

"Feyne."

It caught her off guard when Feyne brought his eyes to her. She expected him to stare blankly ahead, as he had all morning. "I wanted to talk," she said cautiously, "if that's alright with you." He held her stare for a long moment, the gold in his eyes melted by the desert's fever, and she honestly thought that he was going to turn her away. She could already feel the guilt building inside her chest. Suddenly, the sweltering heat swarmed around like agitated hornets. But, to Rin's surprise, the shifter scooted over so that she could slide into the shade.

The shade was like a glass of lukewarm water. Feyne didn't say a word, and neither did she for a moment. Her mind was still bent around the knowledge that he needed to grieve. Rin waved it off. Cruel as it was, there would be time to mourn when they were safe.

"I know—" Rin just barely had the time to open her mouth when Feyne's head met her shoulder. She jumped. The sweat on his forehead seeped into her sleeve, but she didn't throw him off.

"Are you hurt?" Feyne mumbled.

Her brow furrowed, sending a beam of sweat running down her face. "No? I'm fine, or I think I am... I'm not too sure anymore, actually."

Feyne picked up his head. "I never asked. I meant to, but..." his voice fell, "I apologize."

"Hey," Rin said, nudging him with her shoulder, "thank you for asking." The edges of her lips curved, but the smile was empty, and he knew it.

"Just say whatever it is," he sighed, turning his attention away.

Rin tried not to cower. "I know you're blaming Tatsuo for everything that happened." The words blurted from her mouth like they were something never meant to be said. She only wished it appalled Feyne as well. He didn't react.

"Why do you say that?"

Rin stared at the shifter who looked at the world with nothing in his gaze. Maybe she should have waited. Rin shut her eyes. All she saw were the faces. Everyone she passed, flashing through her mind in a flurry of terror and sorrow. "You know why," she said quickly.

"Then you know why I blame him."

Another jab at her chest. She hoped she was wrong. Her hands trembled, and it soon spread to her voice. Anger drove her to speak. "Errogan is to blame. Eretimis is to blame. You're a fool to believe Tatsuo had anything to do with the attack, fire or no fire. And forcing him to hear about his parent's death is the closest to a monster I ever want to see you be, Yreyshin Wuflan." The words kept rolling, her voice kept shouting. "You're in pain. I understand you just experienced a loss greater than most people could handle. Get angry about it, rage about it! Scream at the whole damn world about it and tear it apart to make it right again if you have to! But channel it where it's due, and do not for one second throw that rage at someone who you know would never commit such a sin. Not so the truth will be easier to accept. Because you're better than that—*smarter* than that. What would Scarlette think, hearing what it is you're accusing right now?" Rin's jaw snapped shut as she realized what she said. The words sent a jolt through Feyne's body, lingering heavy in the air between them.

The sun peeked over the rock Feyne leaned against, highlighting the dark tattoo on his arm. Rin forced herself to take a breath. She felt the heat on the back of her head and neck and pressed her palms against her eyes. There was nothing else to say.

Rin dropped her arms down to her sides. Feyne remained hunched over himself when she looked. "We should move out," she said, turning away to find Tatsuo emerging empty-handed from behind the slopes. "There's nothing for us to gain waiting here…" The truth of her words struck hard, and she nearly winced against them. A hand yanked her back. She looked over her shoulder and found Feyne holding her wrist. He didn't look at her.

"I—" It was a breath on his lips, nothing more. Just when Rin thought he was going to finish his thought, Feyne shook his head. She rested her free hand on top of his. Wordlessly, she squeezed it, and stayed until the others headed toward them.

They climbed further south of the highlands they trekked last time. The slopes creased into narrow paths that drafted light breezes, carrying the howls and whispers that Rin forced herself to believe were just the wind. Instead of heading straight up, Feyne took them deeper into the mount. Farther in where it was harder for the sun to reach them, where the wind howled, and the shade felt like sickness creeping across her skin. Hours passed, and they eventually reached a secluded landing on the side of the slopes to rest. She was gazing over the ledge to the distant desert when Genesis snuck up on her.

"W-what is it?" Rin squealed, stifling her yelp.

"Do you feel it too?" he asked. Rin could feel the utter confusion and slight annoyance seeping through the dirtied pores of her face.

"I have absolutely no idea what you're talking about, Genesis…" His name was still driving her crazy. Something like a dim memory that remained just within the shadows of ignorance.

He stared at her for another moment, lingering on her eyes specifically. Rin wasn't even sure the man was breathing until he sighed.

"The air up here is draining," Genesis mumbled. He dropped his stare and sat down on the thin, shale ground beside her. "I suppose it would just seem like a chill to most people." Rin tried not to snarl at the condescension in the stranger's tone.

She snapped without thought. "I think we all witnessed that I'm not exactly like *most people*." She heard the ice spreading through her voice and it surprised her. Genesis saved her life. Yet still, she couldn't shake the constant irritation clawing at her when she spoke with him.

He raised an interested brow, running a hand through his hair. "So you didn't know you're a user. Hard to believe you've gone this long without realizing it," the man mused. "Your eyes alone scream it to the world."

"My eyes?" Rin wrinkled her nose. "What do they have to do with magic?" Ice and frost and frost and ice. What exactly was it clawing at her temper?

He arched his dark eyebrows. "You really know nothing about this stuff, do you?" He wasn't looking for an answer, and it was probably for the best. "The eyes of a user differ from a regular human's. Brighter. More radiant. It's our greatest trademark," he faced forward, looking at the rising heat above the midday desert. "And our biggest give away."

Rin had to admit it was a useful fact. Her eyes always seemed to shine brighter than anyone she knew. "I didn't grow up around magic," she said, bending her knees against her chest. All she wanted was to rest in silence.

He slowly nodded. "No one grows up around magic anymore. And you just learned about this power today?"

A nod.

And then silence. Genesis kept quiet for a minute, staring ahead. Rin snatched the opportunity to steal a glance of his eyes, satisfying her curiosity. Their deep blue practically glowed. It was only when

Genesis caught her stare did Rin think about removing it. He offered her a faint grin, only to be met with nothing.

Genesis finally sighed, losing the smile, and sitting up straight. "Look," he ran a hand through his hair, pulling the unkempt locks out of his face. "I'm sorry that Zarus didn't get out and sent me here instead... I know you wish I was him—"

Her eyes widened. "I don't wish you were Zarus at all!" Which wasn't true. And the horrid truth smacked her in the face right when he suggested it. Was that truly why she was angry? Because she wanted Zarus to be here? She shook her head, rubbing her palms into her eyes. "Yes, I want Zarus out of the fortress," she said slowly so her tongue did not betray her, "but obviously you needed to get out, too. Zarus thought so, else you wouldn't be here. A lot has happened recently," what an exquisite understatement. "Don't apologize for being here. I also realize that we were never properly introduced before, with the life or death crisis and all, so I'm Rin. Rin Nowell, to be exact. It's nice to meet you."

A lonely breeze danced through Rin's hair as it escaped the rocky landscape. She hated keeping all her thoughts bottled up for so long. Because there was no stopping the flood until there was no water left to run. Rin was still holding her hand out toward the wide-eyed man beside her. She fought back the urge to laugh out of sheer awkwardness.

"Also," she added, slowly pulling back her hand after he didn't shake it, "thank you for saving me back there. I would be, you know, dead... if you hadn't. Or worse, apparently. I appreciate it."

Genesis reached out and grabbed Rin's hand before the offer was gone. "Genesis Masquarem. Nice to meet you, Rin." His bright eyes narrowed, and he smiled at her after huffing a laugh. "And don't mention it. You ended up returning the favor, so thank you as well."

He dipped his chin down, and Rin couldn't help a smile of her own. "Besides, the one you should thank is that pissy demon, Zarus. I wouldn't have even known who you were if he hadn't sacrificed... himself."

Rin picked up her head at the sudden pause. It sounded as if reality finally hit Genesis. What Zarus surrendered so he could walk free.

They both fell silent, whistling winds replacing voices. Rin knew all too well the weight of the feeling. Though it took a moment of hesitation, she placed her hand on his shoulder. A shoulder that felt so frail under her touch. Rin sighed, having finally caught her breath and having some to spare. "Do you think he's still alive?" She faced forward, not wanting to look at Genesis upon asking.

Rin heard the hard breath he swallowed before answering. "He's too important to kill." It wasn't anything worth finding relief in, but she supposed she would have to make do.

"Well then," Rin said, finding some strength in her voice and standing up, "I'll just have to see for myself when I get him out."

Genesis scoffed. "And just how do you plan to do that?" There it was, that hint of mockery. Or arrogance? Rin couldn't tell yet.

"Very carefully," she said as she stretched her arms far out toward the azure heavens. Rin spun around and winked, a smile meeting her face in like fashion. "And if that doesn't work, maybe I'll give you a better answer later, Genesis Masquarem." She offered him a hand to get up. Rin knew she had no business smiling. She remembered how long the villagers in Aresan spent mourning after someone passed. She also knew that with all the matters piling up on one another, none of them should sit any longer.

Genesis stared at her in silence, the shadow of a smile holding his lips still. After another moment, the shadow on his face melted into a grin as he grabbed her hand. Rin helped him up, and to her surprise, he shook her hand.

"We'll both see for ourselves," he breathed. Rin stared for a moment before she understood what he meant. Zarus had saved Genesis's life, and apparently he wasn't intent to forget that. She smiled as Feyne and Tatsuo started shuffling about behind her.

Genesis's sigh caught her attention. "I hope whoever his friend is, they're willing to risk our company." He then walked away to meet with the shifter and dragon, leaving Rin staring at the space between his shoulder blades.

***

Rin knew it wasn't his intent, but Genesis's comment dragged through her head like chains through water.

What if Luna refused them? What if they were forced to trudge through the plateau with no supplies, praying to the gods that Tatsuo's injuries didn't kill him before they found help elsewhere? Or something fouler found them first.

Feyne led the party through the narrow, breathless passes. Their path became filled with far more hazards the further they traveled. One misstep would push them into the mercy of the rocky cliffs, or into one of the chasms they avoided. If Rin didn't know any better, she'd think the shifter was taking her straight into the heart of the rock. In some areas, she couldn't even see the blue skies above. The path twisted, turned, and shifted so narrowly that Rin did not understand how everyone wasn't stuck the moment they stepped foot into the nightmarish thoroughfare. They walked until she hadn't seen the sky for hours. The sun already passed its peak on the cliff side, and Rin didn't know how much longer she could go without a drink.

Sweat beaded her brow as she balanced across a ledge overlooking a depthless gorge. She noticed it again. The chill of the air that Genesis mentioned. It sucked her dry.

'The air up here is draining.'

Rin grabbed Feyne's hand to steady herself. She followed him through a long, dim cave hidden in the twists of the mount's walls. The dim light at the end of the hollow was like food to the famished.

When she could see again, she was speechless.

Towering walls of reddish stone stretched a hundred feet into the air, where a small opening of the sky peered into the box canyon like a sunroof. Daylight trickled down from above, but while just short of meeting at the top, the walls stretched further and further until they finally met the ground half a mile apart in each direction. A lake rippled in the center of the grassy clearing. A garden of flowers and herbs led to a stone cabin on the far side of the water where smoke plumed from a chimney. No matter how marvelous the sight of grass and water, Rin felt the draining chill worsen.

She and Genesis helped carry Tatsuo around the lake. He had already excused his spear, and if she had to guess, he was feeling the constant drain, too. The closer she walked to the cabin, the stronger the scent of flowers roamed. The lavender, in particular, was so strong that her nostrils burned with a strange familiarity. They only halted when Feyne knocked on the door.

It felt like ages, but eventually, the door cracked open. Rin's attention jolted to find the woman who would ultimately seal their fate, but Feyne stood in her way. No one said a thing. It was a silence that ripped her patience apart, but after a long moment, the wooden door swung open and Feyne huffed a sigh of relief and stepped in. She was the last to enter.

Dark figures and hushed voices greeted her arrival. Rin sucked in a massive breath as she felt the pressure draining her dry finally lift out of the air. Her eyes adjusted, and she couldn't help grin. The cabin was cozy and warm and smelled of fresh lavender. Large by no means, but it wasn't unlivable. It even reminded her a bit of the homes back in her own village. However, it was lacking something she couldn't put her finger on. Something that had the cozy little space feeling empty.

Feyne stood on the opposite side of the room, speaking in a whisper to a woman who hid in the shadows. *Luna.*

Rin saw her rosy cheeks, thin frame, and dirty gold locks tucked back into a messy braid, and her chest clenched. The remnant daylight lit up the woman's lavender eyes.

A cold sweat broke out along Rin's spine. She gasped, and the woman's eyes finally met her.

"Erin?"

Over frozen mountains and deceitful lakes. Through forests full of demons, wastelands with scurrying animals, and deserts handcrafted by angry gods. After meeting a mysterious and dangerous and broken male who saved her life yet not his own, after coming to love so many new people only for it all to burn away in a single night, after a life she had chosen for herself shattered into fragments of what it could have been. After she felt light course through her body as life and death. Only after all that was Rin to find her way to this little cabin by the hands of Yath Ha—Olru and E'ral themselves—only for her throat to be left dry of all words. All but one.

Rin clenched her fists at her sides, biting back the cry in her voice.

"Mom!"

Chapter Fifty-Five

The shadows clinging to the ceiling of the throne room greeted Zarus as he slowly woke up.

"Are you finally awake?" Eretimis sighed from atop the throne.

Zarus sucked in a breath and stumbled to his feet as the tyrant's impatient fingers tapped against the arm of the throne.

"If I recall," he scowled, sliding his fingers along the two-inch gash running behind his ear, "you weren't the one kicked unconscious by Raia." He didn't give a damn what Eretimis had to say. Zarus didn't care about anything after seeing freedom and letting his only chance of escape slip through his bloodied fingers. His body felt like it tumbled down the summit of the Hylan Peak. His thoughts pounded against his skull.

"Wasting my time will not make this any easier for you, boy."

Zarus forced the threat to course over him. "Then I suggest you get to your point and stop wasting mine." No chains bound him; nothing kept him from attacking.

The calculative eyes of the Tyrant peered over Zarus before he spoke. "I will not bother asking what it was you were trying to accomplish—"

"If it wasn't clear, then I've been giving you too much credit, Eretimis."

Few could read the reactions of the Dark Tyrant, but Zarus learned them ages ago. Eretimis was in a bad mood before Zarus even woke. "You would have frozen or starved to death in the frozen wastes. Demon or not, resistance to a little cold or not. Before you could worry if there was such a place where I would not be able to find you or that impetuous prince, you would have been dead."

"That prince is long gone," Zarus retorted, lifting his chin higher. "If you couldn't find me for three hundred years, then I'm confident he'll be safe for the rest of his life."

The tyrant straightened in his throne. "Trust me when I tell you this, Zarus: a user's life is not so hard to track down. I even found you. Time is something I have to spare." He rose to his feet without warning, looking down at Zarus from his pedestal with sudden wicked amusement. "When I say your heroic sacrifice was in vain, take those words to heart."

Zarus tried to keep his temper cool. He spat a bitter laugh. "And to think, you tried to convince me for years that I didn't possess such a thing."

It was the frankness in the tyrant's voice that threatened Zarus's resolve. "We all have hearts, Zarus. I simply taught you to think without one." Eretimis walked down the steps of the dais. "I thought I succeeded too. Tell me, when did you learn to open portals?"

Zarus watched the lanterns cast dastardly shadows on his old mentor's face. He didn't *just* open a portal, but against all odds, he linked it to the memory of Rin's presence. He didn't cower. Because as long as that girl stayed out of Eretimis's reach, then the tyrant lost. "Right around the time I figured out I was growing too powerful for you to control. You shouldn't leave the door to your study unlocked."

Suddenly, the tyrant stood in front of him, looking into his crimson eyes like a surgeon deciding where to cut first. "Why did you wait all this time to use it?"

Zarus narrowed his eyes. "We both know the risks of using portals: two could cross into each other if they're opened at the same time. I was out of options." Not that he would admit, but he also could never open one after years of trying.

The Tyrant's brow twitched with amusement. "Apparently, we do not know all the risks." His still stare beat down on Zarus's ignorance. "Do you know how portals operate, Zarus? The caster cuts a hole through our universe, scrunching up the fabric and connecting two spaces. There is another aspect that my followers often forget when they open these gateways. If you have to cut a hole and fold, then there is something filling the space between the two openings. A dark, cold, unknown place that unknown beasts lurk in. Beasts that are alone and hungry. It is my guess that they were zylk left over from the War of the Divine, and they hid in this space between nothing before the Divine exterminated them. You never know what might snatch you before you step out the other end."

Zarus swallowed dryly, his face pale in his stupor. "Like I said, I was out of options."

Eretimis smiled at this. "You were my favorite, Zarus. Always prepared for anything, even treachery. But saving Genesis? I thought I freed you from such *humanities*." Eretimis paced, circling him as if he were prey to be studied. "All it took to thaw your heart was a human caught in the snow and a demon back from the dead."

The words felt like death brushing against Zarus's ears. He forced himself to scoff. "Errogan did nothing to my heart other than try to rip it to pieces—literally." Finding his old friend alive was a surprise, but it was clear as day that their friendship died when Errogan fell off that cliff. Nothing remained other than a few unanswered questions. He wished he could tear the grin off Eretimis's face to prove it.

"And what of the girl?" The tyrant asked. "Did she also have no effect on your sudden care for the living?"

"You're a fool if you think either of them means a thing to me," Zarus said tightly.

"And you are a liar, but that is not the point."

Zarus bit down on his snarl. "Do enlighten me."

There was a moment of silence. Zarus reluctantly looked up to the demon's smile before him. A chill wrapped around his spine.

"I would be a fool if I overlooked how easily my best creation was ruined, Zarus. An even bigger fool not to see its uses." Eretimis paced, his dark hair caught in a phantom breeze, hands folded behind his back.

Zarus suppressed the urge to attack this smug bastard. "None of this matters. You're going to poison me with that serum again, and I'll fall victim to your will or die trying." Just the thought of having that sludge coursing through his veins again made him recoil.

Eretimis's step faltered a heartbeat. Just enough for Zarus to catch. The tyrant's tone was short. "The serum is no longer an option."

Eretimis's footsteps echoed like a clock ticking the seconds away. Zarus wasn't sure what it counted down to anymore. "No longer an option," he repeated in a hush. Zarus found himself face to face with Eretimis, who, to Zarus's surprise, did not look too pleased. "Did you finally realize how flawed it is?"

Eretimis stared at him with dark, ungiving eyes. "The serum is as perfect as it can get. It weeds out the beings who are of little use to me and gives me the ability to control those worthy to serve me. I alone am the only being who can use it, given that it was created from my magic." That was news, but it didn't shock Zarus. "It is as perfect as it can get. Near flawless."

Zarus narrowed his gaze. "But..."

"*But*," Eretimis accepted, holding firm to Zarus's stare, "because of the intensity of its effect on the body, it can only be used once without turning lethal."

It was involuntary; Zarus couldn't help the laugh bursting through his lungs. The sharpening throb of his head roared, but the laughter didn't ebb right away. "Now that's a magnificent flaw, wouldn't you say?" he asked, forcing his voice to level out. Although Zarus didn't hide the smirk spanning his cracked lips.

The outburst did nothing to faze the tyrant. "It could be seen as that, but given that you and that princeling are the first to freely walk away after being subjected to it, I would say it was not worth the thought."

The only two options until now were death or puppet. There'd be little reason to perfect the magic completely. What Zarus then didn't understand... "Why would you create the antidote if both results of the first worked in your favor?" Again, Zarus felt the awkwardness of not being bound in chains as he rubbed the area of his arm where those inky veins once spread about. He didn't think he'd ever be able to forget the deathly feel of those veins.

A sigh left the lips of the tyrant, and he once again paced. "It was a fail-safe to cancel out the first serum when I was still working to get the effects right. I never meant for the antidote to be used after I made the control serum." He cast a glance toward Zarus. "I have to admit, I am curious how you discovered it, boy."

Zarus's eyes dropped to the floor. "My will would be a vessel enacting whatever you imposed upon me right now if it wasn't for that prince." He huffed a laugh through his nose, bringing his smug stare back to The Tyrant in front of him. "That's what happens when you leave people to rot: they play dead until you're close enough to strike." Though Zarus didn't know for sure, Genesis probably learned of the antidote by eavesdropping on the guard's conversations. He based Zarus's freedom off of another hunch.

A devil's grin toyed at Eretimis's expression. "Yet you still ended up before my throne, Zarus. What good does a fool's hope do if you accomplish nothing but a gash on your head?"

"It sets another man free."

This time it was Eretimis who couldn't help his swelling laughter. The demon leaned over, leveling with Zarus's; pools of crimson staring into the depthless abyss. "And you made that sacrifice so the boy could run around in the sun for a few days before I catch up with him. Tell me, when were you ever the selfless type? Or is this something else you picked up in the last three hundred years?"

"I'll always make the sacrifice if I get something in return."

Eretimis's smirk deepened. "You have not changed, after all, Zarus. Still looking out for yourself, still acting without consideration to the power I possess."

"I guess so," Zarus agreed, stepping outside of the circle Eretimis walked around him. He paced opposite of the tyrant. "But this time I didn't even have to play in ignorance of your power. You wasted your one and only shot of using the serum. Your arrogance did all the work for me." Zarus spat out another laugh, but it sounded more like a scoff. "Now look at you: mindlessly talking to figure out what to do with me now that your *near flawless* plan fell to pieces at the hands of a human you experimented on one too many times, and a demon you thought as good as dead. So tell me, because I am dying to hear what you plan to do with me next, Eretimis, or are you finally realizing that I won't bend to your throne so easily as I once did? Maybe you're even considering ending my life; after all, a sentence to death seems rather fitting for everything I've done. Because believe me when I tell you this, *your Majesty*," he snarled at the title, "that serum was your best chance of having me bow down to you again. And you wasted it."

Zarus challenged the Dark Tyrant, and not for the first time in that meeting. There was something small and hushed that filled Zarus's head as he watched Eretimis face him. A voice that wasn't quite a voice, but a presence. The same presence that had been haunting him ever since he arrived at the fortress, even a bit before. Although now it didn't feel like he was catching the end of a fading echo. The clarity the presence communicated with sounded like someone whispering right in his ear.

The sensation wasn't too different from Vulyn's warnings, but it wasn't a feeling of dread. A thought in his head of words that weren't his own.

Do not tempt a fate we cannot control, child.

He will stop at nothing... he knows no bounds.

You must find a way to survive until—

Like a blade cutting through a fraying rope, the presence faltered.

Zarus gritted his teeth and looked the Tyrant in the eye. "Nothing else to say?"

The tyrant held his stare a moment longer. The depth in which the demon could look into someone was terrifying. Calculation crept into his expression, but a misleading smile replaced it. "Between you and Errogan, you were always the one that could not hold your tongue. You truly believe there are no other options for me? That I have lost all my chances of making you bow? You of all people should know I am never one to surrender."

'Do not tempt a fate we cannot control.'

The words of the voice echoed in Zarus's head. "What are you planning?"

The tyrant's smile grew deep into malice. "There are more ways than the serum to remold one's soul for my use. I think a certain human we just caught in the desert would do well to persuade your compliance. She would make you think twice about trying to sneak away again."

Zarus's magic riled. He watched wide-eyed as the demon before him slowly turned around and walked toward his throne.

Rin. Eretimis brought Rin to the fortress.

It was a flash, and not one of light. Zarus released his power in a heartbeat. One moment, thick shadows submerged all. The next, a surge of ice stretched out from the floor beneath Zarus's feet and consumed everything in its path. Spiraling rods of ice and frozen darkness erupted from the polished floor in a line headed straight for Eretimis. The magic never struck him, nor did he make it five steps in the tyrant's direction before a dozen demons filed out of the shadows and jumped to restrain Zarus.

The hilts of swords and daggers rammed into his body. They grabbed him. He heard arrows strung back in their bows from the balconies above, among the clatter of armor, as endless soldiers spilled into the throne room.

A savage roar burst from Zarus. Wild and uncontrolled, his ice crawled onto everything holding him back. He thrashed his body free and ran, leaving countless demons screaming as the ice shattered their limbs. He maneuvered through the recouping horde, not caring as they drew their weapons. The slices of steel were scrapes compared to what he planned to do to Eretimis. A storm of shouts thundered behind him, but he didn't bother with the guards. The only thing that mattered in those blurry moments was ripping out Eretimis's heart.

He was too fast for the foot soldiers, but the line of archers above caught him.

The first arrow struck his chest. He lurched over after two more pierced through his leg. Zarus fought against every drop of blood, every sense of survival blaring in his body, and willed himself to rise. He seethed with each limping movement, but the soldiers caught up to him. The pommel of a sword met the top of Zarus's skull. He thrashed against the impact, biting down so hard his vision flashed red as he staggered to his knees. Another restrained his arms behind his back. The first attempt to yank away earned a blade to his throat.

A vicious snarl welcomed the steel. Eretimis found his way to the throne and looked down at Zarus with disappointment. "If only you had not acted with your heart," the tyrant *tsked*, tapping his fingers against the arm of his throne. "Maybe then that girl would not be here in this mess."

Zarus attempted to free himself once more time. The blade cut closer to his jugular, drawing blood with every movement.

"*Where do you have her?*" He screamed at the demon.

That derisive grin stared down at him. "You have more important matters to worry about other than that human, boy."

As if on cue, every demon pulled him to his feet. They forced him forward, but not toward the doors. No, they pushed him up the marble steps leading to the throne. It was only then he realized where they led him.

"No," Zarus whispered under his breath. His pulse pounded like the drums of war. His body fought backwards. *Anywhere but there.* He dug his heels against the steps, pushing himself backwards with all the strength left in his body. The blood loss and uncontrolled surge of magic finally caught up with him. No matter how much he fought, he couldn't keep himself from being forced past the obsidian throne to the red velvet curtain that laid beyond. Nothing kept him from being tossed through the spiraling archways leading to the dark chamber hidden behind the throne—the room where so few had been invited, and no one had made it out in one piece. He was already under the threshold.

Zarus gritted his teeth. A dark mist engulfed his hands as he stomped his foot down and yanked his arm free. Against the strength of the soldiers, he forced himself to turn and outstretched his hand toward the back of the throne. A wisping tendril of shadow magic shot out from his palm at the demon who sat on the other side of it. Yet his control over the magic faltered, stopping just short of its mark. A hollow formed in Zarus's gut.

After all these years, Eretimis still overpowered him.

The weight of a lifetime pressed down upon Zarus's shoulders until everything became a blur. Stripped of his dignity, robbed of his freedom, and thieved of his strength, he didn't fight back as a fog settled over his head. Finally, the soldiers shoved him into the lightless chamber. The curtain drew shut, and like a candle blown out by a draft, his senses stranded him in the depthless darkness. That didn't matter, because Zarus had failed Rin Nowell.

There was little he could do to atone for that, save pray to the gods who had long ago forsaken him.

Chapter Fifty-Six

The velvet curtain fell over the chamber behind the throne. Eretimis whispered a spell to seal it in place, so even if Zarus had been screaming—had he been dying or bashing his head against the walls until he bled out—no one outside of the room would know. Not until Eretimis himself drew the curtain back. There were no disturbances as he paced back and forth before his throne. None, save for the bloodied demon lying prostrate upon the marble floor.

"Now," the tyrant's solemn voice ripped through the silence like thunder, yet the demon below did not stir, "explain to me again why you have returned empty-handed."

The demon did not respond, did not flinch or make to rise from the floor. Eretimis looked down at his silent, motionless subject. It was only when he knelt down and lifted the demon's head by his moon-lit hair did he continue. The shadows of the room rippled around the walls as he spoke. "Do not make me ask again, boy."

Errogan's bruised eyes tried and failed to focus. The demon at last forced his voice to connect with his thoughts. "She is a user." The words were a struggle as blood welled against his teeth.

"Oh?" the dark ruler hummed. "When was it ordered that you retreat upon sight of a measly human magic user?"

A spray of crimson hit the floor as Errogan exhaled. "There was no order," he coughed.

Eretimis nodded. "No order..." he mused, his eyes shifting off of the demon. A dry chuckle left his throat. "No order," he repeated.

The tyrant threw Errogan's head down, splitting right onto the edge of the first step leading to the throne. "I was not aware *you* were the one giving yourself orders, boy." Eretimis let go of Errogan. He staggered on the floor, grabbing the bridge of his nose as blood pooled on the marble. The Dark Tyrant paced back and forth, deep in thoughts nefarious enough to stir the dead.

"We found a mage!" Errogan seethed, struggling to his feet with newly fractured ribs. The bruises seizing his skin suggested a broken arm as well.

"And I told you to bring her back to me," Eretimis said, glancing at Errogan over his shoulder. "Tell me, did you once consider the fact that you are a demon? Or did you simply flee at the first chance from a fight against a human?" His words steeled, slowly dropping his level demeanor until he finally spat out the last two syllables. The intensity of the shadows grew, reaching about to smother anything in their path. The color drained from the corridor as he grabbed more, replaced by grey and black. It was as close to anger as he allowed himself near. "A fight that you lost."

Errogan tried to pick himself up. He raised his head, straining to get out a single word. "I came back only when there was no chance—" A shadow wrapped around his throat.

The intensity of Eretimis's abysmal stare held the magic in place as he strode toward the bloodied demon. The concentrated darkness pulled taut around his subject's throat. "Do not interrupt me if you know what is best for you, Errogan," he warned. "I was expecting more from you. It was a simple task, but you still failed. Even the human has been more useful than you in recent months. He at least led to the burning of that pathetic resistance."

Errogan tensed, ire building up as he found the strength to rise to his knees. Eretimis motionlessly tightened the dark rope around Errogan's airway before he could say anything.

"It makes me wonder what use you are to me if you cannot withstand a human's untapped magic." Finally, Eretimis dropped his stare, dispersing the magic that kept Errogan in check. The shadows receded to the walls, and the color leaked back into the room.

Errogan's gasps for air echoed as he lurched over, one arm catching him before he crashed to the ground. "It wasn't just the girl," he forced between jagged breaths.

"I do not have interest in your excuses, Errogan," Eretimis sighed.

The demon snarled, but he shook his head. Excuses were meaningless. At least he could see that. "My liege," he said, his voice fuller, "I was right in saying there was something unusual about the girl." Blood-splattered and bruising, Errogan looked at his dark ruler.

Eretimis rose a sole brow. "Is that how she bested you?"

Errogan fought off the rage from his expression. "Indeed." Even against the sanguinary beating that left him broken in more ways than one, the demon still found the will to sneer. "What would you say if I told you that our missing Cissrey Kingslin wasn't the last white mage around?"

Eretimis's brow arched, intrigued at what the Moonlit Bastard dared suggest. "I would say you ought to be correct in that assumption if you still wish to have breath in your lungs."

Errogan remained quiet for a moment, searching for the words that might save his life. "It's the only explanation why Rin Nowell healed three people blinks away from death."

Silence reigned over Errogan.

Eretimis didn't give his subject the slightest trace of what he was thinking. A white mage in his grasp would make this entire endeavor on Armiria much more attainable. He was left with whispers on the wind for just over a century now on where to find the damned Key he sought. None of the demons he sent out to search for it had found anything fruitful. Not even he had discovered where it might have been located. His best chance was the sudden surge of magic that sprouted in the Lennaels a week ago, but that discovery only led him to find Zarus, not what he truly desired. Yet a white mage? That would quicken the process...

The conversation of flickering flames seized the room. Errogan wisely opted to stay on his knees and looked wan by the time Eretimis made his decision. Errogan's stare on the Dark Tyrant never faltered.

Slowly, Eretimis descended the steps and halted at Errogan's side.

"Get up," Eretimis ordered. Without another word, he walked to the grand doors. He heard the struggle as the demon behind pained to his feet, but didn't stop.

"How shall I serve you, Your Majesty?" Errogan asked, with barely a breath in his lungs. He nearly collapsed catching up to Eretimis. The stench of his blood smothered the chamber. Yet Errogan still followed the Dark Tyrant.

Eretimis didn't bat an eye. "Pinpoint the mage's location and retrieve her. That was why you rushed back here, is it not?"

Errogan's silence said all it needed, but the demon paused his step when they both met the door. "...And what of Zarus?" Something just short of curiosity lingered in his voice—so well hidden, so well ignored, that Eretimis doubted Errogan was the slightest bit aware of its semblance of concern.

Eretimis glanced beyond the throne to the chamber his old student dwelled in. "The seal will hold him in there for however long I say, but for now," he stated with an eerily calm smile, "we will see how far that strength of his stretches before it snaps." He then swung the throne room doors open and stalked into the hallway beyond.

A white mage. Two of his best creations. All soon to be under his command.

The Dark Tyrant couldn't help but smile at what could be done with pawns of such might as he made his way into the heart of his fortress.

Acknowledgements

This book would not have been possible without the constant love and support of my family, friends, and Christ. Thank you to Ethan, for loving me through every step of the stress; mom and dad, for never questioning my decision to write; Xaikar and Rachel, for encouraging me in my doubt.

Thank you to Sandra Holt and Rebecca Weil for your feedback and savvy eyes.

Writing a book is a long process, and I would not have been able to accomplish this dream without countless people supporting me behind the scenes. From the bottom of my heart, thank you, and I thank God for blessing me with this passion to keep writing.

www.ingramcontent.com/pod-product-compliance
Lightning Source LLC
Chambersburg PA
CBHW031842310726
48972CB00005B/1378